ONE HUNDRED PHILISTINE FORESKINS

One
Hundred
Philistine
Foreskins

A Novel by

TOVA REICH

COUNTERPOINT

BERKELEY

A section of this novel was written at the Yaddo artists' retreat in Saratoga Springs,
New York. The work was completed with the support of the Radcliffe Institute for
Advanced Study at Harvard University.

Library of Congress Cataloging-in-Publication Data
Reich, Tova.
One Hundred Philistine Foreskins / Tova Reich.
pages cm
ISBN 978-1-61902-107-5 (hardcover)
1. Women rabbis—Fiction. 2. Jewish fiction. 3. Satire. I. Title.
PS3568.E4763O54 2013
813'.54—dc23   2012040587

Paperback ISBN: 978-1-61902-280-5

Cover design by Rebecca Lown
Interior design by David Bullen

COUNTERPOINT
2560 Ninth Street, Suite 318
Berkeley, CA 94710
www.counterpointpress.com

Printed in the United States of America

TO SARA TOV

Contents

Part I

Azuva

King Solomon
Made an Aperion
for Himself

It is a matter of record that certain living creatures, feeling the end of life squeezing them in, make one last desperate attempt to break free and do exactly what they want to do and express themselves exactly as they wish to be understood, on their own terms, without consideration of the desires or pressures or disapproval of family and other enemies, or of any being at all who claims ownership over them.

As she readied herself to carry out such an action, HaRav Temima Ba'alatOv, the renowned Jerusalem Bible teacher and beloved guru revered as Ima Temima by thousands of disciples, called to mind the case of the most godlike of all mortal creators, the writer Lev Tolstoy, who in a grand final gesture took flight from the unbearable materialism and vulgarity of wife and other hangers-on and bolted from his estate Yasnaya Polyana in search of the purity he preached and needed—yes, he had to have it right now, he could not put it off another minute, this was his last chance, his final statement—only to be reduced by an old man's illness in the once insignificant train station of Astapovo, where he died the ignoble but fitting death of a holy fool.

Tolstoy was a Russian, as everyone knows, but under the same heading of striking out at the last moment in a pure gesture of unrestrained, desperate fidelity to self, as Temima was preparing to make her own radical statement on this order, she also called to mind a German—a German Shepherd to be precise, her gentile neighbor's dog known as Germy from the earliest chapter of her life when she was a girl growing up in the ultra-Orthodox Boro Park section of Brooklyn and was known in those days as Tema. Howling raggedly day and night, lunging at the end of his rope inside his wretched cage of a yard due to the surrounding Jews' fear-of-dogs gene, Germy's fur thinned and faded as Tema bore witness year after year until one day, when they both turned twelve and Tema was legally and *halakhically* considered a woman accountable for her own sins, and Rabbi Manis Schmeltzer, the principal of the girls' school she attended, maneuvered his member into her mouth to her wonderment that such a curious idea could even be contemplated—Germy finally shut up once and for all. Casting off his chains with the recklessness of nothing more to lose, he leaped wildly through the gate, staggered down the alley that separated their two houses straight into the street to keep his appointment with the oncoming truck driven by Itche the junkman, which smashed into him, killing him instantly, leaving nothing but a pulped and liquefied mess.

From dead dogs Temima's thoughts glided seamlessly to her area of universally acknowledged expertise, the Hebrew Bible—Tanakh—with her specialty, its difficult women, problems one and all, coming to rest on one of her dearly beloveds, her pet, the majestic Queen Jezebel—in Hebrew, Izevel, island of garbage, female spam—who, as the very strict prophet Elijah the Tishbite had foretold, was recycled first into dog food and then, in the natural course of bodily processes, into dog shit in the fields of Jezreel. Jezebel was the model to whom Temima now turned as she made her preparations for a public demonstration that would finally bring clarity to all who took note of it. Nothing remained of that proud old queen but a skull picked fleshless, a pair of inedible feet, the palms of her idolatrous hands—leavings that even the dogs had spurned. The bitch got what she deserved—Jezebel, a name translated on the tongue of posterity to harlot, but oh how noble and true to herself she was in her final hour, Temima could only bow her head awestruck. Staring straight into the eye of her doom without a speck of self-deception or self-pity, her murderer already at her door, even so this proud old dowager makes him wait, takes her regal time, applies her eye makeup like war paint slowly and artfully for this last battle, the outline of black kohl punctuating her death mask, she helmets her hair as befits a warrior queen, she arranges herself at the upper story window of her palace as for a royal audience—and from that elevation she talks down to the killer of her sons and her own designated assassin—Traitor! Usurper! Murderer! Her eunuchs arrayed behind her take stock of the situation, consider their options, give the old lady a little push, flick her out the window, skirts flying up to expose the withered queenly jewel box, blue blood splattering all over the walls, the absurd indignity of that tough old carcass splayed on the ground to be mashed under the hooves of her executioner's mount.

Her eyes rimmed with black kohl expertly applied by Cozbi, one of her two full-time personal attendants, the unwholesome glow of her skin calmed with white powder, Temima Ba'alatOv sat at her window that morning in her private chambers on the upper floor of her house in the Bukharim Quarter of Jerusalem, gazing down on the street below. Her richly embroidered white silk yarmulke was pulled low over her nearly hairless skull, her phylacteries box from the morning prayers was still affixed to her forehead, the tefillin straps still wrapped around her slack arm, her great talit draped over the shoulders of her loose white robe. Women at windows were never good news, she reflected, they never came to a happy end, you didn't need the Bible for that insight. The women for sale in the storefronts in the municipal whore market in Amsterdam, for example, each a different piece of goods depending on the depths of your fantasy and your pocket. She had been window-shopping that night so many years ago with Abba Kadosh, blinded by too much light, and he was explaining to her softly, in his intimate voice that forced her to lean in closer, in his spiritually enlightened mode, how each of these women in the storefronts was an aspect of the feminine emanation of the divine presence, the holy *Shekhinah*, and by offering herself so generously to the broken vessels of the shattered male spirit, each of these beautiful, holy, holy ladies in sheer synthetics and leather studded with nailheads and gelatinous smears of lipstick was performing an act of unparalleled loving-kindness and *tikkun olam*, world repair, for which the reward would be incalculable and the redemption hastened.

What had been leaving Temima transfixed and breathless during that entire trip was her knowledge that Abba Kadosh almost never left his compound in the Judean Desert where he had recreated a patriarchal community with himself as the number one patriarch, but for her sake, for the sake of swaying her to join him as either one of his wives or a concubine, he had taken her on this educational junket to the red-light district of Amsterdam at great personal risk to himself. She was dazed with flattery beyond anything she could have anticipated, like the most simple and inexperienced of girls, she had considered herself above such primitive seductions but in the end she was swept away. She was thirty-five years old when Abba Kadosh became her impresario, but her thighs were still like globed jewels the work of an artisan, her navel like a round goblet, her belly like a heap of wheat, her breasts like two fawns, her neck like a pillar of ivory, her eyes like the pools of Heshbon, her nose like the tower of Lebanon looking to Damascus, her head like a camel, her hair like purple streamers in which the king is entangled—people said of her that her beauty was surreal. She was still ravishing, still smoldering, still desirable despite seven pregnancies, five miscarriages and two live births, both of whom, including the baby buried in the ancient cemetery of Hebron and the little boy not even three years old, she had abandoned along with her husband of over fifteen years, Howie Stern of Ozone Park, Queens, reinvented as Haim Ba'al-Teshuva, scribe and phylacteries maker in the holy city of Hebron in the biblical heartland of Judea and Samaria, known to the alien world as the West Bank—Occupied Territory.

In Judea and Samaria, between Bethel and Ramah, the ferocious Deborah, wife of Lapidot, sat under a palm tree and prophesized, belting out her victory song after the battle against the Canaanites, gloating over her conjured-up image of the mother of the enemy general Sisera sitting at *her* window, gazing into the distance, awaiting the return of the chariot of her triumphant son—in vain, in vain. How long are you going to sit there waiting at that window, Sisera's mom? Your boy is already dead. The savage Yael, wife of Hever the Kenite, in whose tent he had sought refuge, refreshed him with milk, warmed him with her mantle, offered him so selflessly who knows what other acts of lovingkindness to repair his broken vessel, and when afterward he had immediately fallen asleep, as men tend to do, snoring with supreme entitlement, she drove the stake of her tent through his temple and into the floor, pinning him like a trophy beetle spread under glass.

Maybe the time has come for women to stop looking out of windows,

Temima concluded. What are we hoping to see? What are we expecting? What are we waiting for? Abba Kadosh had a mother too, the late Mrs. Hazel Clinton of Selma, Alabama, and Arad, Israel. Temima supposed that she owed Abba Kadosh's mother a debt of gratitude simply for sticking it out and not running off and abandoning the oiled black boy she had called Elmore, who, when in the fullness of time he had anointed himself as Abba Kadosh, prophet and messiah, affirmed her mastery of Tanakh and forced her finally to surrender to her destiny.

Cozbi had carried the lumpy root-vegetable weight of the earthly corpus of her mistress to the window with the assistance of Rizpa, the second live-in personal attendant. They settled Temima in the sagged-out scoop of her capacious ivory wingchair where she presided as upon a throne overlooking the Bukharim Quarter, awaiting the delivery of the brilliant conveyance from which she would offer her final and boldest teaching as she was transported to her personal Astapovo, her fatal encounter with the junkman, the bitch queen's showdown at the gates with her assassin.

She had stopped walking entirely at an appointed hour some years earlier, and without offering any commentary as to whether or not she still was able to, had simply declared one day that she had walked far enough, she refused to take another step, leaving it to her followers to draw from this mysterious abstention whatever wisdom they were capable of, each at her own level. From that time forward, all of her business was conducted in this room, most of it from the vast high bed that was its centerpiece, where she would recline propped up against a bank of white satin cushions under mounds of white satin bedclothes. In her white silk skullcap that bulged with the mortal nodes and knobs of her head, the discolorations and spots on her face concealed by the makeup expertly applied by Cozbi and over which she wore a veil such as masked the blinding flush of Moses Our Teacher, Ima Temima six nights a week presided over her following gathered around the great raft of her bed at least three deep with mouths open to suck in her wisdom. The seventh night, Friday, the bed was transformed into a table, a *tisch* to usher in the Sabbath, a great banquet-sized white damask cloth spread across it, the holy woman HaRav Temima Ba'alatOv enthroned as if at its head leaning against the bolster of her white cushions tearing with hands gloved to conceal the mottled, loose skin underneath one hallah after another set out by Rizpa, her Hasidim, like ravenous birds to whom the old lady tosses some crumbs, stampeding savagely for the smallest blessed leavings touched by Ima Temima and cast out as *shirayim*.

All of this would come to an end this morning, thank God, Temima thought—it had become tainted, idolatry. Her body had grown flaccid and scaly from age, grotesque like a vermin. Somewhere along the way it had happened; as she herself noted, No one escapes. Yet she had not let her inner self go, she was preparing herself—the shells and *klippot* were being peeled away to expose to those with true vision her purest self contracted to the essence of her all-knowing soul still unborn; she had undergone a kind of divine constriction—*zimzum*—reconfiguring herself into the Place that withdraws to leave some space for others. In the same ironic way, though her outward physical presence had swelled and sagged with lumps and ruts, the physical space she now occupied was condensed to this chamber from which she had not emerged in years. The pot was carried in and the pot was carried out by tiny Rizpa, in her past life the cleaning woman Mazal Shabtai of Rosh HaAyin, Israel, brown and wizened like an old shoe. She was bathed and dressed and groomed and made up and then veiled on the changing table of her bed—by Cozbi, the former masseuse Anna Oblonskaya of Tverskaya Street, Moscow, six feet tall without the three-inch stiletto heels she always wore. Anyone who desired intercourse with her—responsa, exegesis, advice, a blessing, a cure, prophecy, prayers, above all the truth about themselves that Ima Temima possessed and selectively dispensed, the meaning of their troubling dreams, what would happen to them, where to find what they had lost, how to remember what they had forgotten—came and petitioned for access from her gatekeeper, her damaged boy, the son she called Paltiel, the child she had abandoned in Hebron who, in his manhood, had found his way through the woods back to his mother, the only male member permitted unrestricted entry into her innermost-inner court.

Behind her, rimming the upper floor of this stately old Jerusalem stone house bequeathed to her by a benefactor whose name was too dangerous to pronounce out loud, room after room with lofty vaulted ceilings and floor tiles stenciled like Turkish carpets that had once comprised her living quarters opened up in a balcony arc overlooking the study hall and synagogue below. She could scarcely believe now that there had ever been a time when she had felt the need for so much space. This was the morning when she would remove her presence from her dwelling place, but she would not fold it up and carry it off to the next station like the God of the Testament with his Tabernacle, she would not bear its contents away with her on long poles always in place for portability, ready to travel; she would not blow it up or burn it down, foxes would not be seen prowling among its scorched ruins. Whether she lived in it or whether she left it, whether she wanted it or whether she wanted nothing more than to be rid of this earthly yoke, the house was hers, it was her eternal possession, that was the deal—those were the terms the mentor with hidden face had laid out, addressing her from behind a mask, backlit with fever.

When she vacated it this morning in a public demonstration of great moral consequence, articulating exactly how she meant to be understood in a form that could not be misinterpreted, Paltiel would simply in the natural course of events complete his takeover. The house would be her reparations to him, to erase from her life book the frozen frame that still screeched in her memory—the child following behind her and weeping as she made her way to the car where one of Abba Kadosh's retainers was awaiting her, Paltiel stumbling after her along the path sobbing, Ima, don't go, please don't go, Ima, until his father, the husband she still called Howie, scribe and phylacteries maker of Hebron, took his hand and said, Come home now, and carried him away. Still, there he would always be, fixed ever after, the little boy branded eternally into her memory as Paltiel, walking and crying, walking and crying, like Paltiel son of Layish when he was forced to give up his beloved Mikhal daughter of the paranoid King Saul to that mafia don and bandit, David son of Jesse, anointed in Hebron and soon to consolidate his kingship in Jerusalem over all of Israel, who had first seigneurial rights on the woman because he had bought her from her father for the bride-price of one hundred Philistine foreskins, he had the receipt.

I've been expecting you, Paltiel, were Temima's words to him that day when, as was inevitable, the wounded and bereft boy came back to her with his dark beard tipped with silver and a bald patch on his head, small and soft-paunched, a grown man in outer appearance only. She appointed him her chief of staff on the spot, number one *shammes*, and gave him full rights and privileges over the property as her authorized squatter. From shreds of chatter gleaned through acolytes who congregated at her bedside each night to drink in her teachings she had heard that he had appropriated the living quarters behind her chamber, converting a portion of it into a private apartment for himself and Cozbi who towered over him, not to mention allocating a room of one's own convenient to the kitchen and laundry for Rizpa, and turning the rest into an administrative complex with banks of computers and other high-tech equipment, everything cutting edge and top of the line, from which he oversaw their entire operation.

The operation, as it happened, was constructed out of air and silken strands, but even so, from what she had been told (she personally collaborated in shielding herself from such matters) the money it brought in had substance. It was a website called MaTov. Paltiel derived touching creative pride from what he considered to be the cleverness of the brand name, a play, on one level, on the intended curse morphed into a blessing that spurted out of the mouth of the pagan prophet Bilaam son of Be'or as he overlooked the goodly tents of Jacob, the dwelling places of Israel spread out in their wilderness encampment in one of the many great comic scenes of the Tanakh, this one featuring a talking donkey. If words could be put into the mouth of an ass, why not also into the mouth of a human dummy by the great ventriloquist above? And what Paltiel was selling in MaTov was her, his own Good Ma, Ima Temima. In lovingkindness she was obligated to repair his vessel that she herself had broken; even as she found his dealings to be squalid she could not deny herself to him yet again, she owed him.

It was all clarified on the website, though Temima herself, of course, had never physically even laid a hand on one of those machines much less, God forbid, worshipped at a screen as at an icon in its designated corner of the room. There was, however, from what she had gleaned, a sliding fee scale, depending on what you were willing or able to spend, ranging from Bronze Standard to Silver Select to Gold Superior to Platinum Premium to Diamond Exclusive—from having your email petition, once it was paid for with your credit card number and your expiration date, printed out and deposited at the foot of the holy woman's bed with heaps of other standard petitions in a white plastic laundry tub or black trash bags depending on how many had come in that day, to having it placed with a number of select others under one of the holy woman's pillows, to having it set on her tray in a fan of superiors where her eyes might fall upon it, to having it read out loud to her with full premium urgency, and, for an added cost, arranging for her blessing or oracular utterance to be communicated back to you in an email reply. The mere proximity to the holy woman of your petition was bound to improve your self-knowledge and your fortune, and the chances of success were exponentially increased if you paid to have your request brought into her aura more than once, with special package deals for auspicious numbers of times—four, seven, ten, thirteen, eighteen, or any combination of eighteen (thirty-six, fifty-four, and so on), forty days and forty nights—all variations on four or forty were deemed incredibly potent. Fees were also calibrated depending on the request, which, Paltiel discovered, since the clientele consisted mostly of women, fell generally under two very broad headings, Ma and Ov—maternal and gynecological. Petitioning that you might finally find your soul mate, for example, was costly, naturally, but not nearly as expensive or as complicated or as resistant to cure or consolation as anything related to the troubles that derived from the womb you came out of or the sorrows that touched upon what went into your own womb and what came out.

It had, of course, not escaped Temima's notice, as a native English speaker though living in Israel more than three-quarters of her lifespan by now, that a playful deconstruction of her name Ba'alatOv could lead to the hermeneutics Mistress of the Ovary, an especially tempting twist because so many of the lessons she drew were derived from and applied to women—Ovum Ovarum, Sanctum Sanctorum. But the fact was, when she had taken the name Ba'alatOv, she had meant it as a respectful nod to yet another of her dearly beloved Tanakhi women, the despised necromancer, the Woman of Endor, mistress of the *ov* and *yedonim*, with the power to raise familiar spirits and ghosts. And a secondary benefit of this name was that, with it, Temima was also sticking a finger into the eyes of the establishment religious leaders, all men, who considered her an aberration and an abomination, a freak and a menace—a witch and a sorceress—placing their bans and *herems* upon her, the way King Saul had done on all mediums and wizards and magicians and possessors of talismans. Yet Saul in his desperation had sought out the Woman of

Endor anyway—just like those ossified and inflated rabbis whose names she could mention if she were so inclined who had come to her in secret and disguise like the johns prowling the red-light district of Amsterdam, and then gone away to take full credit for her brilliant interpretations of the texts to guide them in their perplexity and her responsa to such questions as whether an hermaphrodite should pray on the women's or men's side of the partition at the Western Wall. And doesn't the book tell us in black and white that the Woman of Endor actually succeeded in raising the cranky prophet Samuel from his freshly dug grave in Ramah? Such powers did exist after all—and this witch possessed them. You had to hand it to her, the hag, the crone, she knew her business, she delivered, she was a professional. But that was not why Temima loved her. Temima loved her and honored her, could only bow her head, marvel, and practically weep at how, after all the bad news for the future of the royal line came spilling like worms out of the spectral mouth of Samuel the prophet, and the beset King Saul collapsed, passed out in her kitchen, the good witch would not even think of letting him out of her house after he was revived until first he ate something. Eat something first—then I'll let you go. What do we learn from this? Ima Temima would pose the question to her students. The answer is: All women are witches.

Before the computer operation installed by Paltiel, Temima had of course helped many people in the old-fashioned way, with basic human raw materials, one-on-one, hands on, so to speak. Not only with her teachings, for which students gathered from the four corners of the earth to the Temima Shul to absorb her wisdom, hanging with raw fingertips from the windowsills even in the dead of winter until they were discovered frozen and buried under the Jerusalem snows, but also, in those simpler times, the sufferers would come to her door on their own, or stop her on the street in those days when she made her way boldly already veiled, stop her with their needs and sorrows and struggles and losses, and she would listen and dispense as necessary. In some such way she had found Cozbi on a cold night in an alley off Sabbath Square, makeup congealed on the cheekbone blades under her slanted Slavic eyes, loose platinum-colored hair giving off dull glints of light, chandelier earrings dangling forlornly, in her trademark stilettos, long legs and narrow hips and tight buttocks shrink-wrapped in low-slung red pants, a clinging gold halter top with cleavage and midriff bared, smoking something or other as she slumped against the wall beside a yellow poster enjoining the daughters of Israel not to arouse the feelings of neighborhood residents by dressing immodestly. A young man with a sparse beard and a great cupola of a black velvet yarmulke, the blood rushing to his face, was whipping her in a frenzy with the rope *gartel* he had unsnaked from around the waist of his lustrous black kaftan, lashing and yelling *Pritzeh! Pritzeh!* Harlot! Slut! What, you think this is a stable?—pausing only to amass fresh gobs of spit to aim at her. And she didn't even stir, she didn't flinch or cringe, she just went on dragging on her cigarette or bidi or joint or whatever it was she was smoking, as if all of this disturbance and spectacle had nothing to do with her.

Temima, a formidable if notorious figure in the neighborhood—as much as you disapproved of her you definitely did not want to risk starting up with her—trailed by a band of her students, including her Cherethites and Pelethites, her *kraiti and plaiti*, four husky male acolytes who had become the designated bodyguards she called her Bnei Zeruya, paused in her processional and inquired of the beater and the spitter, "So tell me, Reb Yid, how do you know this is not Elijah the prophet you are assaulting?"

"Eliyahu HaNavi? What kind of idiocy, what kind of *shtoos*? Heresy, *apikorsus*! The Messiah a woman? A whore—a *zona*?"

"Like Rahab the *zona*," Temima nodded with galling calm, "purveyor of *mazon*—nourishment—as Rashi the commentator-in-chief spins it. Which may, after all, be the definition of whore. On the other hand, the Talmud tells us that the mere mention of the name of Rahab the whore of Jericho was enough to bring men to climax."

They took Cozbi home with them that night, her hips thrust forward like a roast on a tray, grinding in intentional provocation as she staggered the entire distance up Yekhezkel Street back to the Temima Shul in the Quarter of the Bukharim.

And not only Cozbi, but Rizpa too arrived on her own at Ima Temima's in her need without the help of a computer in those more primitive and intimate times. To be more precise, in Rizpa's case, she was delivered, levitated from the Satmar girls' school Beis Ziburis across the road between two married ladies, teachers at this ultra-ultra school most likely, with their shaven skulls tightly wrapped in black scarves, in their loose, boxy suit jackets over perpetually pregnant bellies, long skirts, thick black stockings and lace-up shoes, and the severe tight-lipped expression on their scrubbed faces as they deposited their burden in front of Temima and declared, "This one is your type—another lost soul for your collection. Her name is Mazal—but she's not so lucky, poor thing, not so *beseder*." They spoke mostly in Yiddish, mixed in with granite Hungarian— the Holy Tongue, Loshon Kodesh, was not meant to be tainted by daily use in the manner of the insolent and accursed Zionists—but now and then they inserted some Hebrew words they had picked up through osmosis despite themselves from the commerce in the air, such as when they said *beseder*, and to illustrate, in case Temima did not get the point as it related to Mazal, each of them, with her free hand, rotated cuckoo spirals at her temple.

As it happened, the behavior over the course of the last few days of this wretched Mazal they were hauling between them had attracted even Temima's attention from across the street, who could not but notice her coming out onto the upper balcony of the Satmar girls' school Beis Ziburis with a squeegee and a bucket splashing with a dark sudsy liquid, and she would mop furiously, screaming shrilly the whole time, "*Schmutz, schmutz, this place is stinking with schmutz, must get rid of all this schmutz*," using, oddly enough, though she was Sephardi from the Arabian Diaspora, the Yiddish word for dirt, filth. She would overturn the bucket on the stone parapet of the balcony, dumping the slop and contagion onto the street below, onto the head of whoever was passing by; with any luck it would merely be a woman, but it could also be a man, ranging from a *schnorrer* with his hand out begging for a shekel to a rabbi of great reputation with his hand out making a point, a sage before whom everyone rose when he stepped into a room, from the top of the black hat you couldn't tell who was who—she did not discriminate but continued dumping the offal in this way until she was dragged back inside the school building. After an interval, when she reckoned no one was looking, her eyes darting in this direction and that, she would come out again with her squeegee and her sloshing pail and start her whole routine all over again, yelling, "*Schmutz, schmutz!*"—swabbing the floor and dumping the fetid liquid on unfortunate heads, male and female, young and old, Arab and Israeli, Jew and gentile, holy and unholy, passing below, never looking up as they ought to have done.

"She claims that we Satmar Hasidim stole her babies from their hospital bassinets after she gave birth to them and told her they were dead," one of the righteous matrons said to Temima in Yiddish. "I'm not saying yes, I'm not saying no. But just between us, it would not have been such a bad thing for these poor dark *kinderlakh* to be handed over to families that would raise them in the proper religious way. Sometimes extreme measures are necessary in the name of the Master of the Universe."

Temima said, "Leave her here with me. I will call her Rizpa."

"Rizpa—very nice. It means 'floor' in Loshon Kodesh—no? Good. She mopped our floors, so now she'll mop yours."

In Beis Ziburis across the street, as Temima knew only too well, they instructed the girls in how to kosher a chicken and the laws of *niddah* relating to menstrual impurity and ritual bath procedures, all the rules and regulations regarding getting rid of the blood, the chicken's blood, the woman's blood, and so on and so forth, that was education enough for them. Why should Temima have expected them to recognize this reference to the concubine of King Saul, Rizpa daughter of Aya, whose two sons were impaled on the mountainside in a political deal to appease the enemy? Spreading her sackcloth over the rock by the mountainside, Rizpa sat guard there from the beginning of the barley harvest until the rains came pouring down, and she would not allow the birds of the sky to touch the bodies of her sons by day, or the beasts of the field at night.

So here was another womb made crazy by the important affairs of men. Ima Temima ordered that Rizpa be put to bed and that simple, familiar Yemenite foods be carried in to comfort her until she regained her strength, sweet mint teas and *malawah* breads. And once in a while, in those pre-computer days when she still moved from room to room, Temima herself would come and sit at her bedside and listen to her stories about her life in Rosh HaAyin as one of the four wives of the revered teacher Baba Rakhamim, and about all the hens in her backyard with only a single cock who ruled over them, bothered them day and night, wore them out so utterly that, one after another, the hens came right up to Rizpa, then known as Mazal, in her kitchen and willed her to slaughter them and dump them in the soup. But Paltiel had informed his mother that, now, with the far-reaching tentacles of his computer network, they were beginning to make headway in learning the fates of Rizpa's babies; the graves in which they were supposed to have been buried had been opened and discovered to be empty, for one thing, and there was now also an army of Sephardi activists and hotheads ready to grab by force if necessary swabs of DNA from the insides of the mouths of extra dark Satmar Hasidim with extra corkscrewed sidecurls and more refined physiques briskly walking down the streets of Mea Shearim and Bnei B'rak in Israel, Williamsburg in Brooklyn, or Monroe in New York State, bizarrely speaking and gesticulating in Yiddish, and match this evidence against the genetic map of the eternally bereft and inconsolable mothers. Even if the Satmars didn't believe in DNA and regarded it as idolatry, the authorities had faith in science, which in the end mattered, it mattered on this earth.

And not only that. Thanks to the powers of his computers, Paltiel was now happy to report he believed they were also closing in on the pimp who went under the name Stalinsky who had trafficked Cozbi to Tel Aviv in the days when she was known as Anna Oblonskaya with the promise of a job as a childcare provider in the home of an oligarch living in a guarded compound of stupefying ostentation near Herzliah, robbed her of her passport, drugged her, raped her, beat her, and then sold her into prostitution in the Monopol Hotel in Tel Aviv on the corner of Allenby Street and HaYarkon. "In this day and age," as Paltiel explained to his mother, "one-on-one is just no longer cost-effective." One-on-one had to be reserved only for the clients of MaTov who chose the Diamond Exclusive option, which for an undisclosed fee entitled them to a private audience of maximum thirty-minutes duration with the world-renowned master teacher and guru, the charismatic wise woman and reputed miracle worker, HaRav Temima Ba'alatOv, who revealed to them many things about themselves that they both knew and did not know—rendering it all the more imperative, as Paltiel reminded her repeatedly, that she no longer indulge in spontaneous personal ministrations with any single individual, including (and especially since she no longer went out anymore) any of the followers who gathered around her bed to soak in her vibrations night after night. Such simple human encounters were a luxury of the past, Paltiel stressed, they would fatally drive down the market value of the Diamond Exclusive if word got out that the same product could be gotten free of charge if you came to the nightly Torah salon at Ima Temima's bedside and snatched an unguarded opening to lean over and steal what others paid for, deposit into her ear the burden of your troubles and be healed.

Now when the purchasers of the Diamond Exclusive option arrived they would be ushered up the stairs behind Cozbi in full distracting motion and conducted to one of the benches on the balcony that constituted the rear portion of the second floor of the building beyond the living quarters, and that, in the old days, had served as the men's prayer section. There they would sit obediently waiting to be summoned into Ima Temima's bedchamber for their appointment, gazing down at the women's section below, the long narrow sanctuary and study hall with its rows of dark wooden benches and tables and stacks of worn volumes and its satin-sheathed ark housing the holy scrolls and the podium from which the exalted and universally renowned HaRav Temima Ba'alatOv, Ima Temima, may she live on for many good long years, had presided and taught through her veil lest her audience be blinded by her light until she had willingly and deliberately contracted her world to a single room upstairs where she was now sitting at the window, preparing to shed even this paltry four cubits for her final and most instructive stop before the grave.

And while we're on the subject of women at windows and all the troubles this position has brought down upon them, let us also not neglect to mention King Saul's daughter, the princess Mikhal, for whom that extravagant show-off David had actually overtipped with two hundred Philistine foreskins though the asking brideprice for her, true, had been the bargain rate of the mere one hundred at which her value had been assessed. Two hundred Philistines for a yield of two hundred foreskins, think about it, maybe circumcised after they were killed, maybe while they were still alive like Dina's rapist Shekhem and all the men of his town, a major bloodletting, a wild scalping, but David liked to do things big, he liked to make a splash, and Mikhal, after all, was a princess, a Jewish princess, worth every foreskin.

Mikhal, whose loins must have once throbbed for that irresistible bad boy David so that she even betrayed her father to save him, letting him down out of the window of their bedchamber to escape the assassins the old man had sent after him and tucking idols (What? Another Tanakhi lady, like Rachel Our Mother, who could not bring herself to part with her *teraphim*?) in the bed with an absurd tuft of goat hair sticking up on top to trick the pursuers in another of the Bible's great comic interludes. How much bitterness and loathing and alienation must have encrusted the heart of this degraded woman as she stood years later at the window, a prisoner of the harem, staring down at David in his triumph, observing him as he whirled and leaped half-naked in the street like a lunatic in front of all the riffraff and lowlife, despising him in her heart as he led the processional bearing the Ark of God back to Jerusalem.

Temima let out a sharp, caustic laugh, like a bark, the first sound she had emitted all morning not counting her prayers, which launched Cozbi and Rizpa straight to the window. There below, turning into the Bukharim Quarter and propelling himself toward them, was a small man girded only in a loincloth and a fringed garment threaded with azure strings and a snug-fitting white crocheted openwork skullcap drawn low over his head, spinning ecstatically like a Sufi or a dervish and singing with such fervor that rills of drool snaked down from his mouth, matting his beard, chanting more than singing, over and over again, the refrain, "Te-Tem-Ima-Temima-from-Brooklyn."

"It is Paltiel," Cozbi said. "They are coming. We better get ready."

Forgive me, Paltiel, Temima beseeched him in her heart—not denying, as had Mother Sarah, her indiscretion of laughing at some masculine absurdity. Inwardly she begged him to pardon her. Her laugh that to some ears might have sounded contemptuous had just burst out of her in an unforgiving flash before she had recognized him as her own son, in the fraction of a second when she had seen him coldly through a stranger's eyes.

At the head of the great throng that began streaming into the Bukharim Quarter behind Paltiel, heavy with women and girls, but also including multiple kosher prayer quorums of tens of men, surging forward to the front of her shul, dancing, stamping their feet, twirling, clapping their hands, swaying, many bearing musical instruments, drums, tambourines, rattles, bells, roaring, ululating, whooping, chanting the Te-Tem-Ima-Temima-from-Brooklyn mantra, she now also easily spotted her eighth and last child, the daughter Zippi she had with Abba Kadosh. Temima's eyes even in the dimness of age were instantly snagged by the bright yellows and reds of the African kente cloth turban that wrapped the mass of Zippi's dreadlocks and the coordinated robe that cloaked her matronly form, the solid protruding bolsters of breasts and buttocks. In each of her upraised pumping fists Zippi waved a tool of her trade—a double-edged knife in her right hand, a shield to hold back the prepuce in her left. She was a *mohel*, a circumciser, like her namesake Zippora, the reputedly black-skinned wife of Moses Our Teacher, the blood groom too busy having visions and saving the Jewish people to attend to his own sons, forcing her to do the job and sacrifice their boys herself. The third tool of Zippi's trade were her own plump lips, with which she performed the *meziza*, sucking the blood from the wound, and with which she now was chanting Te-Tem-Ima along with the swelling congregation packing the entire area in front of the Temima Shul in the Bukharim Quarter, snaking around the corner to Yekhezkel Street with no end in sight.

It had been because of this child Zippi, now a grown woman, not only already a mother in her own right but also a grandmother, that Temima had finally broken with Abba Kadosh and fled his patriarchal kingdom in the Judean Desert, followed out of the wilderness by Shira, another one of his concubines, who had started life as Sherry Silver and now went by the name Kol-Isha-Erva. The former lead singer and instrumentalist of the once-popular band Jephta's Daughters, which performed for audiences of women only, Shira had been living on a trust fund in the Nakhlaot section of Jerusalem and working part-time as an ecological nature guide when she surrendered to Abba Kadosh, who was madly turned on by her vibrato. Temima now spotted Kol-Isha-Erva easily in the crowd, a thick twisted rope girdling her waist, its trailing length encircling the waists, one behind the other, of the women who were her students in her school for prophetesses, some of them blowing long sustained blasts followed by pulsing beats on upraised shofars, others flinging their arms in the air, their shoulders twitching, ecstatic utterances coming from their lips in an ancient, mystical tongue that no one but fools and children could any longer decipher—the spirit of God had settled upon them so that if anyone wondered what had come over these girls, it could be said of them that they too were among the prophets.

Kol-Isha-Erva had taken her name around the same time and in the same spirit of defiance and revelation as Temima when she had recast her own name to honor the Woman of Endor. A woman's voice is nakedness, you say? Well then, that is how I shall be known—Woman's-Naked-Voice, Kol-Isha-Erva. She tilted back her head to look up to Temima's window, and even through the veil they knew their eyes linked instantly. The two women were closer in spirit than twin sisters still in the womb in body. Kol-Isha-Erva was to Temima Ba'alatOv as Rav Nosson of Nemirov was to Rav Nakhman of Bratslav. She was Temima's scribe and the recorder for posterity of all her stories and wisdom since, like Rav Nakhman, Temima never wrote anything down herself, she regarded writing to be a crime, and as Temima herself used to say, Were it not for the voice of Kol-Isha-Erva, no one would ever hear me and nothing of me would remain.

As Kol-Isha-Erva and her band of student prophetesses were prodded forward by the surging crowd, she flicked her head sideways in a signal to Temima to look in the direction she was indicating. The aperion borne by her four bodyguards, her Bnei Zeruya, was turning the corner and coming into view, preceded by her white-robed knot of priestesses led by Aish-Zara, Temima's girlhood friend from Boro Park, Essie Rappaport, in the tall white mitre of the high priestess and with an Urim and Tumim jewel-encrusted breastplate hanging from a heavy chain around her neck that Paltiel had ordered on the Internet from the Yale University website. Taking her halting and excruciating steps leaning on two canes, the pain of her metastasized cancer creeping along her spine through her hips down her legs, fortified by a fierce inner will, Essie had insisted upon undertaking this arduous final passage in the procession accompanying her beloved Temima. Under no circumstances would she even consider accepting the invitation to be transported beside her teacher in the aperion, which now approached the Temima Shul in the very center of the crowd, like the Tabernacle with its ark and cherubim, its Holy of Holies, in the wilderness surrounded and shielded by the priests and the Levites and the twelve tribes in prescribed formation, the heart at the heart. The four Bnei Zeruya carried it on poles high above the heads of the assembled. They were big men, from their shoulders and upward taller than all the people; the poles went through rings attached to the sides of the palanquin and extended to rest on their shoulders elevated above the throng pressing in on all sides. They passed through the opening into the courtyard to reach the door of the Temima Shul, and set it down ceremoniously on the ground to await her arrival.

King Solomon made an aperion for himself out of wood from Lebanon. Its posts he made of silver, its top gold, its seat rich purple cloth, its interior inlaid with love by the daughters of Jerusalem—the first recorded traveling orgone box. That was your high-end aperion model, and those were the luxury features, fully loaded. When his mother informed him it was her wish to be conveyed through the streets of Jerusalem to the place to which she now intended to go in a palanquin such as King Solomon had made for himself as specified in lyric detail in Song of Songs, Paltiel's job as her chief of staff was to make this happen.

Where in the world could a Solomonic aperion be found in this day and age, even in Jerusalem, the center of the earth where all things converged? To import some sort of equivalent conveyance made out of bamboo or rattan and festooned with colored baubles from an alien and distant place like India or China, and maybe also a white elephant to accessorize it upon whose back the contraption could ride, would be entirely inappropriate for the culture and mentality of the Middle East, which was more camel and donkey oriented. And to build such an aperion from scratch, with the designated precious materials, would be an outlay prohibitively beyond their resources, and would require craftsmen of divine endowments long vanished from the guild—a Bezalel, an Ahaliav, a Hiram of Tyre, an artisan of the skill and genius attributed to Solomon himself. Paltiel had almost despaired, but then, by a stroke of great good luck, while goofing sullenly around on the Internet, his second favorite pastime, he came upon an outfit almost in the neighborhood—in a hilltop trailer settlement outpost in Samaria—that specialized in authentic reproductions of biblical artifacts, garments, incense, musical instruments, vessels, coins, celestial azure dye, and so on, including among its offerings a full Old Testament wedding with the bride conveyed to the canopy by four bearers in what they actually called an aperion, with the appropriate verse appended to the luscious product description.

Accompanied by Cozbi, Paltiel went out to the headquarters in Samaria of this for-profit to personally check out the merchandise. They both agreed, upon close inspection, that it was a depressingly antique heap, a battered crate, resembling more a sedan chair that had seen far better days than what they imagined a royal aperion might be like, gussied up a bit with scrollwork and friezes, arabesques and filigrees to give it a generic Levantine look, but that, bottom line and considering the kind of time pressure they were under, it would serve. They stepped inside to examine the seat, a bench really—a bit worn, a bit hard, the purple cloth some sort of frayed glossy synthetic. Nevertheless they sat there for a while and exhaled in relief, mission accomplished, the close darkness and love veneer applied by the daughters of Jerusalem putting them in the mood. On the plus side, they noted, it was exceptionally solid—sturdy enough to carry five brides at once to a Moonie wedding, and Temima was a woman of great bearing and distinction, a flimsy contraption just would not do, Paltiel did not, God forbid, want any embarrassments.

They speculated that perhaps a century and a half ago a conveyance of this type might have been new, used perhaps to transport a well-fed personage of substance and heft around the country, up and down the hills of the Holy Land, an English baron or lord, a Montefiore or a Rothschild, for example, whose manicured hand with its blinding diamond ring and starched white shirt cuff with gold links would extend out the window and drop coins for the beggars and cripples scrambling in his wake. The windows, they noted approvingly, were thickly curtained, a great advantage in Temima's case, affording her privacy from unseemly stares, not only of spectators who would inevitably be lining up along her route, but also of journalists, photographers, and other assorted rabble and gawkers and predators. After some perfunctory haggling, they signed the rental lease at an extortionist price, which Paltiel wrote off as a donation to the biblical restoration venture. This was the aperion that was now parked at the threshold of the Temima Shul, gently and reverentially lowered by the four Bnei Zeruya who ducked out from under the rods that had rested on their shoulders as they maneuvered it to its reserved spot. They proceeded inside the building and up the stairs, dizzied by Cozbi leading the way to the men's balcony where they were directed to sit down and wait as final preparations were completed for Temima's departure, when they would be summoned to carry her down in a dignified fashion and settle her comfortably inside her chariot.

As they bore her down the stairs, Temima's heart filled with pity for these four overgrown boys she called her Bnei Zeruya though she never really took pains to get to know them; they were not related to each other as far as she knew, she had never troubled to etch into her mind their individual names. It was entirely on account of their mothers that she felt such an ache for them; to her eyes, though they were so muscular and sleek and inscribed with such beguiling tattoos, and, on the surface at least, in the prime of health, they nevertheless seemed to her pathetically mortal, like every mother's son. Yoav ben Zeruya, Avishai ben Zeruya, Asa'el ben Zeruya—these were the sons of Zeruya in the book of Samuel. It made no difference at all to Temima that Zeruya had only three sons; for her purposes, her four bodyguards and bearers were Bnei Zeruya. Zeruya was their mother, Temima taught. Where else in the text did you find sons, and especially sons of such extravagantly wild belligerent instincts, such testosterone sons, identified by their matronymic? They definitely were not mama's boys, Zeruya's sons. Jesus son of Mary was another such case that came to mind, but that was a different story, another personality type entirely with a paternity issue too complicated to go by his patronymic. What was his father's name anyway?

They ferried her down the steps with almost choreographed delicacy and caution in a special transfer chair that had been devised for this purpose as befitted her stature in the world. Temima gazed sorrowfully at her four Bnei Zeruya through the veil with which Cozbi had covered her face, which was glowing alarmingly like the face of Moses Our Teacher as if infected by a fatal disease contracted from God in the thin air of the mountaintop. Speaking through this veil she requested that, before being brought outside and placed in the aperion to embark on the journey that would be her ultimate statement, she be set down for the last time on the *bima* in front of the ark of her sanctuary where her priestesses led by Aish-Zara, hooded in their great white prayer shawls and in their stocking feet, had on so many occasions bestowed upon the worshippers the priestly blessing dictated to Aaron in God's name, raising their hands over the assembled who obediently shielded their eyes from the blinding mystery of it all. This was where Temima herself had taught and preached for so many years to her congregation of women in the main sanctuary and to the men sitting up in the balcony until she had retired definitively to her chamber. This departure moment, her last moment in this holy place, would be especially auspicious for a prayer for the healing of all humankind, she believed, for the sick and the soon to be sick, for the mortality of these Bnei Zeruya decaying in front of her eyes, asking for mercy in the name of their mothers.

Cozbi and Rizpa drew back the maroon satin curtain draping the ark, which, when exposed, revealed itself to be a fireproof steel safe, an authentic bank vault of great weight and thickness, donated by the anonymous benefactor following an act of savage vandalism and pillaging perpetrated by an antagonist who, it was believed by many in the neighborhood, had acted out of a justifiable sense of righteous outrage against this brazen *hillul HaShem,* this intolerable desecration of the Name, committed daily by this female upstart who called herself HaRav Temima Ba'alatOv, the abhorrent liberties she took with all that was sacred and pure and forbidden to her as a woman. The massive doors of the ark were opened with the combination entrusted to the memories of Cozbi and Rizpa, who then, from either side, assisted their mistress out of her portable chair. After positioning her securely upright to keep her steady with her hands clutching the ledge behind which the Torah scrolls were arrayed, they stepped respectfully back a few paces to allow her these final private moments with her girls.

That's what she always called them—My girls. There they were all lined up like debutantes at a ball in their fancy velvet and satin dresses trimmed with gold and adorned with silken embroideries and their soaring ornate silver crowns. On the Sabbath, in the synagogues of her childhood, some man would ask one of them to dance, take her out, give her a spin around to show off his trophy that everyone else reached out to stroke, to fondle, to kiss—lay her down, undress her, open her up, gaze at her, find her place, read her, know her, and when he was finished with her, raise her up and exhibit her exposed—the largest and strongest man would exult in displaying her open at her widest—then dress her again before taking her around for one more whirl now properly decent and placing her back with the other girls to await the next time she would be asked out again. The best moment for Temima, a moment she savored even when she was herself a young girl, had always been when they dressed her again after having undressed her and entered her—when they gave that little tug, such an awkward gesture for a man, the gesture of a father who is not often called upon to dress his little girl, to straighten the bottom of her mantle skirt so that it would not ride up.

Temima inserted her head deep within the ark, inhaling the fragrance of dust and moldy plush, then turned her eyes to the far corner where she knew the wallflower was wedged—the smallest and plainest girl, the one who was never taken out except on the festival of Simkhat Torah, when Temima alone would rejoice and dance with her in the days when she was still dancing. This was the Torah that Temima herself had written secretly, with a quill on parchment and repeated ritual bath immersions in anticipation of inscribing the ineffable name. She had undertaken this radical task in order to know Torah intimately, to penetrate its mysteries letter by letter down to the tiniest thorn of the tiniest *yod*. Later, when she had a synagogue of her own, she bestowed her Torah upon her congregation in honor of her mother who had died when Temima was eleven; only the innermost core of her innermost circle could identify the scribe of this least prepossessing little Torah in the lineup as Ima Temima herself. On its blue mantle the inscription was embroidered in gold thread now frayed and faded: "To the precious soul of Rachel-Leah daughter of Hannah, Rosalie Bavli, may her memory be a blessing, mother of Temima Ba'alatOv, may her candle shed light, may she live on for many good long years."

Temima loosened one hand from the ledge of the ark against which she was supporting herself and extended her arm to stroke the poor little reject. "I still haven't forgiven you for deserting me, Mama," Temima said in English inside the safe. Behind her, Cozbi and Rizpa could hear her muffled voice though they could not decipher the words, and in any case they did not understand the language, but when they noticed that she was beginning to sway and totter, they shot forward to catch her. Temima stopped them with a shake of the head and, speaking clearly in Hebrew so that they could make out every syllable, she said, "Remember what happened to Uzzah when he thought the Ark was slipping off the wagon and he dared to put out his hand to steady it."

Neither Rizpa nor Cozbi could remember, or, for that matter, ever even knew, what had happened to Uzzah, but they figured it was probably not something good. Temima, instead of revealing to them the well-meaning Uzzah's cruel fate, just let go of her ark-safe entirely and stood there unassisted with her back still turned to them. She was recalling how, for almost the entire year after her mother's death, she did not speak a single word except on Sundays, when she would take two trains and a bus out to the cemetery in Queens where her mother was buried still without a gravestone to mark the plot, and she would talk to her mother all through the afternoon, telling her mother everything that had happened to her and everything she had thought and felt that week and who had hurt her feelings and who had humiliated her, and she would cry and cry until she would pass out from grief and longing.

But this time Temima did not collapse. She turned around and faced her long synagogue and study hall with its rows of benches, as she had so many times in the past to preach and teach. One arm encircled the shriveled body of her little mother Torah, its insides the handiwork of a woman and therefore blemished and unkosher and impure, its blue velvet dress threadbare and filmed with cobwebs, its crotch and bottom lightly straddling her hip as if she were carrying a child. With her other hand she pulled the top rim of the great prayer shawl that encircled her shoulders over her head like a hood, drawing it forward so that her veiled face disappeared inside the talit as if into the far depths of a tunnel. With her shrunken little mother in her arms, she walked on her own down the aisle of her synagogue, past Cozbi and Rizpa guarding her anxiously, past her four Bnei Zeruya gallantly awaiting her with the porta-chair, and, without looking back, she stepped out of the door of her shul and through the door of her aperion, their two openings now aligned like capsules docking in space so that it was impossible to distinguish where you were coming from in the world and where you were going.

The transition was executed fluidly, as if she had just been ushered into the next room, and yet Temima's breathing expanded with the sense that she had been released from a black pit like the hole into which Joseph was cast by his brothers, crawling with snakes and scorpions, in which she had been held until sold into the slavery of her position in the world, as if she had just escaped a life sentence. It had been a very long time since she had simply been outside in the free blowing air—years, she thought.

Through the curtained window of her aperion she could feel the dear morning breeze and the sweet warmth of this early spring day. It was the tenth of Nisan, the biblical first month of the year. In four days' time, if she lived, she would sit down to preside over her Passover Seder in the place to which she was now leading her flock, a destination she had not yet revealed to them. She had purposely chosen this day to carry out her wishes exactly as she conceived of them, with no discussion or consultation or opportunity afforded for anyone to dissuade her or modify her plans in any shape or form, because by Temima's calculations, this was the day, in the fortieth year of the Israelites' wandering in the wilderness, that Moses' sister, Miriam, died. The fact is mentioned in passing, Miriam's death, practically a footnote to their itinerary—arrival at the wilderness of Zin in the first month, stopover in the city of Kadesh, and by the way, Miriam died and was buried there—immediately after a detailed discussion of the rituals of the eradication of impurities with the specially mixed ashes of a perfect red heifer. In contrast, Miriam's other brother

Aaron the high priest, creator of the golden calf, dies some verses after on a mountaintop in a ceremonial rite of priestly passage, and is given full honors, with thirty days of mourning and universal lamentation. What do we learn from this? Temima would pose the question to her students. That in the great scheme of things, a woman's place is somewhere between two kinds of cows.

By scheduling her radical action on Miriam's *yahrzeit*, Temima sought to correct this slighting of a woman who had always tried her best to do the right thing. One year to the day after Miriam's death, also on the tenth of the first month as it happened, the Israelites, led by Moses' successor, Joshua son of Nun, crossed the Jordan to the Promised Land, the waters piling into a great heap at the moment the priests leading the way bearing the ark dipped their feet into the edge of the river. Like the priests at the head of Joshua's hordes crossing the Jordan on this day more than three millennia ago, Temima in her aperion with her deflated little mother Torah in her lap intended to ride at the head of her liberated congregation, hundreds strong, to show them the way. She made this point categorically to Paltiel, she would not bend on it, she would not countenance being swaddled in the middle of the swarm like a queen bee, or protected in any way as Paltiel and the others had at first insisted. Nevertheless, they had devised a kind of makeshift seatbelt for her, which she now also rejected, actually uprooting it and tossing it out the window like a spoiled child, punctuating what she had already told them. "This time I'll be transported my way. Next time you carry me I'll be flat on my back with my nose in the air—and you can do it any way you want, I won't stop you." The only prop she accepted was a cell phone with which to communicate her orders, since she alone knew how they would be going; the route as in any fumbling human journey would be winding, it would not be direct, and only she knew where they would end up.

She pressed the autodial to signal the chief of her bearers, the head Bnei Zeruya. "*Sah!*" she ordered.

There was an unexpected lurch as they set off that caused her to almost drop her wasted mother Torah, a calamity that could have mandated a penitential fast of forty days—followed by an exhilarating gust of buoyancy as they raised her in her aperion into the air and sailed forth, cutting through the crowd that parted to allow her to pass to its head. As they swung into Yekhezkel Street and proceeded down to Sabbath Square, Temima leaned back. She was on her way. She closed her eyes to penetrate the deepest levels of inward concentration and connection to the divine as she recited the traveler's prayer while already in motion. Save us from the hands of every enemy and ambush and bandits and wild beasts along the way, and from all the varieties of punishment and suffering that agitate to gather on this earth.

When the first rock struck the side of her aperion, Temima's eyes shot wide open. She strained forward to peer through the curtains of her Solomonic palanquin. They were entering the heart of Mea Shearim just before the point where the street narrows. It was precisely in that direction, into the most narrow and choked straits of pious conviction and certitude, that she intended now to march her flock, even if their course would be lengthened and circuitous and lurking with peril and drag on for forty years—in order to purge them of the mentality of slaves, in order to assert her rights and stake her claim.

Everywhere she looked, black-clad men and women in wigs and housecoats and thick rolled-up stockings were scurrying frantically in and out of stores, shopping desperately as the merciless Passover deadline approached. Against the walls bearded men in white shirts stretched by too much kishke were positioned with blowtorches to fire oven racks and stovetops to a glow, removing every trace and memory of leaven. Temima spotted some joker in a blowtorch queue awaiting his turn with a toaster. Maybe it had been another joker who had thrown that first stone, but then she picked them out in their multitudes, shifting through the masses, boys mostly, some as young as five by her estimate, few older than sixteen with patches of new beard, on holiday from the long hours in the study halls, burning with pent-up indignation, quivering with excitement, their faces flushed and glistening, some with arms already raised, poised for the signal to begin the bombardment. Everywhere there was rumbling and hissing, and above it all a speaker mounted on top of a car thrusting out and amplifying invectives against Temima and her followers. "Impermissible! Desecration of the Name! Blood and Fire and Pillars of Smoke! Worse than the sodomites who were prepared to parade through our streets flaunting their abominations to defile our holy city!"

Against the horn on the car rooftop saturating the airwaves, drowning

out every rational thought, Temima had no way to raise the full nakedness of her woman's voice. All she had was her cell phone. She reached
Paltiel. As soon as her Bnei Zeruya step foot on the narrow portion of
Mea Shearim Street, Temima instructed her son, the road ahead of them
will empty entirely, like the river Jordan. She herself, HaRav Temima
Ba'alatOv, will be stationed aloft in her aperion at the top of the street
for the whole time as her congregation streams by as Moses stood on the
hilltop with his arms held up in the air by Aaron and Hur in the battle
against Amalek. When all of her people pass before her and proceed down
the street and arrive at the great synagogue of Rav Nakhman of Bratslav
on the other side of the Mea Shearim *shuk*, Temima said, she will go forth
to join them. They were to await her coming there at the Bratslaver shul.
It was also Paltiel's responsibility to remind them to gather up as treasures
as many of the stones that are thrown at them as they can carry. These
will form our monument. The stones meant to strike us will be made to
speak for us.

Drawing up the collars of their black jackets to mask the lower portion
of their faces, and with cries of Harlots! Whores! Sluts! Jezebels! Vashtis!
Delilahs!—the stone-throwers were winding up and hurling their missiles.
Streetlights were smashed. Tires were set aflame. Burning dumpsters were
overturned. Great plumes of smoke looped up into the air. Ima Temima
in her aperion borne by her four Bnei Zeruya advanced to the top of Mea
Shearim Street and took her position there like the pillar of cloud that
had moved from in front of the Israelites and stationed itself behind to
screen them as they crossed the Reed Sea and confounded their Egyptian
pursuers. And just as Temima had foretold, the narrow street in front of
them was emptied of people; the only signs of human life that remained
was the trash—the plastic bags and the wax paper from falafels and
bourekas and knishes of every variety, kasha and potato, wafting in the
breeze and plastering themselves with their own grease like some kind
of installation art against the metal grates that had just been slammed
down over the shop fronts.

With cries of Te-Tem-Ima-Temima-from-Brooklyn her congregation
flowed past her aperion into Mea Shearim Street—Paltiel and Cozbi and
Rizpa, the ecstatic band of prophetesses tethered along their rope pulled
by Kol-Isha-Erva, the ailing high priestess Aish-Zara and her consecrated
knot of priestesses, and the hundreds of others, with Zippi, her daughter

by Abba Kadosh, circulating among them, wiping away blood, wrapping gauzes around heads, applying antiseptic to wounds, dispensing bandages from her circumcision kit. Their numbers stretched across the entire width of the street, spreading luxuriantly in the emptied roadway as if it were the Sabbath and all traffic had rested, onto the narrow sidewalks as if they had the right of way. They could pass freely just like men, they were not obliged to step submissively off the curb to give way to a man striding briskly toward them, insulating him from the distraction and temptation that their physical existence signified.

When the last of her followers passed through, Temima set forth in her aperion borne on poles on the shoulders of her four Bnei Zeruya down the deserted street, alone and unaccompanied, with hundreds of eyes upon her peering through shop grilles and, above the shops, through slightly parted curtains of apartment windows. Like an empress on an unfurling red carpet Temima went forth to meet her flock awaiting her alongside the great white synagogue of the Dead Hasidim on Salant Street, near the entry to the *shuk* of Mea Shearim. There through her spokeswoman Kol-Isha-Erva she commanded her followers to file behind her into the marketplace—and as they proceeded, she ordered them to place one by one the individual stones that had been hurled at them and that they had salvaged onto a heap as a remembrance of what had occurred on this day—like the stones that had been gouged out of the Jordan riverbed and erected in Gilgal after Joshua and the Israelites had crossed over, an eternal commemoration, like the stones set on top of a grave as a sign that you were there, you are still alive, they tried to kill you but you're not dead yet. "When the Messiah comes and Rav Nakhman returns to take his rightful place in his empty chair that awaits him inside this shul," Kol-Isha-Erva raised her voice speaking for Temima Ba'alatOv, "he will gaze at this memorial and kiss each stone. He will bless each obstacle that has brought us closer to our redemption."

Inside the *shuk* they were confronted by yet another obstacle placed before them, because, as Rav Nakhman himself taught, God is found in the obstacles, which obliged them to halt there to await its overcoming on the road to the fulfillment of their desire. An old man dressed in tattered and threadbare oatmeal-colored yellow-stained long underwear such as could only be seen in public in Mea Shearim hanging rigid as if electrocuted from clotheslines, was staggering back and forth screaming,

No, no, I won't! I don't want to! I don't want it! No, you can't make me!
Oy,Oy,Oy! His long white beard was flying, the sparse white hair rimming the bald and mottled crown of his head wild and streaming. He had
escaped from his deathbed in one of the apartments above the market,
a fruit stall owner explained to a member of Temima's congregation—
and the news swiftly spread. He had been screaming like that up in his
apartment for three days already—Oy, Oy, Oy!—howling, howling nonstop. He was driving the whole neighborhood crazy with his unbearable
screams, he was inconveniencing everyone, he was taking much too long
to die, it was indecent.

Temima and her people stopped there frozen as the old man darted
back and forth flailing his arms, shrieking No! No! No! within a gradually constricting circle, as if he were being sucked down a hole that was
inexorably drawing him in. In her aperion Temima was singing from the
one-hundred-and-sixteenth Psalm, The cords of death have encircled me,
and the straits of the underworld have found me. She was sending her
message along the waves of the air to this old father, Run, my heart, run
Reb Lev, flee, escape, get away from them! Chasing after him were three
younger men all with dark beards, all of them crying out, Tateh, Tateh,
Tateh, one of them waving a large black velvet yarmulke, yelling, "Tateh,
how can you go outside without your *koppel* on your head?"—the second
crying, "Tateh, Tateh, your little *schmeckel'e* is popping out from your
gotchkes, it's not dignified for a man your age to let people see his whole
business hanging out in the street, it's not becoming"—the third racing
after their ancient father with a wheelchair as if to scoop him up in a net
like a writhing fish already bloodied by the hook.

It was astounding how long it took them to catch the dying old man
so fired was he by his last exalted struggle—long enough for a delegation from among Temima's followers toward the rear of the crowd not
in a position to witness in its full misery this futile resistance at the last
barricade, the group that called itself the Daughters of Bilha and Zilpa,
to enter the hardware store with its goods spilling out into the market
square and buy up every single cleaning implement they could lay their
hands on—so that once the old man was finally trapped and restrained
with ropes and bungee cords and the *gartel* belts from his sons' kaftans
in the wheelchair still screaming Oy, Oy, Oy, No I won't, I don't want
to! No, You can't force me! and speeded away in all his unseemliness

out of sight and out of hearing forever and the aperion set off again followed by the throng out of the *shuk* and up the hill toward Ethiopia Street, throughout the moving mass, women, including Temima's own Rizpa, now had their heads wrapped in turbans made of cleaning rags and dishtowels and they were pumping into the air brooms, mops, squeegees, carpet sweepers, dustpans, toilet brushes, plungers, and so on, chanting Te-Tem-Ima-Temima-from-Brooklyn, and balancing on their heads plastic buckets and metal garbage cans, strainers and colanders, like pilgrims to Jerusalem bearing offerings of first fruit to the Temple.

By now, word was already spreading throughout the city of a wondrous procession making its way no one knew where for a purpose no one could say what as they entered the top of Ethiopia Street, past the compound sheltering the great round domed Abyssinian Church, past mysterious gardens heavy with silence behind stone walls, past the house in which Eliezer ben Yehuda, fanatic resuscitator of the Hebrew language, once resided, its historical marker ripped off yet again by fanatic defenders of the faith offended at the sacrilege of the Holy Tongue deployed for common intercourse, leaving only a gouged-out frame marking the ghostly whisper of a plaque. They veered into the Street of the Prophets, and from there to HaRav Kook Street, pausing at Temima's command in front of the home of the first chief rabbi of Israel, Abraham Isaac Kook, halting at this spot for personal reasons—to grant Temima a few minutes to focus inwardly in silence on the memory of her baby boy named for this towering Zionist mystic—her baby Kook Immanuel, tucked for so many years now in his tiny cradle blanketed with dirt in the ancient Jewish cemetery of the old city of Hebron.

Let me not look upon the dying of the child, Hagar cried as she cast her boy Ishmael away from her in the wilderness. A savage cry came out of Ima Temima—she did not know from what depths within her it had come up or how it had escaped her, she did not know if it was a cry of grief or a cry of shame. And then she lost all connection to that cry entirely, she concluded it had not been her cry after all, it had not come from her at all but from outside of her where it was amplified many times and reverberated over and over again as her aperion lurched forward into the moving traffic of Jaffa Road, bringing progress to a dazed halt as this epic caravan from an apocalyptic age lumbered across the road. The cries were coming from every side—from the ululating women of the east running toward them from the Makhane Yehuda market, skidding on rotting fruits and vegetables, cracking sunflower seeds with gold teeth and spitting out the shells, from the shrieking bands of *klikushi* pouring forth from the Russian Compound, letting out great convulsive fits of lamentation like professional mourners, writhing spasmodically and barking like dogs as if possessed by demons, tearing at their hair and rending their garments. Behind them, riding on broomsticks fashioned from the wood of birch trees, cackling wildly, came the Baba Yagas with long loose ash-colored hair, word having reached them of a great and powerful sister witch making her way in a proud demonstration through the streets of city.

The *erev rav* have fastened themselves to us now, the mixed multitude, Temima noted, the riffraff, the *asafsuf*. She accepted the inevitability of this. Maybe she was not at the same level as Moses Our Teacher of whom it is written that there never arose again in Israel a prophet like Moses to whom God had spoken face-to-face—even more intimately, mouth to mouth. Unlike Moses in his old age, the vigor and moist freshness of Temima's youth had fled her and was gone, it was true, but she too was leading a congregation of obnoxious neurotics and malcontents and complainers from one slavery to another, and to their ranks a mixed multitude of hangers-on and groupies and assorted fans and freaks and misfits with all varieties of baggage were now also attaching themselves as they had to the eternally ripe Moses in his grand exodus from Egypt, as if she didn't have enough problems already, bringing nothing but more headaches.

They proceeded into the Ben-Yehuda pedestrian mall, with this great cast of extras metastasizing wildly on their back, their numbers multiplying every step of the way, more and more fellow travelers joining their ranks like the pilgrims who had once streamed by foot to Jerusalem three times a year to bring their sacrifices on the altar of the Holy Temple. More and more marchers hooked on to them here until the space was packed from end to end, some tagging along out of coarse curiosity and the itch for distraction, it is true, but others also gripped by the hope that periodically seized this superficially Westernized land and threw its inhabitants into spasms that salvation was arriving at last.

The cacophony of sounds was overwhelming, surging in waves that were practically visible to those with eyes that could see as they passed over the crowd, in volume greater even than at Mount Sinai when the chosen people received the Torah. Whereas at Sinai there were only your standard voices and thunder and a trembling mountain and God Himself calling out from the plumes of fire and smoke, here on Ben Yehuda stretching all the way to Zion Square there was also what amounted to a full symphony orchestra of Russian musicians, including a pianist still banging on the grand he dragged out every morning to the mall for busking purposes, now being pushed along on its wheeled platform behind Temima's parade followed by the entire string section, including a harpist, the brass, the winds, the percussions, not to mention several bands of varying configurations of Slavic accordion players in authentic folk costumes, as well as klezmer fiddlers and clarinetists decked out in Eastern European vest and cap concepts. Also latching onto Temima's procession was a clutch of Breslover Hasidim just released for holiday furloughs from prisons and lunatic asylums bedecked in white crocheted skullcaps with pom-poms pulled over their shaven heads down to their eyebrows inscribed with the phrase NA-NA-NAKH-NAKHMAN-FROM-UMAN, which they were also bellowing ecstatically in counterpoint with the official anthem of the parade, Te-Tem-Ima-Temima-from-Brooklyn. They were followed by half a dozen Rabbi Shlomo Carlebach clones strumming the same three holy chords in a minor key on their untuned guitars, two Elvis impersonators, one with a glossy white satin yarmulke topping his slicked black wig stamped with the words BAR MITZVAH OF SEAN SCHNITZEL, to which were glued iridescent sequins to flash the King's proud Jewish roots, and also a Bob Dylan impersonator with a harmonica strapped in front of his mouth like an orthodontic torture device who many in the crowd claimed was the actual troubadour Bobby Zimmerman himself going through yet another stage of spiritual crisis and rebirth and accordingly they approached him for his autograph, which he graciously provided.

Needless to say, more shofars were also added to the tumult—even in this respect Temima's extravaganza was not outdone by Sinai—blasted for the most part by messiahs in white robes astride white donkeys, and there were, in addition, assorted King Davids, one of them a dwarf, in cardboard crowns covered with tin foil plucking harps and lyres and lutes, which, unfortunately, could barely be heard to sooth the anguished soul in the great din. A Moses with horns on either side of his head—not the useful kind that could be blown to contribute to the medley—also honored Temima with his company, and there were, in addition, a good number of competing Jesus Christs from all corners of the globe resurrected for the season conducting choirs of pilgrims who had descended upon the Holy Land for the Easter holiday singing hymns responsively in a babel of tongues, bearing enormous wooden crosses, the two beams lashed together with duct tape, and flagellating themselves with leather whips still reeking of freshly flayed stray cat purchased for this purpose at full retail payable exclusively in dollars or euros from the shops on the Via Dolorosa in the Old City.

Reports of all of this churning activity amassing at her rear were relayed to Temima Ba'alatOv on her cell phone by Kol-Isha-Erva at the head of her school for prophetesses and from the high priestess Aish-Zara leading her band of priestesses. I don't already have enough meshuggenehs of my own? Temima thought to herself, poaching another one of the great Tanakh comic vignettes, the quip of King Akhish when David fled from the manic-depressive King Saul to Gat, disguising himself as a crazy person, scratching at the walls and letting his spit drool down into his beard. If King David could turn himself into madman, why can't your local psychotic also turn himself into King David?

Temima accepted all of these developments with resignation, even a level of tolerance. She had anticipated a circus of this nature, but the prospect would not deter her from setting out from the Bukharim Quarter as her life on earth was constricting, to carry out her final intentions purely on her own terms. Through the window of her aperion she followed the movements of hordes of beggars, male and female, who had also attached themselves to her procession and could not be shaken off. They had descended on the mall in their legions that morning to profit from the flood of tourists funneled in by the high Paschal season, working the growing crowd tenaciously.

Poverty did not confer righteousness; this is what Temima taught. Do not favor the poor in their disputes, the Torah in one of its more progressive passages instructs us in matters of justice. The beggars in their destitution were in principle no holier than the tourists with liquid assets they were scavenging among or than your standard recognizable mall habitués whose ranks also unfolded in great crests in Temima's wake—the youth groups spanning the entire range of the political and religious indoctrination spectrum, right, left, and center, every one of their members identically hooked up and wired to their equipment like marionettes, yelling into their cell phones and flailing their arms in emphatic gestures, squealing, hugging, bouncing up and down in ritual circles; the tough guys strutting in their tank tops and gold necklaces and natal crease décolletage tearing with their teeth great chunks of kebob off sticks, twitching to their inner trance; the gay Arab boys from Nablus and Jenin, eyes rimmed in kohl, openly holding hands on the sinful side of Jerusalem; the Muslim girls in headscarves and tight jeans lugging overflowing shopping bags; the Hasidic men looking for some action, along with the foreign workers, the Romanians, the Thais, the African slaves imported for the dirty work, all with matching unhealthy skin colors due to excessive self-abuse; and swarms of North American shoppers for souvenirs of little olivewood trinkets and Israel Defense Force knockoffs and silver ritual objects who were filling up to capacity the Jerusalem hotels for the Passover festival, including Mr. and Mrs. Peckowitz from Teaneck, New Jersey, he insisting over her shrill protests that they check out the action, join the parade, this was the authentic Israel they were finally seeing, videoing with his new camera given to him as a going-away present by their son the mob massed in front of them in every stage of its progress through the Ben-Yehuda pedestrian mall down to the end of King George Street, past the mausoleum of the Great Synagogue evoking the destroyed Temples of Solomon and Herod toward the open space of French Square where the entire procession was alarmingly brought to a dead halt by a phalanx of police mounted on horses in full body armor with rodentlike masks and helmets, at which point Flo Peckowitz screamed, "What did I tell you, Stanley, you schmuck? It's a terrorist attack! They're drawing us all to one spot so they can kill every last one of us in a single stroke, the lousy Nazis. The ingathering of exiles—follow the leader to Israel like lemmings—one great big concentration camp—so we can all be wiped out with one bomb and they can finish the job for Hitler once and for all. That's what we call efficient—the *final* final solution! Stanley, you're such a pathetic schmuck, how many times do I have to tell you?"

Then came the explosion, and, as if shot from a cannon, the multitude of hangers-on flew off in every direction, to be recycled in the endlessly absorbent crevices and chinks of the stones of Jerusalem, leaving in the street only Temima Ba'alatOv in her aperion borne by her four Bnei

Zeruya and her original flock of several hundred who had set out with her that morning in unquestioning obedience and loyalty—We shall do and then we shall listen!—following wherever she would lead.

Before they could move onward, however, they were held up behind barricades that were swiftly and efficiently erected, with all the steel professionalism of catastrophic expertise, as the sirens brayed and the medical and emergency and security personnel poured in and the area was thoroughly combed for additional bombs for which this first one might have been designed as a diversion. French Square was a particularly sensitive spot—the prime minister's official residence was nearby, the Women in Black held their weekly vigil against the occupation in this place they had renamed Hagar Square, it was a crossroads where old sins rotted on gallows for all to see and contemplate. In the end, though, it had been a meticulously controlled blast, detonated, as it happened, by Israeli sappers when a lone suicide bomber, girdled in a vest studded with explosive charges with dangling wires visible under a sweatshirt, was observed running in agitated circles in the middle of the square, completely oblivious to the traffic swirling around from all sides and would not listen to reason that might have resulted in a lifesaving defusing. Now the bomber lay alone, the sole casualty, a pulped heap almost exactly in the center of the square as the religious squads arrived in their fluorescent orange vests and rubber gloves to clear away the mortal remains.

That evening Al Jazeera released to YouTube the martyr's traditional farewell video. In the history of suicide bombings, it had been a notable and shocking twist when women began to blow themselves up, including mothers of young children, risking the immodest exposure of a recognizable body part when they were ripped apart, damaged goods exalted by the promise of the restoration of their virginity in paradise.

This time there was an even further variation on the theme. The martyr this time was a dog. According to the narrator of the video, the dog's name was King George. King George was shown staring straight ahead into the camera with his lugubrious eyes against the background of a black, white, and green Palestinian flag with a Kalashnikov planted on either side, his long, mournful brown head framed by a black-and-white checked keffiyeh folded at the peak like Yasir Arafat's in the symbolic shape of a full river-to-sea Palestine.

"King George has chosen his fate willingly and with joy in his heart, with absolutely no tremor of fear and the words *Allah hu akhbar* on his lips," the voiceover intoned. "Tomorrow King George will be a *shahid*. Tomorrow King George will no longer be treated like a dog. Tomorrow the gates of paradise will open up to him without a checkpoint and he will be welcomed inside as a holy martyr by seventy-two virgin bitches at his eternal disposal, but as our imams remind us, the pleasure will not be sensual—it will be spiritual." The dog, people remarked in the comments below—there were millions of hits—looked exceptionally melancholy, and progressively even more depressed as the narration proceeded and came to its end.

Afterward, a huge protest surged up from the animal rights delegation against the government of Israel for blowing him up instead of making a greater effort to entice him with a biscuit, while pundits seized on the material to deconstruct the symbolism and rich ambiguities of a dog martyr. Many people who had been on the scene recalled having seen this dog roaming the streets of downtown Jerusalem that morning, dressed in a canine sweatshirt with a hood inscribed with the logo for Yeshiva University of New York, a costume that, in retrospect, appeared exceptionally incongruous in the heat not to mention bulky on a creature who overall gave such a gaunt, neglected, unloved impression. Flo Peckowitz remembered having seen him too, and even if, looking back, she conceded that maybe she ought to have reported the beast as a suspicious object, at the time she had thought his getup was absolutely adorable, and though the dog seemed to be entirely alone with no owner anywhere in sight, Flo nevertheless had asked out loud where she could get a sweatshirt like that for her granddaughter's puppy Fluffy, and a deep disembodied voice from somewhere in the distance was heard to intone, "The Source of Everything Is Jewish," as if God Himself had answered her from the mountaintop.

As government agents and military personnel exited the scene and fanned out into the alleyways to penetrate the populace with the mission of hunting down the late King George's human handler, who had taken a pit stop with a Moldovan hooker on Pines Street and neglected in the end to trigger the charges from afar, four police officers astride their horses, on highly classified orders from the very top, were detailed to ride alongside Temima's procession to keep guard over her to wherever her heart's desire was guiding her.

Still, it was especially treacherous maneuvering through the protesters camped out in front of the prime minister's residence, to cut a path between the fors and the againsts on every issue, from territory to religion to reparations to imprisoned spies languishing in terminal stages of horniness, and so on and so forth, through the jungle of signs on poles brandished like paddles, through protesters in chains, in coffins, in cages, in concentration camp costumes, through women in green, women in black, women in white, women in blue and white, through tent cities and shiva-sitters and shofar-blowers and megaphone-screamers and forty-day-hunger-strikers stretched out in sleeping bags. For this purpose the head of state's official quarters was placed on earth. Who made you lord over us? Korakh demanded, backed up by the collaborators Datan and Aviram, and two hundred and fifty bigshots called up to the tribe—who made *you* the boss, Moses?

From within her aperion Temima took all of this in and shook her head. Enough with you already, sons of Levi! It was past noon, she was weary, it was time for her nap, but this was for her a day like no other, a day that was neither day nor night, she had to endure. Still she asked herself again now as had become her habit of late with the advancing years—lifting the curtain to peer out she posed the same question to herself yet again, Is this something I will miss when I am gathered back to my mothers?

The procession continued along Azza Street and looped into Radak Street on instructions from Temima communicated by cell phone to the four bearers of her aperion, her Bnei Zeruya. This was the route that Temima had laid out in advance for her penultimate journey. She had always liked Radak Street from the days when she had walked the city to establish her exact place in the world after her flight from Abba Kadosh in the wilderness with only Kol-Isha-Erva at her side, just one faithful disciple accompanying her in those days to soak in her words—the canopy of its old trees, the privacy of its old stone houses, the dignity of its old dwellers, the narrowness of its old roadway that now, in her triumphant return passage, swelled with her people from seam to seam, heralded by the four horsemen of her apocalypse.

She could have chosen a different route. There were other circuitous paths in the new city along which she could have led her people to arrive at her destination, and naturally she had also weighed the instructive value of taking them through the Old City, with all of its biblical visual aids, and beyond its walls to the City of David on the flank sloping down to the Kidron Valley and the pools of Silwan. She could have brought them through the ravine of Gehinnom, where our rebellious ancestors built shrines to their idols Baal and the Molekh, putting their own children to the fires as blood offerings—the Valley of the Slaughter, the prophet Jeremiah called it, hell on earth itself—then up to the plateau atop Mount Moriah where the Holy Temple once stood destroyed for their sins as Jeremiah had foretold, where our righteous forefather Abraham brought his own son Isaac to sacrifice him, bound him to the altar and raised the knife to slit the boy's throat at the Lord's command—the closest spot on earth to heaven itself.

To ascend the Mount, though, they would have been obliged to acknowledge the Western Wall, and this was a site that Temima on principle shunned, not because of the unfair and demeaning partition of space between the worshipping men and the women; under the aspect of the divine, how could that signify? No, she avoided this mosh pit because of the flabbergasting idolatry of praying to stones. Not for nothing does the text make a point of noting that no one to this day knows the exact place where Moses Our Teacher was buried (by God himself, as Rashi the commentator-in-chief notes—or, even better, Moses buried himself, as we all do), lest they turn it into a shrine and prostrate themselves before it. And then Temima, in her bed in the Bukharim Quarter that had become like a prison to her, had the dream that directed her how to go.

It was a dream in threes, like the dreams of Pharaoh's head baker and head cupbearer that troubled them one night in the dungeon of the king's chief steward, the dreams that revealed to them who will live and who will die, interpreted with merciless prescience by their fellow inmate, that show-off, that suck-up, that crybaby, that pretty boy Joseph, possibly a closeted homosexual. In Temima's dream there was a house with three impossible entrances—one was so low that only a flat cart could fit through, the second was even lower and much narrower to give access only to a small animal, the third was high up with no way to get to it—but there was no door to this house in the expected place of a size or shape that a normal human being could reach or pass through. In her dream Temima was either inside the house trying to get out, or outside attempting to get in—she herself did not know which. Though her form in her dream was that of a fetus, she knew with utter certainty it was she, she never questioned this at all in her dream or even experienced it as strange. Inside the womb of the fetus that Temima recognized as herself was another fetus that she knew was her mother, and within the womb of her mother fetus there nested yet a third fetus, an even more miniature Temima—like matryoshka dolls, homunculi, golems within golems. The skin of all three fetuses was transparent so that Temima could clearly see through them one inside the other. The tiniest fetus was struggling to get out of the mother fetus, who was laboring to get out of the biggest Temima fetus, who was attempting to get out of, or perhaps into, the house—but it was all in vain, they were helpless, as if stunned, paralyzed, again and again they were sucked back into the space they were struggling to escape from as into a vacuum or a black hole.

It was so horrifying that Temima squeezed out a stifled scream that brought Cozbi and Paltiel, in bedclothes hastily thrown over their naked bodies, flying to her room to cut the cord and liberate her from this nightmare. But in the last second before she woke up, through the transparent skin of the largest fetus that was herself, Temima could see the heart beating, with its blood vessels lit up in red and blue like the street map of a city. This was the map on which Temima traced the route she was destined to follow on this day.

When she arrived now at the vanguard of her procession to the end of Radak Street and the house of the president of the State of Israel was revealed as if on a stage before them, Temima received the final confirmation that she had chosen the correct path. They had reached the third major station on their road, the last preordained stop before she would come to her destination, when, at one and the same moment, she would enter and exit.

For the first time in her journey that day Temima poked her head fully out through the window of her aperion, to the great exultation of her people whose cries of Te-Tem-Ima-Temima-from-Brooklyn grew even more rousing at this glimpse of her craning her head out to try to view for herself, as much as was possible through her clouded eyes and the veil fluttering in front of her face and the talit hooding her head, the events unfolding before them that Kol-Isha-Erva at the head of her school for prophetesses was reporting from the scene into Temima's cell phone bulletin by bulletin.

The president's wife is standing on the upper story balcony of the house, leaning against the parapet, Kol-Isha-Erva was reporting. Her face is blotched, puffy, bags under her eyes, hair in curlers, wearing only a lacy bra. She's screaming, "I can't take it anymore, I can't take it!" She's sobbing. People are coming out of the house behind her, moving toward her very slowly. She's climbed over the parapet now. She's sitting on the ledge with her legs dangling down—fresh pedicure, pink panties—crying, shoulders heaving. Now she's screaming again, "I'm jumping, I'm going to jump!" A bunch of kids are standing outside the gate. They're yelling, "Jump, lady—go on, your majesty, jump!" The people behind her are getting closer, very carefully it looks like, creeping up, no sudden movements, don't want to alarm her. They're talking to her. She's turned around now, maybe to hear what they're saying, her back is to us. Now she's sliding down from the parapet, holding on with both hands, she's hanging there from the ledge over the ground below, the lower half of her body is swinging, rolls of fat between bra and panties, significant cellulite. She's let go with one hand now. Now she's let go the other. She's dropping, she's falling, can't tell how many meters to the ground. They're waiting for her down there—it looks like almost the whole staff is gathered there, holding out plastic trash bins. Thank God, they've caught her—she's saved. She's in a dumpster, she'll be recycled. They've put on the lid.

A garbage truck was maneuvering past them toward the president's house as the procession now wended its way up Jabotinsky Street headed by Temima in her aperion borne aloft by her four Bnei Zeruya with the four armored policemen mounted on their horses riding two on each side. Kol-Isha-Erva thought she recognized the driver. She thought she had also seen him earlier that day—in the *shuk* of Mea Shearim, sweeping up the stale human refuse with a brush broom, and then later on again in French Square, among the squad of salvagers scooping up the carcass of the dead dog. But she dismissed her ruminations as unworthy. She was stereotyping menials, she admonished herself, they all looked alike to her, she couldn't tell them apart, and even if an injunction against stereotyping did not exist so far as Kol-Isha-Erva knew in either the Written or the Oral Law, as a woman who had started in a secular place and who could not quite purge herself of the common naive values that had formed her, Kol-Isha-Erva was overcome with shame by the baseness of her private associations and prejudices, she shook her head hard now as if to knock them out of her mind like foul water in her ears.

From Jabotinsky the procession swung right, in accordance with Temima's instructions, into David Marcus Street, continuing unimpeded and without further incident past the Jerusalem Theater that was featuring an adaptation of S.Y. Agnon's unfinished novel, *Shira*, moving onward alongside a descending stone wall with strange sealed doors set flush in the masonry evoking Temima's nightmare, following the wall down the hill as they turned left and very soon after came to an abrupt stop on Temima's clipped command to the head of her Bnei Zeruya—*Poh!*—at an iron gate. The huskiest of the policemen accompanying them now alit from his horse, proceeded to the gate, unlocked it with a key he drew flamboyantly out of his pocket, threw the gate wide open, mounted his horse again, and nodded to his companions, at which signal all four swiveled the tails and the great defecating rumps of their beasts toward Temima's congregation and trotted off. Not a soul was surprised by this fanfare of special protection. It merely confirmed yet again how Temima was set apart by an extraordinary endowment of divine personal providence.

There are eight entrances in the stone walls that surround the leper colony in the heart of Jerusalem, but this was the main entrance and it was the grandest, and through it HaRav Temima Ba'alatOv in her aperion and her entire flock entered and left this world.

They marched down the central pathway toward the hospital building rising straight ahead in front of them with the words JESUS HILFE carved into the pediment from the days when the nuns and deaconesses of the order of the Moravians had ministered to the lepers, proffering the help of Jesus with punishing ecstasy. On either side of the path were fruit bearing and shade trees, olive and pomegranate and almond, carob and spruce and palm, and ancient gnarled cactuses, and there was a great stone cistern in which the water had been collected when the colony had been almost entirely self-sustaining and few healthy outsiders were condemned to enter to provide services and be infected. They passed the ruins of the herb and healing gardens with early spring sprouts of poppy, sweet pea, and hyssop, sage and lavender and nasturtium, haphazardly tended in therapeutic programs by youth groups afflicted with physical handicaps and mental retardation after the last lepers had been extruded and put away no one knew where.

They paused in their forward advance to wait politely as two ancient turtles took their time making their way across the path as if in deep conversation, reminiscing on over a century of lepers who had lived and died in contaminated isolation and quarantine within these walls, taking note, perhaps, that now it seemed the patients were returning after all, but unwilling to tax their constitutions by letting themselves grow too excited about this new development.

Kol-Isha-Erva climbed the steps to the landing in front of the main entrance to the hospital. Standing under the Jesus Hilfe inscription, gazing out over the assembled massed below her made up preponderantly of women, and speaking in the name of HaRav Temima Ba'alatOv, she said, "*Ha'maivina tavin*—in other words, She who understands will understand."

There was a savage scramble as the members of Temima's congregation swarmed in every direction to stake out for themselves the best squatting spaces within the hospital itself, with some of the less enterprising souls in the end forced to find shelter on the balconies or outside in the gardens. Cozbi and Paltiel claimed for themselves, as was their right, a suite of rooms on the ward floor, on the staff's side of the partition still in place that had segregated the patients from those who had cared for them with exemplary pious strictness, since, as we learn in Leviticus, even stones and houses can be stricken with *zora'at* and must undergo purification. Rizpa was allotted a designated room next to the laundry and the kitchen, which, to the wonderment of all that only served to elevate and confirm in their eyes the powers of HaRav Temima Ba'alatOv, was already fully stocked with provisions of all sorts to last an indeterminate length of time, as if it were a bomb shelter. No one questioned these miracles. They believed in Temima and the higher forces that hovered in her radiance to protect and provide for her.

In the midst of this frenzy, a hidden chamber on the patients' side of the ward was discovered to be already occupied by a man wearing a keffiyeh on his head flowing down over his shoulders to the middle of his back who would not turn around to face those who stood frozen in the doorway and would not respond when they addressed him—an Arab squatter perhaps, perhaps, even more troubling, a leftover leper; the members of Temima's flock who had stumbled upon him backed out of the entrance and slammed the door. Later, when Temima was apprised of this situation, she commanded with cold severity, "Do not raise your hand against the boy, and do not do anything at all to him"—summoning the words of the heavenly messenger addressing Father Abraham in the nick of time as he raised the knife to slaughter his son.

Temima Ba'alatOv, meanwhile, was borne onward in her aperion by her four Bnei Zeruya around the hospital building on its left side, along the terraced stairs to the dark secluded garden in the northern corner. From the moment they had entered the leper colony she had closed her eyes, displaying no curiosity at all about the new surroundings she had labored so hard to attain, opening them again only after her aperion had been set down and she had been carried with respectful delicacy out of it by her four Bnei Zeruya and conveyed into the small apartment at the edge of the garden and laid down on the bed that had been prepared for her made up with crisp white linens, tucking in her little mother Torah that she was hugging to her breast like a plush stuffed animal cozily beside her. A Tanakh was already set out for her on the bedside table, and beyond that across the room there was another table covered with a white cloth with a small vase of blood red poppies in the center and a chair for Kol-Isha-Erva to sit on when taking down Temima's words.

She stretched out her hand toward the Tanakh on her nightstand in a gesture as if to claim it, then pushed it away from her. "Blot me out please from Your book that You have written," Temima said softly. She closed her eyes again in a sign of great physical weakness and exhaustion, and Kol-Isha-Erva looked discreetly away when she noticed the old-lady tears being wrung out from under the creased lids as if from a rag. "The Talmud tells us that there are four categories of people who are considered to be the living-dead," Temima said, speaking in almost a whisper with her eyes still shut. "A blind man, a poor man, a childless man, and a leper. To that we now add a fifth—a woman. This is not commentary, it is simple logical deduction. I have had the misfortune to enter the Promised Land. Unlike Moses Our Teacher, I have not been spared."

■|■|■

More Bitter
Than Death
Is Woman: Azuva

The Teachings Of HaRav Temima Ba'alatOv, Shlita
(May She Live On For Many Good Long Years)—
Recorded By Kol-Isha-Erva At The "Leper" Colony Of Jerusalem

IN THE awareness of the Presence and the awareness of the congregation, in the convocation of the heights and in the convocation below, and at the personal behest of our holy mother, HaRav Temima Ba'alatOv, shlita, I am privileged to be appointed scribe charged with taking down for us transgressors the teachings of Ima Temima and with recording events of note as they transpire during our sojourn here in the Hansen's Disease treatment center compound of Jerusalem. Every syllable I write is read aloud to Ima Temima for final approval. Thus, I am justly admonished by Ima Temima at the outset for referring to our present place of habitation as the Hansen's Disease treatment center rather than "leper" colony. When I humbly suggest with utter reverence that the term "leper" is no longer acceptable usage and is universally deemed offensive, Ima Temima bestows a wise smile upon me and offers that I am regressing to my pre-enlightenment stage when my woman's voice was clothed rather than naked. "Who told you that you are naked? The serpent, most naked and wily of all beasts—to shut you out of paradise, and to shut you up." This is a teaching of Ima Temima in the "leper" colony of Jerusalem.

On the explicit instructions of Ima Temima, this journal is to be called "More Bitter Than Death Is Woman," a verse from the book of Ecclesiastes—by the author known as Kohelet, the nom de plume, some say, for King Solomon himself, gripped by melancholy and depression. With total reverence, I raise my wily woman's naked voice to speculate on the appropriateness of this title, suggesting with great diffidence that it might perhaps be construed as misogynistic: Full of traps and snares is woman, Kohelet goes on to rant, not even one in a thousand is any good. If it really is Solomon, Ima Temima remarks with a dark laugh, he should know, since he kept in his harem a total of one thousand women, wives and concubines.

Yet very correctly our holy mother goes on to chide me for slipping into the pitfall of conventional self-censorship and excessive concern about public perception. It is then that Ima Temima puts forward a teaching of radical import: Kohelet was a woman. This is evident, Ima Temima demonstrates, not only from the obvious feminine form of her name, but also from the fact that the feminine conjugation of the word "said"—*amrah* Kohelet—is used in attributing this seemingly most woman-bashing of observations, providing the ironic clue to its true authorship and meaning for anyone open enough to grasp it. "Most people simply don't penetrate behind the mask," Ima Temima elaborates. "Kohelet passes herself off as a prince in the Davidic line, but it's not the first or last time in history that a woman author has been forced to create a masculine persona in order to be listened to, much less to be taken seriously. And who but a self-hating woman can better deploy the voice of a man to be more expressively self-hating than even a self-hating Jew? And how much more so if the self-hating woman is also a self-hating Jew? But once you recognize the voice as the voice of a woman you understand that only a woman would know better than anyone else on earth how bitter we are, yes, more bitter than death—and for good reason."

ON THE morning after our arrival at the "leper" colony, an event occurred that threw the entire camp into great consternation and even inspired a goodly number of doubting souls to take sudden flight through any opening in the walls that would permit them egress, some even clambering over in faithless panic when doors would not yield, to return to the fleshpots of Egypt. That morning, as many members of our flock were strolling the grounds to explore our new headquarters, and as the Daughters of Bilha and Zilpa under the direction of Rizpa, one of Ima Temima's two treasured personal attendants and our domestic management associate, were hauling in the bags of fresh provisions that had been left outside the gate—fruits, vegetables, dairy products, baked goods, as well as the first delivery of supplies for the forthcoming Passover festival—an unusually large and heavy object came flying over the southern wall into our compound, striking the head of our circumcision engineer, Zippi, cherished daughter of Ima Temima by our mutual ex-husband, the late Abba Kadosh, a'h (peace be unto him), knocking her out cold. This was doubly unfortunate as Zippi is the primary health care provider for our community; in cases of illness or accident, it would have been she who would have been called upon to be our server.

A decision was made to defer informing Ima Temima, who in any event at that very moment was engaged in the standing meditation of the morning prayer and could not be disturbed even if the world were coming to an end, God forbid. Rizpa ran for help to the apartment we had all noticed on the western side. This, by all accounts, is the home of a senior-citizen physician, allocated to him and his family as their place of residence in exchange for his on-call service to the "lepers" in nighttime emergencies. He had been granted the right to continue living there for the remainder of his natural life even after the last of his clients had been purged. Rizpa soon came back to report that the apartment was in shambles and abandoned, and she went on to add that the unmistakable ghosts of the bodies of the doctor and his wife were imprinted on their beds like stains in a substance that she likened to a white chalk, as if they had slowly decomposed there.

Thank God, by this point, Zippi was already opening her eyes and beginning to complain in her own inimitable way that contributes so richly to the diversity of our congregation about all the people who were in her face; the impact of the object that had struck her had been vastly diminished due to the kente-cloth turban she was wearing packed with heavy foam rubber to give it added stature and presence, which, thank God, protected her precious brain from severe trauma like a bicycle helmet. I venture to suggest that perhaps everyone should be required by law to wear a bicycle helmet in this perilous life at all times; this is not necessarily also the opinion of Ima Temima, I hasten to add by way of a disclaimer.

Two of Ima Temima's bodyguards, from the loyal Bnei Zeruya contingent, soon arrived with a hospital stretcher and bore Zippi off to her designated room attached to her clinic on the staff side of the hospital ward, where she continues the healing process. Blessed be God, day by day.

The missile that had been hurled over the southern wall and that had struck our dear Zippi on the head and landed on the ground with a dull thud was revealed, upon inspection, to be a dead goat. This discovery only served to increase the fright of some of our people, provoking even more of those challenged by a lack of commitment and self-esteem to begin scraping the walls in a desperate effort to flee, though not a soul would have prevented them, God forbid, from following their passion simply by walking out through the gate—we are pro-choice as a matter of principle and policy. The animal-rights supporters and vegetarians among us, with whom I include myself, were horrified by this shocking cruelty and disrespect to the remains of an innocent life created by the Almighty on the sixth day, just a little before He created man, and, as an afterthought, woman. If some mentally challenged individual has something against us, why did he have to take it out on the carcass of a poor goat? Why couldn't he have thrown something else to make his point—a trash bag stuffed with used condoms or tampons, for example, or a toilet seat?

Some of the more right-wing-inclined witnesses to this event that morning ventured that this goat-o-gram was a threatening message from Arabs living nearby, in East Jerusalem or Abu Tor, or even farther away, in Judea and Samaria where their flocks can be observed grazing on the terraced hills that belong to us, the Jewish people—our birthright, they emphatically declared; it was a signature act of the Arab mentality that needed to be understood for the sake of survival, they insisted—zero regard for human or animal life. There were also those who insisted that this dead goat special delivery was a spiteful act of hostility on the part of the ultra-Orthodox, a hideous warning to us as women for daring to overstep our bounds. It was nothing less than a scapegoat, they declared, laden with the filth of our sins, like the he-goat chosen by lottery that the high priest dispatched on Yom Kippur day with a man designated specifically for this task, to a desolate place where it was cast off a rugged cliff straight to Azazel, to the realm of demons and Djinns, of the anti-God. It followed, then, that those who had flung the scapegoat into our precincts regarded us as the polluted and sin-stained denizens and worshippers of Azazel.

For this reason, because of the possibility that the gruesome present we received that morning involved a priestly rite, our own high priestess, Aish-Zara, was summoned for a consultation. She arrived as quickly as was humanly possible on her two canes, supported by some of her subordinate priestesses, one of whom, a woman practically a senior citizen, I realized for the first time, was in an advanced stage of pregnancy. (I ask her forgiveness here in these pages—it was simply crude ageism on my part to mistake the forthcoming miracle of life for a watermelon-sized uterine fibroid.) Without touching it directly lest she be defiled by death, Aish-Zara leaned forward on her canes and proceeded at once to examine the goat. There was no discernible red woolen string tied to the head of this goat as would have been done with a scapegoat in the days of the Holy Temple, may it be rebuilt speedily and in our time. Nevertheless, on the principle of ruling more stringently in indeterminate situations when there is doubt regarding a commandment originating in the Written Law itself, and in the event that perhaps the red string might have slipped off as the animal was soaring over the wall into our premises, the high priestess Aish-Zara passed her canes to two of her acolytes and raised her hands over the head of our dead goat to recite the words that the high priest would have intoned over the scapegoat before sending it to its doom in the wilderness, after confessing the mad and malicious sins of the people: Please, HaShem, they have erred, they have been iniquitous, they have willfully sinned, I beg of You, please, forgive them.

As the bystanders clustering around the dead goat, in imitation of the example of Aish-Zara, prostrated themselves and fell on their faces crying out, "Blessed is the name of His glorious kingdom forever and ever," Ima Temima's son Paltiel, by her first husband Haim Ba'al-Teshuva, accompanied by Cozbi, the other treasured personal attendant of our holy mother, came rushing over, cutting through the crowd that gave way to them as was their due to survey with their own eyes the source of the commotion. They had hastily thrown bathrobes over their bodies, their faces were still puffed and dented by sleep, and on their feet were slippers—Cozbi's were lustrous red synthetic-satin backless stiletto heels with fuzzy pink pom-poms, which added even further to the disconnect between her impressive height and that of Paltiel, who, even in situations that are not comparative, can be described as vertically challenged. (There is no offense intended here, heaven forbid; with regard to this physical attribute, Ima Temima has requested that I note in these pages that Paltiel resembled our ancestors who were privileged to live during the periods of the First and Second Temple based on the scientific evidence of low-ceilinged domiciles unearthed by archaeologists.)

Cozbi gave the rapidly putrefying and bloated carcass one quick look and announced, "I know goat. She is goat of cheese-maker from Silwan, Ishmael, very cute guy. She is lady goat. See titties? All dried up." Cozbi went on to explain that the cheese-maker was morbidly superstitious about burying his dead goats in his own pastures lest the bad karma of death curdle the milk of the rest of the flock, and so it was his practice to get rid of the evidence by loading the remains into his truck and dumping them somewhere in West Jerusalem, preferably one of the more posh neighborhoods such as Baka or Talbieh. It was Cozbi's opinion that the appearance this morning of the cheesemaker's dead goat on the very valuable real estate of our "leper" colony in the heart of Jerusalem was either sheer coincidence or else something akin to an instant message from the cheesemaker meant for her, a friendly way of just saying hi and reminding her of old times. She did not go on to elaborate, but suggested instead that it would be best to stop making such a fuss over rotting goat flesh or read any deeper meaning into its emanation, either earthly or heavenly, but to bury it at once and forget about it.

"She already stink," Cozbi said, with great refinement pinching the wings of her nostrils between two exceptionally long ebony-lacquered fingernails. "Get Bnei Zeruya to bury her in garden. She will turn into hummus—make desert bloom."

Later that day, when a suitable interval arrived in which to inform our holy mother of the events of the morning, Ima Temima plunged into a discourse with eyes closed, as if in private meditation, on the vision of the minor prophet Zekharia of the original flying saucer—a woman representing wickedness packed into a tub of some sort pressed down with a leaden weight being borne by two other women with wings like the wings of a stork soaring on the wind to deposit their load in the land of Shinar, home of the tower of Babel, scene of one of humankind's first rebellions against God. "Welcome to Bavel. I am Tema Bavli, your official guide." Our holy mother opened her eyes and added, "The flying goat is the one kid that father bought for two *zuzim*. We sing her praises at the close of the Pesakh Seder. She is the herald of our redemption. *Had Gadya!*"

HALLELUJAH! Every soul sings the praises of HaShem. I am thrilled to record that our beloved teacher and the illuminator of our souls, HaRav Temima Ba'alatOv, shlita, our holy mother, Ima Temima, was blessed with the strength by the merciful Master of the Universe to preside over our Passover Seder on the night of the fourteenth of Nisan, four days after our arrival at the "leper" colony.

Mattresses bedecked with brilliantly colored cloths were carried down to the great hall on the first floor, the chosen venue for our Seder, and arranged in a ring for the purpose of allowing us to recline as free women liberated from slavery. Three mattresses were piled one on top of the other for Ima Temima, as befitted the lofty position of our holy teacher. I hasten to note here that the strictures in the Written Law regarding the malignant eruption of plague inside the walls of a house or in any of its furnishings were waived with regard to our mattresses; the "lepers" who had slept upon them for so many years along with their secretions and seepages, the drools and droppings and discharges of all their bodily fluids from all of their orifices, had been exorcised, their mattresses had been purified by the clean and healing air of our holy city of Jerusalem. Nevertheless, when, in the feebleness of my faith, I expressed upon our arrival some concern about contagion or contamination that might have been absorbed by these mattresses ("hazmats," I called them, in the poverty of my faith), Ima Temima reassured me in scientific terms that we were well-vaccinated and well-immunized by the Creator of the Universe since we as women have all already been stricken.

Everyone arrived to the Seder dressed in their best finery. Ima Temima, in full glory and selfhood, veiled as always like a bride being led to the altar, was robed in a majestic white satin *kittel* of surpassing elegance, in compliance with the injunction to glorify a mitzvah. In my white Bedouin dress embroidered with blue thread that I had purchased from a nonprofit organization promoting the handiwork of indigent Palestinian women, I was honored to recline on the mattress at Ima Temima's right that I had covered with a madras cloth over the organic micro-toxin super protection pad. Aish-Zara, in high priestess regalia, including an azure robe with its border of little tinkling bells and pomegranate globes stitched to the hem and a band wrapped around her forehead with the words HOLY TO GOD inscribed upon it reclined on her mattress at Ima Temima's left. (It is permissible, I am assured by Ima Temima, to note the resemblance between the priestly headband and the hippie headbands so many of us, in our foolishness, tied around our heads a lifetime ago to keep our brains from exploding.) Rizpa, in a dress adorned with Yemenite embroideries, the work of master seamstresses, and Cozbi, in an Armani number with a Russian lapdog, a white Pomeranian she called Abramovich, in her cleavage for warmth, and Jimmy Choo shoes, all gifts from Paltiel, were in attendance.

There were no children present in accordance with Ima Temima's express orders handed down prior to our departure for the "leper" colony. "We are finished with sacrificing children," Ima Temima had declared as a teaching. This absence of children, however, led to a minor though unfortunately public sibling-rivalry incident early in the proceedings as to who would be honored with the asking of the so-called Four Questions. As the youngest offspring of Ima Temima, Zippi, our circumcision engineer and primary health care provider, claimed this right by custom and tradition. For his part, as the sole surviving child from Ima Temima's only legally sanctioned marriage, Paltiel, our chief operating officer who runs the business that contributes so much to the maintenance of our organization, insisted that the honor be accorded to him. Zippi stamped her foot and pouted with her full lips with which she performs the oral *meziza* ritual, sucking up the blood of the circumcision insult, while Paltiel's face flashed red as an open wound and he raised his arm as if to strike. Thank God, before the matter could escalate, Ima Temima settled it as the mothers of all mothers do. "Children, you must share," Ima Temima said, adding as a teaching that sharing does not come naturally to the human animal, it goes against the grain, and therefore must be taught, though, regretfully, it is a lesson that girls learn only too well.

Ima Temima then assigned the Four Questions to Zippi, who belted them out in gospel fashion, riffing on the tune of the emancipated slaves of America, "Glory, Glory Hallelujah," The Battle Hymn of the Republic, bringing the entire congregation to its feet, swaying and dancing rapturously. Paltiel, in compensation, was accorded the role of the Wise Son of the Four Sons, but because on this night that was so different from all other nights the Four Sons had undergone gender-reassignment therapy and were transformed into the Four Daughters, and also, it may be assumed (with no offense intended), not to be outshone by his half sister Zippi, Paltiel delivered his lines in a shrill falsetto at full screech, which, Ima Temima has permitted me to note in these pages, some in our congregation regarded as a disrespectful caricature and mockery of the naked voice of a woman. Later, in reviewing this matter, Ima Temima recalled the story of how, in order to cure a prince who would not come out from under the table where he sat gobbling because he was convinced he was a turkey, the holy Rav Nakhman of Bratslav crawled under the table and gobbled along with him, declaring that he was a turkey too. *Ha'maivina tavin*—She who understands, will understand.

On the great white cloths that had been spread on the floor to serve as our Seder table inside our ring of reclining mattresses, tea candles floated in glass bowls filled with saltwater—flickering eyes in pools of tears. Though the effect was otherworldly, entrancing, trippy, I raised my woman's naked voice with utmost respect to caution against fire hazard, especially at those mystical heights when the holiness would become too much for us, and we would helplessly be seized by the need to worship through dance. Ima Temima only said, *HaShem ya'azor*—and indeed, during the exultation of the *Dayenu*, at the verse: If he had just given us their money and not split the sea, that would have been enough for us, the hair of EliEli, one of my prophetesses, a luxuriant cascade (and, I might add, an excess of vanity like a shampoo commercial that I have been after her for some time now to bring under control), began to sizzle and fry as she was swinging it about in all its shining splendor and burst into light like the burning bush as she was transported to another spiritual realm. And God *did* come to our aid, exactly as our holy mother had foreseen, so that we were able to quickly smother the flames with someone's poncho, the only residue of the mishap a smell like singed chicken feathers lingering through the night.

It is true that Ima Temima has on occasion commented that we tend to go overboard with candles to manipulate emotion, in Shoah commemorations for example; it is a form of idolatry, Ima Temima has taught, we must reject the intervention of votives, they are the arousal and aphrodisiacal toys of the goyim in their dark caves and naves prostrating themselves in adoration of blood and the agony of sacrificed sons. But with respect to the candlelight at our Seder, Ima Temima was laid-back and mellow, calling it "an elegant touch." To give credit where it is due, the candles were an expression of the good taste of our dearest Zippi to whom I, too, was like a mother when we all lived together as gatherers in the wilderness under the protection of our hunter-in-chief, the late Abba Kadosh, a'h, our dominant male figure.

I am enjoined to move on to the heart of the matter and achieve closure, but with the full knowledge of the Omnipresent, and with the full knowledge of Ima Temima, I have been given permission to digress yet again, for the sake of moral instruction, by relating one further incident that occurred early in our Seder. As we were lifting the cover off the matzah to expose our bread of affliction and raising our Seder plate like an offering in open invitation to all who are in need to come into our "leper" colony and eat, both Aish-Zara and I, almost simultaneously, noticed that our beloved Ima Temima was in considerable distress, twisting on the elevated pile of mattresses that was like a royal divan as if seeking a more comfortable position to ease a sharp pain. Naturally, I rose at once to the assistance of our holy mother—and thank God, our crisis management rapid-response intervention soon led to the discovery of a dried chickpea under the bottommost mattress of the thick pile of three upon which Ima Temima was reclining, which, the moment it was removed, brought instant relief. Ima Temima was our princess and that was the pea.

"*Kitniyot* alert!" someone yelled out, no doubt a stickler Ashkenazi member of our congregation for whom legumes are prohibited on the Passover with almost the same force as the five grains of leaven specified in the Torah. Immediately, Rizpa, our domestic management associate, came forward and stood trembling before Ima Temima, as if to take her rightful punishment like a well-drilled soldier for this dishonorable lapse in housekeeping. That is what we all assumed was the explanation for Rizpa's coming forward, until we discovered, to our astonishment, that she was confessing that it had been she who had deliberately concealed that single little dried chickpea under the mound of mattresses reserved for our holy mother in order to give expression to her Sephardi heritage, in which legumes are permitted on Passover; it had been a private subversive act of identity politics on Rizpa's part, she had never expected it to be discovered, she had not counted on the ultrafine supernatural antennae, the sensitivity of a spirit such as Ima Temima. Now she was overcome with shame, begging forgiveness for causing even a moment's discomfort to our precious mother—that had never been her intention, God forbid.

"*Kitniyot, shmitniyot!*" Ima Temima said, flipping a hand to illustrate how trivial the concern was.

As if a spigot had been turned on full force, fat tears began pouring unchecked down Rizpa's leathery brown cheeks, surprisingly large and copious for such a tiny woman, as if her entire body were nothing but a sack filled with gallons of tears. "Even some of our rabbis have called the *kitniyot* ban a stupid law," Ima Temima went on. "Those are their very words—quote-unquote, 'stupid law.'" But Rizpa would not be comforted; by now she was letting out great racking sobs, her whole body shuddering.

"Come to me, my holy, holy Rizpa, come lie down beside me, mommy," Ima Temima said, clearing a space on the mattress for the bereft little woman, who curled up like a lost kitten beside our beloved mother burying her face in the maternal warmth and wept and wept as Ima Temima stroked her head and murmured over and over until her spirit was restored, "You are so good, my holy, holy Rizpa, you have worked so hard, you have suffered so much, how you have suffered, we owe you so much, forgive us for not recognizing you, forgive us for taking the labor of another woman for granted, we should know better, forgive our ingratitude, mommy."

YES, TRULY, thank you, Rizpa—and, thanks also to our heavenly mother and father, we lacked for nothing. Bottles of wine were placed conveniently within everyone's reach, and we were directed by Ima Temima to drink down to the dregs each of our four cups. "It is a mitzvah," Ima Temima said. "Do not for one second think you don't deserve it, do not deny yourself." And Ima Temima taught by example; Aish-Zara and I had the honor and privilege to be the royal cupbearers for the evening, charged with offering the wine to our queenly mother, lifting the lower part of the veil modestly, like a bride's under the canopy, and tipping each of the four cups to the holy lips until they were drained.

Also gracing our table were heaps of round *shemura* matzot, burnt to perfection at the edges, guarded every second, like the dead before burial, at every stage of their production process lest they be exposed to moisture and the danger of fermenting into *hametz*—strictly supervised from the harvesting of the wheat to the kneading and shaping by hand to the baking in the oven for no more than eighteen minutes, God forbid, to the sale of eight pieces for thirty dollars minimum in a cardboard box barely distinguishable in taste from the matzot themselves. Aish-Zara and I glanced at each other when we noticed one of those emptied boxes with its print in bold black letters. They were Bobover matzahs, produced by the Hasidim of Bobov. Aish-Zara, who had grown up in Boro Park, Brooklyn, very near to Ima Temima's girlhood home, was the daughter of a Bobover Hasid, and even now with her illness in the incurable terminal stage she was still dealing with many painful unresolved issues concerning her childhood. For a moment I feared that a rush of recovered memories and the effects of post-traumatic stress disorder would seize our Aish-Zara, but, to my great relief, in the joyous spirit of the evening, she leaned toward me, she blessed me with her playful smile that exposed her dark gums with almost every tooth knocked out, and whispered, "At least they're not Pupa matzahs. Pupa is much more constipating." Aish-Zara's ex-husband, the wife-beater and abuser, was a Pupa Hasid.

In the center of our table there were two tall goblets of equal height, one filled with wine for Elijah the prophet and the other filled with water for Miriam the prophetess. Water was Miriam's sign, she was an Aquarian—the water over which she stood watch when her baby brother Moses was hidden among the rushes to save him from Pharaoh's death sentence against all newborn Hebrew boys, the water over which she led the women in song and dance with timbrels and drums when the Israelites crossed the Reed Sea on dry land with the Egyptian chariots in pursuit, the water of the well that, it is said, escorted them in her merit during the forty years of their wandering in the wilderness. There was also a magnificent Seder plate in the center of our table, fully loaded. In addition to the usual shank bone and the bitter herbs and the greens and the egg and the red paste of the *haroset* to commemorate the bricks our ancestors were forced to make during their enslavement in Egypt—in addition to all this familiar antipasti there was also a piece of gefilte fish (turd-shaped rather than sliced, unfortunately) to symbolize water. "For our Miriam mermaid," Ima Temima taught, "to whom we dedicate our Seder on this our first Pesakh in the 'leper' colony of Jerusalem."

Let us now at long last give Miriam some credit, our holy mother declared. Moses, Aaron, *and* Miriam led us out of Egypt, the prophet Micah said—but Micah was only a minor prophet after all. Miriam—her name contains the word bitter—was on the cutting edge of independent women in that she never married, we were horrified to learn from Ima Temima; there is no explicit mention of her marriage in the plain, unmediated text, Ima Temima taught, an unacceptable omission from the point of view of the sages, and so it was ordained that the wife of Caleb son of Yefuneh, a woman known as Azuva—her name means the forsaken one—was none other than Miriam, broken into wifehood and submission under an alias. "But for us," Ima Temima taught, "her name will be neither Bitter nor Forsaken. For us her name will be Snow White—because Miriam-Azuva-Snow White was the noblest 'leper' of them all."

Gevalt, the teachings about Miriam-Azuva-Snow White that dripped from the holy tongue of Ima Temima in the course of our Seder that night, were like honey, they sweetened the innermost soul and touched upon the most private sorrows and disappointments of each one of us, leaving us breathless. By the time we opened the door to the prophetess Miriam and invited her to cross the threshold into our space along with her escort for the evening, the prophet Elijah, and sip from their cups, it was as if her bitterness and abandonment had been transformed into nectar and we had all become one with her, an exalted band of dancing holy "lepers." For speaking ill of her brother Moses on the matter of his having taken for himself a "Cushite" woman (no offense intended against African Americans or other people of color, our holy mother was quoting straight from the text), who may or may not have been his wife Zippora the Midianite, Miriam was stricken with "leprosy." She turned white as snow; it was all about skin color in the end—black and white. For the sin of evil gossip she became like the dead who emerges from her mother's womb with half her flesh eaten away.

"Leprosy" is legendary for its contagiousness, Ima Temima reminded us in the most stunning teaching of all—so from whom did Miriam-Azuva-Snow White catch it? The answer is—from her little brother, Moses. And from whom did Moses catch it? The answer to that one is, from the original carrier, God Himself—first, a mild case at the burning bush, then a virulent case that erupted on his face rendering it so alarmingly incandescent he was obliged to cover it with a veil before meeting his public after spending forty days and forty nights without food or drink on the mountaintop in close quarters with the leper-in-chief, the original carrier, who spoke to him mouth to mouth. Mouth to mouth, that will spread it for sure—and who but Moses has ever been so honored in this way? With Miriam the infection was also communicated, for good measure, directly by mouth, when her heavenly father spit in her face—that will also do the trick—leaving nothing but skin white as death, rashes and lesions, nodules and sores, and a Jewish nose hanging by a scab liable any minute to fall right off. Beware the plague of "leprosy," the text cautions us. Remember what the Lord your God did to Miriam on the journey when you left Egypt.

As we reclined on our mattresses nodding our heads straining to absorb in its full relevance this teaching of Ima Temima, Cozbi threw the door wide open, perched her hands on her hips, and in a clear, strong voice for all to hear greeted our holy guests. "Welcome to leper colony, *tovarishchi*!"

"Pour out Your wrath against the nations that never knew

You, pursue them in fury and destroy them from under Your heavens," a few of the more traditional members of our flock chanted to usher in Elijah the prophet, herald of the Messiah. In response, there was only a still, small voice as by the flickering lights of the floating wicks a black shadow seemed to flit into the room and vanish deep within the bowels of the hospital. But by far the greater number of our people rose up clapping and dancing in greeting and lifted their voices fully to welcome Miriam the prophetess with her song, "Sing to the Lord because He has triumphed so mightily, horse and rider He hurled into the sea," as a white bird flew into the hall through the open door, setting off a panic in the welcoming committee and among many others in our congregation as well, who ducked down, covering their heads, shielding their eyes, swatting at the bird with their hands and napkins and assorted utensils as it whirled disoriented above them. "Rejoice," Ima Temima said. "It is the spirit of Miriam-Azuva-Snow White. It is the live bird that the high priest sets free when the 'leper' is cured."

The bird was throwing itself against the walls in confusion and terror as it sought wildly for a way to escape back to the open air from this cell it now found itself trapped in, squirting out the green glop of its excrement and scattering the debris of its white feathers as it smashed into the stone walls again and again and then dropped onto the floor that was also our table, a forlorn little heap in a puddle of spilled wine. Cozbi's lapdog Abramovich dove out of his mistress's cleavage in excitement, panting and leaping and circling comically, scampering with his tongue hanging out toward the deflated morsel now that it had crash landed—only to be frustrated by Rizpa, who swiftly gathered up the throbbing little parcel in both hands and carried it to Ima Temima, setting it down on the very spot on the reclining mattress where she too had sought comfort earlier that evening. Ima Temima stroked the bird exactly as Rizpa had been stroked, and from the depths cried out the prayer of Moses Our Teacher when his sister Miriam the prophetess, the original girl babysitter who had looked after her little brother so faithfully when he was only an infant in a basket drifting on the water, was stricken with "leprosy": "*El-na, refah-na la*! I'm pleading with You God, heal her, I beg of You!" The bird raised its head to gaze at Ima Temima with defeated eyes, then lowered it again, tucking it into its own breast, and surrendered. With arms lifted and furious emotion, our holy mother called out to the heavens above to awaken the quality of mercy for all of us lowly and rejected and shunned and despised "lepers" of this earth, echoing with fierce conviction the words of the holy society upon completing the ritual preparation of the dead for burial: "She is pure! She is pure! She is pure!"

IT WAS close to three in the morning when our Seder came to an end, but, because of the injunction that the more one tells the story of our liberation the more praiseworthy it is, Aish-Zara and I, despite our profound exhaustion, were honored beyond what we might ever have thought we were worthy of to be invited to Ima Temima's apartment in the secluded garden on the northern side of the "leper" colony to continue the discussion until daybreak, like the five sages in Bnei B'rak who reclined around the Seder table so engrossed in recounting the exodus from Egypt through the night that it required the barging in of their students to remind them the hour for morning prayers had arrived. Ima Temima requested that we bring along with us a few bottles of wine and some glasses to lubricate our conviviality, as wine gladdens the hearts of all people, women not excluded, and, in any case, Ima Temima said, the directive to stop all eating or drinking by midnight or after partaking of the last bit of afikomen matzah, whichever came first, applies only when children are present at the Seder—and there are no children in this perilous place to which we have come.

Ima Temima was propped up against the cushions in bed in a pale nightdress and a shawl but without a veil, having already been readied for sleep by Cozbi and Rizpa, our holy mother's two treasured personal attendants. The room was dimly lit with only a few candles, and a second chair had been brought in for Aish-Zara. Immediately we filled our glasses almost to the brim and toasted each other with the blessings of life. As we sat there sipping our wine, in complete love and trust, with Ima Temima breaking the silence now and then to impart yet another holy teaching, I was awestruck once again to find myself on this night that was so different still in the innermost inner circle with such heavyweights the likes of Ima Temima and Aish-Zara, my rebbes and my teachers. It is very much my wish not to speak of my own journey in these pages or to reveal through these words any personal information about myself in all my insignificance that might lead to the stealing of my identity—but for a girl like me, Sherry Silver from Park Avenue, Manhattan, New York City, a dropout from Juilliard, by avocation a seeker, by training a harpist morphed into a thereminist, which so attuned me to sound waves and vibrations, good and bad, seamlessly glissandoing me to my present career as executive director of the school for prophetesses—for such an undistinguished resume to be included at the core of our revolutionary enterprise with two Boro Park girls at the level of HaRav Temima Ba'alatOv, shlita, and the high priestess Aish-Zara, the former Tema Bavli and Essie Rappaport, respectively, from Brooklyn, New York, was more than I would ever have dreamed. I thank God every day for bestowing this gift upon me.

And most wondrous of all, something I learned for the first time during those early morning hours as we sat in the private quarters of our holy mother after our Seder, Ima Temima and Aish-Zara, despite having grown up within a block of one another, first met only in their junior year of high school and in an entirely different Brooklyn neighborhood—at the Williamsburg branch of Beis Ziburis (the very same girls' school, by an amazing coincidence, that had its Jerusalem branch across the road from Ima Temima's former headquarters in the Bukharim neighborhood, from which our holy mother had liberated Rizpa from slavery), though before the year was over, at the age of sixteen, Aish-Zara (known as Essie Rappaport at the time) was pulled out of school by her father and married off to the Pupa Hasid from Mea Shearim, Jerusalem. It was not until many years afterward that Ima Temima and Aish-Zara met again—after the first shock and insult of sexual intercourse which, despite years of reruns, never fully ceased to stun her (Aish-Zara has released me to use

her experience for the sake of providing consolation and hope
to other women similarly dumbfounded) with a husband who
would not have recognized her face if he passed her in the street,
after thirteen children, numerous beatings, the loss of her breasts,
her womb, her teeth, her hair, the lobe of one ear sliced in two
when an earring was ripped out and half the other ear bitten off,
the burn marks of cigarettes that had been stubbed out all over
her body, after mortal illness and bone weariness and chronic
pain to the point of utter exhaustion and indifference as she was
being beaten practically unconscious by a squad of men in black
returning from prayer when she refused to move to the so-called
women's section in the rear of the Number One municipal bus
on its way back from the Western Wall (yes, Aish-Zara is our
very own Rosa Parks)—only after becoming a survivor of all this
persecution and suffering had Aish-Zara ventured one day into
the Temima Shul in the Bukharim Quarter that had always been
right there for her in the neighborhood. With both hands, Ima
Temima had beckoned to her on that day to approach through
the crowd pressing in to soak up the words.

"Welcome, Essie," Ima Temima had said. "I've seen you many
times on the street. I've been expecting you. I've been waiting
for the day when you would come to me of your own accord."

It was not long after that reunion that our holy mother had
informed her that she would no longer be known as Essie Rappaport. From that day forth she would be called Aish-Zara, the
anointed high priestess, rendering by this decree null and void
the physical blemishes that would have disqualified her for this
office had she been a man, which, according to conventional
thinking, were as nothing in the face of the overriding blemish
of her femaleness, of her original disfigurement as a *nekaiva*,
derived from the Hebrew root for opening or hole—like all of
us, a walking sexual organ under wraps. But aren't men also
intrinsically blemished, Ima Temima asked, mutilated eight days
after birth by the covenant, not to mention the deep hole a man
is born with that could never be filled from which a rib had been
gouged out, fashioned into woman, the gaping void where his
lost feminine had resided when he was whole and complete?

Ima Temima set the wineglass down on the nightstand and called to us to come sit on the bed. But because of the lateness of the hour and all the wine we had consumed, neither Aish-Zara nor I could at first absorb the fact that such an exclusive, extraordinary, once-in-a-lifetime invitation was being extended to us even as our holy teacher continued to insist, patting the mattress emphatically to make it all the more clear that we must approach, and drawing back the quilts to communicate that we must also all share the warmth and comfort under the covers. At last Aish-Zara and I got the message. We set down our glasses on the table, slipped off our shoes, and, reeling from the wine and the unanticipated honor, I took Aish-Zara's arm to assist her and we obeyed the call. Before we could take in the meaning of it all, there we were, the four of us, including Ima Temima's little mother Torah, under the covers. It reminded me of the pajama parties, the girls' sleepovers from my childhood, and despite myself I began to giggle as we used to giggle then from fantasies of monsters that seemed so real and the realities of sex that seemed so unbelievable.

The giggling, as always, was contagious and quickly spread among us so that I for one, already sloshing with all the wine I had taken in and despite being at least a generation younger than my present bedmates, experienced some anxiety about my own personal bladder control as bursts of laughter crested in great waves and then subsided, leaving us gasping and panting. As soon as we had made ourselves as comfortable in the bed as it was possible to be alongside such a luminary of nearly divine proportions—it was as close as we would ever get to "mouth to mouth"—Ima Temima announced that we would be engaging in an experiment. We would test the dictum of the sages that *mozi-shem-rah* turns you into a *mezorah* by speaking ill of people, gossiping through the remainder of the night and then checking in the morning light to see if our skin had erupted in "leprosy," in pustules and sores and turned white as snow and we had become symptomatic (since of course, as Ima Temima had taught, we women were, by definition, already "lepers" in various stages of the disease, from carriers to latency, from virulent to terminal). "You mean you're actually giving us a *heter* to talk *loshon hara*—special permission just for us?" Aish-Zara asked in astonishment—and Ima Temima confirmed that indeed yes, we *were* being given a dispensation to indulge the evil tongue to our heart's content. "Uh-oh—L.H.M.F.G," Aish-Zara sang out in a girlish voice, "*Loshon Hara* Makes Fire in Gehenna—remember that from Beis Ziburis?" And Ima Temima together with Aish-Zara collapsed in laughter, like sorority sisters reminiscing at a reunion, and even I, who did not attend Beis Ziburis (I went to Brearley, but that is of no account), was drawn in simply by the infectiousness of the mirth.

At first it was difficult to descend to the level of gossip in the presence of a righteous icon of such world renown, but Ima Temima nevertheless urged us on for the sake of the experiment, helping us to get started by inquiring if we had noticed any couplings at the Seder, given the intimate romantic atmosphere created by the glimmering candles in the darkened hall, the internal temperature-heating properties of the wine, the bodies laid out in a reclining state especially on the polluted mattresses, which might have had the added effect of relaxing the risk-averse with the sense that all was lost anyway like at the outbreak of a decimating war, and, truth to tell, also the awareness of everyone present that Ima Temima's external vision was limited especially in the dark due to the ravages of senior citizenship (in contrast, I hasten to add, to our blessed teacher's internal vision, which remains unrivaled among mortals), and therefore our holy mother might not be in a position to see what they were up to. Yes, there had been a lot of that kind of activity going on, we acknowledged—mostly women with women either by sexual preference or due to the dearth of men, but every man present, regardless of how unblessed, had someone, either female or male, and each of the Bnei Zeruya was spoken for—one with my prophetess, EliEli, I recounted, the girl who got so turned on during the *Dayenu* she nearly set her hair on fire and immolated herself, another with someone I didn't recognize, and the other two with each other, which is really a big waste, I said, because they are such hunks.

As another wave of laughter gathered force threatening to engulf us, Ima Temima asked if either of us had observed Paltiel and Cozbi during the Seder. Both Aish-Zara and I understood what was behind that question; Ima Temima suspected that, bottom line, Cozbi, who may or may not have been Jewish—she definitely did not look Jewish—was using Paltiel to further her own career or other ambitions whatever they might be, we didn't even want to begin to speculate. "Like an old couple," Aish-Zara reported. "They didn't look at each other once or say even one word to each other all evening."

Mention of Cozbi brought to mind the precious little lap-dog Abramovich that she had snuggled between her breasts and caressed all evening at our Seder, so to salvage the mood that was beginning to darken with the specter of maternal disappointment, I began jabbering on about the great relief I had felt that my cat, Basmat (named in honor of the daughter of that wild man, Ishmael, and the wife of that caveman, Esau), a feral stray I had rescued from the humane society just before she had been scheduled to be put to sleep, was safely upstairs in my room when Cozbi opened the door and let the bird into the hall. As I was going on with my idle chatter I could picture Basmat's body stiffening, her back arching, and then it was as if I could actually see her pouncing on the bird, sublime in her ruthlessness. The sequence of images was so vividly and blasphemously ridiculous, considering the burden of signification that had been loaded onto that bird, that I erupted into hilarity again and, I admit to my horror, a small amount of hot moisture, maybe a thimbleful at most, trickled out of me to my eternal mortification. Even as I recall it a screech leaps from my mouth like a cartoon balloon before I can snatch it back as if it were filled with hot air and floated upward on its own.

Ima Temima stroked my head with the same tenderness as she had the bird's head before me and Rizpa's head before that, murmuring, "It's okay, Kol-Isha-Erva dear, it happens. Just try your best not to get any on my mother." In my confusion I had not even considered such a horrifying possibility. I was among the privileged who knew that every letter of this precious scroll tucked in the bed with us had been inscribed by Ima Temima's own blessed hand; soiling it in such a way would have been an intolerable calamity for me, life would have lost all meaning.

But, pulling the little mother Torah safely out of harm's way, Ima Temima immediately went on to comfort me in the words of the kabbalist poet ushering in the Sabbath queen. "Don't be ashamed, don't feel disgraced. Why be so downcast, why do you moan?" I beg forgiveness here for focusing so much on myself, but I do so entirely to showcase the powers of our holy teacher, Ima Temima. The truth is, by this point I was well past the giggling stage of grief and it required all my inner strength to hold back the tears. In my heart of hearts, I wanted nothing more at that moment than the privacy to open my mouth wide and to wail and wail.

"They cry out and are not ashamed," Ima Temima said, paraphrasing from the book of Psalms, as if my inner needs and my longings had been utterly transparent. With not the slightest hint of embarrassment, Ima Temima's mouth opened wide and great cries came forth. Ima Temima was howling like a jackal in the night right there in that bed we were all sharing in the "leper" colony of Jerusalem. Soon Aish-Zara and I joined in and were howling too, our holy mother had given us permission, we were howling together all three of us at the top of our voices without self-consciousness or shame, purging the dross from our souls, cleansing and purifying our spirits, all sense of time fading. Afterward neither Aish-Zara nor I could pinpoint the moment that Ima Temima had shifted from wordless animal howls to the song of the heavenly seraphim in the celestial vision of the prophet Isaiah, *Kadosh, Kadosh, Kadosh, Adonai Zeva'ot*, the mantra we also chant in our prayers, Holy, Holy, Holy, Lord of Hosts. We legatoed into *Kadosh, Kadosh, Kadosh, Adonai Zeva'ot*, chanting it over and over again without end, *Kadosh, Kadosh, Kadosh*, until our very selves were blotted out, our personal identities were erased and the dawn came up and our students rushed in crying, Our teachers, the time has come.

Part II

Yiska

Here's Your
Wife, Take
Her and Go

In the turmoil immediately following her mother's death, the soul still in its unsettled and agitated wandering state, neither in this world nor the next, Tema's father assigned to her, their only child, the interim task of sitting guard over the body, which by the strictest law must not be left alone for even one second until it is pinned down under the weight of the earth and can cause no more harm.

Tema was eleven years old at the time, and what horrified her above all was not the waxen pallor of the corpse, or the fumes of liquefying organic matter already diffusing into the room, or even this cold stranger's obstinate refusal to respond when Tema addressed her so politely. It was the open mouth, hanging down slack, like a dog's—that was simply unbearable. Tema tried to slam that mouth shut, shoving the chin upward with the palms of her own hands, but it was hopeless—it just dropped down again and slung there, revealing everything, the deepest and most private secrets of the family.

She looked around the room—it was her parents' bedroom—for a cord or a belt to strap around the face and hoist up that jaw no matter how unseemly and ridiculous such a contraption would be, like a gauze bandage wrapping for a toothache in an old-fashioned slapstick farce. There on top of the bureau, as always, her mother's collection of three head-shaped wooden wig blocks were positioned on their stands—one for her everyday *sheitel*, one for her Sabbath and holidays *sheitel*, and one for her fanciest, most expensive *sheitel* reserved for very special occasions such as weddings. In a playful mood one evening a year or two earlier, as Tema was engaged in a favorite pastime, watching her mother getting dressed to go out—attending especially to how her mother, as if she were completely alone and unobserved, leaned forward with utter concentration toward the mirror to apply the red viscous clown gash of her lipstick and then blotted it on a tissue, sending up a stale spit odor mixed with the oversweet artificial fragrance of the lipstick's perfume and the crushing smell of her mother's impenetrable unhappiness that would nearly ruin Tema for life—on one of those evenings when she was once again keeping her mother company during this eternally fascinating feminine ritual, Tema had taped a photograph of her mother's face to the front of each of the three heads on the wig stands, indulging the creative license of a child's capricious arts and crafts project. Her mother had never taken down those pictures, and now her three faces were staring back at Tema from the wooden heads on their stems on top of the chest of drawers. The special-occasions head was alarmingly bald, its wig on duty on the unresponsive woman they claimed was her mother lying there on that bed with her mouth hanging open like a dog, the face grotesquely made up, a long pearl earring like a teardrop inserted through the slit of one earlobe.

From this mannequin on the bed, Tema's eyes moved to the nightstand, where she noted once again her mother's favorite book, Leo Tolstoy's *Anna Karenina* in the Modern Library hardcover edition translated by Constance Garnett—a very fat volume, nearly one thousand pages long. This is what Tema took to wedge under that chin and prop it up, succeeding at last to clamp shut that mouth with the moist scarlet rim of the lipstick that had exposed the fleshy tongue, the teeth packed with gold fillings, the obscenely dangling pink uvula—until her father, Reb Berel Bavli, strode back into the room, accompanied by the professional *shomer* who had been hired to take over bodyguarding duty from Tema, to escort the remains and recite the chapters of Psalms through all the stages from transferal to the funeral home to awaiting burial after the ritual cleansing away of all earthly nonsense and artifice including wigs, makeup, and jewelry, the purification with poured water, the plugging with earth of all the orifices, the dressing in plain white shrouds for the grave. With barely a glance at Tema or her mother, in a kind of backhanded stroke as if in passing without breaking his stride, Reb Berish flicked the book out from under his late wife's chin, releasing the jaw to flop right down again and cast open the mouth in that imbecile expression. To Tema, the drop was audible. Reb Berish just shook his head. "At least you didn't stick in there a holy book with God's name," he said. "Forty days you would have to fast."

It is true that she could have used the Tanakh on the nightstand on her father's side of the two pushed-together beds for this purpose, to elevate her mother's chin and seal her lips, since it was more or less the same thickness and heft as the Tolstoy, but the presence of the divine name on its pages and especially the unmentionable Tetragrammaton between its covers rendered it unthinkable, even to one as young as Tema was then, to defile such a holy volume by contact with the dead. The Hebrew Bible was a book you just did not fool around with. You did not deface it, you did not underline in it, you did not scribble comments or exclamation points or question marks in its margins or doodles or drawings of idealized girls' faces and fantasy hairdos during the numbingly boring Bible and Prophets classes, and if by some misfortune it fell on the floor you picked it up reverentially and kissed it in the hope of the unforgiving author's forgiveness.

Nevertheless, though Tema exploited only the work of a mere mortal to prop up her mother's face and restore it from the face of a dog, she still undertook over the course of the following year of mourning a series of mortifications of the flesh, including fasting from food and drink every Monday and Thursday when the Torah is read in the synagogue, and also a *ta'anit dibbur*, fasting from speech all week excluding Sunday after school, when she would take two trains and a bus out to her mother's grave plot still unmarked with a stone in the Old Montefiore cemetery in Queens and pour out her heart like water lashing her mother's face.

On top of that, she privately undertook several additional personal corrections, including sleeping with rocks packed in her pillowcase like Jacob Our Father in Beit El on his flight from his brother Esau to Haran, as well as the Tikkun Hazot, awaking at midnight every night and sitting barefoot on the cold floor of her locked room in a rent nightgown to mourn the destruction of the Holy Temple and the exile from Jerusalem for our sins almost two millennia ago with the prescribed prayers and lamentations, a trove of ashes from sheets of notebook paper burned in an empty lot sprinkled on her head. She also recited the Tikkun HaKlali, the ten psalms specified by the holy Rav Nakhman of Bratslav, and often for good measure she would even recite the entire book of Psalms, all one hundred and fifty of them, as well as immerse herself three hundred and ten times in her improvised mikva, which consisted of the bathtub filled with ice-cold water. All of these mortifications she undertook to repair the damage she had inflicted on her spiritual core when, while lying in bed awake, she could not in her weakness resist the temptation to explore herself in a place she could only think of as "down there," somewhere on an uncharted map like the South Pole, or, while asleep, when she had no control over her thoughts or actions, she would be assaulted by a dream that she could never remember but that would startle her into consciousness with spasms of shocking intensity—spasms so powerful and so unlike anything else she had ever experienced that she wondered why human beings did not occupy themselves with trying to reproduce this sensation every minute of every day and night, but, at the same time, she understood without having to be told that, whatever this was, it could only be a sin, religion had surely been invented to keep this thing under control.

Now and then over the course of that year, someone would take her father aside in the synagogue or in one of the stores on Thirteenth Avenue to remark that Tema looked like she was losing too much weight or that Tema had become "such a quiet girl." Reb Berel Bavli would simply absorb these presumably well-meant bulletins regarding the troubling changes in his daughter and shrug his shoulders, putting out both of his large hands with their meaty palms upward in a wordless gesture that translated, What do you expect? The girl just lost her mother.

For thirty days following his wife's death, Reb Berish abstained from trimming his fiery red beard, a personal vanity he privately indulged, but Rosalie Bavli, Tema's mother, was, after all, his second wife; his first wife he had divorced on the day after the anniversary of their tenth year of marriage when she had still failed to produce an offspring of any flavor. The woman he took shortly afterward, the woman who became Tema's mother, was nearly fifteen years his junior, in her early thirties at the most by his reckoning when she departed this world, they were almost of different generations not to mention different sexes.

On the *shloshim* after her death, following the prescribed thirty days of second-stage mourning, Reb Berish bared his throat to his trusted barber for a nice beard trim, commissioned a local synagogue hanger-on to say Kaddish during prayers three times a day over the duration of the eleven months' mourning period for his late wife, Rosalie—Rachel-Leah Bavli—who had failed to plan ahead and leave a son qualified to perform this service in her behalf, and he let it be known to everyone in his circle as well as to professional matchmakers that he was now in the market for remarriage. He also threw himself even more intensely than ever into his business, which was prospering beyond his wildest dreams, providing the most highly regarded, strictest kosher certification to meats of all kinds based on his years of experience as a *shokhet*, a ritual slaughterer, now employing a sizable staff of authorized personnel, butchers and overseers, and branching out to a whole range of other food products in addition to meats. The Berel Bavli logo—the double-B seal of approval, evoking the two tablets of the Ten Commandments—was worth its weight in gold, a guarantee of the highest, most trustworthy level of supervision. Of course, by the time his second wife Rosalie passed away he no longer worked hands-on, so to speak, as a *shokhet*, but there is no doubt that the accumulation of years he had spent standing in pools of blood cutting the throats of cattle and sheep and fowl and inspecting their entrails gave him a realistic perspective on physical mortality that extended to humans in the image of God as well, not excluding women—a perspective that could not be expected of a sheltered child such as Tema assigned to sit watch beside her freshly dead mother whose mouth hung open like a dog's.

Even so, during that first year following the death, Reb Berish took sufficient heed of the trouble signs in his daughter that were being brought to his attention with increasing frequency, and based on the advice of his rabbi, the Oscwiecim Rebbe, he took Tema out of the neighborhood girls' school, Beis Beinonis, which was considered slightly more to the permissive side, and transferred her to Beis Ziburis off Bedford Avenue in the Williamsburg section of Brooklyn, which was reputed to be a stricter institution that kept the girls rigorously focused on what was expected of them regardless of personal problems or life situations. Reb Berish banged on the door of Tema's bedroom one morning after he had tried to open it by turning the knob, which was how he discovered that she had installed a lock to carry out her mortifications in private, and informed her that he would be driving her to her new school in half an hour, after which she would be going there and back on her own on the subway—which was how Tema discovered that she would be switching schools.

It was also during that year before the stone was unveiled over the grave plot that Reb Berish married again without informing Tema of his intentions or even that he had been looking much less found a bride. A small, private ceremony, without music of course out of respect for the recently deceased, was held in the living room of the Oswiecim Rebbe, who officiated under a tablecloth held overhead as a *huppa* canopy by four old Jews dragged in from the street along with their folding shopping carts. Afterward, the rebbe's wife pushed aside the great maroon volumes of Talmud and other books of law on the long dining room table where her husband usually presided and served some schnapps in little fluted paper cups and slices of sponge cake on napkins, and, as a special treat, because it was she who had been the successful arranger of this match, a plate of herring, each piece skewered with a toothpick topped with a brightly colored decorative cellophane frill.

Naturally, Tema was not present on that occasion. She met the new wife the next morning after her father had already gone off to shul for prayers and then onward to his business when there was a knock on her door in the wake of a tread that she could tell was not his. Tema opened the door to a woman in a pink chenille bathrobe who inquired with a heavy Eastern European accent where the linen closet was located. She needed to change the bedsheets.

Her name was Frumie Klein, she was seventeen years old, and Tema recognized her instantly as one of the older girls from Beis Beinonis known collectively as the "refugees" who were coming into the high school during that period from a black hole referred to as "over there," where terrible but not surprising things were happening to the Jewish people too shameful to talk about but which everyone accepted in the cosmic scheme as predictable and no doubt deserved punishment for our sins against the Master of the Universe acting through his evil agent, Adolf Hitler, may his name and memory be blotted out. Frumie, originally from a cosmopolitan, secular Budapest family where she had been known as Felicia, was a silent, gaunt girl of fifteen when she arrived from a displaced persons camp aboard an American troopship setting sail from Bremerhaven and was collected at the dock in New York City by distant ultra-Orthodox Boro Park relatives who regarded it as a great mitzvah that could only redound to their credit in the divine ledger to take in such an orphan, may such misfortunes as befell this poor girl never befall any of us.

Over the ensuing two years Frumie occupied herself with eating steadily mostly in secret and with stealing small change from her host family in order to buy facial creams and lotions from the drugstore to cope with a devastating case of acne, a mask of pus pimples and inflamed sores that all the ladies sitting in the balcony of the synagogue remarked was so unusual in Hungarian women, universally acclaimed for their flawless complexions and for the skincare secrets they possessed, which produced legendary cosmetics magnates female by sex and Jewish by race.

By the time Frumie turned seventeen her petty thefts were discovered, her face was permanently scarred, cratered and pitted in texture like the landscape of the moon and medium-rare in color, her figure had filled out, especially the womanly parts, ballooning breasts and buttocks cinched by a cartoonish small waist, a caricature of voluptuousness. A decision was made to marry her off as soon as possible while she at least had her youth. With the guidance and encouragement of the Oscwiecim rebbetzin, Reb Berel Bavli, though a bit on the older side, was presented as a suitable candidate—still vigorous and in the prime of life, extremely well-off financially and a good provider, with only one child from a previous marriage who was no longer a baby and would likely within the next few years also be married off herself. One morning, standing across the street from Beis Beinonis alongside Reb Berish as the girls were filing into the school with their books and looseleaf binders pressed to their bosoms, the rebbetzin pointed out the merchandise, confident that her client possessed an expert eye that could quickly and accurately appraise the livestock. A few days later, a deal was struck.

When Tema turned twelve, Frumie was already pregnant with the first of the daughters she would produce almost each year—five by the time Tema herself left home and lost track. Though she had the opportunity to run into Frumie again several decades later and repay her in some measure for the small motherly kindnesses she had extended during their time together, including slapping Tema hard across the face to stir up the blood in her cheeks by way of cautionary congratulations when she got her first period, and supplying the sanitary pads and belt, and offering intimate guidance related to bathing and body odor and so on and so forth, she completely lost all contact with the little girls, her half sisters, to the point that, years later, when she would on occasion try to summon up their names, inexplicably they would elude her. In her mind, she would refer to them by the names of the five proto-feminist daughters of Zelophekhad—Makhla, Noa, Hagla, Milka, and Tirza—who very respectfully had stood before Moses Our Teacher and all the chieftains in the wilderness at the entrance but not inside the Tent of Meeting and collectively petitioned for their rightful parcel of land among their tribesmen of Menashe as their father, Zelophekhad, who had died for some unmentionable sin, had left no sons and heirs. Doubly punished their father Zelophekhad had been, or, more precisely, punished twice as hard—whatever this sin was that he had committed must have been in a class unto itself—punished not just with death but also with having as progeny only daughters and no sons to inherit his portion and perpetuate his name, a compounded form of death, like leprosy—erasure and obliteration. Oh yes, said the Lord who knows everything, both text and subtext, Rightly the daughters of Zelophekhad have spoken.

But what she was above all eternally grateful to Frumie for was the endlessly tactful, entirely ungrudging and unresentful way she left her alone, asking almost nothing at all from her throughout those years they lived under one roof, not even occasional help with the whining little girls throwing their tantrums or babysitting duties for a moment's relief. It was thanks to Frumie's policy of benign neglect that Tema was left free to read undisturbed through all of her mother's small but treasured collection of books that she had claimed as her rightful inheritance, including the *Anna Karenina*, which she reread once a year around the time of her mother's *yahrzeit* throughout her adolescence and thereby entered into her complicated lifelong involvement with her divine but disapproving and intolerant Reb Lev.

And not only that. Because of the benevolent, even conspiratorial, blind eye that Frumie turned, every Friday on her way home from Beis Ziburis, when school ended early in anticipation of the Sabbath, Tema was able to stop off at her local branch of the public library and totally free of charge take out the maximum of four books from the "adult" section even when she did not yet quite qualify by age, aided and abetted by a lax, perhaps subversive, librarian, possibly an anti-Semite, Tema sometimes speculated, sniffing out rebel or apostate material. Tema would carry these library books home on Friday afternoon, crushed to her heart under her schoolbooks and spiral notebooks and looseleaf binders, spirit them into her bedroom, tear up some pieces of paper and insert them between the pages where the words BROOKLYN PUBLIC LIBRARY were stamped on the outer edges of the closed volumes, so that, in reading the books on the Sabbath, opening and closing them and turning their pages, she would not be forming these words and thereby violating one of the thirty-nine categories of labor prohibited on the Sabbath by in effect writing, for which the punishment is death or being totally cut off from your people.

Lying on her stomach on the floor of her bedroom with the door slightly open as everyone else slept and her father's male snores rattled that silenced house, Tema would read very late into Friday night by the hallway light left illuminated for the entire Sabbath, since switching on the electricity was tantamount to igniting a fire, another one of the thirty-nine forbidden categories of work—and she would also read through the entire Sabbath afternoon as everyone obeyed the fourth commandment and rested on the seventh day within those close, musty walls, knocked out by the heavyweight lunch of the bean and meat and potato *cholent* stew that had simmered on the stove on a low flame under a metal sheet for twenty-four hours, never lifting her eyes from the page lest she forfeit her focus on the letters and words as the sun set and darkness descended. Without any outside interference, Tema would read unmolested a minimum of four books almost every week, making her way through the adult literature section of the library in alphabetical order, from Aeschylus to Zola, checking out four new books every Friday before the Sabbath after returning in perfect condition the four she had read, never marking or soiling them in any way or folding down the corners of their pages to indicate her place or smearing snot on them, since the injunction against desecrating holy books with which she had been inculcated carried over to a respect for all books in general.

In this way, in spite of the fact that Beis Ziburis allocated only the minimum of two hours a day to secular general studies to meet government education requirements, from four to six in the late afternoon, under the apathetic instruction, considered good enough for these girls, of terminally exhausted and battle weary teachers who would trudge into their school to earn a few extra dollars after having just survived a day of toil and abuse at the nearby public schools, Tema managed, thanks to Frumie's silent collusion and the amateur course of independent study she had designed for herself, to gain through these alien books at least a glimpse of what else lay out there in the world. And she managed also, by penetrating these works, to begin to acquire her mastery of the interpretive powers that she would later bring to the holy texts—the texts that even then already gripped her above all others and broke her heart with their sheer cruelty, with the coldness and finality with which they, no less than these strangers' books, dismissed and excluded her.

Women, slaves, and children are exempted from studying Torah. That is the first axiom stated by the second Moses—Rabbi Dr. Moses son of Maimon, the formidable medieval philosopher and physician known as Rambam or Maimonides. To Reb Berel Bavli, man of action and appetites, Maimonides' dictum meant that even if a woman appeared to be studying, in reality she was not. It was an illusion since she was exempt; it was impossible since her mind was not suited as Maimonides the rationalist correctly pointed out; it could encourage lasciviousness, Maimonides the moralist cautioned.

Still, Reb Berish was not worried. A girl with her nose all the time in a book who never even bothered to look up to give you a little smile once in a while was not exactly high on the charts in the hoo-ha department. Whatever she was doing by herself all the time with those books, it was not something to be taken seriously. It was like a hobby, nothing more, a phase that would soon pass when she was married off and had children of her own and no time to waste on such *shtoos*, such nonsense and extracurriculars.

Reb Berel Bavli was a busy man; he had more important things on his mind than to monitor this moody girl's reading habits and materials. He had a growing business and a growing new family to deal with—though unfortunately, year after year, no son yet, and he such a virile specimen, ruddy and robust, condemned to drown in a quagmire of pink; it was as if someone were playing a joke on him, making him look ridiculous. There must have been something wrong with this fat Frumie too, just like with his other wives. Had she taken the trouble to give him a son for a change, with his years of experience wielding the knife, he could have, like Abraham our father, circumcised the boy on the eighth day after the birth and initiated him into the covenant himself with his own hands instead of delegating this sacred task to a surrogate acting in his behalf. Had this lazy Frumie cared enough about him to produce a son instead of just another tiresome version of a female, when the boy turned thirteen and became a bar mitzvah, responsible for his own sins, with what joy Reb Berish would have boomed out in front of the entire congregation his gratitude to God to be released from the punishment of *this one*—and he would have pointed with such pride to his own strapping son in his image, may the evil eye spare him.

Reb Berish was not responsible for his Tema in the same way. When Tema turned twelve, the age at which a female (who matures more quickly than the male and, it follows, more quickly becomes overripe and wilts) is legally and *halakhically* accountable for her own sins, he was not charged with making sure she study Torah, as he would have been for a son who was not exempt. Still, around the time of Tema's twelfth birthday, which, as it happened, coincided roughly with the establishment of the State of Israel, Reb Berish did privately mark her passage into adulthood by noting as he presided at the head of the Sabbath table that she was the same age as Germy, the dog that belonged to the goy next door—and the average life span for a German Shepherd, for your information, was, or so he had heard, more or less the same as for the Nazi regime—twelve to thirteen years. "A very old dog, an *alter cocker*. Makes you think, no?" Which led to his next observation, concerning the newly established Jewish state: "We'll know already soon what this world is coming to when the people over there in Eretz Yisroel start talking to dogs in Loshon Kodesh." A few days later, Tema approached Germy safely locked up where he could do no harm for all of his twelve years in the neighbor's backyard due to the surrounding Diaspora Jews' fear-of-dogs. She looked into his demented eyes and his moronic open mouth with the tongue hanging down. "*Higi'a hazman*," Tema said to the dog in the Holy Tongue. Your time's up. And, like an executioner, she opened the gate.

Years later, she would mentally flip to the image of the wild dogs in the Valley of Jezreel lapping up the blue blood and tearing the royal flesh of her beloved majestic Queen Jezebel, and she would forgive herself in some measure for opening the gate that day and liberating the Brooklyn descendent of those dogs, the wretched Germy, to go forth and almost instantly meet his fate with that wreck of a truck, its bells jingling as it clattered down the street driven by Itche the junkman. But in the months that followed the event itself, the image that gripped her was of a pulped and bloody mess in the middle of the road moments after a brief canine burst of hope and exhilaration at having been set free at last. This was the image she would return to again and again in those days, like a dog returns to its own vomit, as the author of the book of Proverbs said, reportedly King Solomon.

On a Sunday morning at Beis Ziburis not long after the fateful meeting between Germy the dog and Itche the junkman, the girls were reviewing for a final exam on the second book of Samuel that they had just completed under the instruction of their Prophets teacher, Miss Pupko, a sallow-faced young woman eighteen years old, recently engaged to be married, who had just graduated from the school the year before and was translating verse by verse, chapter by chapter from the Hebrew directly into Yiddish. Suddenly Tema's daydreams were brutally interrupted by the words in chapter nine of Mephiboshet, the crippled-in-both-legs son of Jonathan, groveling before the bandit kingpin David who had just promised him a permanent seat at the royal table and restored to him all the lands of his grandfather, the crazy King Saul: "What is your servant that you have shown such regard for a dead dog like me," Mephiboshet said, so hideously obsequious. Tema raised her hand and asked permission to leave the room, which was the only way to earn the privilege to use the toilet to relieve yourself.

In all her years at Beis Ziburis, Tema had never once used the toilets for the purposes for which they were intended, to relieve herself—including by crying—they were too filthy and public. She exercised extreme self-control throughout the long day, she held everything in until she came home, then dashed through the house straight to the bathroom; the women of her family knew what to expect and they all gave way. Now Mephiboshet the dead dog sent Tema wandering through the halls of the dingy firetrap that was Beis Ziburis, the peeling and flaking walls, the gashed and stained linoleum, the smashed light fixtures and exposed wires, the cracked windowpanes, all of it in violation of building codes and officially condemned by municipal inspectors but considered good enough for the girls by the overseers of the school, who kept it in operation through private arrangements with elected city officials.

There was a door that Tema had noticed many times but never opened. This time, though, she turned the knob and went through, down the stairs into the cellar. She switched on a light and, by the grimy yellow wattage, she gazed around her, surveying the hundreds of cans of food of all kinds and sizes that filled the shelves along the walls and spilled over into great mounds and heaps on the floor. Some of the cans were fairly new, but others had torn or missing labels, the metal smashed and dented, rusted and bloated and exploded, so that even as she stood there taking all of this in she could hear toxic popping noises that caused her to turn around and come face-to-face with the principal of her school, Rabbi Manis Schmeltzer, the only male on the premises all day until four in the afternoon on weekdays when the defeated public school teachers plodded in to provide the minimum mandatory secular instruction. For some reason, the principal's presence down there in the cellar did not surprise her in the least.

"I guess you never got around to giving those cans to the poor starving children we collected them for," Tema said.

"Ah," said Rabbi Schmeltzer, quoting from one of the great comic scenes of the Torah, "And the Lord opened up the mouth of the ass. And I thought you were such a quiet girl. Everybody tells me you never say a word. Who would have ever imagined you had such a fresh mouth on you?"

He laid both of his hands on top of her head as if he were about to bless her, but instead he pushed her down to the cement floor of the cellar onto her knees, even though everyone knows that a Jew may never kneel before another human being. A Jew bows down only before God, Tema had been taught, but maybe that rule applied only to men, such as Mordekhai the Jew who refused to prostrate himself before the grand vizier Haman, thereby aggravating the villain even more, rendering him nearly apoplectic, nearly bringing about the annihilation of the entire Jewish population of Persia and Mede, one hundred and twenty-seven principalities from India to Ethiopia, a death sentence that required a major knee job, with Mordekhai the court Jew's full support and encouragement, on the part of his hot niece Hadassah/Esther to get it repealed. "This should shut you up," Rabbi Manis Schmeltzer said. He unbuttoned the fly of his trousers and took out what he called his *bris* and shoved it into her mouth, which he called her *pisk*, and began *schuckling* back and forth as if he were swaying in prayer with particular concentrated *kavanah* and focus—all of which Tema observed with an odd detachment, as if it were happening not to her, not to Rosalie Bavli's daughter, but to someone else, she didn't even bother to try to raise her voice to protest in some way as even Bilaam's ass had complained in that great comic scene in the Bible—even that donkey had dared to inquire what it had ever done to deserve this.

When he was finished with his business, Tema turned her head to the side and vomited on some corroded cans with their contents splattered and disgorged. "This will be *tsvishn uns*," Rabbi Schmeltzer said as he reassumed his usual disguise. "Between us—get it? One word about this, and I will simply let it be known that you're out of your mind, crazy, like your late mother, may she find some peace at last. You're a smart girl, Tema Bavli, I'm sure you get my point. It will not help your marriage prospects one little iota if anyone ever hears about this, believe you me. Number one, what were you doing cutting class? Number two, what were you doing alone down here in the cellar anyways? Try to explain all that to your father and to the ladies auxiliary and to the entire congregation of Israel."

Tema returned to the classroom, slumped, head lowered, seeking to enter as unobtrusively as possible. "*Gai avek!*" Miss Pupko cried out sharply in Yiddish. Jolted, Tema raised her eyes despite her ardent wish at the moment to remain invisible. Was the teacher ordering *her* to get out? Could the news have already spread so rapidly like a plague? But then Tema recognized this as the translation into Yiddish of the words of King David's son Amnon to his half sister Tamar, right after he was done raping her—"Get up, Get out!" Amnon had barked to the Jewish princess Tamar, and then to his royal attendant, "Get this thing out of here and lock the door behind her."

As Tema made her way to her desk in the back of the room and sat down, turning her head from the swampy girls' smell of stagnant menstrual blood and underarm sweat to stare out the streaked window, Miss Pupko continued with the lesson, leaning in toward the class. "Memorize these words, girls, wear them like a seal on your heart if, heaven forbid, you are ever tempted to give in to the evil inclination. 'And Amnon now hated her with a very terrible hatred, the hatred he hated her with was much greater than any love he had ever felt for her before.'"

They were up to chapter thirteen. Tema realized she had been out of the room for four chapters and look at all that had happened in the meantime. She wondered what happened to princess Tamar who, following the rape, was taken in like a casualty to her brother Absalom's house, and two years later he exacted his revenge, setting up their half brother Amnon to be terminated. But beyond that, concerning Tamar's fate, not a word. Did she take her own life from shame? Did her brother arrange to have her stoned in an honor killing for disgracing the family by letting herself be violated? The text is finished with her, except perhaps indirectly when it informs us that Absalom had three sons with names not listed, and one daughter, a beauty called Tamar. Jews name their children after dead relatives.

Miss Pupko gave Tema a lacerating glance. Between the two of them, there was a long-standing entrenched tension. The teacher was exceedingly aware that Tema conducted her own private study of Tanakh and had even memorized entire books, including such long ones as Isaiah and Psalms, to the point that you could just spit out one word and this strange girl could supply the entire sentence that encased it complete with chapter and verse citation. Who would ever marry such a freak, and motherless besides? She was like some kind of *illui*, a prodigy who had mastered the complete Talmud, except that an *illui* was an honored category reserved exclusively for boys—in a girl such precocious flashes of brilliance were simply bizarre and superfluous and disturbing, there wasn't even an accepted feminine form for the term. Miss Pupko felt in her heart that Tema had nothing but contempt for her knowledge of the Scripture, and she was keenly wounded. Tema regarded herself as too good for this review, Miss Pupko thought bitterly, there was nothing she could learn from it, that was why she had stayed out of the room so long, doing her business, whatever it was, in the toilet or wherever.

"Tema Bavli," Miss Pupko bellowed, "Read!"

Slowly and deliberately Tema turned back toward the stifling, puberty-laced interior of the room from staring outside through the grimy window down into the street where she had been observing Rabbi Manis Schmeltzer opening the door to his car illegally parked in front of a fire hydrant, removing the CLERGY sign from the windshield, flipping the sign along with his black fedora hat onto the front passenger seat, cupping his black velvet yarmulke and readjusting it on his head, hoisting the tail of his glossy black kaftan in order to slide his haunches more comfortably into the driver's seat—and then she pictured him jiggling his hindquarters, easing them into the bowl of the seat with a palpable sense of well-being, and jutting his chin forward toward the rearview mirror, drawing back his lips and baring his teeth like a primate to examine them proprietarily before inserting his key into the ignition and setting forth with a roar. Tema gazed at Miss Pupko in complete confusion. "Aha, so you weren't paying attention," the teacher said. "You don't even know the place."

When school ended, Tema walked to the subway station intending to make her way home to purge herself in privacy, to brush her teeth thoroughly and rinse out her mouth, to stand under the shower for as long as possible before someone started banging on the door. But since it was a Sunday, with no secular instruction, late afternoon in early summer but still daylight, Tema went instead in the other direction almost without being fully aware of her movements or that she had made any particular decision at all, and she boarded the train that would take her to the second train that would take her to the bus that would bring her to the Old Montefiore cemetery in Queens where, once, her mother could always be found waiting to listen to everything.

But ever since the stone had been unveiled over her mother's grave, a slab of granite with the minimal inscription entirely in Hebrew from right to left—name, date of birth and death in accordance with the Jewish calendar linked by a minus sign, and the generic double-edged one-size-fits-all compliment for females from the book of Proverbs, A WOMAN OF VALOR WHO CAN FIND—Tema's visits had grown more and more infrequent. Her mother was no longer there, no longer nearby, she was packed away, sealed off, she no longer cared. And this was what Tema also felt now as she approached the grave in the twilight with the darkness beginning to descend, her mother moving even farther away from her to a cold point in the distance.

"Mama, Mama!" Tema began screaming into that distance, her cries bouncing from headstone to headstone in the cemetery emptied of all other living beings. She bent down to gather a handful of pebbles and small rocks and granite and marble chips that had cracked off the gravestones, but instead of setting them down on her mother's grave as a sign that she had come by to visit, she began throwing them, pelting her mother's monument with missile after missile. Horrified by her actions, Tema broke out in sobs, "I'm sorry, Mama, I'm sorry!"—and she fell down on the plot as if splayed on her mother's body with her arms hugging its headstone, crying so hard, crying like she used to cry when she was a little girl, her entire body heaving until the breath seemed to be sucked out of her and all her moisture drained, and she swooned, collapsed from sheer physical depletion.

She woke up in the pitch dark and began staggering around the cemetery like the abandoned children Hansel and Gretel in the Black Forest fairytale, only at least they had each other whereas she was entirely alone, utterly lost and with no bearings at all as to where she was in the world, groping in the darkness until she fell partway into an open grave awaiting its dead the next morning, grasping onto one of the two mounds of soft, freshly dug up earth that rose on either side. This is where she was found at dawn by the caretaker of the cemetery making his first rounds. For the remaining weeks of that school year Tema was sick in her bed. She never took the final exam on the second book of Samuel for the Prophets class or in any other subject for that matter, and they didn't bother with makeup tests either since, as the principal Rabbi Manis Schmeltzer himself so wisely pointed out, "Who are we kidding? Let's face it, it really doesn't make a difference one way or the other in the overall life schedule of these girls."

During the first stage of her illness Tema barely responded at all. But after about a week she returned from wherever she had been; she recognized that she was completely altered, that she had undergone an event terrible and undeniable, that she had given up one form of bondage in exchange for being bound to something else—she would never be free. She had come back from the dead with secrets, with forbidden knowledge, weighed down by a calling. The first person she saw when she opened her eyes was Frumie sitting with legs apart on a chair at the bedside in her pink chenille bathrobe stretched taut and pulled open to expose a patch of the great smooth mound of her pregnant belly with a dark line trailing downward from the plug of her navel. "Oh my God, why did you leave me?" Tema cried out, and her voice came up as if from below—deeper, riper, the voice of the blood of her mother crying out to her from the ground. Frumie's head sank low over her belly, her hair tightly bound up in a married woman's headscarf. "I'm sorry, Frumie, I don't mean to hurt you," Tema said. "Such a life is just not meant for me."

For much of the remainder of the period that Tema lived under her father's roof, until she left home at the age of twenty or so, one of the signature refrains by which she was tagged within the family was her rejection of "such a life"—and as if to elaborate by way of a concrete example, she would inevitably specify that she was never getting married. While she was still in school at Beis Ziburis, her father, Reb Berel Bavli, dismissed it as an adolescent trifle, though from time to time as the years accumulated, at the expanding Sabbath table with more and more miniature female offspring lining the sides flowing from his seat at the head as from the source of the river, when Tema would once again be provoked to restate her refusal with respect to marriage, Reb Berish would lean back in his armchair to allow more scope for his ample gut, blow his nose into his napkin, give out a loud and succulent belch to which he felt fully entitled as the sole and dominant male, feeder of all these female mouths, and he would launch into some variation of "*Takkeh*? You should excuse me if I have to comment with a *greps*—but is that so? Not getting married? You think maybe you're too good for anyone, Miss Hassenfeffer? So, tell me something if you don't mind, what else will you do with yourself if you don't get married? Bang your head against the wall? Spit wooden nickels? Dance a kazatzka? Nu, so I'm waiting to hear—explain me already."

The matter, however, grew far more urgent after Tema finished high school and still refused to budge from her position as, one by one, like ducks in a shooting gallery, each of her classmates either became engaged or was married and some could even be spotted already pushing a baby carriage down the street. Tema alone was taking no steps to begin real life. The time had come for her father to pay attention. A girl could not forever remain in such a holding pattern; before you knew it a new crop, younger and fresher, would be moved to the front of the shelves, and she would have to be sold off at a bargain price past the expiration date, cut-rate goods, remainders, as is. Meanwhile, though, for his sins, under no circumstances would this prima donna daughter of his consent to fill this gap in her life in a respectable way by teaching at Beis Ziburis, for example, for which she was remarkably qualified though she herself claimed she did not know enough.

Reluctantly, therefore, Reb Berish gave Tema permission to attend night courses at Brooklyn College just so she would have something to do with her time during this limbo; she could after all make some practical use of this dead space by working toward a degree in elementary school education, for example, which, God willing, he hoped and prayed she would never have to complete, though it was a very good backup career for a woman if it came to that since it fit so compactly into the schedule of a wife and mother. During the day, Tema continued with her own private curriculum of Jewish studies behind the locked door of her room at home, and for a brief period she came into his office part-time several days a week at her father's insistence, to contribute to her "room and board," as he put it, helping out with the phones, especially with handling complaints, until the day the other ladies, the secretaries and the book-keepers, listened wide-eyed as the boss's daughter explained to a caller that No, that wasn't rat feces in the box of chocolates, it was the candy itself, and even if it was rat feces, the Berel Bavli *hashgakha* seal meant that it was one-hundred-and-ten-percent kosher, you can count on it, *ess gezunt aheit*, eat in good health.

Privately, Reb Berel Bavli put out the word to all the yentas on the circuit that he was now in the market for a suitable *shiddukh* for his daughter, Tema, and naturally he got in touch with every one of the recommended matchmakers operating in the territory. The professional assessment was that Tema Bavli was an exceptionally beautiful and brilliant girl. Both of those attributes were on the minus side. Also on the minus side was the fact that her mother had died young of circumstances that were not exactly clear, from a physical or a mental problem, either of which was not good news, either of which could, God forbid, be inherited by the children, may they multiply. In addition, certain rumors did not exactly improve her prospects, including reports by witnesses that she had often been seen coming and going from the public library, which suggested that she polluted her mind with English books and other garbage. Finally, the matter of her having been found one morning in an empty grave in a cemetery reportedly after having experienced some kind of mystical vision that many suspected could more accurately have been described as a nervous breakdown of some sort was common knowledge in certain circles, and though this event had occurred several years earlier when she was considerably younger and more impressionable and understandably still overcome by the loss of her mother, unfortunately it did not help in the delicate situation of pinning down a girl's destined mate.

On the plus side, however—and this, by universal agreement of the professional matchmakers, was a tremendous plus—the prospective bride's father, the distinguished Reb Berel Bavli, was an extremely wealthy man. In comparison to this, every other plus paled and was not worth mentioning, even and including the plus of Reb Berish's well-documented record as a benefactor of many worthy causes and his numerous notable charitable acts such as his weekly custom of putting each of his little girls on the meat scale every Friday morning and then distributing their weight in top rib or chuck roast stamped with the Berel Bavli kosher seal of approval to the poor for the Sabbath stew. The consensus, then, of these experts who dealt day in and day out with delivering perfect matches from heaven was that, with regard to Tema Bavli and her special situation, they should narrow the search to a young man acclaimed to be brilliant and diligent, a beacon in holy studies, a *talmid hokhom* of the top caliber, but also dirt-poor. Once the couple was married, may it be in a good hour, the boy would sit and learn all day, while the wife would have babies, and her father, Reb Berel Bavli, would support them for as long as necessary, maybe forever.

With this plan in mind, they plunged into the search. One suitable candidate after another was put forward, all of whom, without exception, Tema refused to even consider. She stuck her fingers into her ears and made clacking noises with her tongue to drown out a recitation of their glowing qualities. She ran to her room, slammed the door, and locked it from within.

In desperation, Reb Berel Bavli made a decision to bring his daughter to his spiritual guide, the Oscwiecim Rebbe, to talk some sense into her. There was no question of refusing to go to this consultation. Reb Berish made it crystal clear that should that be the course Tema chose, he would wash his hands of her for good; she could go sleep in the streets for all he cared and eat from the garbage pails and squat down to pish and cock behind a bush.

The Oscwiecim Rebbe was already in place in his designated chair at the head of his dining room table in which only he was permitted to sit and which stood empty as if occupied by his ghost when he was not there to fill it. Behind him in the shadows stood his son, Kaddish, his chief *shammes* and right-hand man. Reb Berish, his major donor, took a seat to the rebbe's right, with Tema standing before them to their left like a defendant in the dock, and the rebbetzin, with her everyday oxblood-shoepolish-colored wig slightly askew on her head and in her flowered housecoat with the sleeves pushed up to her elbows, listening in through the open kitchen door as she continued rolling and shaping more than two hundred matzah balls for the forthcoming Sabbath's chicken soup.

Stroking philosophically his long white beard yellowed around the mouth by tobacco and tea, the rebbe mumbled a few perfunctory questions in Yiddish to Tema since he was already familiar with the main points of the case through her father and chose to avoid being troubled by her side of the story. After a brief consultation with his wife, who now stood beside him mopping the sweat from her forehead with a dishrag, the rebbe announced his diagnosis that Tema was possessed by a dybbuk, the naked soul of a dead sinner condemned to wander the earth in restless torment, possibly even the girl's own mother, who had invaded the vessel of Tema's body to take refuge there. It was this dybbuk that was speaking through Tema's mouth insisting she would never get married, the rebbe explained, these were not the words and certainly not the thoughts or desires of a respectable and sensible girl like Tema Bavli herself from such an outstanding and reputable family.

It would be necessary to expel this dybbuk from the vessel of Tema's body, and since they already had her there in the room, it made perfect sense to proceed with the exorcism at once. Tema briefly considered turning and running out of the house of the Oscwiecim Rebbe to make her escape, but where could she go? She was trapped as if in a dream in which she was both actor—or acted upon—and observer. It was a Thursday evening in early winter, darkness was descending. Ten men were rounded up, trudging in from the street in their galoshes with their shopping bags, to make up a minyan. The rebbetzin turned on a lamp, and for atmosphere she lit the candles in all of her Sabbath sterling silver candlesticks, which approximated, since one is forbidden to count, the number of her children and grandchildren, close to one hundred.

She directed Tema to remove her shoes and stockings, and pointed to the chair in which Tema must sit. Pinning Tema in place for the procedure with one arm encircling her neck in a kind of headlock and the two fingers of her other hand pressing down firmly on Tema's pulse where the demon resided, the rebbetzin whispered urgently into Tema's ear, "Push! Push! Push that dybbuk out, daughter!"

At the same time, the rebbe, her husband, was stationed at Tema's bare feet, which were resting on a stool. At his wife's behest, he was holding out a bowl to catch the exiting demon while intoning Psalm ninety-one over and over again, forward and backward, for what seemed like an eternity—You who sit in the high mystery, You who rest in the shade of Shaddai—his eyes glued to Tema's big toe as it was sinful for his gaze to stray any higher up for the sign of the blood that must trickle down to mark the exit of the dybbuk.

"Shmiel," the rebbe's wife called to him from her end, "do you see anything yet?"—but the rebbe only shook his head despondently. The rebbetzin brought her mouth close to Tema's ear and hissed, "So nu, what about getting married already? We don't have all day. I have fifteen kugels to make for Shabbes!"—but Tema raised her hand, the one that was not being pressed down by the rebbetzin at the pulse, and motioned with her index finger from side to side—*No.*

They were dealing with an exceptionally stubborn dybbuk who was not cooperating at all, the rebbetzin indicated to her husband. A more extreme measure was now called for to finish this business. Dutifully, the rebbe gave the nod to Kaddish, who joined forces with his mother at Tema's head with a shofar clutched in his fist, which he raised to his mouth and blasted directly into Tema's ear, into the very same ear that she had plugged with a finger when the names and attributes of eligible young geniuses scouting for a rich bride were presented for her consideration. The rebbe's son Kaddish now filled that ear with a ringing so intense that Tema thought she was hearing voices, and all of the voices were chanting in chorus, *No, No, No.*

Over the course of that winter, Reb Berel Bavli dragged his daughter Tema from rebbe to rebbe to straighten her out even as he recognized that his search for a cure would inevitably leak out into the community and lower the value of the goods in the marketplace.

The Chernobyler Rebbe listened to the whole story as transmitted by Reb Berish, then brought his face as close to Tema's as was decent within the constraints of modesty and, expelling sour whiffs of constipation, he enunciated very deliberately as if to a person who is deaf or mentally deficient or an alien, "Listen to me, young lady—act normal! Even if you are not normal, you must act normal. Remember my words—Act Normal!"

The Kalashnikover Rebbe's face puffed up in a fury, turning blazing scarlet and blaring, "What this little *nudnik* needs is a few good *potches* in *tukhes* to knock some sense into her head!" as he came charging toward Tema wielding his cane, only to be deflected in time by the massive slaughterer's forearm of Reb Berish who said, very deferentially but firmly, "Excuse me, rebbe, but *I* am the father."

The Brooklyner Rebbe recommended a psychiatrist on Central Park West who, though secular himself, had been thoroughly vetted by the religious leaders so that there was absolutely no danger whatsoever that he would inject heretical or forbidden ideas into the vulnerable heads of his ultra-Orthodox patients such as lascivious thoughts about their own mothers or murderous feelings toward their fathers, or attempt in any immoral way to brainwash them by opening sinful valves of temptation for relief. In fact, with his exclusively *haredi* practice, talking was kept to an absolute minimum in his treatment room; his specialty was dispensing and renewing prescriptions for drugs and medications at a good clip. Tema sat in his crowded waiting room filled mostly with men and a few depressed older women clumped together, all of whom, from the tiniest variations in their Hasidic uniforms, could be zoomed-in on the map to their exact neighborhood and even in certain cases their block in the five boroughs of New York City and the counties beyond, but she left before her appointment when a young Hasid rushed in with his earlocks and fringes flying, feverishly agitated and shaken, and went around the waiting room, from person to person, demanding that each one in turn tell him if it was really true that he looked so crazy since as soon as he had walked into this fancy building just a few minutes ago, the doorman had pointed him to this office—the office for the nutcases.

Through the long brooding nights of that winter, after Tema returned home from Brooklyn College where she took courses in Western philosophy and Eastern religion, and ravenously devoured in the library anything she could lay her hands on—every footnote was precious—

about the punished life of the charismatic and uncompromising Puritan dissident Bible teacher Anne Hutchinson, confident that all this extracurricular study was only a minor deviation from her contract with her father that he had neither the time nor the interest to scrutinize, after reading into the early morning hours Tema would switch off the light and lie on her back in the dark in her girlhood bed with her eyes open wide listening to the night noises of the house. Terrors were lurking everywhere, she could sense them closing in upon her as they had when she was a child. The steam hissed in the radiators, monster shapes were pitched onto the ceiling of her room from the headlight beams of passing cars, toilets flushed, appliances cycled on and off, she could hear Frumie's heavy, eternally pregnant tread making its way through the hallway down the stairs to the kitchen, the sucking sound of the refrigerator door opening, the scraping of the chair being pushed back as Frumie sat down at the table with a deep sigh to eat in peace whatever food in whatever combinations and quantities her heart desired. She could hear the little girls whimpering in their beds, or crying out from some Black Forest nightmare, she could hear her father lumbering down the hall into and out of their rooms to attend to them.

One afternoon, while her half sisters were napping or away at their nursery programs or kindergartens, as Tema was preparing to set out to college she passed the partly open door of her parents' bedroom. Frumie was sitting at the very edge of the bed staring numbly ahead, completely dressed as if to go out, in her black coat with the white mink collar and cuffs and her matching white fur hat and her boots and her gloves and her black patent leather pocketbook in her lap, and what seemed to be a fully packed suitcase on the floor beside her. Her eyes registered Tema leaning in the doorway. Tears were coiling down her blotched, ravaged cheeks. "I was going to leave for good," Frumie said, "but look at me"— and her hand brushed against the globe of her pregnant belly. "And who will take care of the girls? And how would I live without a penny to my name? And where would I go anyway?"

Later that evening, sitting in the lounge after philosophy class with Elisha Pardes, having the coffee that had become an illicit pleasure, drinking in public a strange brew from a strange cup with a strange man, their foreheads drawing closer like magnets in the intensity of their talk, Tema told herself it would not be a betrayal of Frumie to describe their encounter that day, which had imprinted itself on her mind like a bruise. Elisha was a married yeshiva boy of medium height, slight in build, pale transparent skin as if he were not quite of this earth or in a perpetual state of recovery from a grave illness, dark eyes with long heavy lashes. When they were together strangers often asked them if they were brother and sister, more because of their shared aura of being set apart in the same place rather than their physical resemblance—to which Elisha would always answer, "All Israel are brothers—even the sisters are brothers." He supported his growing brood of daughters by devoting his days to rigorous holy studies for which he received a stipend from the prestigious Ivy League Academy of Advanced Higher Jewish Learning Kollel, but, like Tema, he had also been granted special permission to take some secular courses in the evenings, because his rebbes believed that a measure of flexibility might save this brilliant, restless mind from tipping over to the side of apostasy and rejection, this rare soul from being snatched away by the mystics and ecstatics.

When she finished relating to Elisha how she had found Frumie sitting on the edge of the bed in desolation with the packed suitcase beside her, for a reason she could not fathom and never anticipated, Tema went on to dredge up an account of all of the rebbes her father had hauled her to against her will over the past few months to force her into marriage as if she were chattel in some kind of medieval bondage, and all the suffering and humiliation that had been inflicted upon her. Elisha listened pensively, and when she was done, for a long time continued to remain silent, tugging at his wiry black beard. Finally he said, "You should go see the Toiter Rav. The Toiter will have the answer. I will let him know."

The elevator up to the Toiter Rabbi's penthouse on Fifth Avenue was operated by a uniformed attendant and actually opened up in the apartment itself rather than in a common hallway, an astonishing revelation that Tema had not expected and had never experienced before, as she had also never before inhaled the smell of marijuana, or even heard the word. The young acolyte waiting to greet her as she stepped out of the burled-wood casket of the elevator, luminous in his white robes rent at the collar and his crocheted skullcap pulled low over his hair so that only the two ringlets of his earlocks dangling down were visible, explained that the cloud of smoke that filled the room by day and the cloud of fire by night was a celestial drug, a healing essence that eased the eternal agony of the rebbe, since every Toiter Rav was always in excruciating pain, terminally ill and dying. That was the Toiter's condition, it was his state of being. Moreover, there could never be a son to succeed him, and were a son to be conceived or actually born to him, the boy would die in the womb or before the age of two at the latest, as had been the fates of Yaakov and Shlomo-Efraim, the two sons of the original Toiter, Rav Nakhman of Bratslav. Because he had no sons, he was considered dead, like a leper or a blind man, and so he was known as the Toiter, the Dead One—his followers, the Dead Hasidim. The present Toiter now at death's door was the eleventh in the line and the next one was already waiting in the wings to take his place, he too already mortally sick and dying, and so it will be from one *zaddik* of his generation to the next until the true messiah arrives may it be quickly in our time.

Tema was led through a labyrinth of sumptuously furnished and carpeted rooms with cloths draped over the mirrors in their gilt frames. In every room she passed, and in distant rooms beyond them, she could see unshaven men clothed in white garments ripped at the lapels milling around in stocking feet as if floating, or sitting on low stools with their head in their hands like mourners, in woeful or meditative poses, or swaying in prayer in small clots, and she thought, too, that she had glimpsed Elisha Pardes standing alone and apart with his thin arms raised as if in agonized petition, the mouth on his pale face open as in a scream but no sound coming out—and soon she lost all sense of where she was in the world and how she might ever find her way out again.

At last she was led into a small room with no other furniture but a plain pine wood box in the middle of the floor. Her escort who had accompanied her up to this point now backed out of the room as from the presence of a king and closed the door. A thin swirl of smoke curled up into the air from the open box in the center of the room, and the smell that was quickly becoming familiar to Tema suffused the space. Soon the joint itself from which the smoke was emanating levitated before her eyes, and the withered hand that was holding it emerged and beckoned to her to draw nearer.

Inside the box the Toiter Rav was lying supine wrapped in pure white linen shrouds; only the veil that would ultimately conceal his face and the mittens that would enclose his hands had not yet been placed on him by the saintly members of the holy burial society. The skin of his cadaverous face was drawn tautly back exposing his stained teeth and his black gums, outlining the contours of his skull so close to the surface, and even through the shrouds, the bulges and lumps of the tumors that riddled his body were everywhere discernible, but in the deep hollows of his eye sockets something still glittered like a jewel at the bottom of a well and his eyes continued to laugh.

With his free hand the Toiter began to stroke Tema's cheek, murmuring in a voice that seemed to be coming from below, "Such a *krasavitsa* you are, what a beauty, skin like velvet"—and his hand descended to her breast where it rested gently, cupping without moving, and he said in a still, small voice, "Ah, my Shunamite, allow me—this may be my last time. I can feel your heart throbbing, throbbing. You don't have to say a word—I feel everything, I know everything about you. There are only two ways out for you. My way is one way. It is not your way—not yet. You will find your way for now. You have not yet completed your task on this earth. Your task is great. You are my regent, a shadow Toiter. Remember, I am always with you—my rod and my staff. Your mother and your father may abandon you, but the Toiter will never leave you. The main thing is not to be afraid at all."

As winter faded Tema began setting off to school earlier and earlier in the day, directing Frumie to explain to her father if he happened to notice that she needed to spend time in the college library to look up information in books that could only be found there and nowhere else in order to complete her homework. She would often walk the entire distance to school as the weather grew warmer, some four or five miles or so by her calculation, making her way slowly and meditatively, as if in a stately solo processional, stopping off regularly at the Israel kosher delicatessen on Coney Island Avenue near Avenue J for a glass of tea and a piece of apple strudel, which she would take lingeringly while reading one of her books. After a while, the young man in the white boat-shaped paper hat who worked behind the counter brought her the tea and cake as soon as she sat down. One day, as he was placing it in front of her on the Formica-topped table, he demanded to know in an accent that was distinctively New York but not Brooklyn, more Italian than Jewish, why she never ate any real food, like a tongue sandwich maybe, or maybe some chopped liver. She raised her eyes from the pages of her book and took him in for the first time—short, stocky, curly dark hair already thinning, intense eyes set a little too close together, a few days' growth of beard, an unlit cigarette drooping from his mouth.

"My father's a butcher, so I'm a vegetarian," Tema answered, and she lowered her eyes back to her book.

From then on, if the restaurant wasn't busy, or even if a few other customers were there, already slurping their mushroom barley soup or gnawing their pastrami on rye, as long as the boss was out, he would make himself comfortable in the chair opposite hers, straddling it backward, leaning over to plant his elbows on the tabletop between them and settling his chin in the sling of his joined hands. He would stare at her relentlessly with fierce concentration as she continued to ignore him and read, now and then disengaging slightly from her book to lift her glass to her lips for a sip of tea or pressing a finger down onto her plate to suction up a crumb of pastry and place it on her tongue like a lozenge.

Tema recognized that this open association with a young man however unsuitable he obviously was would not help her at all in the treacherous marriage minefield. She understood very well that her father would be livid when word reached him, as inevitably it would, that she had been seen talking to a strange boy in the public arena, and she also knew without question that she would earn no points whatsoever by virtue of the fact that she herself hardly uttered a single word—it was this obsessed guy who mainly was doing all the talking. Even so, she continued to stop off at the Israel delicatessen on her walk to school to test where this new danger was taking her and she never demanded that he get up from the seat he had staked out opposite her and leave her in peace, she never slapped his face or complained to the boss or called the cops, all of which he interpreted as warm encouragement.

His name was Howie Stern, she heard him say as she continued turning the pages of her book. His father worked at Ratner's on Second Avenue, a waiter like Howie himself, though the old man was a card-carrying union member whereas for him, Howie, this gig at the Israel kosher deli was only temporary; the trunk of his pop's Chevy was so stuffed with little black bowties that they erupted and overflowed like a steaming manhole whenever you opened it. His mother was a custom girdle and brassiere fitter in Ozone Park, Queens, mostly an Italian neighborhood, for her information, distinguished by Mafia types among whom there were some who had even made stabs at recruiting him for stuff she wouldn't want to know about, which explained why he hopped boroughs to work at this menial and anonymous job in Brooklyn.

He was a Zionist and an artist, in that order; those were the two main facts you needed to know about him, he told her, the rest was commentary. He had dropped out of yeshiva to earn money to fulfill his consuming dream of making aliya to Israel, yes, ascent, ascent to the heights of the Holy Land, ever upward, the sooner the better, where he planned to immediately enlist in the army—to put on a uniform and fight to defend the Jewish homeland. "If you will it, it is no dream," Howie declared, quoting Theodor Herzl, the father of modern Zionism, but, meanwhile, the closest he could come to the fulfillment of that dream was the Israel restaurant on Coney Island Avenue in Brooklyn—and he swept his hand morosely before him in the direction of the trays of kishke and knishes, the tubs of potato salad and cole slaw. Once he made aliya, though, between wars and annual reserve duty, which he would fulfill with overflowing joy in his heart, his ambition was to learn the craft of a *sofer*—to enable him, as a scribe of the parchments folded inside mezuzot and tefillin boxes, to earn a living by channeling the main element of his art, Hebrew calligraphy, in the name of heaven. Eventually, God willing, he hoped to master the trade to such a high level that he could write entire scrolls including the Megillah of Esther and the holy Torah itself.

One day he presented to Tema a sheet of paper rolled up like a diploma, which he opened before her after giving the table a quick cleansing swipe with a foul-smelling rag. At first glance the image he displayed in front of her eyes seemed to be that of a naked woman with fantasy-defined breasts and hips such as might appear on a calendar in a men's locker room or in any dirty magazine, but, when you examined it more closely, you saw that it was a mosaic made up of thousands of minute parts that Tema of course recognized at once as Hebrew letters. "Micrography," Howie Stern declared proudly. "Recognize yourself? It's a picture of you. That lady is you—made up of the whole Song of Songs, the whole thing, every single letter and word, all eight chapters and one hundred and seventeen verses."

Later that evening, in the lounge after philosophy class, she cleared away the coffee cups and cookie crumbs and unrolled Howie's offering in front of Elisha Pardes, who stared at it for a long time in silence twisting as usual the coils of his beard. "To paraphrase what Shekhem son of Hamor told Jacob's sons after he had raped their sister Dina," Elisha spoke at last, "Ask anything you want of me, including my precious foreskin and the foreskin of every single guy in my town, and I'll give it to you—as long as I get the girl."

What she should ask of Howie Stern soon emerged with pure clarity from the hints embedded in Elisha's words. Because she had accepted his first gift, Howie was emboldened not long after to present her with another, this time with trembling hands—a small, flat object folded into wax paper such as might be used to wrap a corned beef sandwich with a pickle.

"I'm giving you the most precious thing I own," Howie said as he slid the package in front of her. Tema made no move to claim it, so Howie himself peeled back the wax paper to reveal a crisp new United States passport, opening it lovingly and flattening it out on the table to show off a mug shot of his street-battered face, and then flipping through the entire booklet to reveal one blank page after another.

"I'm trusting you with my life. I'm giving it to you to hold on to until I get the money together to make aliya to Israel. It's very valuable—you know what I'm saying?—and I live in a lousy neighborhood, so the main thing I'm asking is you should keep it in a safe place for me—okay?"

Tema sat frozen in her seat staring at this object that was like lifeblood for him. She reached out to draw it closer. She picked it up with two fingers as if it were a spider, slipped it down the front of her sweater and tucked it into her bra, from where it instantly gave off a small puff of aroma like an atomizer, smoked meats and brine.

Not long afterward, Tema asked for what she wanted, putting her proposal before Howie, laying out the terms on the table without embellishment. It was quite possible, she told him by way of incentive, for him to get to Israel much sooner than he had ever imagined, to live there in far greater comfort than he had ever dreamed of for as long as he liked, even to enjoy what amounted to a grant to cover in full his training as a scribe, provided he agreed to two things.

The first thing he would have to agree to was to marry her. Her father, an extremely wealthy man as it happened, would support them in style for as long as was necessary, even forever if that's what it took. Her father already considered her damaged goods anyway, so he was in no position to reject her marriage even to the poor schlemiel deli worker she had been seen talking to at the Israel restaurant like some kind of slutty *pritzeh*. Thanks to Howie, Tema informed him, her reputation was now completely mud, ruined beyond repair. Howie could trust her on this—her father would come through with the money after arriving at the dead-end conclusion that Howie was the best she could do under the circumstances. There was absolutely no doubt in Tema's mind that her father would stamp his Berel Bavli kosher seal of approval smack on the flank of their marriage and proceed to do the right thing by her for all to see.

The second thing Howie would have to agree to, Tema went on, was that, even though they would be married in the eyes of the world and the law and of Moses and Israel, it would be a marriage in name only. Privately, between the two of them, where it counted the most, they would live like brother and sister. What Howie needed to keep in mind above all else, Tema stressed, was this: she would only be like a sister to him, nothing more. If he ever dared to try any funny business with her, to make moves on her in the slightest degree in private in a way that crossed the line from brotherliness, for example, she would walk out on him immediately if not sooner, no ifs, ands, or buts. Her father would rally to her side and cut him off completely while continuing to support her generously since she would not hesitate to accuse him of all manner of atrocities. And even if he threatened to exercise his masculine prerogative under religious law by refusing to give her a *get*, she wouldn't care; it made no difference to her one way or the other if he gave her a divorce or not—she had no intention of remarrying anyway, she had never wanted to get married in the first place, all she wanted was to get out of her father's house; marrying him was an act of necessity and survival on her part, even, you might say, of desperation. To put it simply so that Howie could grasp the big picture, Tema elaborated, what they would have between them would resemble a marriage between an alien who needs a green card and an American citizen; for the alien such a marriage was the only way in, and for Tema such a marriage was the only way out. So that's the deal, he was never to touch her, never, Tema summed up for Howie—take it or leave it, and she folded her arms in front of her chest, staring at him grimly.

"But what about my health?" Howie said finally, practically whining, passing a hand forlornly across his crotch to make his point. "How about my needs?"

Tema barked out a sharp laugh that caused almost everyone in that restaurant to stop chewing and turn around to stare.

"What are you laughing for?" Howie asked sullenly.

"Don't worry," Tema said, "I'll find an outlet for you. Scout's honor." And she drew his passport out from inside her sweater, placed her left hand flat upon it, and raised her right hand as if taking a solemn oath.

They were married at the end of August at the Roosevelt Hotel on East Forty-fifth Street in Manhattan. Tema's father, Reb Berel Bavli, pronounced "Roosevelt" to sound like "rooster," and in honor of the occasion he personally with his own hands slaughtered hundreds of hens and cut the throats of a herd of cows for the impressively lavish smorgasbord and the elaborate wedding feast that people could not stop talking about for many months afterward. The morning after the wedding an article about it appeared in *New York Times*—not an announcement in the society section but on the front page itself, as Reb Berel Bavli had privately arranged with the New York City police commissioner to close off the entire block in front of the hotel between Madison and Park Avenues so that the ceremony could be held outside in the street under the sky as the dusk settled into darkness. At the bottom of page one of the *Times* there was a photograph shot from the roof of the Roosevelt Hotel showing a sea made up of the tops of thousands of black hats, and in the corner, if you looked very closely, a lonely white dot, the crown of the head of the bride, Miss Tema Bavli, later to be known as HaRav Temima Ba'alatOv, Ima Temima, her face so heavily veiled with a white satin cloth of such weight and thickness that she could not see her way at all and had to be guided by her stepmother the refugee, Mrs. Frumie Bavli, and her mother-in-law the corset fitter, Mrs. Mildred Stern, to her place under the marriage canopy like the condemned, blindfolded on the road to the gallows.

One week after the wedding Mr. and Mrs. Howard Stern boarded the Zim Lines *SS Zion* in New York harbor. Howie's eyes misted with emotion as he gazed up at the blue-and-white flag with the Star of David of the Jewish State hoisted proudly on top of the ship, waving in the breeze like the flag of any other normal and legitimate country in the community of nations with a fleet of its own. The newlyweds, traveling with thirty stiff new leather suitcases, one of them stuffed exclusively with toilet paper at Tema's insistence since she had heard that the still-very-young state had not yet evolved to a civilized level in that department, were installed in a first class cabin. Waving from the deck to family and friends, including Elisha Pardes who was standing alone in the distance with arms raised, palms uplifted, and the mouth on his wan face in the shape of a silent scream, and whom she acknowledged with a discreet nod, Tema left her homeland and her birthplace and the house of her father and set sail for Israel, never to return.

You Shall
Give Me the
Firstborn
of Your Sons—
and You Shall
Do the Same
for Your Cattle
and Sheep

On the morning of Passover eve, April 1968, Haim Ba'al-Teshuva, as Howie Stern was by then already known, scribe and phylacteries maker, joined a group of brash ideologues who had responded with blazing enthusiasm to a small newspaper ad—WANTED, FAMILIES OR SINGLES TO RESETTLE ANCIENT CITY OF HEBRON; FOR DETAILS CONTACT RABBI M. LEVINGER. That morning, Passover eve, eighty-eight yearning souls, men and women, many bundling along their children, made their way in caravans from every corner of the land of Israel to the Park Hotel in Hebron, once the summer resort of choice of the Jordanian upper classes for the cool, dry air of the ancient city. Rabbi Moshe their leader boldly set down on the reception desk an envelope stuffed with cash, advance payment in full to the Arab owner of the hotel for accommodations.

For the remainder of that day the pioneers toiled together in a spirit of common purpose, with an intensity such as Howie Stern had never before experienced even during the euphoric six days of the miraculous war less than a year earlier that had restored the biblical heartland and the holy city of Jerusalem itself to the Jewish people. Making their preparations for the forthcoming festival, they cleaned and scrubbed, they banished every trace of forbidden grains and leaven from the portion of the kitchen allotted to them and stocked it with the Passover supplies they had carted along for this exodus to the pith of the Promised Land.

When night fell, they celebrated their Seder at a spiritual height so exalted all traces of their physical and mortal bonds seemed to have been overcome, rendered meaningless and beside the point. Afterward, the women and children collapsed two or three to a bed in the hotel rooms, while the men found places to stretch out their bodies on the cold floor of the lobby without even a stone to place under their heads for a pillow, such as Father Jacob had when he stopped to rest in nearby Beit El on his flight from his brother Esau to Haran, and in his dream he saw a ladder with angels ascending and descending, and God Himself appeared to him and said, This ground you are lying upon I will give to you and to your offspring.

Two days later, Rabbi Moshe their leader announced to the world that the Jewish people have returned to this ground, never to leave again. This ancient city of Hebron belongs to us, it is the site of the Cave of Makhpela, the tombs of our patriarchs and our matriarchs, which Father Abraham purchased at the going rate of four hundred shekels of silver from Efron the Hittite as a burial place for his wife Sarah. Without haggling, without asking for any special treatment or consideration or favors or deals, Father Abraham purchased it at full price, retail, fair and square; it was the legitimate estate of his descendants in the line of the son he had with Mother Sarah, Father Isaac. We, the Jewish people, have prudently and with commendable foresight kept the receipt, its authenticity available for anyone's examination in the book of Genesis, chapter twenty-three, verses sixteen through twenty.

Howie Stern, in his new life as Haim Ba'al-Teshuva, scribe and phylacteries maker now at long last of Hebron, had always been struck by the deep and wondrous implications of the Hebrew word for receipt—

kabbala. A follower of the great mystic Rabbi Abraham Isaac Kook, Howie abided by the teaching that every Jew is holy, and, by extension, everything touched by a Jew is holy—and Jews touched a lot of receipts. But when it came to the receipt for Hebron, its sacred powers were truly kabbalistic, it transported you to a state of breathless ecstasy and selfless willingness to be consumed in the mystical fires.

Howie's wife, Tema, did not join him in this adventure. She remained at home in Jerusalem, not only because she had serious moral and intellectual reservations about the Hebron offensive, and not only because she did not like living in squalor or roughing it, but also because after nearly twelve years of marriage and a single bout of sexual intimacy with her husband in name only—a copulation episode that may have lasted no longer than a minute in time but felt like an eternity—Tema was in the very last stages of pregnancy. Howie had thrown himself upon her with savagery and violence, screaming, "Hey, I'm fucking you! I'm fucking you! Look guys, I'm fucking her!" His triumphant cries would have been more repellent had they not also struck her as so pathetically comic that she was in danger of insulting him unforgivably by erupting into laughter. Nevertheless, she managed to control herself—taking it like a man—lying there on her back without resisting, her eyes open wide, observing the progress of an oversized juke bug scuttling along the ceiling who didn't get very far.

She had made a deal with Howie, and she was doing the honorable thing by living up to her part. The deal was—if he instructed her in the skills of a scribe, which no master *sofer* would risk imparting to a woman, and if he guided her in the writing and completion of a Torah scroll in accordance with the strictest rules and regulations, she would allow him a single shot at possessing her—she would let him "know" her; that was the euphemism in the text she had just written out letter by letter, as if this alone were the portal to complete knowledge and ownership of a woman, with no equivalent or reciprocal knowledge or possession of a man by a woman. That was the bargain she had made with her husband-in-name Howie Stern, who reinvented himself as Haim Ba'al-Teshuva, the penitent who had returned from sinfulness to full faith the minute he learned that the seed he had sown with tears would bear joyous fruit.

When her little mother Torah was completed, from the first word, *Bereishit*, to the last word, *Yisrael*, over three hundred thousand letters, each one inscribed painstakingly with a turkey feather quill and specially prepared ink on parchment made from the skin of an unborn calf, one-hundred-percent kosher in every respect except that it had been created by a rogue scribe who was a woman, hopelessly impure no matter how many times she immersed herself in the ritual bath, she did not renege on her agreement. She was a good sport. She lay down on her back and paid up.

Afterward Howie rolled off her, and though entirely spent and panting, managed to inquire, "How come I don't see no blood?" By way of an explanation, she told him a story about how every day in the springtime when she was a little girl, with her neighbor's dog Germy locked in his holding cell observing her, lunging at her from the end of his chain and barking madly, she used to climb the trellises bolted to the sides of her family's garage at the end of the driveway, even in the skirts she was required to wear. She would climb those trellises every day in the spring in order to gather bouquets of roses to bring to her mother and extract a ghost of a smile. And every day when she came down from the trellises her flesh was torn by the thorns and splinters, and blood streamed down her face and arms and legs. That was how she had lost it, she told Howie, that was why there was no blood left.

Now, on this Passover eve, April 1968, standing on the terrace of the apartment her father had bought for them on Ben-Yefuneh Street in the Baka neighborhood of Jerusalem, watching Howie set off in his Peugeot heading into the Judean Hills past the tomb of Rachel Our Mother who had died in childbirth on the road to Efrat, driving onward to join his band of hotheads and reclaim the ancient city of Hebron, she pressed both hands against the massive heaving mound of her womb as she was seized by the insistent force of her first contraction. She recognized that a process had begun that would have to come to completion one way or another. The course had been set. No power on earth could stop it.

Supporting her belly from underneath, she waddled back inside to the small study attached to her bedroom, and sat down with her legs apart on the edge of a straight-backed chair by the window to consider how to proceed. What her father had bought for them was actually two apartments, which they had combined into one by knocking out the dividing wall. Howie had his own bedroom on the other side in what had once been the second apartment, though they kept a proper master suite with the two beds pushed together in a room that the former owners had dedicated as a memorial shrine to their son, killed in the 1956 Suez War. This official conjugal chamber was set up for the sake of public image, to forestall the gossips, and for the same reason she visited the ritual bath every month in compliance with the laws of family purity required of a married woman still in her childbearing years so that the ladies could comment to each other in the market the next morning that they had noticed Mrs. Stern coming home from the mikva last night, may the barren soon rejoice with her sons gathered around her, amen.

Her father would have preferred to buy in the Rekhavia section, which he regarded as more dignified and established, its streets named for distinguished commentators and sages. But Tema had insisted on Baka, with its streets called directly by the names of biblical characters, plain and simple, a few women's names too. And even though Ben-Yefuneh was not in the section of Baka mysterious with lush gardens and old abandoned Arab stone houses, there was for her a measure of ironic justification in settling on a street named for Caleb son of Yefuneh, whose first name in Hebrew, Kalev, written without vowels, consisted of the same three letters as the word for dog, *kelev*. Her life had come full circle; once again, she found herself on the street of the dog. Reb Berel Bavli let his daughter have her way with regard to choice of location despite the fact on the ground that he was the one writing the checks because bottom line he was investing not in real estate but in progeny. Whenever he was in touch with her, usually by telephone which, whether the connection was clear or not, required shouting due to the accepted etiquette for long distance, he never failed to boom out across an ocean and a continent, "So-nu? Something cooking in the pot already? What—I didn't pay for enough rooms for you maybe?"

Now, sitting in the study of her Baka apartment looking out to Ben-Yefuneh Street as the labor pains surged up in shorter intervals and with greater intensity, she reflected on her situation. She was a woman past thirty with a history of five miscarriages all in the first trimester of her previous pregnancies about to give birth to the only baby she had ever carried to term. The sensible course to follow would be to call a taxi at once to convey her to the nearest hospital. Nevertheless, she remained in her place, unable to take action.

To complicate matters, it was the eve of Passover. Almost every Jew in the city was occupied with the frenetic last-minute preparations for the festival. There was no Jew who did not have a Seder to attend. She too had houses that would open their doors to her as another needy soul and welcome her to their table now that her cowboy husband had headed to the hills to resettle the Holy Land with a critically urgent mandate that could not be put off for another minute; his priorities were fixed even with a wife on the perilous cusp of giving birth to his only child. She was aware with grim resignation that already on this day the hospitals must be severely understaffed, and, the longer she waited, the fewer would be the professionals on duty to attend to her. She would end up being delivered by the Arab janitor on the stone floor of the hospital lobby beside a slop pail and a squeegee. How had it happened that she had lived and sustained herself and arrived at this season with no one to turn to? How had it come to pass that she was so utterly alone?

The pains were growing more regular but were still tolerable—and so her thoughts drifted to the preposterous idea of approaching her renowned Jerusalem teacher of Tanakh, Nekhama Leibowitz, in whose classes she shone and whose *gilyonot* handouts with questions on the Torah portion she wrestled with weekly, coming up with answers so startling and original that they shook even the pedagogic rigorousness of her legendary teacher, at times thrillingly, at other times with horror over the basic assumptions that had been tossed out and the boundaries that had been crossed.

She could picture Nekhama in her tiny apartment at this very moment, with her blind husband settled in his familiar corner, her plain little woolen beret perched at an angle on her head covering her hair, signifying her status as a married woman. Despite the prominence she had carved out for herself as a celebrated teacher of Tanakh to both men and women, territory that had until then been almost exclusively the domain of men, the skin of her hands would still be rubbed raw in the soapy basin, her fingers bloodied from peeling the potatoes, she would scrupulously carry out the menial chores traditionally assigned to women in preparing for the holiday—this was the model she set forth for other women, stepping on the line firmly and publicly, but not, God forbid, overstepping or blurring it.

There was no doubt in her mind that Nekhama in her lovingkindness would make an effort to help her, even with the strict Pesakh deadline looming, from the immutable Written Law itself that could not on any account be put off. But was it truly possible to seek her out now, at such an hour and for such a reason, as Mother Rebekah had gone to seek out and inquire of God when her pregnancy was killing her, crying, Why me? Why me?—a simple human question. Nekhama would ponder the question in her usual circular way, answering with yet another question from the point of view of the commentators: What is so hard here for Rashi? What is troubling Rashbam? What is bothering Ramban? What is Hazal's problem? And Tema would cry, My teacher, that is not the correct question. The correct question is right in front of your eyes, What is so hard here for Mother Rebekah? What is troubling Tema?

Just picturing this scenario exhausted her, and she made her way heavily into the adjacent room to lie down on her bed. She might have turned to Elisha Pardes, her other teacher, but she knew he was not in Israel at this time because, had he been there, he would surely have summoned her at once to his side. As the Toiter successor he was no doubt at this moment in the Fifth Avenue penthouse preparing for the Passover, with his wife and daughters and his disciples already in mourning over him. The veil had already been lowered over the face of the previous Toiter, and the mittens drawn up on his hands after the still glowing roach of his joint had been prized loose from his fingers. He had been gathered back to his fathers. The first time Elisha came to Israel as the new Toiter, not long after Tema's own arrival, he dispatched a disciple down to Jerusalem to bring her up to him in Haifa. As the car drew up to his villa on the top of Mount Carmel, she saw him walking toward her from among the pine trees, where he had gone for a session of *hitbodedut*, to pour out his heart to God in seclusion like a child pleading with his father. His hair and beard had turned shimmering white, he resembled Elijah the prophet coming like a vision out of the Carmel. He had aged devastatingly in so short a time, he looked like a man of seventy years.

Tema turned to her escort and asked, as Mother Rebekah had asked of the servant Eliezer of Damascus who was delivering her to be the wife of his master Abraham's son, Isaac, Who is that coming toward us from the woods? The answer came, That is my master, the Toiter.

Like Mother Rebekah who had fallen from her camel in a kind of swoon when she first laid eyes on Isaac and had drawn her veil over her face, Tema's knees grew weak as she stepped out of the car, and she buckled onto the concrete, covering her face with both her hands in mortification.

Elisha the Toiter Rav lifed her by the hands and led her into the villa, to a private room stark white overlooking the sea, with a bunch of red poppies in a crystal vase in the center of the table, and he closed the door. He fell on her neck and kissed her, and raised his voice and wept as Father Jacob had wept with recognition when he first set eyes on Rachel Our Mother, she was so lovely in face and form. She was his sister / his bride, he said to her, she was the Toiter's shadow, his mirror image, his locked garden, his sealed fountain. Her name would no longer be Tema, he said to her, she would be called Temima—because she was blameless and without blemish, perfection, she was the pure *Ima*, the holy Mother. He placed his left hand under her head and with his right hand he caressed her. Love is as fierce as death, he said to her—and so they knew one another, and, finally, after all the years of grieving, reborn as Temima, she was comforted for the loss of her mother.

Thereafter, whenever he came to Israel, several times a year, a car would be sent to bring Temima so that she could study at his feet for the duration of his stay, sometimes for as long as a week—an extraordinary privilege and an honor to be singled out in this way by one of the giants of the generation, as she explained to her husband, Howie Stern. In the first years he would arrive by ship to the port of Haifa and never venture out of the Galilee, going as far as Safed or Tiberias but no farther, because, as he told her, more of the Holy Land would be just too much for him, he could absorb it only in small doses. It was like reading the Torah, he elaborated. Often he was obliged to stop at the first words of the third verse—"And God said"—he could not go on, it was too overwhelming; think about it—God said, He spoke, it was more than enough to take in. "But what He said is, 'Let there be light,'" Temima responded with a laugh, and playfully she switched on the light to reveal their naked bodies, his already sickly and wasted, and she added, "I just wanted you to see for yourself that it's Rachel this time, and not poor Leah with her bloodshot eyes from too much weeping."

Later on, when he began to arrive by plane, he would go no farther than Jaffa, where she would stay with him in a specially prepared suite of rooms overlooking the harbor from which the prophet Jonah set sail to Nineveh. His depleted body was already bruised and diseased as if it had been thrashed around in a storm, swallowed up in a darkness like the grave and then exposed to too much sunlight, and like Jonah he would beg to die, and like Job covered with scabies he would declare, Perish the day I was born and the night in which it was announced that a male child had been conceived. Nevertheless, after each of her miscarriages—five in all, all surely sons, since the Toiter can never produce a male successor of his own blood who could survive—he stroked her hair and comforted her with the words of the holy Rav Nakhman, There is no despair here in the world at all, and he set before her a meal of olives and bread and wine and figs, urging her to eat. "Why should we fast?" he would say to her as King David had said after the death of his baby son by Bathsheba, the woman he had stolen from another man. "Can we bring him back again? We are going to him, but he will never come back to us."

She must have dozed off, because now she started into alertness from a clenching pain and found herself soaked, lying in a wet pool. Her water had broken, liquid was gushing out from between her thighs beyond her control, but the answer had been revealed to her through her ruminations in the realm between here and there. She needed to go find Ketura. It had been Ketura who had taken care of her after each of her five miscarriages, tending to her with blessed devotion and discretion, offering the excuses to Howie that the mistress is indisposed due to female problems—that was sufficient. It was amazing how easily a man could be deceived simply because he did not pay the correct sort of attention, it was a side benefit of not being taken seriously that a woman could count on.

Temima knew exactly where Ketura lived: on El-Wad Road in the shadow of the Temple Mount with its Golden Dome, in an apartment Temima had rented for her. She had been to visit her there on several occasions in recent months since the Old City of Jerusalem had been breached and opened again to Jews, bringing money to Ketura to tide her over after Howie had dismissed her from their service when Temima had conceived from the single time he had flung himself upon her to collect what was owed him. Officially, Ketura was their Arab housekeeper, but soon after she arrived at their home from the Makhane Yehuda market she also began serving as Howie's handmaid, his *pilegesh*, the "outlet" that, in their original negotiations in the other Israel—the Israel kosher delicatessen on Coney Island Avenue in Brooklyn—Temima had vowed to Howie she would provide for him for the sake of his health, to take care of his needs.

Temima had found Ketura begging on the Agrippas Street side of the market with an exquisite mocha-skinned baby swaddled in a towel lying in a discarded grapefruit crate some distance from her by a garbage dump. The baby opened his eyes, a translucent pale color, gray almost blue like ancient glass, and stared at Temima. "I just can't bear to watch the boy die," Ketura had whispered when Temima had placed a coin in her hand that day in the market, even in violation of her principles against encouraging women beggars who exploited their children because she had been electrified by the remarkable scar in the shape of a black bird with outspread wings stretched across the face of this cast-off woman. Since there was no justice, at least let there be mercy.

Ketura had just come out of the wilderness, from the patriarchal compound of Abba Kadosh, who had disgorged her with her baby. She left with her child in her arms, calling him Ibn Kadosh because he was his father's son. The scar that had taken the oracular shape of a bird had been seared with acid onto her face by her father and brothers when she had first dared to brazenly step out on her own. Abba Kadosh had never had a woman so mystically branded. The bird beguiled him, it excited him, it pleased him to trace its outline on Ketura's face with his finger, its wondrous shape, the wings outstretched across the cheeks emerging from the hump of her soaring refined nose. Howie, on the other hand, avoided looking at it, especially in intimate moments, and deep down he churned with resentment at Temima for this cynical fulfillment of her promise by providing for his needs and his health with damaged goods. Now, ten years later, the boy with skin like brushed sable and eyes like ice and a bearing like an exotic young prince, along with his brutally scarred mother, had been cast out once again.

Temima folded some hand towels and packed them between her legs to absorb the flowing liquid. Wrapping her head and shoulders in a great woolen shawl, with dark glasses masking her eyes and a basket on her arm filled with the Passover macaroons that Ibn Kadosh loved covered with a white cloth napkin, she set out on foot from her apartment on Ben-Yefuneh, east on Yehuda Street, then up Hebron Road in the northward direction, away from Hebron and all of its madness toward Jerusalem and all of its madness, and passed through the great stone walls of the Old City by the portal of the Jaffa Gate.

It was already late afternoon, the air was cool and crisp, traffic had stopped, the streets were silent and deserted as each citizen took shelter inside a warm house with the ghost of a blood smear on the doorpost to protect the firstborns and found a seat at the brightly lit Passover table. Every few steps along the way Temima was obliged to pause and lean against some inanimate support, bracing herself, moaning and massaging the writhing globe of her belly as the spasms gripped her relentlessly, wave after wave. By the time she reached the Via Dolorosa through the winding alleyways of the Old City bazaar, all of its shops shuttered and locked fast, she was doubled over with the pangs of labor, like a film run backward of Miriam mother of Yeshua HaNozri making her way along the street of her boy's future agony, with no place to give birth and begin the story.

At last she reached Ketura's apartment on El-Wad Road and collapsed against its door, her wracked body brushing against it as she slumped to the ground—and the Djinn who appeared before her was Ibn Kadosh in his white underpants. He informed her that his mother was not at home, she had a job that night at the King David Hotel—in the kitchen, he stressed, lest Temima assume it was a private commission in the bedroom of a paying guest; she was working the communal Seder on this night for the rich tourists. He asked her what she had brought for him, and sat down on the floor to eat his macaroons.

Within the hour Temima's baby was born, extracted by Ibn Kadosh in his white underpants with almond and coconut crumbs stuck to his fingertips on the prayer rug of the living room floor, a procedure not so different from the kidding of the goats he tended on the slopes of Silwan, Temima creating much more of an uproar than the other animals, straining and bearing down frantically with sweat streaming down her cheeks flushed bright red, bleating nonstop, Mama, Mama, Mama!

When Ketura returned home at dawn, in a headscarf and long tailored coat over her tight jeans and spangled halter top, she found Temima still sprawled on the floor covered with a fuzzy pink blanket stamped with the image of a Barbie doll that Ibn Kadosh had spread over her. The baby boy, still attached by the umbilical cord, was grazing at her breast. Ketura cut the cord and gathered up the pulpy mass of the placenta. She took it into her small kitchen and sliced off a section, hacking the remainder into two chunks like liver, one to be planted in a pot to bear a life-giving tree, the other to be wrapped in clear plastic and stored in the freezer for future emergencies. The fresh piece of placenta now sitting on her scarred countertop she dumped into a wooden bowl and minced with a chopping knife, then stirred it into a tea with lemon juice, sugar, cinnamon, and mint leaves. She brought this infusion to Temima in a glass even before setting about the task of cleaning up the new mother and her infant, wiping away the blood and mucous.

She squatted on the floor beside Temima and fed her spoonful after spoonful of the tea until the glass was empty. "It is very good for you," Ketura said over Temima's squeamish objections. "Yolk-sac tea. It will save you from the sadness of after birth."

"But is it kosher for Passover?" Temima asked.

"You see?" said Ketura. "Already you are joking." And she smiled with such pleasure the wings of the bird on her face stretched out even wider as if preparing to take flight.

A week later, Temima woke up in her bed in her Ben-Yefuneh Street apartment after a longer-than-usual undisturbed sleep, her breasts painfully hard like two boulders, swollen and engorged, the front of her nightgown stained with great blots of starch-dried milk and milk still seeping. She wondered why her baby boy, as yet unnamed, had not cried for his usual feeding, and experienced for a moment the pride of a mother with an unusually good child who so considerately sleeps through the night.

The next morning the baby was to be circumcised. Howie had agreed by telephone, after consultation with rabbinical authorities over the fine points of which mitzvah or obligation trumps the other, to tear himself away from their holy mission of settlement at the Park Hotel in Hebron where he and his comrades were still entrenched, and to come to Jerusalem to partake of morning prayers at a nearby synagogue on the eighth day after the birth during which the holy commandment of circumcision, the *brit* of his first and only son, would be performed and a simple festive mitzvah meal would be offered.

Holding herself very carefully, Temima descended from her bed, her body still tender from the poundings and lacerations of childbirth, and shuffled to the cradle in the corner of her room to check on the baby. Where he should have been lying, she found instead a note from Ketura informing her that, on Howie's orders, she had taken the boy to Hebron to be circumcised in the Ibrahimi Mosque. "I'm sorry, Temima," Ketura wrote. "I really need the money."

Ketura returned late the next day without the child, telling Temima that they had decided it was in the boy's best spiritual interest to remain with his father at this unprecedented messianic time. She put out both her hands palms upward and shrugged her shoulders and the wings of the bird seared across her face drooped mournfully. There was nothing she could do about it; they were all crazy, she said. The child was being cared for by one of the women in the hotel group who had given birth a month earlier—a convert with long false eyelashes called Yehudit Har-HaBayit, formerly known as Rapture Reed, Ketura had heard, the daughter of Christian evangelicals from Idaho in America, ardent believers in the State of Israel as the herald of the Second Coming. Now Yehudit Har-HaBayit suckled two babies without favoritism, one at each breast, a wet nurse in a sustained state of exaltation.

Ketura herself had not been present at the circumcision that morning, having been requested as an Arab and a Muslim and also as a kind of impure "leper" due to the ominous discoloration of her skin, the bird of prey sprawled across her face, to leave the chamber containing the tombs of Abraham and Sarah while the ceremony took place. She stationed herself instead, as a form of protest, on the seventh step leading up to the mosque that had been erected over the burial cave, which was as far as the Jews had once been allowed to ascend for so many years, peering with longing through a small hole in the masonry at their heart's desire, the mothers and fathers denied to them. She could hardly see anything at all, but she was able to report that she had heard from conversations around her that the gentleman who had carried out the circumcision was Temima's own father who had just arrived the day before from Brooklyn to do the job. She handed to Temima a note from Howie in a sealed envelope, which Temima slipped unopened between the pages of her Tanakh, at Genesis, chapter twenty-two.

Her father, Reb Berel Bavli, showed up at Temima's apartment the next night still high from the audacious event the day before, raving with enthusiasm for the entire resettlement project to which he had already made a substantial financial contribution, announcing that he now intended to establish it as his number-one charity, above even supporting the Oscwiecim Rebbe. Imagine, he cried, the first *bris mila* in Hebron since the massacre of 1929, when sixty-seven of our people were slaughtered by the Arab murderers, may their names and memory be blotted out, and the rest, Jews who had lived there for hundreds of years, were banished from our second-holiest city. Well, watch out boys, we're back—believe me, you putzes, we are definitely back, and this time, we're here to stay! The first bris in Hevron in almost forty years—that we have been kept alive and sustained to reach this day!—and in the Me'aras HaMakhpela no less, by the grave of our forefather Avraham Avinu himself of all places, the very same Avraham who performed the first recorded circumcision in Jewish history, the original *mohel*. And who of all people is given the honor to perform this one, with his own hands, for his own grandchild, his only male descendant? I'm telling you, Tema'le, tears were running down my face, and you know me—I'm not the type who usually cries because of a little blood. In thirty seconds flat—a new record!—I snipped it right off, good-bye and good riddance, quicker than a wink, faster than you could say Moishe Pipik. The *sandek*, Rabbi Moshe, the leader of the movement himself, who was given the honor to sit in the chair of Eliyahu HaNavi and hold the baby on a pillow on his lap while I did my business, couldn't believe it was over—it should go in the *Guinness Book of Records* for the fastest bris ever, I'm telling you, someone should write to them, even with my jet lag and my reflexes not so ay-yay-yay I broke the record. The baby didn't know what hit him, he didn't even have a chance to let out one good holler before I sucked the blood from the cut with my own mouth and spit it out into a cup, and then I wrapped his little *schmeckel'e* up in a piece of gauze, it was so delicious, a delicacy like a chicken neck, a *gorgel*, and just as he was getting ready to yell bloody murder I dipped some gauze—a different piece of gauze, needless to say, not the same one I used on his little you-know-what—into the *bekher* filled with nice sweet wine and stuck it into his mouth, and he sucked away happy as a lambchop. I'm telling you, Tema'le, this is a grade-A baby, and I know from grade-A, believe me. He looks just like his father, the spitting image, also with a pot belly, also bald, all he needs is a beard and they could go on the road together and do a comedy routine in the Catskill hotels, on the borscht belt, Maxi and Mini. Then Howie announced the baby's name: Pinkhas—Pinkhas Hevroni, may he grow up to Torah, to the wedding canopy, and to good deeds. Hevroni, you know what that's for, of course, and such an honor it is for him to be the first boy to be circumcised in the Me'aras HaMakhpela in Hevron, he'll never forget it, he will go down in the history books. And Pinkhas, so that he should be blessed with the balls, the *baitzim*, you should excuse the expression, to stand up and do the right thing by our people in times of danger, when God is so mad at us for our sins He is ready to wipe us out like a bunch of cockroaches—to stand up like Pinkhas son of Elazar son of Aharon the *kohain*, who took his spear in his hand and went straight into that tent, he didn't think for one minute should I / shouldn't I, he stuck that spear right into those two, that bigshot from the tribe of Shimon, what's his name?—stuck it into him right there, while his *schlang*, you should excuse me, was *schtupped* in a place where it had no business being, in that shiksa from Midian, that temptress who leads men to sin, may her name be erased forever. That's the kind of boy we want our Pinkhas Hevroni Ba'al-Teshuva to grow up to be—am I right, Tema'le? And afterward, I'm telling you, such a meal we had, a kiddush like you wouldn't believe, right there in the Makhpela, courtesy of yours truly—super deluxe, catered five stars, one-hundred-percent kosher for Passover, nothing but the best for my grandson, with real tablecloths and napkins and dishes and silverware—no paper or plastic for our young prince, Pinkhas Hevroni Ba'al-Teshuva—and with flower centerpieces and waiters in uniforms, all Arabs by the way, so much for their principles when you wave a few dollar bills in front of their noses, that's the Arab mentality. I'm telling you, it's amazing what you can accomplish, even in so-called Occupied Territory, even in the wild West Bank, with a little money and a little hutzpah. Every kind of smoked fish and salad you can imagine we had—twelve stations, meats like you never saw, and I know from meats, wild ox and leviathan just like in Gan Eden—cakes and fruits, mountains of *shemura* matzah that cost me an arm and a leg, drinks like you wouldn't believe, hot and cold, including the world's best kosher wine to toast a *leHaim* in honor of the occasion, and even two ice sculptures, one molded in the shape of the Holy Temple, may it be rebuilt speedily and in our time, filled with pickled lox, and the other in the shape of the Tomb of the Patriarchs, filled with pickled herring.

I'm telling you, Tema'le, you missed an event of a lifetime, I'm sorry to say. You should have been there. That's where you belong. What kind of mother and wife are you anyways? Your baby is there, your husband is there—what are you doing here, if you don't mind my asking? Howie tells me he sent you a letter asking you to get off your *m'yeh*, you should excuse the expression, and come right away—so tell me already, what are you waiting for, the Moshiakh?

Temima listened to all of this without a word. She did not offer her father refreshments, not even a glass of water or a cup of tea. When finally he paused long enough for her to conclude that he had come to the end of his story, she stood up and said, "You must be very tired, Tateh, from your jet lag and from beating the world's *brit* record and from dealing with the caterers—and I am in great pain. I gave birth to a baby a few days ago and now they've stolen him away from me. My breasts feel like they're going to explode like bombs"—and she blushed crimson from the ordeal of being obliged, in her urgent desire to end this meeting, to offer her father intimate information about her woman's body.

At the door, Temima asked after Frumie, and her father made a slicing motion like a karate chop down the front of his chest. "Cancer, very bad. They cut them right off, yup, both of them"—and then he left, without even a light kiss or a fatherly embrace, it would have been too awkward and unseemly after such news about Frumie, and also after being made privy to details about the state of his own daughter's equipment, all this talk of breasts, even for a man like Reb Berel Bavli whose life's work with creatures had eviscerated him of every shred of sentimentality about flesh and mortality.

Howie telephoned the next morning on the pretext of informing her of the name he had given to their child. "Pinkhas is not a name I would have chosen," Temima retorted coldly.

This response provoked from Howie a fiery outpouring on how the land of Israel had just been handed back to the Jewish people on a silver platter, it's a miracle that only a blind man or a fool would spit at and reject. He then went on to inquire if she had read the note he had sent to her with Ketura. "I've already paid with interest for your writing," Temima replied. "I don't have time to read any letters from you. I'm sick with fever and sores because you snatched my baby from my breast. What kind of animal are you anyway? Even Hannah was allowed to wean her boy Samuel before turning him over to the corrupt bosses in Shilo. Even that fanatic Abraham allowed Sarah to finish weaning Isaac in the natural course of events, and made a party to celebrate the milestone before he took him up to the Moriah to slit his throat and sacrifice him." And she slammed down the receiver with a crash to prevent him from hearing her sobs.

She cried for six weeks without pause, even in her sleep she wept in her bed, and in the daytime she wept at the window of her apartment on Ben-Yefuneh Street, looking out as if seeking the one her soul longed for, never leaving the house lest the expected one show up and she not be there to greet him. Yet it was beyond her power to amass the energy and will to rush to his side, sweep him up in her arms, and flee with him to safety. This was a child conceived in a compromising deal with a man she scorned, carried off to a place she could not justify or bring herself to. She who had been forsaken by her own mother, she should have done better by her own child. Maybe she just did not love him enough, poor thing. The best she could offer him was to dress herself in sackcloth, to wail and refuse to be comforted, and go down mourning to the depths of *Sheol*.

Throughout this time, Ketura did not leave her side. As Ibn Kadosh was dispatched for food and supplies, Ketura squeezed and pumped milk from Temima's breasts to ease the swelling, at times suckling from them herself but never emptying them entirely, to wean them gradually until they dried out. She placed frozen cabbage leaves over Temima's breasts to soothe them, rubbed olive oil into the nipples to soften them, brewed teas from sage and peppermint leaves to prevent infection, and she defrosted a portion of the placenta she had saved, ground it up, and stirred it into the food she prepared for Temima, without even notifying her of this added ingredient, to lift the heavy cloud of sadness that crushes the spirit after childbirth. But for a mother whose baby had been torn from her as had been Temima's lot, Ketura reflected with keen distress, since she herself had been an accomplice, even the garnish of the placentas of half the women of China might not suffice.

When the child was about six weeks old, Howie telephoned again ostensibly to let Temima know that they had moved from the Park Hotel in downtown Hebron to an Israeli military compound overlooking the city. This, of course, was something that Temima was already aware of, as the tortured internal ideological debates of the Hebron settlers who were insisting they would never move from this place in which they had established a foothold at such personal cost and travail seared the news day after day. But not to worry, Howie assured Temima, even though the government considers us a royal pain in the rear, we sealed in cement a major deal with the big enchiladas: first, a new city will be built for us overlooking Hebron, to be known as Kiryat Arba, and then the old Jewish quarter in the heart of Hebron itself, Beit Romano, Beit Hadassah, the Avraham Avinu courtyard, and so on, will be restored to its original grandeur. For Temima's information, her father, Reb Berel Bavli, had already purchased for them the best villa in Kiryat Arba and the best apartment in Hebron, sight unseen, still only a dream, fully paid-up, no mortgages, no headaches whatsoever. So there was nothing to be concerned about, Howie went on, there was no risk in abandoning our stronghold in the Park Hotel. Hebron is ours now and forever, it is ours in this day as it was then, even if meanwhile we are living in tents on an army base with a communal kitchen and the latrines in the mud. As the Gemara teaches us, the land of Israel is acquired only through suffering. He asked again if Temima had read his note, and when she did not respond, he said, The main thing is, I'm inviting you to come and live with us. This is where you belong—your baby is here, this is your home.

"Is there a Jacuzzi on the army base?" Temima inquired.

Howie groaned. "How come you're still such a JAP, Tema?"

"Maybe when they put in a Jacuzzi, I'll think about coming," Temima said, and she hung up the phone.

She began to venture out of the house, returning to her Tanakh classes with her steadfast teacher, Morah Nekhama Leibowitz, who with a swift, curiously raw female appraisal took note of Temima's restored trim shape and asked about the baby.

"In Hebron," Temima said, "with the settlers. His father kidnapped him for his *brit* and I haven't seen him since."

"Ah," Nekhama said, "already they are sacrificing the children to the Molekh. *Avodah zara*, idolatry. As the prophet Jeremiah says, 'The number of your cities has become your gods.'"

And then, in a manner strikingly alien for her, so rigid was she in keeping to her program, in a gesture that Temima appreciated as the fumbling attempt of an incurably formal spirit to comfort a desolate mother with the nearest thing to a touch that she could muster, Nekhama returned to the final portions of the book of Exodus, even though it was already late spring, almost summer, and they had completed those sections months ago—posing a question without even covering herself modestly by channeling it through the male commentators: "If the Holy Temple was created as the permanent dwelling place for the earthly presence of the Master of the Universe, why do you think its artifacts—the ark, the altars, the table, and so on and so forth—continued to have the original design of rings with poles through them for ease of portability, a quick getaway, so to speak, from the days of the Tabernacle when our ancestors were still wandering in the wilderness?" And even more atypically, Nekhama answered her question relying on her own authority rather than that of the sages, even throwing in another colloquialism meant to brighten the face of the stricken mother who had endured such a blow. "Because the heart of the matter has never been land, it has always been Torah. Have Torah, Will Travel, as they say on the great frontier—that is our ticket."

More and more now, Temima left the apartment on Ben-Yefuneh Street, which had become for her increasingly suffocating and unbearable with remembered pain. This was when she began to take up with intense seriousness and concentration the practice of *hitbodedut*, which she continued over the years in different forms. In those days, she would throw a shawl over her head and shoulders on the cool Jerusalem nights and seek a solitary place, in the woods or the fields where she could hear, as Rav Nakhman of Bratslav had heard, the unique song of each blade of grass. She would converse with God in her own language and in her own way, supplicating Him, spilling out everything in her heart as to a mother, no matter how shameful or frivolous.

At first she sought out secluded spots in the western part of Jerusalem, parks and gardens, Ein Karem, the Sultan's Pool, the leper colony, Gehinnom. With time, she ventured alone deep into East Jerusalem, beyond the walls of the old city, along the slopes near what was said to be Absalom's tomb, by the springs of Gihon and the pool of Shiloah and Hezekiah's tunnel. She stood alone among the crumbling gravestones on the Mount of Olives one dark night, wild dogs prowling nearby, her arms raised to the heavens, confessing to God yet again with strangled cries the terrible guilt that was churning within her for abandoning her child, for allowing pride and perverse principle to override her maternal responsibilities to this blameless boy, for colluding by her stubbornness in letting go of him so passively.

As she beat her breast in anguished confession again and again, God answered her by sending a gang of Arab boys to fall upon her and throw her to the ground. Their hands began groping at her woman's body—breasts, belly, buttocks, between her thighs—she who had always felt herself to be set apart and chosen, and yet, in the end, she was no different from other women, the geography of all her hidden places was known to any stranger and imbecile and thug. Her mouth open but no scream issuing forth as in a nightmare, she struggled to detach her spirit from her body and nullify her inconsequential physical self with thoughts of God. This is what a woman who casts away her own child deserves, this is what a woman who wanders alone in such a place in the dark of night deserves, this is what a woman who presumes to take on the spiritual calling of a holy man deserves.

Then, as suddenly as the attackers had descended upon her, they were gone, taking flight like a flock of crows rising from carrion. Coming toward her now she recognized Ibn Kadosh in a white loincloth, brandishing a sword like an epic warrior, braying like a wild donkey, obeying the command of his mother Ketura, who had charged him with following Temima at a distance in her perilous night wanderings. Temima is a holy woman who must be allowed to move freely, Ketura had said to her son, but we her followers must follow her wherever she leads, and guard her in her comings and goings from all evil.

Her wanderings continued through the summer into the fall. She walked the length and the breadth of the city of Jerusalem and its surrounding areas, east and west, by night and by day, her Tanakh in her cloth bag slung across the front of her body like an ammunition bandolier. Now and then she would sit down to rest, on a bench, or a stone parapet, on the ground under a tree, and occasionally in a café where she would order some Turkish coffee or a mint tea and, once in a while, something to eat.

That is how she found herself late one afternoon in early autumn as the High Holidays were drawing near in a café on Ben-Yehuda Street, with her Tanakh open before her at the chapter on the binding of Isaac on the altar on the top of Mount Moriah where the Golden Dome of the Rock and the Al-Aqsa Mosque of the Muslims now stood—the chapter that would be chanted very soon on Rosh HaShana—and she decided that the time had come to break the seal and read Howie's letter. Though he had composed it in the spring at the end of Passover, he began with the Kol Nidre language of Yom Kippur coming soon upon them: All my vows, my oaths, my obligations with which I once pledged and bound myself I now repent of, I deem them absolved and annulled and voided, with no power over me. I no longer will consider you my sister. If you want your child back, you must come to Hevron and live with me as my wife in accordance with the law of Moses and Israel.

Temima folded the letter, slipped it back into its envelope and reinserted it between the pages of her Tanakh, this time at the Second book of Samuel, chapter three. She raised her eyes at a grating noise, followed by coarse shouting, and saw the manager of the café, his face red and glistening with perspiration, scuffling with three young men dressed entirely in white with exceptionally long sidelocks descending from their crocheted white skullcaps in waves down to their waists. She recognized them as the trio of Bratslaver Hasidim who staked out the spot in front of the café, singing and dancing until they brought themselves to a climactic pitch, then passing around a large empty tin can with its Kibbutz Beit-HaMita pickles label still affixed.

"I know these guys," the manager said to Temima as she approached, a great chrysanthemum of saliva spraying forth from his mouth. "They'll order every last thing on the menu, then give us a blessing in the name of the Dead Hasidim and walk out the door without paying one lousy *grush*."

Temima nodded her head to soothe him with her understanding and sympathy, and assured him he had no cause for worry; let them eat their fill to their heart's content, they were growing boys, she would cover their costs entirely—and she returned to her seat to continue her studies.

Out of the corner of her eye, she could take in every inch of the surface of the small round table nearby that the three were clustered around filling up again and again with the dishes they had ordered, their sidelocks tucked into their collars so they would not dip into their soup, their heads bent low over their bowls and plates, beaking their noses into their food as they stuffed it into their mouths in voracious heaps, sometimes with utensils, mostly shoving it in with their hands, gesticulating passionately with those very hands, spitting out moist, half-processed gusts as they argued with rising passion and fervor the legal correctness of taking the initiative and blowing up the mosques on top of Mount Moriah, purging the ground in preparation for the Third Temple, scorching the earth and bringing on the redemption. Someone had to do it, the idols had to be smashed, it could not be put off any longer. Maybe it was unfortunate that good people would have to be destroyed along with the bad, but the time had come to get the show on the road, the *geula* is coming, redemption is at hand, the question was not what but when: We must pose this question to the Toiter Rav, we must ask the Toiter when is the right moment in this apocalyptic time, the Toiter will know, the Toiter is in direct communion with the Master of the Universe—Come on, boys, let's go, the Toiter is sitting just a few blocks away, thank God, right here in Jerusalem the holy city.

Temima gave out a sharp little laugh. How could the Toiter be here in Jerusalem? He never came as far as Jerusalem, and besides, he was too frail to travel even to Israel, too sick, and even if by some miracle he had been conveyed to Israel, not to speak of Jerusalem, surely she would have been notified—it was ridiculous to think he was in town.

The three Bratslavers stopped eating abruptly, swiveled sharply to face her in unison, and demanded to know what exactly she thought was so funny. Temima stared at them blankly, but they insisted, Don't deny it, you were laughing, we heard it.

The Toiter is in Jerusalem for the holidays, they went on. The Toiter wanted to go to Uman at this time of year, to the grave of Rav Nakhman of Bratslav of blessed memory near Kiev in the Ukraine because the holy Rav Nakhman has promised whoever visits his grave around the time of Rosh Hashana and gives a coin to charity and recites the ten psalms of the Tikkun HaKlali, that person will be cured of the sin of wasting his seed and nocturnal emissions and *keri* and polluting the very place of the original covenant, the *brit* itself, and, by extension, he will be cured of all his other sins as well. But those cursed Russian anti-Semites, they would not let even the holy Toiter into their stinking country, not for all the money in the world, they refused to give the Toiter a visa, those rotten, atheistic communists, may their names and memory be blotted out forever and ever, may their kingdom perish from the face of the earth. And so, instead of to Uman, the Toiter has come here to the holy city of Jerusalem. The Toiter is at the King David Hotel, for your information, in the Royal Suite on the sixth floor, complete with Jacuzzi for the sake of his health.

The three Bratslavers left the café soon after, turning their faces as dusk descended and shading their eyes to look from afar and survey the Old City of Jerusalem and the Temple Mount with its mosques rising above it. Temima got up, paid their bill and her own, and set out for a ritual bath—not the regular mikva she used to visit in her neighborhood to divert the busybodies, but another one entirely to which she had never gone before—where she immersed herself for the first time since giving birth six months earlier.

She returned to her apartment on Ben-Yefuneh Street and removed the drab maternity smock she was still wearing. She dressed herself with great care, in a white silk blouse and a flowing skirt of crimson velvet, a silver belt around her waist, embroidered slippers on her feet, a long pearl in the shape of a teardrop in one ear, kohl outlining her dark eyes, and on her head a diaphanous white veil that came low over her face. She was the vision of a matriarch, Mother Sarah, who passed herself off as her husband Abraham's sister to save his life from kings wild to possess her for her lambent beauty.

Carrying only her little mother Torah wrapped in a shawl like a baby in her arms, she made her way that night to the King David Hotel, where she announced herself at the reception desk only as Temima; she had an appointment to see Rabbi Elisha Pardes, she said. He knew her, she added; he was expecting her, he had sent his messengers to inform her to come. Within minutes, one of the Toiter disciples robed in luminous white came down and escorted her up to the Royal Suite on the sixth floor.

Temima did not emerge from the private quarters of the Royal Suite of the King David Hotel for more than a month, through the holiday season, commencing with the rise of Rosh HaShana, curving up to its peak on the day of Yom Kippur, and sloping down to trail into the new year with the rejoicing over the Torah. Everything she required in the way of food and drink was left on a tray outside her door, always with a vase of fresh flowers. All of her personal needs were satisfied within. The clothing she arrived in she cast in the depths of the wardrobe. Once a day she would put on the white dressing gown with the gold crown of the King David Hotel crest embroidered over the heart, her long black hair streaming down her back, and she and the Toiter would stand in opposite corners of the room to practice *hitbodedut*, like Isaac and Rebekah pleading for a child. When the Toiter returned to New York at the close of the holiday season, Temima left the hotel, putting on again for the first time the clothing she had worn when she arrived. She carried her little mother Torah in her arms wrapped now in the talit that Elisha had given her as a pledge, with a neckpiece embroidered in gold and silver threads, and azure fringes, which she sent back to him at the end of ten days together with a note informing him that the father of the baby she is carrying is the owner of this prayer shawl.

Within a week the talit was returned to her with a note pinned to it—HOLD ONTO THIS UNTIL OUR SON IS READY FOR IT. The Toiter also revealed to her that the dynasty would be restored through Temima; moreover, he let it be known to her that, should something happen to him, she would be the Toiter regent until the boy grew up. Meanwhile, he wrote, she must go to Hebron to live with her husband as his wife. Let all the world regard the boy as the son of Haim Ba'al-Teshuva until the moment arrives for him to reveal himself. In that way, perhaps, the angel of death will be deceived.

When the time came for Temima to give birth, the familiar ideological debate sprang up again among the Hebron settlers in the military compound overlooking the ancient city, their numbers significantly increased by supporters from all over the land of Israel who had dropped everything to join the cause and give meaning to their lives. Among the women, the discussion was naturally most heated. On the one hand, the more fiery spirits insisted that, from this time forth, every child should be delivered in Hebron, in the Cave of Makhpela itself optimally, to establish the precedent of the permanence and normalcy of Jewish life cycles on this ground from death to birth to death; there were enough skilled women who could assist, and there was even a licensed midwife practitioner among them, Shifra-Puah, who could handle just about any complication that might arise—and, bottom line, God would help. Even if, in the meantime, the birth itself would have to take place up here in one of the tents of the army camp, it could still be asserted that this child was born in the holy city of Hebron, and thereby the stake of ownership would be dug in even deeper.

Virtually all those who gave birth during this period, even first-time mothers quaking at the unknown, were shamed into having their babies in this way, their women comrades closing a circle around them in the tent, swaying in prayer, waving sprigs of rosemary and myrtle, chanting and beating on drums.

There were, on the other side, a few cooler voices who advocated that they take advantage of the resources available to them through the military. Within half an hour the laboring mother could be transferred to a cutting-edge hospital facility in Jerusalem with the best-trained specialists and top-of-the-line high-tech equipment, conveyed in a cortege of army vehicles mowing down everything in its path, lights flashing, sirens blaring—or she could be transported by helicopter, they could arrive in a great swoop like a spaceship from another planet spiraling down to earth. We may be stuck in Hebron with the toilets in between the olive trees, but we are enlightened Westerners, we are not some kind of uncivilized tribe from a Third World runt of a country.

Especially in Temima's case, when her time came, the more moderate voices grew stronger and more insistent—not only because Temima was over thirty and had given birth so far to only one child hardly a year earlier under the most primitive conditions, and not only because it looked as if this second baby was coming into this world somewhat prematurely and complications might ensue, but above all because from the moment Temima had arrived in Hebron, she was recognized as a woman set apart by extraordinary powers and gifts who must in every way be protected. Even as she entered the camp that first day there were unmistakable signs. It was nearing the end of October and the rain was pouring down as if all the fountains of the deep had split apart and the windows of heaven had opened. The prayer for rain that had just been recited on Shemini Atzeret, at the end of the Succot festival, had obviously done the job. Giving off a majestic radiance, Temima made her way through the compound to her tent like a queen on a road from which all obstacles had been cleared away as the rain pounded down; everyone was soaked to transparency while she alone remained completely dry, untouched by a single drop. She was hailed at once as the reincarnation of the holy Rebbetzin Menukha Rachel Slonim, the granddaughter of Rabbi Shneur Zalman of Liadi, the first Lubavitcher Rebbe, founder of the Habad dynasty, who had come to Hebron with her family in the year 1845, blessed with the power to walk between the raindrops, and it was said of her that never once had she been touched by rain.

Now of course this holy woman Menukha Rachel Slonim, who became known as the Matriarch of Hebron, to whom both Jews and Arabs in their need had turned for blessings and guidance and solace, lay in the old Jewish cemetery below, not only drenched by the rain and mauled by all the other natural elements, but her grave crumbling and befouled with garbage and filth, desecrated with all manner of noxious waste, human and inhuman. Yet Temima's reputation as Menukha's *gilgul* acquired even greater force by the next morning after her arrival when it became known that the tent of the Ba'al-Teshuvas had sprung a leak directly over the spot where the entire family slept, yet not a single drop of water had fallen upon them. The simplest solution would have been to move the mattresses, but by pressing in on Temima and huddling under her wing the family was sheltered and kept dry. Temima turned on her side to face the baby her husband called Pinkhas, who lay practically beneath her with his eyes wide open, watchful and on guard, as if to prevent her from ever leaving him again and shield her from all harm, she stroking his head murmuring, I'm here, mommy, it's okay, no one can hurt me, this is how it is meant to be—while from behind her Howie moved in, raised her nightdress to the level required for his purposes but no higher, and, without any preliminaries, asserted his rights and staked his claim.

From the time of Temima's arrival in Hebron, the child her husband called Pinkhas would not leave her for a minute. She carried him every-where in a pack on her back and, when concern was expressed about the burden of the extra weight for a woman in her condition, Temima would place one hand under the child's rump behind her and the other hand flat on the globe of her taut belly in front of her and respond that she felt herself to be perfectly balanced from both sides.

She was excused from serving her shift with the others in the com-munal kitchen, the laundry, the nursery, the entire sphere of women's workplaces, not because she was pregnant—almost every woman of childbearing age was pregnant except, for the most condensed interval possible, those who had just given birth—but due to the general consensus, stunning in that it elevated a woman but not without precedent in Hebron because of the reputation already associated with the celebrated Menukha Rachel Slonim, that a better use of Temima's powers would be to position her in a place from which she could impart her wisdom to everyone's benefit. The first thought was to breach the ancient Jewish cemetery of Hebron, abandoned now for forty years since the massacre of 1929, the Tarpat pogrom, even at the risk of inflaming the passions of the local Arabs, to clean up the gravesite of the holy Rebbetzin Menukha Rachel Slonim and to set up a pavilion with a canopy there under which Temima could preside comfortably on a nice lawn chair and receive students and petitioners, but this proposal was rejected because of the danger of the evil eye to a pregnant woman who flaunts the promise and hope of life in a place saturated with death.

Temima herself spurned the concept of the evil eye; she found no support for it in the plain, unmediated text. Not only was it a form of superstition and idolatry, as far as Temima was concerned, but whatever malevolent power it possessed if indeed it existed at all was acquired only through human beings' collusion with it to their own detriment through misguided belief. Nevertheless, out of deference to those who would have been horrified by the presence of a pregnant woman planted in a graveyard holding court there, she set up her chair on the top of Tel Rumeida, in front of the stone ruins that sheltered the tombs of Ruth the Moabite and her grandson, Jesse, father of King David, alive and everlasting.

For the remainder of her pregnancy, with four armed soldiers surrounding and guarding her at all times—the first emanation of her Bnei Zeruya quartet—Temima sat there almost every day like the prophetess Deborah under her palm tree. When the weather was warm she sat outside in front of the stone archway of Ruth's tomb, and in the winter months she sat inside beside a small heater attached to a generator in the army jeep, the child her husband called Pinkhas playing quietly at her feet, careful not to disturb lest she grow angry and leave him again.

Men and women, Arabs as well as Jews, would come to the wise woman Temima with their griefs and woes, with all the disappointments and worries that vexed them, and she would illuminate for them who they are and reveal to them their innermost worlds. Then there were those who would simply climb the hill for a respite, to gather at her feet and learn with her. The thread she was drawing out from the texts at that time as her pregnancy advanced in Hebron, the city in which David was anointed and ruled for seven years before consolidating his kingdom in Jerusalem, related to the dynasty that would lead, in the end of days, to the Messiah son of David. Above all, Temima sought to illuminate the line of women—maligned, disgraced, meek, adulteress—who lay down compliantly to receive the seed and pass it on: Leah the unloved, mother of Judah; Tamar, Judah's harlot, mother of Peretz; the convert Ruth, supplicant at the feet of Boaz the landowner, the great-grandmother of King David in whose aura Temima now sat. And then there was the mother of Solomon through whom the line of David would snake onward into the messianic age culminating in the minister of peace—Bathsheba, wife of Uriah the Hittite, plucked dripping from her bath and impregnated with a doomed child by David the king, who then marshaled his royal clout to get her husband, Uriah, to sleep with her too so that the cuckold would believe he was the father and take the blame.

With regard to the birth of his child, Temima's husband, Haim Ba'al-Teshuva, scribe and phylacteries maker of Hebron, was among the strongest advocates for it to take place in the army compound, the closest they could come at this moment in time to the heart of the ancient holy city of Hebron itself. The spiritual honor and privilege of an entry into this world in such a sacred place by far outweighed any advantages that modern science could provide in an approved hospital, in Howie's view. Besides, he argued, compared to the floor of the hovel in which poor Pinkhas was delivered by an Arab urchin whose hands had been who knows where, the military compound and the loving support of experienced women could only be considered state-of-the-art. Temima was a strong woman, as every Hebron woman was expected to be, she had survived far worse.

Nevertheless, when the time came, he found himself sitting glumly in an army helicopter opposite his wife, the child he called Pinkhas, about fifteen months old, curled up in her lap. Shifra-Puah, the authorized midwife, had expressed concern about the early onset of labor that might necessitate special care for the newborn not available on the military base—no Jewish child could be wasted, especially given the wildly spiking demographics of the surrounding Arabs breeding full time like rabbits. On the basis of Shifra-Puah's recommendation, the rabbinical authorities that Howie consulted then ruled that danger to life overrides even the mandate to settle the land of Israel.

When they touched ground at the Hadassah hospital, Howie was faced with the humiliating task, in the presence of all the onlookers—doctors, nurses, and other medical personnel who had gathered around instantly— of peeling Pinkhas, wailing as if bereaved, out of his mother's arms as Temima was ushered into a VIP suite. Her father's shekels, no doubt, Howie reflected bitterly, spoiling and pampering her as usual. He passed the next few hours entertaining the child, mostly in the hospital cafeteria, where the little boy, who had not that long ago evolved into an upright biped, spent most of his time pulling the levers on vending machines that Howie kept feeding with coins spitting forth candies and salted snacks and sugared drinks. When at last they were summoned back into the room, Temima was sitting up in bed against a bolster of cushions, cradling in her arms an infant in a white crocheted cap swaddled in a blue blanket. It is true that this baby was much smaller than Pinkhas had been at birth, weighing just over two kilos, and he was much darker and more wizened, but the expert opinion was that he was sufficiently well formed to thrive without artificial support. Ketura with her savagely burned face was leaning over the bed offering a cup with a straw poking out for Temima to sip from—like a bad omen, Howie felt, another source of embarrassment to him due to the intimate nature of his prior relationship with this Arab handmaid before he had returned in penitence and metamorphosed into Haim Ba'al-Teshuva. What is she doing here in the middle of our nuclear family at such a time anyway? Howie shivered with loathing and disgust.

"It was a hard birth," Temima reported to Howie. By now, the child he called Pinkhas had found his way into her bed, under the covers, rooting into her side. "Thank God I had Ketura's hand to hold," Temima said. And Ketura showed Howie her hands, pierced with the stigmata of Temima's fingernails, the Braille by which her agony could be read, the glyphs of her travail, the blood that had streamed down drying now in a palette from mud black to mottled orange.

"An extraordinary baby, may the evil eye not befall him," Howie heard someone say, and he turned his head to take in what appeared to be an older man with a long white beard sitting in a wheelchair in the corner of the room. He had not noticed him until now just as he had not noticed the potted plant, so central was the vision of the mother and child.

"Oh, I'm sorry, Howie, I should have introduced you," Temima said. "This is my teacher, the Toiter Rav."

"The Toiter!" Howie rose to his feet and swiveled around breathlessly. "Forgive me—my back was to you. What an honor—such an honor!"

The Toiter smiled gently. "Never mind," he said. "I'm at the hospital, as you can see," and he indicated the wheelchair. "I came to bless the child. May he eat butter and honey. May he despise evil and choose good." He raised both of his hands, which were trembling like Father Isaac when he realized he had blessed the wrong son, passing them in benediction in the airspace over the newborn, and declared, "His true name is Immanuel. I would be honored to perform the *brit* in the Makhpela."

Despite the unsteady hands, Howie agreed at once to have the Toiter wield the knife upon his son, so awed was he by the offer from such a mythic holy man. Eight days later, by the tomb of Father Abraham in the Cave of Makhpela, the Toiter performed the circumcision much to the disapproval of Reb Berel Bavli, who on this occasion was demoted to the position of *kvatter*, handing the baby over to Howie's father, the waiter from Ozone Park, Queens, Irwin Stern, who sat in Elijah's chair as *sandek* with a pillow across his lap upon which Reb Berish deposited the baby as on an altar. The Toiter turned to Howie and said, "With your permission, since the mitzvah is incumbent on the father, I am fulfilling the role of the father." He raised the skirt of his gold-striped kaftan and swagged it upward, tucking its edges into the *gartel* around his waist so that it should not impede him as he worked on the infant. Hunching over the baby, in deep concentration, his tongue sticking out from between his teeth, he sliced off the foreskin and, bending in even closer, he placed his mouth over the wound to suck up the blood—"His hands shaking like nobody's business," Reb Berish reported later to his wife, Frumie, who was recovering from a hysterectomy at Maimonides Hospital in Boro Park, Brooklyn. "Such a klutz, you should excuse me, I wouldn't hire him to kill even sick chickens. It took him a year and a Wednesday to get the job done, the baby was hollering bloody murder for five minutes straight, they couldn't shut him up. Where do they get all their money from anyways, those Toiters? The Oscwiecim rebbetzin says they're all meshuggeh, and they have some kind of anonymous meshuggeneh donor who supports them, maybe Howard Hughes."

When the baby was quieted at last, the name was announced—Kook

Immanuel son of Haim—may his two-hundred-and-forty-eight body parts and his three-hundred-and sixty-five veins recover fully, by his blood he will live, the sign of the covenant sealed in his flesh.

The good convert Ruth, in front of whose tomb Temima had once presided, is a success story. The boy she gave birth to, Oved son of Boaz, grew up to become the grandfather of King David, but while he was just a baby he was the delight of Ruth's former mother-in-law, Naomi, who took him to her bosom and became like a mother to him, inspiring the matrons in their Bethlehem village to remark to one another, Naomi has a son again, though between you and me, her daughter-in-law Ruth is better than seven sons. But for Temima in her tent not far from Bethlehem, in the military compound overlooking Hebron during the period following the birth of her son Kook Immanuel, there was no wise mother Naomi at her side to turn to when her baby let out a piercing shriek in his sleep and woke up as if bludgeoned from the nightmare of being born, and there was no trusted mother to confide in when, a week or so after the circumcision, the wound itself having mostly healed, she began to notice blisters and sores breaking out in the area of the covenant, swellings and rashes and inflammations and whitish discolorations such as are described in the chapters in the book of Leviticus devoted to *zora'at,* what is commonly translated as leprosy, immediately following the section on the uncleanness of a woman who has just given birth.

Temima acknowledged to herself that what she was observing could have been contracted from the mouth of the Toiter in the course of the circumcision when he performed the *meziza be'peh* to suction up the blood, and she recognized the danger of the public disgrace and defamation that could ensue were she to bring the matter to the attention of the official medical and health authorities. She knew it was necessary to act immediately for the sake of the child, but her first instinct was to cover up—to take the precautions of allowing no other hands but her own to touch the baby, of never changing his diapers in front of the eyes of another, never leaving him for a minute. She slept with him on a mattress at one end of the tent, with Howie, on account of the blood of her post-birth impurity, accepting exile to a separate mattress at the other end of their tent along with the child he called Pinkhas, both babies wailing through the night.

In this way, Temima allowed a period of time to elapse from when she first noticed the eruptions, until one morning, entirely without planning consciously, she slipped her little mother Torah into her cloth sack and her baby Kook Immanuel into a shawl slung like a pouch across the front of her body with his face pressed toward her so that he could nurse at will, and announced to Howie that she was going down to the Makhpela for a session of *hitbodedut*, to meditate and cry out in solitude.

"But you're not alone," Howie retorted, pointing to the baby. "Leave him with me."

"He's a body part," Temima said, and she stepped forth from the tent with Howie following behind carrying the whimpering child he called Pinkhas, as Temima went to find the four soldiers who had stood watch over her from the days when she used to sit on top of Tel Rumeida at Ruth's tomb. "Where's your faith, Tema?" Howie demanded. "What do you need those guys to guard you for anyways? It's safer down there in the Makhpela than in the streets of the Bronx, in case you want to know."

At the Makhpela, Temima's security contingent stepped discreetly back to grant her the privacy required for the proper practice of *hitbodedut* as she approached the cenotaph draped in a heavy cloth embroidered with Arabic calligraphy and lavish Islamic designs marking the spot somewhere in the caves below where Mother Sarah lies. It was to bury his wife Sarah, after all, that Abraham bought this field from Efron the Hittite for the inflated price of four hundred silver shekels. Sarah was living nearby when she died, in Kiryat Arba, which is Hebron, and Abraham came up from Be'er Sheba to take care of the final arrangements.

Temima rested her forearm against the side of the long domed monument that was Sarah's tomb, pressed her brow into her pulsing wrist, and closed her eyes, awaiting the words that would come pouring out of her mouth like the cries of a daughter to her mother. It seemed to her as she leaned against the stone mound that she could feel the rise and fall of the maternal breast and the lump of the stopped heart behind it, and from its very depths a smothered voice—Oh yes, we were living apart by then, he in Be'er Sheva, I in Kiryat Arba which is Hebron. I would never live with the old man again after he took my son up to the mountaintop to sacrifice him. I should never have let the child out of my sight for one minute, I should never have left him alone with the old man—I'll never forgive myself. The boy was never the same again. The Isaac who went up that mountain with the old man never came down again. That Isaac was slaughtered, burnt on the altar as an offering. No, I never saw the old man again after that, and the ghost of my Isaac rising from his own ashes, he also never saw the old man again except when he came with his half brother Ishmael to bury him here, somewhere alongside me I'm told—the death ride is mercilessly solo. But at least the old man spent the money to buy this plot. I set my mind on this field and I took it. I am your original Woman of Valor. (Here she gave out a bitter laugh; she was famous for her inappropriate laughter.) He was always hearing voices, the old man—but the true test is to distinguish the voice that is meant to be disobeyed.

Temima opened her eyes and looked around. There was Ketura on all fours with a bucket beside her, swabbing the stone floor around Mother Sarah's tomb with great flourishes of her rag. From this sign she recognized at once that the voice she had heard was a voice meant to be obeyed, and she understood its message. She signaled her four bodyguards, and instructed them to convey her and the infant, along with this Arab cleaning woman, directly from the Makhpela to Jerusalem. In less than an hour, an armored tank with smoke puffing out of the gun from the soldiers' Noblesse cigarettes pulled up in front of Temima's building on Ben-Yefuneh Street. She got out with the infant, followed by Ketura, and entered the apartment.

"You've taken the correct steps according to the book," the Toiter said to Temima when she informed him by telephone of the situation and all that she had done. "Seven days of quarantine outside the camp. After seven days, if there is no spread, wait seven more days, just to be sure he's clean. Then wash his clothes and return to the camp. Over this entire period of two times seven days, recite nonstop if possible the ten psalms of the Tikkun HaKlali, which are guaranteed to cure all problems related to that troublesome part of the body, adding also Psalm fifty-one, especially verse nine, 'Purge me with hyssop and I will become pure/ Wash me and I will become whiter than snow.' Also, at the same time, remember to give as much money as you can to charity so that his life's breath may be mingled with the air of the land of Israel, which is entirely free of the taint of sin."

"And if it spreads?"

"If it spreads, then it's the plague of *zora'at*. You must dress him in rags and let his hair grow wild and tie a mask over the lower portion of his face to cover his mouth and hang a string around his neck with a bell attached that will ring whenever he approaches so that people will know that contagion is coming and they will turn away and shun him. And because he is still only a baby and cannot yet speak and call out for himself, you must pin to his shirt the words he would have been required to cry out to warn others that he is drawing near—'Impure! Impure!' The added advantage of this will be that no one will envy him, and the evil eye will not be alerted. This is his fate. He is a Toiter. A Toiter is always afflicted."

Temima set the telephone down on the bed and stretched out to rest with one arm covering her eyes and the other hand spread out flat on the rising and falling chest of the baby lying on his back beside her as the Toiter went on to describe in detail the ritual that must be enacted when the plague is cured, God willing. Two pure birds are required. Slaughter one of them over an earthen pot on top of running water. Dip into its blood a piece of cedar wood, hyssop, some scarlet stuff, and the living bird. Sprinkle the mixture seven times on the baby to purify him. Then release the living bird to fly free over the fields.

Meanwhile, with the buzz of the Toiter's voice in the background, Ketura removed the baby's diaper as he lay on the bed with his mother's hand resting upon him and concentrated on applying the first of a pharmacopoeia of remedies to the infected area that she mixed from natural ingredients in different combinations and proportions, ointments and creams and lotions she concocted from lemon balm, aloe vera, sage, tea tree oil, the wax from honeycombs, prunella, vitamin C, mushrooms, rhubarb, and parsley leaves. As Ketura continued to experiment over the course of the ensuing days, it became apparent to Temima that Howie had not been convinced by her explanation for her sudden disappearance, though, as it happened, it had been the truth—her claim that she had heard the voice of Mother Sarah at the Makhpela that required her immediate return to Jerusalem. For several hours every day, Ibn Kadosh now stationed himself on the floor in the hallway directly in front of her apartment door smoking green tobacco that he rolled himself into cigarettes and whittling slingshots while running a tape recorder at top volume blasting the voice of the child Howie called Pinkhas lamenting and crying, Ima, Ima, come home! Come home now, Ima! The neighbors were complaining, whatever Howie was paying Ibn Kadosh she knew she could top, yet Temima could not bear to silence the voice of her child even at the cost of allowing herself to be publicly shamed as a bad mother; the least she could do for this child whom she had already wronged so many times in his short life was to let him be heard.

She went out into the hallway and stood with her hands on her hips staring down at Ibn Kadosh sitting on the floor leaning against the wall. She could see that he had grown, dark and lanky and still so handsome, his eyes the color of smoky crystal under rich lashes, a silken gauzy shadow over his top lip. She assured him she would be returning home soon, he could communicate that to Howie, but Ibn Kadosh simply shook his head, continuing to whittle with his knife, a cigarette dangling from the corner of his mouth, muttering that the mister had ordered him not to stop blasting the tape outside her door until she came back with him and brought the new baby back too, that was the deal, she could expect him here every day at her door blasting this tape until she was ready to pack up and go.

The chopped placenta had never cheered Temima up, and the elixirs Ketura was brewing and smearing on the baby were creating a mess and having no effect either, so one day soon after Temima bound Kook Immanuel to her chest in the sling of her shawl and crossed the railroad tracks from Baka to German Colony, making her way through the streets of Talbieh to the mysterious door like a cyclop's eye set flush into the stone wall surrounding the leper colony. The doctor who occupied the apartment inside the wall in exchange for on-call night duty to the lepers opened the door himself to let her in. He was dressed only in a loose pair of khaki Zionist shorts and brown leather Old Testament sandals even though he was expecting her; she had arranged this appointment in advance, giving as her name Miriam Gekhazi, and the baby's name as Uziyahu, taking this precaution despite the fact that she had been assured he routinely saw patients on the side for a fee who required treatments of a highly confidential and sensitive nature, that he was scrupulously discreet. Temima stared at the sag of the doctor's bare chest with its curlicues of white hair, and then her eyes were drawn to the long chain with a knob at the end like a torture instrument trailing from his hand. He noticed the trajectory of her gaze and shot her a sly smile. "From our toilet tank," he explained after a teasing pause. "My wife yanked it off again. Some people just don't know how to flush with delicacy."

The back wall of the salon of his apartment in which they were standing consisted entirely of sliding glass doors, and through them Temima could see the small private garden reserved for the doctor and his family, and beyond that the grounds of the leper colony where some sisters in their starched white uniforms were strolling with arms linked on one side of the path, and on the other side, the contorted figures of the inmates making their way, painfully performing the hopeful act of taking their exercise on feet that had been eaten away and that they could no longer feel.

"Nu—so how can I help you?" the doctor said, startling her from this distraction, catching her off guard and almost pushing her over into tears by the offer of help.

She extricated the baby from the shawl, sat down on the divan after telegraphing to the doctor a glance requesting permission, lay the child on his back across her lap, and undressed him. The doctor pulled a pair of spectacles from the pocket of his shorts, set them on his nose where they slipped down until they wedged themselves against the craggy red bulb at the tip, and leaned in to examine the baby's genitals. After a long interval, during which Temima was heating up to acute apprehensiveness, he stepped back, recognized once again the mother's existence, and declared, "Healthy, completely healthy!" From a cupboard against the wall he took out some tubes of salve and told her to apply this medication to the infected area four times a day, adding to these instructions the admonition to above all keep the area clean, and then, raising his voice almost to a shout, he lectured her sternly about the danger of constricting the infected area by binding it too tightly—"Such as with that schmatteh you schlep him around in!" the doctor said, pointing to her shawl. "Naked, naked is best of all, like in the Garden of Eden before the snake. Loose and free—natural, nothing is healthier than natural!"

Temima lowered her head and accepted all of his assaults; she was his supplicant, his slave. She drew out of her bag, in which she had already hoarded the tubes of medicine, an envelope with one thousand American dollars in cash as agreed in advance and set it unobtrusively down on the coffee table instead of handing it to him directly so as not to incur the danger of embarrassing him. He picked it up immediately, tore open the envelope and let it flutter to the floor, counted the bills one by one, folded them into his pocket, and pronounced, "Good, nice and green, healthy like lettuce—*beseder*!"

With the baby in her arms now loosely diapered and bundled, Temima made ready to leave when, as if something else had just by chance occurred to her, she turned to the doctor and asked if he would be willing to take a quick look at one more thing. His expression turned bemused, wily. "If the one-more-thing is on you, then please, with pleasure, no charge for looking." Temima showed him a nodule on her lip, and a bump on her ear, as well as a spot on her neck, each of which he examined attentively without comment. "Anywhere else?" he asked. So Temima allowed him to look at the others, in the private places, which the doctor inspected closely and lingeringly, pronouncing in the end, "Healthy, completely healthy!"—advising her to eat foods such as spinach and lentils and soybeans rich in the right kind of protein, which would also benefit the baby when it would be piped in through her breast milk. Then, as he was letting her out the door, he switched tone and added gravely, with the entitlement of authority, "This is not coming from heaven, you know—not the disease, and not the cure, not the blessing, and not the curse. You have a choice. Choose life if you want to live—you and your child."

Over the next few weeks it seemed to Temima that things were beginning to fall into place, that her life was taking on a semblance of control. She was not asking for happiness, happiness was not a guaranteed right to pursue, especially in Israel; she was asking only for the right not to be consumed by the land, she was asking for a normal child untouched by danger. The baby improved day by day, until all signs of the outbreak had disappeared entirely; no one would ever have to know there had even been a stigma. She called the Toiter to report the good news. Together they reconsecrated themselves to the child.

They agreed that she would contact Howie to inform him of her return—that she was using her remaining time in Jerusalem to put the apartment up for sale and arrange for storage of all their furniture and possessions in anticipation of the day in the near future when, God willing, the Kiryat Arba villa her father had bought for them would be ready and they could move out of their tent in the army camp overlooking Hebron. She asked Howie to call off Ibn Kadosh and his tape recorder, to drive him out of the Ben-Yefuneh Street building. With the telephone clamped to her ear by her hiked-up shoulder, the baby naked in her arms reaching out with his pudgy hands to tug at the wire, Temima watched from her window as Ibn Kadosh slowly made his way down Ben-Yefuneh Street toward Bethlehem Road carrying his belongings including the tape recorder in his sack, his mother, Ketura, over whom he now towered, faithfully at his side. She speculated whether, when they arrived at Hebron Road, they would turn left in the direction of the Old City of Jerusalem or right toward Hebron, as she gave Howie the date and time to send the bulletproof car to pick her up and bring her and the child back to the compound. "What do you need a military escort for?" Howie demanded in frustration. "Who do you think you are anyways, Queen Tut? It's a zillion times safer here than on Coney Island Avenue. You're coming home to Hevron, Tema—to the Me'arat HaMakhpela, for God's sakes, the second holiest site in the Jewish world next to the Western Wall."

The third holiest site is the tomb of Rachel Our Mother. When Temima with her baby Kook Immanuel and her little mother Torah reached this domed shrine by the side of the road as they were traveling in the bullet-proof vehicle back to the army compound overlooking Hebron on the appointed day, she asked the driver to stop to allow her to make a brief pilgrimage. Rachel Our Mother was the least maternal of the matriarchs, and yet, of the four, she above all the others had come to most stand for the idea of mother—the voice heard in Ramah, weeping for her children, refusing to be comforted, the Jewish Our Lady of the Highways, wailing and crying bitterly for her children as they pass her in fetters trudging off to exile, greeting them from the roadside as they return to their borders dancing the hora.

Temima brought her little mother Torah up to the tomb of Rachel Our Mother and brushed her against it, in a kind of ritual greeting of soul mates. Temima's mother, Rachel-Leah, lay alone and unvisited in her grave in the Old Montefiore cemetery in Queens, and here was Rachel Our Mother buried alone on the roadside, excluded from the family mausoleum at the Makhpela, the couples' club. This was her punishment, according to the commentator-in-chief Rashi—to lie alone forever for so contemptuously selling a night lying with Jacob in exchange for a bunch of mandrakes with forked roots that Reuven, the eldest son of her sister and rival-wife, Leah, had pulled shrieking out of the earth, giving off their intoxicating scent redolent of all the possibilities and risks of love and death that enshrouded Rachel Our Mother and those she elected to gather under her veil.

When Temima returned to the military compound a fragrance clung to her, enveloping her like a cloud so intense that people came out to sniff what was in the air. And instantly, as when she had arrived the first time and walked between the raindrops, the sense was renewed and restored of a presence among them endowed with special powers that practically made them bow down as they stood at the entrances of their tents and observed her passage. Soon Temima was holding court again, either up in the army camp itself in the intervals between men's prayer quorums three times a day inside the tent that had been designated as the synagogue, or down in the heart of Hebron at the Tomb of the Patriarchs, under the vigilant eyes of her four bodyguards, where she presided by the cenotaph of Mother Leah, privileged to lie beside Father Jacob for eternity. Wherever she sat, she was never without her two children—Kook Immanuel on her lap or loosely suspended in a sling on her back or front, Temima's fingers encircling a chubby ankle or wrist like a shackle, the child her husband called Pinkhas playing quietly on the floor at her feet, pushing a toy army jeep with one hand and, with the other, clutching a handful of her skirt.

At the Makhpela, Arabs and Jews, men and women, made their way to the holy woman reputed to be endowed with mystical powers—seeking her out for blessings, advice, consolation, cures, foreknowledge and self-knowledge, the interpretation of dreams, restoring the memory of what they had once known and forgotten, leading them to the discovery of what they had lost, from a lost earring to a lost child, for, as Temima taught, When you find sixty-nine objects you have lost you will find redemption.

From all over the land of Israel and from outside the land they risked their lives and ventured into this danger zone to the learned woman sage with questions pertaining to ritual or law, renowned rabbis arrived in disguise or secretly dispatched lackeys to seek out responsa they would later claim as their own to questions ranging from artificial insemination to autopsies, soul birth to brain death and all the confusion in between, whether a woman may elect to take on the risks of cosmetic surgery, six months marinating in oils of myrrh and six months in perfumes and female ointments, whether a man may be counted as a member of the minyan for prayer if he had been born as a woman who had undergone a sex change, and so forth. In the synagogue tent of the military compound, learning circles gathered around the great wise woman, forums for rigorous study, not only men and boys in mixed classes but, often at Temima's specific behest, drawing on her own priorities, women and girls exclusively, which permitted her to nurse Kook Immanuel as she taught with a blanket draped over her shoulder for modesty, and many of her students were breast-feeding their babies too, including the convert Yehudit Har-HaBayit with newborn twins at her breasts, she who had once so joyously offered herself as a wet nurse to the infant Howie kidnapped and named Pinkhas on his circumcision day, from whom the little boy now turned away in alarm whenever she batted her false eyelashes and bared her long teeth to smile and beckon to him, running to Temima and burrowing his face in her lap.

Temima's recent encounter with Rachel Our Mother by the roadside inspired her to devote these sessions to an exploration of the narrow range of authorized feminine categories a woman can inhabit regardless of who she was as an individual. Borrowing from the methods of her revered teacher, Morah Nekhama Leibowitz, she unfolded the discussions through questions, but rather than questions that perplexed commentators or sages she dwelt on the simple human questions, her own and her students', evoked by the plain text, with no mandate to manipulate the answer to arrive at an acceptable foreordained conclusion within the constraints of the orthodoxy. Who was Rachel Our Mother as a woman? Temima asked. There's evidence in the text that she was the beloved of her husband, Jacob, though he spoke cruelly to her when she lamented her barrenness and effectively cursed her with an early death when she stole her father's little idols. But did she love him in return, was she even attracted to him as he so dramatically was to her, or, in the overall scheme of things, are her feelings irrelevant and beside the point? And who was Rachel Our Mother as a mother—childless for so long that she turned to her husband and cried, "Give me sons or I'll die," when what she really might more correctly have said was "Give me sons *and* I'll die?" How did it come about that a woman who died in childbirth, leaving behind the newborn, Benjamin, and his brother Joseph, a little boy with a lot of big personality problems, a woman who in the end had engaged in very little actual mothering—how did it happen that she above all other women emerged as the symbol of the ideal mother whose abiding love for her children renders her inconsolable, the mother her children could rely upon to be in the same spot in perpetual grief for their suffering, the mother who always cares?

"Because the best mothers are those who let go of their children," Yehudit Har-HaBayit answered, her twins now asleep in a double stroller parked outside the tent. Rising from her seat, she continued, "Look at Hagar with her son Ishmael when they were dying of thirst in the wilderness. Only when she lets go of Ishmael and casts him away from her under one of the bushes into God's hands is the boy saved—hallelujah!" She began to move toward Temima. "You have to learn to let go of your child. That's what makes you a good mother—like Rachel Our Mother, who let go by dying." With everyone's eyes fixed upon her, Yehudit Har-HaBayit planted herself in front of Temima with both arms outstretched—waiting.

The heaviness of the silence bore down in the tent, replacing the air, until the moment that Temima acknowledged what was being asked of her by raising Kook Immanuel ceremoniously like an elevated offering and passing him over into Yehudit Har-HaBayit's hands open before her, palms upturned to receive the child. It was the first time during the nine months of this baby's life outside of Temima's womb not counting his circumcision that she had fully released him into the hands of another.

From across the room as he sat on this alien lap the baby Kook Immanuel would occasionally give out a doleful whimper, or lurch forward toward his mother with longing, but Temima could see from his clear eyes and calm breathing that he was safe and at ease, and after a while the eyes closed and he was sleeping tranquilly in the arms of the stranger. After that day, Temima began to set him down on a blanket in the center of the learning circle, and her eyes would follow him calmly as he crawled off to a corner of the tent before someone would go to scoop him up. When the days were warm, she would occasionally leave him outside in a nursery enclosure with other babies supervised by teenagers responsible and mature much beyond their years, the eldest sisters to dozens of siblings; and more and more frequently, when Temima went down to sit by Mother Leah's tomb in the Makhpela, she left him in the charge of another woman, usually Yehudit Har-HaBayit, who had illuminated for her the faith of maternal letting go. As the sages commented, From all of my teachers I have learned, but from my students more than from all of them.

Now at last Temima was also able to resume her regular practice of *hitbodedut* with the luxury of true solitude, seeking an isolated spot on the hilltop overlooking Hebron among the olive trees a safe distance from the perimeter of the military compound even in the dark of night to beseech and converse with God—trusting Howie, before she set out, to watch over the baby, handing over the baby to him along with a bottle of warm milk freshly expressed from her breasts. Just such a bottle covered in blood she found in his stroller on the day her husband, Haim Ba'al-Teshuva, scribe and phylacteries maker of Hebron, with the child he called Pinkhas strapped in a carrier on his back, pushed Kook Immanuel in his stroller at the head of a demonstration along Al-Shuhada Street lined with Arab shops and businesses to reassert sovereignty over what had once been the heart of the Jewish quarter of the old city. Since the blood is the life of the flesh, when the body was prepared for burial the blood-stained bottle was slipped inside the tight swaddling of the blue-and-white Israeli flag with which the stroller at the head of the procession had been bedecked. It, too, was soaked with the blood that had streamed down from the wound when the stone struck the baby's forehead and sank in and he slumped over. The tiny corpse with all of its bloodied artifacts that had been transformed into body parts was then wrapped by his mother in the talit with its silver-and-gold-embroidered neckpiece and azure fringes, a small package to be shipped into the dark belly of *Sheol*.

Thousands of people from all over Israel and from outside the land as well poured into Hebron for the funeral of this innocent baby so savagely cut down. They marched in the procession as it snaked its way down from the army compound on the hilltop through the heart of the city and its teeming casbah into the ancient Jewish cemetery breached for the first time since 1929 when the sixty-seven corpses slaughtered in the pogrom of Tarpat were deposited in a mass grave. Brandishing placards on sticks emblazoned with the words KOOK HAI! and NEKAMA!, and blowups of the baby's face with his bright hopeful eyes and rosy cheeks, wave after wave of raging mourners surged forward. Israeli military personnel heavily armed crouched behind sandbags or stood at alert with their weapons poised along the entire route as helicopters hovered overhead, helpless to halt the advance or to quell the calls for revenge with fists punching the air or to suppress the incendiary cries of the child's unvanquished spirit living on.

At the head of the procession, the bereaved father, Haim Ba'al-Teshuva, scribe and phylacteries maker of Hebron, was pushed in a wheelchair surrounded by masses of men in knitted yarmulkes with fringes hanging out of their untucked white shirttails. His head bound in a turban of white gauze and his arm in a sling from the wounds inflicted upon him by the stones with which he too was pelted, and from using his body as a shield to protect the child he called Pinkhas riding on his back, Howie cradled in the crook of his uninjured arm the tiny wrapped package of the dead baby, Kook Immanuel, rocking him back and forth and singing over and over the lullaby—"No, no, no, no, we won't go from here. All of our enemies, all those who hate us, all of them will go from here. Only we, only we, we won't move from here."

Behind the throng of men came the multitude of keening women with the stately figure of Temima in front, a long shawl on her head draping over her shoulders and down her back that she clutched together with both hands at her throat, her dry eyes concealed by dark glasses, supported on either side by her students to whom at one point she turned and said, "There is no word in the English language for a parent who has lost a child, but we have one in Hebrew—*shakula* for a mother, *shakul* for a father—because we Jews have always needed such a word, the way Eskimos need words for ice." And she coughed out a hard subversive laugh, like Mother Sarah.

Over the loudspeaker came the eulogies of the rabbis and leaders, their voices cracking, rising and falling in outrage and grief, breaking into shouts and sobs. The Lord gives, the Lord takes, may the name of the Lord be blessed. The little wrapped package containing Kook Immanuel with all of his bloody body parts was lowered into the freshly dug grave that awaited him, and the men dumped shovelful after shovelful of dirt on top of it until there rose an imposing mound. Howie was helped out of his wheelchair and supported on either side as he stood up in order to recite the mourner's Kaddish for his dead son—Exalted and sanctified is His Great Name. At the far edge of the cemetery Temima could see the cadaverous figure of the Toiter clad in rent white garments with his arms raised to the heavens and his hands clenched into fists, the silent scream drowned out by the mourner's Kaddish emerging hoarsely from his own lips—He Who makes peace in His heights, May He make peace on us and on all Israel, And now say Amen—and she watched as his body crumpled and collapsed prone on the ground with the arms outstretched, prostrate with grief.

The father of the dead baby, Haim Ba'al-Teshuva, scribe and phylacteries maker of Hebron, was assisted back into his wheelchair, which was then pushed down the long aisle created by the two rows of men facing each other that had formed like a wake from the vessel of the mound over the gravesite that would ferry the child to the next world. As he made his way forward in his wheelchair down the aisle he received from each of the men on either side the ritual consolation—May the Presence comfort you among the other mourners of Zion and Jerusalem.

The baby's mother, who one day would be revered and beloved as the holy woman HaRav Temima Ba'alatOv, Ima Temima, moved forward alone as if floating and entered between the two rows to collect her portion of the consolation. A voice called out, "Men only! Men only!" She heeded it at once, turning back and resuming her place among the women. "He's right," Temima said. "We are all Mother Rachels. We cannot be comforted."

More Bitter
Than Death
Is Woman: Yiska

The Teachings Of HaRav Temima Ba'alatOv, Shlita
(May She Live On For Many Good Long Years)—
Recorded By Kol-Isha-Erva At The "Leper" Colony Of Jerusalem

IN THE awareness of the Presence and the awareness of the congregation, in the convocation of the heights and in the convocation below, and at the personal gentle admonishment of our holy
mother, HaRav Temima Ba'alatOv, shlita, I beg forgiveness for
neglecting my duty to set down for us transgressors the teachings
of Ima Temima, and for putting off my task of recording events
of note that have transpired over these past months here in the
"leper" colony of Jerusalem. Over the course of this difficult
period of adjustment during which I have been so remiss in my
responsibilities as scribe and collector of recovered memories,
our numbers have diminished relentlessly. Through the grinding attrition of impoverished faith and weak commitment, our
general population has declined to a census of fewer than one
hundred, mostly women assessed at thirty silver shekels apiece
between the ages of twenty and sixty, ready to bear arms for
battle. Of the two senior women in our ranks above the age of

sixty, valued at ten silver shekels a head, our elders before whom we are enjoined to rise and whose aged faces we are bidden to glorify as the Torah commands us, Ima Temima alone remains, increasingly frail in body but still a towering presence in spirit and mind.

Now during the haze and stagnation of our sluggish Jerusalem summer days, Ima Temima continues to privately delve into the mysteries of the text within the cool stone walls of the secluded apartment, the sacred inner sanctum to which only the chosen few are given access, among whom I am honored far beyond what I deserve to include my unworthy self. Yet there are some warm, blessed evenings when the entire remnants of the congregation, the embers rescued from the blaze, are still privileged to soak in the teachings at the feet of our veiled holy mother presiding above us from the wheelchair pushed by our domestic management associate, Rizpa, into the dark northern garden outside the door of the private quarters and planted beside the fresh mound of the grave as yet unmarked with a headstone under the ancient oak tree of our other esteemed elder, our high priestess, Aish-Zara, za'zal, may the memory of the righteous be a blessing—a brutal loss. Ima Temima, for reasons too profound for us to grasp, has forbidden us to mourn, and so I along with all others of lesser understanding are still suspended in the first of the five stages of grief—denial and disbelief—unable to move on and get past it and achieve closure.

Aish-Zara, za'zal, was lowered into the ground with only a talit wound over her shrouds, without even a coffin, the wasted form, the tumors and craters of her punished body thinly mummified for all to behold. Yet despite our holy mother's ban against mourning, on one of those warm summer evenings, while sitting in the garden recounting for us the *midrash* about the sealed casket in which Mother Sarah, alive and breathing, was transported to conceal her radiant beauty by her husband, Abraham, across the border to Egypt when a famine devastated the land of Canaan, Ima Temima gazed down at the fresh mound of earth of the grave, still soft and fragrant, and cried out, "Essie, Essie, why did you leave me?"

My thought patterns at that moment naturally legatoed to my ex-student, EliEli, who turned out in the end to be a false prophetess, it pains me to report. EliEli, of the lustrous, swinging hair that nearly consumed her in flames like the incinerated altars of the prophets of Baal on Mount Carmel when she danced so rapturously during our Passover Seder, is among those who now are no longer with us, but in her case it was not a voluntary departure. Holding aloft in defiance a splintering wooden cross, the two beams lashed together with bandages, she was unceremoniously expelled from our compound mounted on the shoulders of one of the four Bnei Zeruya, the very one with whom she had been observed engaging in inappropriate behavior after the *Dayenu*—and the gate was shut fast against both of them. It grieves me to add on good authority that she did not even have the decency to cover her private parts with undergarments for her disgraceful exit, her legs clamped around the neck of her bearer. Nevertheless, I consider it my duty, with the sanction of our holy mother, to report this gross detail. She was cast out of the "leper" colony as the "leper" is cast out of the city; there is not much lower you can sink.

On those rare occasions now when Ima Temima requires to be borne aloft by four strong men, the place in the Bnei Zeruya quartet of EliEli's accomplice is taken by one of my prophetesses, a woman weighing in at over one hundred kilos whom we call Aishet-Lot, whose specialization is visions of the past rather than the future. That alone signifies that she can carry a load. Aishet-Lot has never been heard to speak a single word, however, so extreme an observance of a fast of speech has she taken upon herself that I have at times worried if she is in reality verbally challenged or perhaps afflicted with a case of post-traumatic stress disorder due to the insult of the sages' injunction against excessive conversing with a woman that had plunged her into a lifelong state of oral paralysis. Yet, contrary to popular belief, such extreme silence is an attribute to be prized in a prophet just as being hearing impaired ought to be prized in a mental health provider. (With apologies for this personal digression, which I permit myself only to honor such differently abled individuals as

Aishet-Lot, my own amazing therapist wore a hearing aid when I first became his client at age six; by the time my treatment ended at age nineteen when he declared me fully cured, he was completely hearing impaired—i.e., "deaf.") As for Aishet-Lot, she has found many creative ways to express herself without words in delivering her brand of past prophecies. Of course, there is the added benefit that her muteness assures utter discretion in confidential spheres, and so, due to severe staff cutbacks, she has also been selected to assist our petite Rizpa as personal attendant to our holy mother, above all with the heavy lifting, an interim arrangement that was made permanent after the night that Cozbi disappeared for the last time.

As it became increasingly unavoidable to face the fact that I had a problem on my hands with EliEli, our holy mother, HaRav Temima Ba'alatOv, shlita, directed me once again to the fundamental text of chapters thirteen and eighteen of the book of Deuteronomy in which the identifying features of a false prophet are laid out. There was no question that EliEli fit the bill—a possessed dreamer of dreams, speaking in the name of the Master of the Universe, even shocking us now and then by pointedly dropping His forbidden name "Yahweh" as if He were a celebrity pal of hers with whom she was on a first name basis, offering signs and portents some of which given the odds even on occasion came true, all for the purpose of enticing our people to follow and worship other gods that they knew not and to test us to see whether or not we truly and exclusively love the Lord our God with all our hearts and souls and everything we have.

Nevertheless, Ima Temima allowed me to find my own way to the resolution of this challenge and at my own rhythm, never undermining my authority as executive director of the school for prophetesses by invading my space and handing down peremptory orders from above as to how to manage this infestation on my turf. Instead, to help guide me, our holy mother offered a subtle teaching concerning the seven women in the Tanakh whom the rabbis of the Talmud classify as true prophetesses. First among the Talmud-designated prophetesses is Sarah, whom Ima Temima calls Yiska—from the root *sakha*, she gazed—because of her penetrating visionary powers, her ability to look directly at what was what without deceiving herself. Yiska, who in the text is identified as one of the daughters of Haran, Abraham's brother who died in Ur of the Chaldees, is none other than Sarah, the Talmud states. And though some sages had their doubts about this, and especially given the added complication that it would have made Abraham her uncle as well as her husband (not to mention also her half brother as he confesses later on), Ima Temima always refers to Sarah as Yiska in homage to this clear-eyed, sophisticated realist.

The other six prophetesses in Israel, according to the Talmud, are Miriam (our very own Lady of the "Lepers"—Miriam-Azuva-Snow White), Deborah, Hannah, Abigail, Hulda, and Esther. In the plain text of the Tanakh, however, Ima Temima taught, there are only four women explicitly labeled as prophetesses—Miriam, Deborah and Hulda (both called nasty names by the Talmud sages for their alleged arrogance in their dealings with men), and Noadia. Noadia is only a bit player, with a cameo mention when Nehemia implores God to keep in mind for retribution how this prophetess, among others on his revenge hit list, had unduly alarmed and vexed him.

With respect to how my apprentice prophetess EliEli fits into this food chain, I will say in my defense that I had at first assumed, perhaps too hastily, that the somewhat self-important and presumptuous name she had chosen for herself was a reference to the opening verse of the song of David in Psalm twenty-two—Eli Eli (My God, My God), why have You forsaken me? I now realize that in her personal brain pan, the main ingredient was the "My" rather than "God."

I must have been in a willed state of denial because, looking back, I can no longer repress my memory of the night I came upon her sitting by a bonfire in a far corner of our "leper" colony, in a clearing encircled by dry tangled brambles and nettles, the leaping flames a true hazard to our community, liable to spread as wildly as her dangerous proselytizing and ignite a conflagration. As EliEli sat by the fire along with several co-conspirators, members of her support group, none of whom is any longer with us, in a high state of ecstasy the source of which I now openly acknowledge to have been not entirely spiritual, she chanted over and over again the seventeenth verse of that same psalm from which her name is derived—Psalm twenty-two—in a bizarre free translation I had never before heard: "Dogs surround me, evil ones encircle me, they pierce my hands and feet." *Pierce* my hands and feet? Where did she get *pierce* from in that verse? Was she talking *stigmata*?

Yes, I admit that the horrifying thought did pass through my mind then and there that her chosen name EliEli was not after all a reference to the song of David, but to the reported final cry in Aramaic of the false messiah Yeshua HaNozri, dying on the cross, ripping us off to his very last breath. I am abashed to confess it did occur to me even then there might be a false prophetess in our midst, but in my own defense I must point out that at the time, with our beloved Aish-Zara, za'zal, suffering so unendurably and with each passing day drawing this dear soul further and further away from us to the next life, I felt I just simply did not have the energy to deal with issues related to a borderline personality like EliEli.

Then one night, as I was sitting by the bedside of our precious Aish-Zara, za'zal, strumming an oud and riffing a tune to the words of the prayer for the sick recited during the Torah reading— Oh God, bless Essie daughter of Pessie (unfortunately, I did not know the name of the mother of Aish-Zara, za'zal, and so I simply grooved with the rhyme) with soul healing and body healing along with all of sick Israel—and Aish-Zara, za'zal, was lying on her bed with her mouth open and dry lips drawn back rendering her face even more skull-like, rattling in her throat and wheezing through the black holes of her nostrils having drifted for this interval into a pocket of relief from pain thanks to the marijuana tea I had brewed and fed to her with a teaspoon, Rizpa announced her presence with a considerate padded knock, pushed open the door, and informed me that she would take over death and dying palliative care hospice duties while I went to Ima Temima, who had summoned me to appear without delay.

It was well past midnight when I arrived at the sacred

apartment. My prophetess Aishet-Lot was sitting in the garden outside the door keeping guard, knitting on automatic by moonlight at a frenetic clip with fat needles and thick rough yarn white as salt, a frothy puddle of woolen matting rising at her feet like sand falling in an hourglass.

With a slight nod, Aishet-Lot granted me entry. I found our holy mother already in bed as would be expected at that hour alongside the cherished little mother Torah, which seemed to have grown a few feet longer judging from the bulge under the blanket defining its form, the upper portion of the scroll with its two wooden tree-of-life rollers protruding like the horned pigtails of a child who had just had a nightmare with the cover drawn securely up to her chin.

"Kol-Isha-Erva," Ima Temima said with eyes closed when I entered the room, one hand clutching a roller of the mother Torah as if to pick up its pulsing message in the transmission of a cryptic oracle, "my sources tell me that you must find your prophetess EliEli at once and root out the abomination. Whatever she says to you, you must not believe. It is a sadistic religion. In its intercourse between men and women, there is no such thing as brother and sister."

I will not defile these pages devoted to the teachings of the holy HaRav Temima Ba'alatOv, shlita, and to instructive tales from our journey here in the "leper" commune of Jerusalem by setting down in full detail what I witnessed when I entered the den of my ex-prophetess EliEli. Suffice it to say that those Christian theologians who advocated castration for self-flagellants as a safeguard against sexual arousal while engaged in this perverse activity had a point. The erotic tension in that room was constricting, like a bulge in the throat, it vibrated like instruments with every string drawn too tightly liable any minute to snap as the whips lashed and the blood flowed in an orgy of self-scourging and penitential mortification, men and women flogging their own lacerated naked backs and occasionally the raw proffered backs of others.

EliEli, as if in a trance in another realm, red in the face, slick with sweat, saw me at last standing in the doorway taking all of this in. She approached as if floating on an ozone layer cloud

and held out to me her bloodied whip to use for my own penance, saying to me, "With this you too can do the will of My
Father in heaven and be my mother." Frankly, about the last
thing in the world I wanted was to be the mother of this mixed-
up girl—that's all I needed for my sins. Sweeping the tail of her
whip in the general direction over the writhing self-help group
in the room, including the member of the Bnei Zeruya whom she
had enabled with her enticements, all of them aware of nothing
but the rhythmic stings of the whip and their own ecstatic self-
mutilation, EliEli added, "Just as they do His will and therefore
are my brothers and sisters." She was paraphrasing from the
gospel of Matthew—the New Testament!

At that point all I could do was remain in my place without
raising my woman's naked voice to answer a word to this spiritually disabled child in her altered state. I could only silently bow
my head—not just in an effort to dodge the furious arcs of the
flailing whips, but above all in awe at this further testament to
the powers and divine energy of our holy mother, Ima Temima,
who had once again foreseen and understood everything.

IN THE spirit of full disclosure, and with the unqualified approval
of HaRav Temima Ba'alatOv, shlita, I have already described
the brazen departure from our "leper" colony of the pollution
of my mutinous false prophetess EliEli and her loathsome sect.
It is now my burden to move onward with the task of laying out
a complete account of the mysterious disappearances and reap-
pearances of our holy mother's personal attendant Cozbi, the
former masseuse, Anna Oblonskaya of Moscow, Russia, which
began the day after our Passover Seder and climaxed with her
final vanishment shortly before the passing of our beloved high
priestess, Aish-Zara, za'zal, revealing evidence that annihilated
all hopes for her return. The matter is of particular sensitivity, not
only because of the suspicion of foul play involved in every sense
of the word, and not only because of the confidential and privileged position in which Cozbi had served in relation to our holy
mother, but above all because of the way in which it impacted
the fragile spirit and self-esteem and life choices of Paltiel, the

son about whom Ima Temima openly admits to feelings of guilt, fist pounding heart, with regard to the traumatic and scarring maternal abandonments he was forced to endure as a very young child for the sake of our holy mother's divinely ordained mission.

When Paltiel awoke in the early afternoon on the first day of Passover, the place beside him in the bed usually occupied by Cozbi was empty. Only the imprint of her long naked form remained on the stale sheets along with the vapors of her perfume and the stains of her female effluvia. These details of the Cozbi case that I offer here, however distasteful, have been garnered from several sources, including Paltiel. Our holy mother has commanded me to give a full and uninhibited account of what happened, to relate it as if it were a story, someone else's once-upon-a-time-in-a-faraway-land.

Paltiel did not think much of Cozbi's absence that afternoon, assuming she had risen earlier to attend to her duties at his mother's side. The only irregularity was that her lapdog, Abramovich, was gone too, and he knew that his mother in general abided by a no-pets policy in the private quarters because of the sacredness of the texts handled there and because of a trauma suffered as a young girl in relation to dogs in particular, he could never remember the details. But he figured that Cozbi had taken Abramovich along this time for some fresh air—the dog had lapped up more than its share of wine at the Seder the night before—either tying it with a rope to a tree stump in the northern garden outside his mother's door (not to stereotype, but based on personal experience, Russians do not seem to be overly solicitous of animals, including human animals) or tasking someone else to care for the dog, as she occasionally did. Paltiel spent most of that day lounging and napping in his room, bone-weary from the late hour at which the Seder had ended, with heavy limbs and pounding head from all the wine he too had consumed and constipated from going overboard on the matzot. Maybe Cozbi should have cared enough to take him out for an airing too, he commented bitterly to me later.

The next morning, he awoke earlier than the day before. Cozbi was still not there. He dressed and went outside, where he came upon the entire congregation gathered in front of the "leper" hospital. Above the crowd, on the landing leading to the entrance under the words JESUS HILFE carved into the pediment, was Aish-Zara, za'zal, and all her priestesses, draped and hooded in their long white prayer shawls, bestowing their priestly blessing with hands raised palms downward and fingers parted so that God Himself could peer through the lattices to fulfill their prayer to bless and be gracious to and watch over and grant peace to and shine His face upon His flock, whose backs were turned from this awesome spectacle lest their vision be seared by its white-hot holiness. But as for Paltiel, he personally did not turn his eyes away from the sight, thinking, as he later remarked to me before his final departure from the colony, It's only a bunch of females up there with a bloody gash, a stinking *koos* between their legs. For the sake of our holy mother, let us glide over this crude misogyny of the son. I must note here with sadness that this was the last public appearance of Aish-Zara, za'zal, before she withdrew to focus her energies on full-time dying, which required all of her remaining strength.

Afterward, the congregation dispersed, many to bring a version of the Passover sacrifice on improvised altars of small stone mounds, offering up instead of the Paschal lamb mostly pigeons they had bagged in the "leper" colony and slaughtered, a priestess standing by to collect the trickle of pink blood in a paper cup. Paltiel wandered about the grounds inquiring if anyone had seen Cozbi's little doggie, Abramovich, since the night of the Seder. This was the approach he had devised to save face; he had processed it as an insult to his masculine self-image, a form of neutering, to allow it to be publicly known that he could not account for the whereabouts of his woman, so, God forgive him, he used the dog as a surrogate. Nobody could remember having seen Abramovich lately, but one or two people did mention that they thought they had heard his distinctive shrill yip, somewhat muffled, but maybe that was just an auditory illusion because the dog barked so much and at all hours of the day and night, it was as if his grating sound lingered on the airwaves like an irritating tune that had been played so relentlessly in the background you could not shake it out of your head. In any event, if Abramo-vich were around, one woman conjectured, the smell of roasting flesh on the altar barbeques would have launched him off of his satin cushion and sent him scampering over for a bite, drooling like his Russian cousins, Pavlov's dogs. There was not a single expression of sorrow or regret that Abramovich might be lost. Clearly, this hound was not a favorite in the camp, regarded by many as more privileged than some of the humans, which was not news to Paltiel who also shared a similar feeling in his own way, especially when he allowed himself to compare the pittance of affection that Cozbi occasionally doled out to him with the way she doted every second on the puny rodentlike mutt.

As Paltiel went about our "leper" colony continuing to inquire after Abramovich, several of our members also mentioned that, by the way, they had not seen Cozbi either since the Seder— nor, as it happened, had anyone noticed her either leaving the "leper" compound or entering it. Naturally, as he admitted to me later, it did cross Paltiel's mind that he could get the informa-tion he was seeking most directly and efficiently simply by going to his mother's apartment to which he was granted unrestricted access—perhaps Cozbi was working an extended shift, for example. But for self-empowerment reasons he elected not to involve our holy mother until the very end, which, from my personal point of view, was all to the good as Ima Temima was progressively caught up as the days and weeks passed in the agony of the dying of our beloved Aish-Zara, za'zal. Instead, after making the rounds in the wake of Cozbi's first disappear-ance under the guise of searching for Abramovich, Paltiel found his way to the kitchen where he liked to drop in now and then for a little nosh even when we had been headquartered at the Temima Shul in the Bukharim Quarter. The Daughters of Bilha and Zilpa under the supervision of Rizpa, our nurturing domestic management associate, were busy crushing matzot and cracking eggs for a *matzah brie* lunch. As Paltiel reached for a coconut macaroon, Rizpa drew close to him and with her characteristic discretion whispered into his ear, "Where is Cozbi? Not since the Seder do we see her. She is sick?"

The next morning, when Paltiel awoke and opened his eyes, Cozbi was there in her usual place in the bed beside him, her long naked body blotched with bruises, giving off a rank odor as if it had risen from the swamps or the sewers.

This was the pattern that continued over the ensuing months. Paltiel would wake up to find Cozbi gone, and then a few days later, when he opened his eyes in the morning, there she would be again, her sleeping body twisted in the soiled linen, skin splotched and discolored and ravaged, reeking of the nether-world, Abramovich stuffed like a rag between her breasts. When in his frustration he could muster up the nerve to probe where she had gone off to, which was, he insisted, his right, she would gaze at him through lowered lids smeared with mascara and eyeliner as if he were not quite in focus or not quite present and flip him some words—Vampire. Dracula. Baba Yaga. Gypsy. Werewolf. Alien. Satan. Djinn.

She hardly had the energy to toss out even those syllables much less to fulfill her responsibilities to our holy mother, pass-ing the intervening days between disappearances mostly in bed as if recovering from a near-fatal illness. Our saintly Rizpa, in addition to her other duties, which now also included ministering to Aish-Zara, za'zal, in the terminal stage, would come to Cozbi when she could with some puréed food and tenderly feed her suffering sister against whom she passed no negative judgment spoonful by spoonful with little success, giving up in the end and setting down the bowl on the floor for Abramovich to finish off.

"Another kidnapped soul," Rizpa said to Paltiel on one of those occasions, her heart brimming with pity in contrast to the anger-management issues he was dealing with after each disap-pearance stunt—and, of course, Paltiel grasped the reference to this little woman's enduring bereavement, from the days when he had channeled the Internet in the service of finding her nut-brown babies who had also disappeared, abducted from their cradles.

The strain on Rizpa was becoming unbearable, and so, at the request of our holy mother, who by this time had ordered that Aish-Zara, za'zal, be conveyed in her death bed to the inner sanctum of the northern apartment in order that she might be escorted to the gates of the next life by her closest friend who loved her profoundly, I detailed my prophetess Aishet-Lot to Cozbi's slot as Ima Temima's second attendant. One exceptionally clear night at the height of summer, at the end of the month of Tammuz during the three weeks of mourning beginning with the breaching of the walls of Jerusalem by the Romans in the first century of the Common Era and climaxing in the tragic destruction of our Holy Temple, may it be rebuilt speedily and in our time, as Rizpa and I sat in the private chamber of our holy mother, Aish-Zara, za'zal, sleeping fitfully on her back, our two senior wise women holding hands across the gap that separated their beds, Ima Temima turned to Aishet-Lot who was knitting furiously under the window, a bright crescent moon floating in the sky behind her. "Tell me where Cozbi disappears to," HaRav Temima Ba'alatOv, shlita, said to my prophetess. Aishet-Lot turned around and looked back, pointing with her fat knitting needle to the open parenthesis of the crescent moon with one star in its dip framed in the window behind her. "Yes," Ima Temima said, "it is as I thought."

The waning moon also shone through the window of Paltiel's room that night, and for the first time in all those months he dared to reach out his hand to Cozbi whose back was turned to him in their bed and stroke her flank, only to be informed, in more words than she had managed to string together during that entire period, that their relationship had been downsized to brother-sister status. By morning Cozbi had gone missing again. It was then that Paltiel finally turned to his mother.

Walking and sobbing, walking and sobbing, Paltiel made his way to his mother's chambers in the northern corner of our "leper" commune and plunked down with implicit entitlement on the bed. In reviewing this moment with me later, HaRav Temima Ba'alatOv, shlita, made reference to the one-hundred-and-twenty-sixth Psalm, the Song of Ascent often chanted before the grace after a meal, in which those who sow in tears walk along weeping, carrying their bag of seeds. "How terrible it is if one must walk while crying, the need to cry must be so unbearably overwhelming," our holy mother taught. "For crying, one should at least be given the grace to stop, not to be forced to go on, as on a death march. This is the most painful kind of crying." But then Ima Temima noted, with a mother's tender heart, the happy ending—the walking-crying bearing bundles of ripe sheaves, reaping with joy.

Moreover, in recalling the encounter, our holy mother, accentuating the positive, pointed to an unexpected and in some measure a gratifyingly therapeutic streak of acting-out on Paltiel's part when he settled himself on the bed and described his last confrontation with Cozbi. Mimicking her heavy cigarette voice in a provocatively exaggerated way and dropping his articles in mockery of her Slavic accent, Paltiel reported that she had announced to him, "You are brother to me, mama boy. I am sister to you." He went on to inform his mother that as far as he was concerned, with respect to this vulgar slut Cozbi, he was now left with two options—either to dump her or to kill her. Ima Temima recommended the former, counseling him to leave our "leper" colony to assert his own dignity and self-respect, and to return to the Temima Shul in the Bukharim Quarter from where he could continue to run the operation and from which Cozbi would be strictly barred by designated enforcers.

As for the second option, in discussing the exchange with me afterward, Ima Temima wondered out loud if the boy's father, Howie Stern, reinvented as Haim Ba'al-Teshuva, scribe and phylacteries maker of Hebron, whom she seemed to have always regarded as mentally challenged, was actually some kind of variation on an "idiot" savant, as demonstrated by his prescience in naming the boy Pinkhas. For the man who had entered our holy mother's quarters walking and weeping brokenhearted like Paltiel son of Layish when his beloved Mikhal was wrested from him and reclaimed by her husband, King David, as his property rightfully acquired with the payment to her father King Saul of her price tag of one hundred Philistine foreskins plus a big tip of an extra one hundred thrown in for good measure—that same man went forth like the zealot Pinkhas son of Elazar son of Aaron the high priest who had raised his spear and rammed it through the guts and groins of the fornicators, Zimri son of

Salu, a chieftain of the tribe of Shimon, and the idol-worshipping shiksa, Cozbi daughter of the Midianite elder Zur.

Pinkhas son of Elazar son of Aaron the high priest has his fade-out in the Tanakh at what must have been a phenomenally old age in the closing chapters of the book of Judges, as strict as ever. By the end of his days he is high priest in Beit El, where the Ark of the Covenant was then housed. Speaking for the Lord as His oracle, he rallies the Israelites to battle against their brothers of the tribe of Benjamin, perpetuating a bloody civil war in which thousands are slaughtered and Benjamin is nearly wiped off the face of the earth. With her finger pressed to these verses, my prophetess Aishet-Lot rose from amid the heaps of white wool streamers she had knitted that encircled her like a salt mine and brought the open book of Judges over to our holy mother after Paltiel left. Ima Temima nodded in complete understanding, and with noble generosity praised my prophetess Aishet-Lot with the words, "I see you have enlarged your vision from the past to the future."

The verses that Aishet-Lot was pointing to in which Pinkhas takes his farewell bow are in the middle of what it pains me to say is one of the most offensive sections of the Tanakh—the story of the concubine of Gibeah. This poor *pilegesh* is violently raped all through the night by a gang of men in Gibeah in the territory of the tribe of Benjamin where she and her master had stopped in their travels. When the Benjaminites of Gibeah are finished with her, they dump her at the door of the only house in town in which the travelers could find hospitality, her hands clawing the threshold. In the morning, her master loads her lifeless body onto his ass and hauls it home. He carves her up into twelve parts with his knife, hacking through the bones, dispatching the pieces of his violated property throughout the borders of Israel with the message, Take heed, Take counsel, Such things have never happened in Israel.

Are there truly some things left that have never happened in Israel? That is my question.

Paltiel departed from our "leper" colony that evening. Rizpa followed behind dragging one of his suitcases and a plaid vinyl bag filled with his favorite dishes in plastic containers that she had prepared for him as he made his way to an exit on the David Marcus Street side where a taxi waited. About a week later a package was found at the door of Ima Temima's apartment in the northern garden. I raised my woman's naked voice to express my concern that it might be a suspicious object, cautioning against handling it lest it blow up in our faces, but our holy mother overrode my security concerns and commanded Aishet-Lot to open it at once. Inside was the mangled shriveled carcass of Abramovich, barely recognizable, poor thing, next to a blackened waxy human ear of indeterminate gender except that from its piercing a long gold earring hung that no one could have mistaken as belonging to anyone other than Cozbi—the same earring that had jangled so prettily in happier times when she had crossed the floor in her three-inch stilettos to open the door on Passover eve to welcome Elijah the Prophet and the prophetess Miriam-Azuva-Snow White to our Seder.

MENTION of Elijah the Prophet moves me at this time under the aspect of the shattering life-cycle events, birth and death, that followed soon after the shocking revelations of the Cozbi case to legato in my thoughts to Rabbi Elijah, the formidable eighteenth-century Lithuanian Talmudic genius known as the Gaon of Vilna. Our own formidable Jerusalem Tanakh genius HaRav Temima Ba'alatOv, shlita, would on occasion cite the Gaon of Vilna in definitively identifying who among our women could rightly be included in our priestly tribe, in the lineage of Aaron, the first high priest. Such positive ID became a matter of particular sensitivity in our post-modern age, when traces of Aaron's DNA could be found on the Y chromosome of men from Africa to India no matter how alien, automatically conferring upon them the honor of priestly status by virtue of patrilineal descent, the indisputable manifest destiny of genes.

We women, of course, do not possess a Y chromosome, I thank God for this every morning in my prayers—Blessed are You Lord our God King of the Universe Who has not made me a man. Amen. Ah women. In determining who among our women could rightly be classified as a *kohenet,* therefore, our holy mother ruled according to Rabbi Elijah, the Gaon of Vilna. Surnames such as Cohen, Kahan, Katz, and so on and so forth, were all well and good and might or might not indicate that the individual so called descended from the priestly line. But, as the Vilna Gaon is reported to have decreed, if a person's name was Rappaport, that person was a certifiable priest, conferring upon her not only the extra burden to always be on the best exemplary behavior that is laid upon the back of a daughter of a priest (the harsher punishment of burning, for example, if she is caught in adultery), but also the right to partake of all the privileges and honors accorded to the men of that holy caste (eating the best cuts of meat of sacrificial animals, being called up first of the pack to the Torah).

The majority of our priestesses, maximum four in all remaining at our "leper" colony at that time, were certified to have descended from family trees with Rappaport signatures from either the maternal or paternal branch, including our beloved high priestess Aish-Zara, za'zal, née Essie Rappaport, and also including the nearly senior citizen priestess whose advanced stage of pregnancy I had noticed for the first time the day after we arrived here, when the dead goat came flying like a nostalgic image from a painting by Chagall over the stone wall of our "leper" shtetl. I admit now that I cannot (perhaps due to an extended senior moment of my own) recover the memory of her original given first name, and neither she nor to my deep regret Aish-Zara, za'zal, is with us any longer to enlighten me. In any case, it is sufficient for me to assert at this time that she was a guaranteed genuine Rappaport. As for her first name, when she was initiated into the sacred mysteries of the priesthood she took the name Tahara, with all its complex allusions to purity.

The priestess Tahara Rappaport's birthing travails began in our "leper" colony just a few days after the hideous body-parts parcel was delivered to our holy mother's door. Her water broke on the eve of the Ninth of Av as we began our fasting and lamentations over the destruction of our Holy Temples, two catastrophic blows dealt us by an astonishing coincidence around the same day of the same month half a millennium apart, proof positive that they could only have been delivered by the hand (anthro-pomorphically speaking, in the language of human beings) of the Almighty Himself. Tahara's harrowing labor lasted through the night, and by early afternoon of the next day, the Ninth of Av—the day on which some say the messiah is slated to be born and coincidentally the purported birthday of the false messiah Shabbtai Tzvi—the child was delivered. As the first day of the newborn's mortal journey on this earth advanced and darkness descended, our beloved Aish-Zara, za'zal, drew her legs up onto her bed, biblically speaking, took her final breath, let out her final mortal gasp, her agonized death rattle, and was gathered back to her mothers.

On that Tisha B'Av eve, HaRav Temima Ba'alatOv, shlita, delegated me to preside at our communal recitation of the Scroll of Lamentations composed by my colleague the prophet Jeremiah—Alas, how the city once teeming with people sits solitary, like a widow weeping, weeping through the night, no one to comfort her from among all who once loved her. The divinatory powers bestowed on a personage of such expanded consciousness in such close communion with the spiritual realm as Ima Temima rendered our holy mother's inspiring presence in our midst out of the question that night. Ascending to the heights, our holy mother saw with the certainty of pure inner vision that the precious soul of Aish-Zara, za'zal, would depart from her body within the next twenty-four hours, on the Ninth of Av itself, a day on which so many other calamities befell our people, this one only adding to the list. It was unthinkable—impermissible—for Ima Temima to leave the side of Aish-Zara, za'zal, at such a time, a matter of danger to the soul overriding all other sacred obligations. I accepted my mandate from our holy mother, therefore, and with humility took my place at the head of our mourners of the destruction of Jerusalem sitting on the floor of the great hall of our "leper" hospital in stocking feet, candles flickering in the dark sealed by their own pools of melting wax to the cool stones.

The reader intoned from the Scroll of Lamentations. In the siege of the Lord's wrath, starving women ate their newborn babies. Tenderhearted women with their own hands cooked their children. (Thank God, at least they cooked them first, I thought to myself; our holy mother has instructed me not to delete this transgressive thought, which is valued as an expression of positive rebellion.) It was soon after we chanted that verse about these desperate acts resorted to by mothers who, as a crucial element of their job description, are merciful, that the first anguished scream of the laboring priestess Tahara Rappaport cut through the reading, jerking every head up from the texts in which they were following along by candlelight.

OVER THE next twenty-four hours of Tisha B'Av not only did I not eat, since fasting is required, but I also did not sleep as I shuttled back and forth between birth and death—the room in which Tahara was undergoing her ordeal, the most well appointed in the hospital, in all likelihood once reserved for the Moravian prioresses who held dominion over the "lepers," only recently evacuated by Cozbi and Paltiel and then promptly claimed by our chief health care provider and circumcision engineer Zippi—and our holy mother's apartment in the northern garden where Aish-Zara, za'zal, was moving irretrievably toward the end.

By this point, Aish-Zara, za'zal, had been lifted up like a baby from her bed in the arms of my prophetess, Aishet-Lot, and set down in the bed of our holy mother. The two old friends now lay side by side under the covers, along with Ima Temima's little mother Torah. As sometimes happens in the final hours of this life, our precious Aish-Zara, za'zal, was blessed with unanticipated moments of alertness and lucidity, during one of which she blurted out that her priestess Tahara Rappaport had always reminded her a little of Mother Sarah-Yiska—a true cynic!—and now she was also, like Sarah-Yiska, about to become a superannuated alter-cocker old mother, a big joke, everyone who hears about it will have a good laugh, haha. At that, she and Ima Temima collapsed into a fit of giggles in each other's arms, like the old high school girlfriends they had once been. I was adjured to come to them as often as possible with bulletins from the birthing room. I must not hold back a single morsel. They did not want to miss a thing.

For the record, I must at this point register my complete disapproval of the birthing facility at our "leper" colony, which was in every respect substandard and unprofessional and, bottom line, especially in this case, irresponsible. Here was a woman by my generous estimate over fifty-five years of age minimum, a *Guinness Book of Records* contender, most likely menopausal and hormonally challenged giving birth for the first time so far as I knew—a primipara, heaven help us. There was no medical support system in place in the event of complications threatening to the life and holistic wellness of mother and/or baby. There was not a single certified obstetrics practitioner present, not even an unlicensed midwife with some experience to assist in the procedure with the curious exception of the centerpiece herself, Tahara Rappaport, who purportedly had medical training as a specialist in infectious diseases, ministering to the plague-and-contagion-ridden expendables of Africa until she gave up in despair or saw the light (often one and the same life-altering event), and returned to the faith to take up her new vocation as priestess. Given her present situation, of course, Tahara was in no position to attend to her own needs, and so the entire show was being run by Zippi armed only with her circumcision kit.

I also feel it is incumbent on me to note here, with no pretensions to self-congratulation and with the full sanction of our holy mother, that twice I raised my woman's naked voice to express my objections to the lack of quality care transpiring right in front of my very eyes; I could not allow myself to remain a silent bystander, I needed to speak truth to power. When I dared to raise my woman's naked voice in the first instance, I regret to say that Zippi did not hesitate to dis me in public in front of everyone present by calling me a dried-up old fossil from a prehistoric age, a bougie from a bourgeois town, and to tell me in no uncertain terms to mind my own bee's wax. This from the very same Zippi who was practically like a daughter to me when her mother and I were among the co-concubines of the late Abba Kadosh, a'h, in his patriarchal kingdom in the wilderness (a reality now so beyond visualization it seems like a dream).

In the second instance, our holy mother conceded that yes,

given the age of the laboring mother, conventional thinking might indeed lead to the conclusion that perhaps it would be more sensible if the so-called "patient" were transferred from our "leper" hospital to another type of hospital. But though there is hardly any description in the Tanakh of women actually giving birth, an activity that is in fact mostly attributed to men in the form of begats, there does exist an honorable mention of the Hebrew midwives Shifra and Puah, aka the mother and sister of Moses Our Teacher, who coped under the most adverse conditions during our enslavement in Egypt, the straits of Mizrayim and the parting of the sea evoking the narrow birth passage from confinement to release, our holy mother declared. We must therefore place our faith in God and in Zippi, both combustible personalities, both with self-esteem issues albeit of different sorts, both quick to anger. Ima Temima turned to Aish-Zara, za'zal, dying in that very bed, and inquired if she happened by any chance to know with regard to her priestess Tahara Rappaport now in her dotage in the throes of parturition who the father of this fetus might be. Aish-Zara, za'zal, the life seeping out of her, raised one skeletal hand and pointed a trembling finger upward in the direction of the heavens above as if to say, God alone knows.

"God the father," our holy mother nodded, "the usual suspect—also responsible for the miracle birth of that other old lady, Sarah-Yiska."

It was then that HaRav Temima Ba'alatOv, shlita, never disappointing, entered into a discourse on the identity of the father of Isaac, offering one of the more radical, some might even say blasphemous, teachings I had ever heard emerging from those holy lips. Calling attention to the incriminating opening verses of Genesis twenty-one—And the Lord *pakad* Sarah as He said He would, and He did to Sarah what He said He would do, and Sarah became pregnant and gave birth to a son for Abraham— our holy mother remarked on the absence of any active participation by Abraham, no mention of Abraham "coming" to Sarah as the generator of Isaac, for example, as he "came" to Hagar for the birth of Ishmael. Our holy mother pushed even further, beaming the full power of the mystical lasers on the meaning of the word *pakad*—translated traditionally as "remembered" or "noticed," the word used to describe what it was exactly that the Lord did to Sarah-Yiska. "*PaKaD,*" Ima Temima enunciated precisely. "Scramble it up, replace the *P* with an *F* since they are after all the same letter in Hebrew distinguished only by one little dot to harden or soften them—and what do you get? *DaFaK,* knocked, knocked up—in contemporary usage, *be'laz,* fucked. God literally fucked Sarah-Yiska as He figuratively fucked Tahara Rappaport as He fucks over all of us since time immemorial."

I must at this juncture interject that I was simultaneously stunned and thrilled by the language used by our holy mother; it was not language I imagined the girls at Beis Ziburis were exposed to (though it was quite common in the enriched program at my high school, Brearley), but Aish-Zara, za'zal, did not blink. A feeling of liberation exalted me from this teaching; it was as if I were suspended above the ground in midair with my fists punching furiously at the heavens.

"No wonder Abraham is so upset when he's forced by Sarah-Yiska to kick out *his* son Yishmael," Ima Temima went on to clarify. "But the old man doesn't even flinch in the next chapter when the Lord commands him to return *His* son Isaac as a burnt offering. He rises up early the next morning to get the job done, saddles the asses, even gives the kid the wood to carry up to the mountaintop for his own immolation on the altar there; let the boy dig his own grave—just following orders. Even when an angel is dispatched to demand a stop to the madness in the nick of time, the old man pleads, Just let me wound this naked boy a little to squeeze out a drop of blood—or so says Rashi the commentator-in-chief."

HaRav Temima Ba'alatOv paused at this point, digging no deeper to penetrate the heretical implications of this extreme teaching, simply putting it out there like a ticking bomb. Summoning my prophetess Aishet-Lot who had been knitting unperturbed at her usual ferocious rate in her seat under the window throughout this head-reeling teaching, our holy mother whispered some words into her ear. Aishet-Lot turned immediately and lumbered out of the sacred quarters on what was clearly an urgent mission. *"HaShem ya'azor,"* Ima Temima assured me with respect to my objections to conditions in the birthing room as soon as Aishet-Lot was dispatched. "God the father will help. But as a backup, there will also be a midwife. I have just made arrangements."

TAHARA RAPPAPORT was placed naked in an ancient metal tub that had been found somewhere in the hospital, possibly used at one time for washing the clothing of the "lepers" or, even more alarming (no offense intended), bathing their diseased bodies. The tub was filled with warm water to ease the transition for the newborn from forty weeks of cushioning afloat in amniotic fluid. The child would be born in water in emulation of the second birth of Moses Our Teacher set afloat in the river among the reeds. The first thing baby Moses' eyes saw when he opened them was a naked woman, Pharaoh's daughter at her bath. Tahara Rappaport was also regarded as a king's daughter, as are all Jewish women, all of us princesses whose entire honor is interior. Tahara the princess was also naked inside her tub of water set in the center of a magical circle that had been chalked onto the stone floor of what was now officially the headquarters of our health care provider, Zippi. The entire room was soothingly lit with candles in aluminum cups, strewn with rosemary and myrtle and other fragrant herbs, the doors and windows thrown wide open as a symbolic invitation for easy entry or exit, depending on your perspective. The women of our community who had given themselves permission to get in touch with their inner female in the service of this birthing were stationed along the circumference of the mystical chalk circle encompassing the laboring mother to offer their spiritual and emotional support and embrace. Most of them were clad only in white shifts like nightgowns, a few were naked, generally the younger and firmer goddesses, all had their hair loose and uncovered, every knot and tie in hair and garments undone to encourage through the power of suggestion full openness without any obstructions for the passage of the new life. From each woman's neck a charm or talisman hung—the open hand of a hamsa or a cameo amulet inscribed with the ineffable Name, the Tetragrammaton, along with the names of powerful first-tier angels to ward off evil spirits, especially the winged demoness Lilith who preys upon women in childbirth and targets newborns with deadly spite. Since the mourning of the Ninth Day of Av precluded music, the women in the circle were limited to pounding with the palms of their hands on the stretched sheepskin tops of small clay drums they held in the crooks of their arms, speeding up the rhythm and banging with greater urgency at increased volume as Tahara's contractions gained force and her screams grew louder. To these rhythms, some women gyrated and shimmied their pelvises and stomachs in circular movements like belly dancers, and there were even a few who took it upon themselves to mirror vicariously Tahara's contortions with each spasm and to echo her cries, as if they too were in labor. But most of the women by far spent the hours intoning Psalms nonstop over and over again to the doleful chant used for the recitation of the Tisha B'Av book of Lamentations—especially Psalm twenty, May the Lord answer you in times of trouble; Psalm one-hundred-and-eighteen, From the straits I cry out to You, O Lord; Psalm one-hundred-and-twenty-six, Those who sow in tears will reap in joy; Psalm one-hundred-and-thirty, From the depths I call to You, O Lord—Lord, listen to my voice.

The voice of the priestess Tahara Rappaport was hopelessly lost after seventeen hours of screaming—from animal cries to otherworldly shrieks, from yelling curses at God the father to roaring Shut up, for God's sake, just shut up, you witches! at the women chanting psalms or banging drums or belly dancing with tinkling bells, screeching Cut it out, you ridiculous primitives! with particular fury at the ones who were sympathetically mimicking her every contraction. And then there were her general all-purpose howls—You're killing me! Knock me out, knock me out! Give me an epidural! What am I doing here? Get me to a hospital, you idiots! Get me out of here! Writhing and twisting as she screamed, she struggled to break through the webbing of cords wrapped around the tub swaddling her in place, leaving free only the great round dome of her taut belly with the navel popped out, her pendulous, veined breasts with their darkened, créped nipples, her head thrown back with her long grizzled gray hair streaming over the side. The cord that kept her in place had been obtained at mortal peril by one of the women who had set out without even an armed escort to Bethlehem right in the neighborhood of the seething Dheisheh Arab refugee camp, to the burial place of Rachel Our Mother who died in childbirth, where she encircled Rachel's tomb seven times with the cord that she brought back to bind Tahara in the tub during labor for good luck.

Two strong women, soaked to the skin, were stationed by Zippi on either side of the tub to keep it from tipping over as Tahara thrashed about, while two others were assigned the task of refilling it as the water splashed over the sides from Tahara's wild flailing. Zippi herself, like the captain of the ship with a periscope, peered now and then into the birth canal for signs of emerging underwater life. Once, she even tried to insert a cherry-flavored lollipop into Tahara's mouth remarking, "My mama says it's okay even on Tisha B'Av, because today is your special day," which Tahara promptly spat out and sent flying like a projectile. But Zippi's main task during this stage, as she defined it, was to massage Tahara's belly, kneading it in spiraling circles with both hands each time a contraction came on, crested like a wave, and subsided, all the while exhorting huskily, "Breathe, Tahara baby, breathe—hee-hee-hoo, hee-hoo-hee!" panting along rhythmically by way of example.

In this fashion Zippi offered her services as she envisioned them until the spasms gripped Tahara so relentlessly and so close together with no respite or relief that she yelled Shut up, Zippi! and toppled her tormentor onto her rear end with legs cycling in the air by sliding the tub from within upon its slick of water and crashing it into Zippi bending over to coach her. In the same desperate maneuver, the priestess Tahara Rappaport also finally succeeded in tearing the cords with which she was trussed like a turkey and broke free at last, as if it were she herself who was being born out of a caul. It was at this point, I am pleased to report (and, I might add, her mother was also so pleased to hear), that our health care provider Zippi displayed the good-natured sweetness that I have always known she possessed buried deep down somewhere within her that I remembered from when she was just a little girl. She collected her dignity, pulled herself up from the wet floor with no signs of embarrassment or resentment, readjusted the lofty white turban on her head, smoothed down her dress, and said, "Lord, girl, the way you're carrying on, you'd think you're the first one in the history of mankind to ever give birth." She gazed good-humoredly at Tahara who was now on all fours in the center of the circle, her breasts and belly hanging down pendulous like great wrinkled overripe melons the gatherers had passed over. Squatting in front of her, Zippi tenderly parted the rumpled gray hair that concealed Tahara's face like a shaggy dog's, and tucked a hank behind each ear. "No need to check out the other end, Tahara girl," Zippi said. "I can see from your eyes you're ready to roll."

As if on cue, the midwife strode into the room at that moment, just as the cervix of the priestess Tahara Rappaport had dilated to ten centimeters and the baby's head began to crown between the old mother's legs like the dark furry center of a sunflower. Strikingly tall and slender, covered from head to toe in a black burqa, only the eyes of this midwife, liquid and beautiful with long rich dark lashes, were teasingly visible through the shadowed panes of a rectangular mesh patch. I must say that at first I was a bit dazed by our holy mother's decision to enlist a Muslim midwife to deliver this Jewish child, but it was not an issue I could afford to probe, and certainly not at that critical moment; I accepted the wisdom behind the choice as only one more mystery beyond my grasp. I suppose I should add that it also troubled me to see that the midwife's hands were already encased in the sterile white latex disposable gloves, especially because those hands were carrying the birthing stool of dubious hygiene, a battered contraption smeared with decaying organic matter composed of two cinderblock-like stones connected by two planks with a space between them—think your basic crude outhouse toilet. Ignoring Zippi entirely, the midwife brushed past her as if she were invisible, not even a player, setting the birthing stool down on the floor beside Tahara frozen on all fours like a terracotta animal on a lawn in sensationally bad taste, pausing to stare in open wonderment at the immodesty of the naked belly dancers and goddesses of the drumming circle.

By then Tahara had already lost her woman's naked voice and could no longer scream. The coming of the midwife cast her even further away into another realm entirely; she became subdued and docile as if under an enchantment more powerful than any chemical anesthetic, submitting without resistance to being helped up onto the birthing stool and surrendering. The priestess Tahara Rappaport sat obediently on the birthing stool, her bottom positioned to disgorge downward through its opening, her back hunched over, elbows on parted knees, head in hands, her face scarlet and streaked with perspiration as the midwife chanted hypnotically in an unearthly falsetto, Push, Vashti, push! We all simply assumed it was Tahara whom the midwife was addressing as Vashti, the name of the spurned Persian queen who had flatly refused to appear before the king with the substance abuse problem and his drinking buddies, thereby paving the way for our salvation via the sumptuous beauty pageant queen Esther. But everybody knows that Vashti is also one of the most common names given to cows in the State of Israel. So, speaking for myself, I must confess that I was somewhat offended by this Arab's demeaning characterization of Jewish women. Nevertheless, I understood that this was not the time to raise my woman's naked voice in protest. Maybe this midwife that our holy mother had sent us for reasons beyond my comprehension was actually a veterinarian, it was not a decision for me to question. I trusted that the deeper meaning of our holy mother's message would in good time be illuminated.

The priestess Tahara Rappaport continued to sit on the birthing stool, pushing and straining, her pelvis jerking in spasms as if in orgasmic throes until everything that had been loosened inside her came gushing out—the baby along with all of the birth junk from the uterus itself not to mention all the fecal matter and fluids from the two nearby orifices.

Oblivious to all the excrement and muck, the midwife deftly

caught the infant and held her up in the air head downward, one hand, now ungloved, pinioning both of her ankles like a chicken about to have its neck slit and with the other hand smacking her resoundingly on the scrawny tight buttocks, setting her crying lustily for good reason. Even through the smears of blood and the coating of cheesy white film, the dark spots on her pale skin and the protrusion above her natal crease were plainly visible. Here was our very own Vashti—a "leper" with a tail. This was the real explanation, some sages say, for the queen's refusal to obey the king's summons to appear at court for a command performance and display herself like a trophy wife in front of all the carousers. It was not some sort of legendary feminist rebellion; she just didn't like the way she looked, a feeling we women can truly appreciate.

The midwife spoke for the first time. "If a kid like this is born where I come from, we smash its head against a rock right away." The voice was the voice of a man, and the hands were the hands of a goatherd.

I made my way back to Ima Temima's quarters to report on the final outcome of the birthing experience. Though as a general rule our holy mother was in the habit of spending large portions of the day in our "leper" colony sitting up in a chair, either inside the apartment praying and grappling with the texts, or on rare occasions if the weather was mild in the garden under the oak tree meeting by appointment with spiritual seekers, I found our two senior wise women that Tisha B'Av afternoon still lying side by side in the bed. In an act of supreme lovingkindness, Ima Temima had elected to remain as close as possible in earthly space to Aish-Zara, za'zal, separated only by the thin fabric of their nightdresses and the skin of their physical beings throughout the dying woman's agony for the sake of offering comfort to the struggling soul laboring to be released from the straits of the mortal coils, a kind of reverse birth. Gazing upon these two entwined sisters, I recounted, "The first thing we all noticed when the midwife held the baby up were the two defects—the spots and the tail."

A profound silence followed as our holy mother took this in, channeling it through attributes of wisdom even the existence of which I could not venture to fathom. "Kol-Isha-Erva," Ima Temima spoke at last, "think carefully. Were these two things truly what you noticed first?"

It was my turn to draw deeply from whatever impoverished well of cognitive awareness I possessed. Finally I said, "I guess the very first thing I truly noticed were the genitals. Isn't that what one always looks for first? I took note that it was a girl. Then the spots and the tail."

"Three birth defects then," our holy mother responded. "Three damning stigmas."

It is not for me to presume how much of this teaching was absorbed by the consciousness of Aish-Zara, za'zal, as she lay in that bed beside our holy mother with eyes sealed, her breaths vibrating in thin rasps. But I can testify that before her final passage our beloved high priestess was blessed with one more moment of what as executive director of the school for prophetesses I would with no hesitation whatsoever call end-of-days prophetic vision. It occurred at twilight on that Tisha B'Av day as I joined the vigil in our holy mother's chambers reading psalms along with Rizpa and Aishet-Lot—Even when I walk in the valley of the shadow of death I will fear no evil because You are with me, Your rod and Your staff they will comfort me.

As if she were startled by a stunning realization she had been grasping for all her life, the cavernous eyes of our high priestess Aish-Zara, za'zal, flashed open and she cried out, "The Queen the Messiah, here she is!" Mustering the last shreds of her strength she clasped Ima Temima around the neck with both arms and kissed our holy mother passionately on the lips. Utterly spent, her arms dropped, her head sank onto Ima Temima's breast, and she remained in that position, her depleted upper body splayed across Ima Temima as our holy mother stroked her back, singing softly in an aged voice, deep and gravelly, a Yiddish lullaby, Sleep, sleep my dear little bird, ay-lululu-lu-lu-lu. Over and over again Ima Temima sang this simple melody, caressing and rocking Aish-Zara, za'zal, for an hour at least as we sat there silent privileged witnesses until the words of the *Shema* rang out from the lips of HaRav Temima Ba'alat Ov, shlita—"Hear, O Israel, Adonai is our God, Adonai is One," and, after a haunting pause, the acceptance of the death sentence, "Blessed is the True Judge."

A long tear crept down the sides of our holy mother's face from the corner of each eye. Rizpa and Aishet-Lot approached the bed diffidently and lifted the body of our high priestess Aish-Zara, za'zal, off of our holy mother and laid her gently on her back in her own bed, her released soul still hovering in mid-air seeking the open window like an agitated bird desperately searching for a way out. The two personal attendants assisted Ima Temima onto a chair, which was drawn up close to the bed. The hands and feet of Aish-Zara, za'zal, were already bloating and growing waxy, an organic smell of sweet rot was beginning to radiate from her, her nearly toothless mouth hung down open and slack. Our holy mother reached for the Tanakh on the bedside table and wedged it under the chin of Aish-Zara, za'zal, to prop up the jaw and close the mouth. Then HaRav Temima Ba'alatOv, shlita, pulled the cover over the vacated face that no longer truly resembled our high priestess Aish-Zara, za'zal, her essence no longer present, and said, "In keeping with the mitzvah to honor the dead I take it upon myself to serve as the *shomeret.*"

Instantly, with no prior consultation, the three of us came forward as one to offer ourselves in place of our holy mother as guardians over the body. We were overcome with concern that the task of sitting up all night beside Aish-Zara, za'zal, keeping watch over the remains so they would not be left alone even for a second would be too taxing, frail with age and desolated by this loss as Ima Temima was, and especially after a twenty-four-hour period of fasting. But HaRav Temima Ba'alatOv, shlita, would not hear of it, refusing absolutely to cede to anyone else this service of lovingkindness to the dead, or even to compromise by agreeing to shifts in which we would each take a turn as *shomeret.* The only concession our holy mother made was to eat something from the tray of salads and fruit that Rizpa had already set out in the front room while my prophetess Aishet-Lot and I during this brief break sat watch over the withered corpse decomposing on the bed. It was a tiny body, yet even so it was too large to stuff into the refrigerator in the apartment for preservation purposes, and, despite the irrefutable holiness of Aish-Zara, za'zal, we were bewildered to discover that her remains were so quickly giving off a rancid stench even on that musty Jerusalem night, though not one of us would dare to dishonor the dead by making reference to it either in words or by facial expressions or by, God forbid, the gesture of placing a hand discreetly under our noses.

Within ten minutes Ima Temima returned from the brief repast, resuming the role of dedicated watchwoman, companion to the dead, even as the three of us also remained through the night, listening in awe as our holy mother intoned all one-hundred-and-fifty psalms entirely from memory in a remarkably young and strong voice. After the verse "Although my father and mother have abandoned me, the Lord will take me in" from Psalm twenty-seven, Ima Temima reminded us that, although Aish-Zara, za'zal, had been cut off by her family for what were judged to be heretical activities impermissible to a woman warranting complete shunning when she left them to join our flock, and although she was regarded as dead by her husband and children who had already sat shiva over her for seven days of mourning, it was nevertheless our responsibility to find a way to inform her thirteen children, ten sons and three daughters, of the actual passing of their only mother and of the funeral and burial that would take place the next day here at our "leper" colony as well as of their obligation to sit shiva again, this time for true and proper cause. "What they decide to do with this knowledge once we have fulfilled our duty to pass it on to them is their choice, God help them," our holy mother said. The task of dispatching a member of the Bnei Zeruya with the mandate to seek out at least one of the children of Aish-Zara, za'zal, to deliver the news and to spread it to the others was delegated to me, a commission I welcomed with gratitude. After that, Ima Temima did not interrupt the recitation of Tehillim again until Psalm one-hundred-and-thirty, arriving at the verse, My soul longs for the Lord more than watchmen for the morning, watchmen for the morning. Here, our holy mother paused and declared, "When morning comes, I will oversee the *tahara*."

From these words we understood that HaRav Temima Ba'alat Ov, shlita, was yielding to us the actual performance of the purification rites involved in the *tahara* process in favor of a supervisory role, and in my heart I thanked God for this. It must surely have been an extremely painful decision for our holy mother to refrain from active participation in what is considered to be among the highest acts of lovingkindness one person can perform for another, a thankless task, and especially in this case the sacrifice must have been doubly hard, since the recipient of this *hessed* would be Ima Temima's soul mate, Aish-Zara, za'zal. Moreover, I can personally attest to our holy mother's extraordinary skill at preparing the dead for burial, from the days when the two of us came out of the patriarchal compound in the wilderness of the late Abba Kadosh, a'h, and Ima Temima quickly became known throughout the land of Israel as a one-woman holy society, traveling anywhere day or night to perform a *tahara*, especially for women who had no one, the nameless and marginalized. But this time, to my immense personal relief, there was an implicit acknowledgment of the limitations that come with age. Now, under the scrupulously demanding eye of our holy mother, the hard labor and heavy lifting involved in the *tahara* were to be left to us, to Rizpa, Aishet-Lot, and myself, joined by a fourth woman, Zippi, who strode into the room and promptly let out a loud Phew!—clapping her hands against her nose and shaking them out as if they had accidentally dipped into some foul pool. In the spirit of special indulgence of one's own child our holy mother overlooked this outburst possibly disrespectful to the dead had the spirit of Aish-Zara, za'zal, heard it, and opened the proceedings at once by paraphrasing from that great depressed authoress Kohelet, "As she came out of her mother's womb naked so must she go—as we wash a baby at the beginning so we wash her at the end."

The wasted and ravaged body of our precious high priestess Aish-Zara, za'zal, was laid out naked under a white Sabbath tablecloth on a wooden bench, the feet pointed toward the door, the hands arranged palms upward in a gesture of supplication. "Essie daughter of Sarah-Yiska," the four of us recited in unison (since we did not know the name of the mother of Aish-Zara, za'zal, this was the name HaRav Temima Ba'alatOv, shlita, instructed us to use), "we of the holy burial society ask your permission to perform this *tahara* on you. We beg your forgiveness for any disturbance we might cause you or for any mistake we might make."

We proceeded to wash the body with water ladled from a pail, exposing only the section we were working on to protect the dignity of the dead like a surgeon performing an operation, barely able to gaze out of pity at the cavernous webbing of scars where the breasts had been gouged out, the savage gash through which the womb had been eviscerated, the evidence of beatings and cigarette burns that had been inflicted upon her. We combed the sparse white hair remaining on the head of Aish-Zara, za'zal, we cleaned out all of the orifices, the ears, the nostrils, the mouth, and so on and so forth, all the holes down the body front and back and packed them with sand, we cut her nails and scraped under them with a toothpick, bemused to discover the remains of a glossy mother-of-pearl polish on her toenails, which we were instructed to remove. As we labored our holy mother sat in the chair directing us, closely monitoring our every move, all the while chanting from the Song of Songs—Her head is like the finest gold, Eyes like doves, Cheeks like beds of spices, Hands like golden rods, Thighs like marble pillars, Her mouth is sweet, She is completely delicious, This is my beloved, This is my darling, daughters of Jerusalem.

The two heftiest women in our group, Aishet-Lot and Zippi, raised the naked body of Aish-Zara, za'zal, and stood it up on its feet holding her rigid form steady in that position as Rizpa and I carried out the actual purification ritual of *tahara*, pouring water from buckets in a continuous stream down her head and body like a shower for a total immersion as in a ritual bath, and afterward we dried her thoroughly. We covered the bench she had been resting upon after drying it too, spreading the great white talit over it in which Aish-Zara, za'zal, used to wrap herself to bless our congregation, first tearing one of its fringes to render it unusable for any future holy service.

We dressed her in her plain white linen shrouds sewn by hand by the women of our "leper" colony—the cap, the veil, the trousers, the socks, the mittens, the tunic, the jacket, the sash wound around the waist knotted in the shape of the three-pronged pitchforked letter *shin* for one of God's aliases, *Shaddai*—"Like the white garments donned by the high priest only once a year on Yom Kippur day to enter the Holy of Holies," Ima Temima said. Here at last was an outfit tailor-made for Aish-Zara, za'zal. Honey, I was tempted to say, With all due respect, this is you! Ima Temima sent Aishet-Lot outside into the northern garden of our "leper" colony to collect some dirt from the Holy Land, which we sprinkled over the eyes, heart, and private parts of Aish-Zara, za'zal, who now totally clad in her white shrouds at last truly took on the ultimate aura of a high priestess. We drew up the edges of the great talit she was resting on and folded it over her completely, tucking in its corners, wrapping her in a tight, neat little bundle as Ima Temima cried out with intense feeling, "She is pure! She is pure! She is pure!"—and we lit a memorial candle at her head.

"Aish-Zara, za'zal," we intoned repeating after Ima Temima, "we beg your forgiveness if in any way we have offended your dignity as we carried out this *tahara*. We have now completed our task according to custom and tradition."

"Thank you," a muffled voice responded in a whistling note followed by a sharp little bray of a laugh—all four of us can testify that we heard this, it was a miracle—and a small brown bird that had been perched on the sill of the open window fluttered its wings and flew off.

THE FUNERAL was held soon after, on that very same morning, the tenth of Av before noon to escape the stifling heat of the day. Every member of our community gathered in the dark shaded northern garden of the "leper" colony outside the door of Ima Temima's apartment where the grave had been readied under the ancient oak tree to receive Aish-Zara, za'zal, in the winding sheet of her talit. It had been dug with somber devotion by Aishet-Lot and the three remaining Bnei Zeruya, who were also given the honor of pallbearers, carrying Aish-Zara, za'zal, out on her bench and setting her down beside the shocking hole in the ground of her open grave. Our holy mother, cloaked and hooded in a prayer shawl and completely veiled, accompanied by the little mother Torah tucked securely into the corner of the wheelchair like a beloved stuffed animal without which a small child will refuse to go anywhere, followed behind in the procession to escort the dead, pushed by Rizpa who was helpless to suppress the sobs that gripped her. Though proximity to the impurity of the dead except in the case of the closest relatives is forbidden to a member of the priestly caste, HaRav Temima Ba'alatOv, shlita, had ruled that Aish-Zara, za'zal, was like a mother to our priestesses, and so they too were present, their white prayer shawls draped over their heads, three priestesses in all remaining to us now in our "leper" colony, including Tahara Rappaport who had risen from her bed and was breast-feeding her tightly swaddled baby under her talit.

Our numbers had been reduced over our sojourn in the "leper" colony approaching extinction, it is true, but on that morning of the funeral of Aish-Zara, za'zal, they were vastly multiplied by the added presence of by my estimate well over one hundred (a Jew is forbidden to count other Jews directly) members of the family of our cherished high priestess—children, grandchildren, and great-grandchildren—who stood some distance from us separated by gender, the men and boys on one side, women and girls clustered in a tighter space on the other side close to but not touching the stone walls. It was a dizzying sea of black hats and long black kaftans, wigs and headscarves and loose dresses brushing the ankles, but that was not the most striking feature that set them apart, nor were the white surgical masks they all wore over the nose and mouth, presumably as a precaution against exposure to the pollution of "leprosy" rather than anxiety about contaminating us. What was most striking about them above all was how large they all were, almost without exception, even the youngest among them, not only well above average in height but also big-boned and heavy, some bordering on the plus-sized; it defied the imagination to absorb the facts on the ground that these specimens had emerged from that hollowed-out little white package lying there on the bench. The only logical explanation was that the Pupa abuser who begat them was a giant, which rendered the visual of him ramming a raw fist into such a small creature as Aish-Zara, za'zal, even more intolerable.

By all accounts he himself was not there that morning. It was possible, however, to distinguish among this throng a few who were the actual children of Aish-Zara, za'zal, by the obligatory mourning rent in their garments close to the heart, and so I approached one of them, a daughter naturally, since I knew from mortifying experience that none of the men would be willing to speak to a woman, and would, in fact, simply look right past me as if I were invisible if I attempted to address him. After expressing my sympathy for her loss, I inquired of this daughter, a large matron with a brown mustache and matching wig, if she could tell me the name of the mother of Aish-Zara, za'zal. Once again the celestial powers of Ima Temima were stunningly affirmed for me when this daughter informed me in Yiddish that she in fact had been named for her mother's mother, for her maternal grandmother, Sora—our very own Sarah-Yiska, precisely as Ima Temima had foreseen. I was then able to insert this name in its proper place when I sang for all the assembled the *El Maleh Rakhamim*, which was the honor given to me thanks to the training I had received at Juilliard before dropping out—God full of mercy, grant a proper rest at the highest levels of the most holy and most pure to the soul of Essie daughter of Sarah—and it did not faze me in the least that every single male member of the family of Aish-Zara, za'zal, had his fingers plugged into the depths of his ears and was droning in a monotone as I sang lest he God forbid sin by hearing my woman's naked voice.

The eulogy was delivered by HaRav Temima Ba'alatOv, shlita, at first in tones so soft and intimate that all the assembled were obliged to lean in to hear. I pictured the crowd as if from above, resembling a copse of trees all bending in one direction from the gust of a mysterious squall lashing them from behind.

"My darling Essie," our holy mother began, addressing Aish-Zara, za'zal, directly, as if they were alone in a room, as if it were a personal conversation to which we were only by chance fortunate to be privy, "my dearest friend, my teacher, my rebbe"—and our holy mother went on to speak achingly not of all the suffering and injustice endured by this tiny creature now lying blotted out on the bench at the lip of her grave, not of all the humiliation and contempt and sheer dismissal of the terms of her very existence inflicted upon her, but rather our holy mother recalled the monumental courage and defiance this little heroine had displayed. "When you assumed your rightful place as our high priestess and took on the name Aish-Zara," Ima Temima said, "we recognized immediately that for you no name could be more fitting. Because you are like the strange-fire, the *aish-zara,* that the two elder sons of the high priest Aaron, Nadav and Avihu, brought to the altar in the sanctuary on the incense pan. Like them you served God in your own way. For their boldness God consumed them in an instant flash of flames, just as moments earlier He had lapped up with fire the burnt offering and the fat parts of the ox and the ram. Nadav and Avihu were just another ox and ram to God, another sacrifice, our God has a taste for blood and fire, and so their father Aaron was forbidden to mourn—Aaron was silent, the Scripture reports. We too shall refrain from mourning, mommy, we too shall remain silent, but we shall honor you by continuing to serve God in our own way, following in your path wherever it leads."

Our holy mother then turned away from Aish-Zara, za'zal, raising both arms to the heavens and in powerful tones, bold and young, taking on God Himself. "We know You exist because You created our world in Your image. You are a cruel God and it is a cruel world—but I have no fear at all. I shall not move from this place, I shall not leave this 'leper' colony, until You put an end to all the injustice and oppression, until you call a stop to all the sorrow and suffering. *Yitgadal Ve'yitkadash Shemai Rabbah.*

Even if my protests incite You to grow more savage and furious, to heave up the entire universe and turn it back to water, to astounding emptiness and void, I shall not move from this spot until You swallow up death forever and wipe away the tears from every face. Exalted and Sanctified May Your Great Name Be."

There was more, but in the interest of full disclosure I must insert at this point that I was unable to hear every precious word of our holy mother's eulogy and was obliged to reconstruct the entirety of the message afterward by consulting with others to obtain the complete transcript that I have yet to fact-check. It was a great personal loss for me, this goes without saying, but a necessary one since early on in the course of Ima Temima's talk I detected restless murmurings in the crowd coming from the direction of the family of Aish-Zara, za'zal. As a precautionary measure, therefore, sensing the danger of brewing violence, I moved unobtrusively to a corner, pulled out my cell phone, and dialed automatically the number programmed in to alert our friends in high places of impending trouble. As our holy mother was drawing the comparison between Aish-Zara, za'zal, and the sons of Aaron the high priest, shouts rang out from the crowd—*Apikorsus*, Heresy, *Hillul HaShem*, Desecration of the Name, and so on and so forth, the usual garbage flung at us over the years. By the time Ima Temima came to the plea to our cruel, savage God, a few stones were thrown, mostly pebbles, mostly by the children in training, I observed with sadness, the pebbles they happened to bring along with them in their pockets as they must have been forewarned against touching anything of ours, all of it saturated with contamination and impurity, which is probably why no one was hurt, thank God. It might have escalated in some way, however, these things can sometimes spread faster than "leprosy," but before that could happen we heard the thumps of a loping four-legged creature though the trot was clearly not that of the police horses I might have expected.

Charging into the crowd at that moment came an Arab astride a huge bellowing camel baring its teeth. His long robes were flowing, his red-and-white checked keffiyeh was drawn across his entire face except for the eyes, he was riding as if through the drifts of a sandstorm on the desert dunes, one hand grasping the camel's reins and the other cutting through the air with a glittering saber, slashing at the wind while ululating shrilly as he drove the entire crowd of masked strangers to the exits and pursued them out of our "leper" compound, disappearing along with them just as the sirens could be heard and the police wagons drew up.

All that was left to remember our guests by were steaming piles of hoo-ha nuggets dropped by the camel, which I can only conjecture are not particularly beneficial to the soil for organic fertilization purposes since the desert is not as a rule known to bloom except through the sheer force of willpower of Zionist pioneers, though our creative domestic management associate Rizpa did later gather up the dung to use for cooking fuel. It remained for us, the embers salvaged from the blaze, the last inhabitants of our "leper" colony, to bury our dead.

As we stood there in reverent silence, Aishet-Lot descended into the grave and the body of Aish-Zara, za'zal, was passed with the utmost delicacy and respect into the safety of her arms by the three Bnei Zeruya working in a relay like rescuers at a fire. Aishet-Lot laid our dear high priestess down lovingly at the bottom of the grave like a baby in its cradle, and ascended. For a few seconds it seemed to us as we gazed into the depths of that pit that our poor Aish-Zara, za'zal, swaddled in her white talit like a receiving blanket was stirring in distress, as if struggling to find a more comfortable position, and then it was as if she had found her place, as if she let out a low sough of relief at the prospect of never having to be bothered again, and she gave herself over to sleep.

A shovel filled with dirt was placed in the hands of HaRav Temima Ba'alatOv, shlita, whose chair had been brought up to the very rim of the grave. The honor of being the first to cover Aish-Zara, za'zal, with the earth from which she had come was given to our holy mother, who tipped the shovel downward, letting the dirt spill slowly into the grave onto the body nestled below. Then we all took turns with the shovels and spades that had been supplied, thrusting them into the piles of dirt that rose

on either side of the grave and emptying them on top of the unre-
sisting body of Aish-Zara, za'zal, until the grave was filled and a
soft fragrant mound rose above it into which a temporary hand-
written marker was sunk—ESSIE DAUGHTER OF SARAH-YISKA,
AISH-ZARA, ZA'ZAL, with a simple drawing as if outlined by a
child of two hands raised in blessing, thumbs arcing, middle and
ring fingers separated, to indicate the resting place of a priest. In
a year's time, God willing, we shall unveil a suitable monument
over the grave of Aish-Zara, za'zal. Our three remaining priestesses to whom Aish-Zara, za'zal, was like a mother chanted the
mourner's Kaddish standing in for her own children who had
fled—exalting, sanctifying, glorifying, blessing the Name of the
Holy One, praising God despite everything.

That very evening I was summoned to the quarters of our
holy mother. I expected to find Ima Temima already in bed after
these strenuous days filled with so much stress and loss, but was
surprised and I must add reassured instead to see our holy mother
sitting in a chair drawn up to the table on which the Tanakh was
open to Leviticus, chapter twelve. There were no signs of mourning in the room, not even a memorial candle, and Ima Temima
made no reference at all in the course of our conversation to the
passing of Aish-Zara, za'zal, or to any of the incidents that had
occurred during the purification and burial rites that had taken
place that very morning. Pointing to the text spread open on the
table, HaRav Temima Ba'alatOv, shlita, reminded me that this
was the section of the Torah devoted to the impurities of skin
eruptions commonly classified under the heading of "leprosy."
But the portion begins with the strictures relating to the impurities of a woman who has just given birth. If a woman gives birth
to a boy, she is considered to be in the untouchable state of a
bleeding *niddah* for seven days followed by thirty-three days
of a secondary degree of impurity, our holy mother reminded
me; if it is a girl, the untouchable menstrual *niddah* stage lasts
fourteen days, followed by sixty-six days of generalized uncleanness. Why the difference? Ima Temima asked. Because the baby
girl, a female like her mother, is herself also a sack of blood, and
doubles the impurity.

Turning now to the subject of the baby girl who had just been born to the priestess Tahara Rappaport only the day before, our poor little Vashti, Ima Temima noted that the child already has three counts against her, possibly even four, because in addition to being a female leper with a tail it was very likely that she was also a "bastard," a *mamzer*, a devastating label slapped upon an innocent soul mandating extreme forms of discrimination and ostracism. This, I knew, was a subject that our holy mother had probed very deeply and was acutely sensitive to, as Zippi, the daughter that Ima Temima had borne in the wilderness to our mutual husband, the late Abba Kadosh, a'h, had been publicly classified by some mean-spirited authorities as a *mamzeret*.

Having laid all these cards out on the table like a Tarot reader, HaRav Temima Ba'alatOv, shlita, gave me my orders. My mission was to go at once to the priestess Tahara Rappaport and inform her that in fourteen days' time from the day she had given birth, at the completion of her first period of extreme bloody pollution in accordance with the strictest interpretation of the text, on the twenty-second day of Av, she must pack her bags and take her baby, Vashti, with her and leave our "leper" colony forever. "Inform her that you will give her some bread and water on that morning and send her on her way with her girl child," HaRav Temima Ba'alatOv, shlita, commanded with a finality that left no opening for argument or discussion. "You may also want to add that my personal advice based on what awaits the child in this life is that she take her into the wilderness and lay her on a rock, abandon her there like a superfluous newborn Chinese girl. Tell her to expose the daughter to the elements for her own good, and to the birds of the sky."

Part III

Haya

They Have
Gone Astray
in the Land,
the Desert Has
Closed in
on Them

Over the seven days of mourning for the murdered baby, Kook Immanuel, stunned citizens from all across Israel, many with their children in tow, set aside their fears of venturing into the wild West Bank and flowed into Hebron to offer comfort to the bereaved parents—and, in the process, to demonstrate with their bodies their outrage that such atrocities were possible in their own land that was their God-given birthright. From common folk to dignitaries at the highest spheres of government and the religious establishment, they made their way defiantly through the treacherous streets of the Jewish people's second holiest city up to the military base on the hilltop, almost every tree and wall along their route plastered with heartbreaking black-and-white posters of the baby's shockingly innocent face overlaid with streaks of bright red blood gushing down like tears along his chubby cheeks from the black hole in his forehead like a third eye, and the stark words electrified in lettering evoking death camp barbed wire, SLAUGHTERED BY TERRORISTS, shrieking the savage tale.

So great was the number of mourners who kept streaming in that the shiva was moved from the family quarters to the synagogue, the largest tent on the compound. Temima sat on the floor in her stocking feet in the women's section to receive the female comforters, an army blanket thrown over her head that she did not raise for the entire period of the seven days of mourning, her lips moving as she rocked back and forth, reciting Psalms from memory but no sound emerging from her mouth, voiceless like the barren Hannah praying for a child in the Tabernacle so that the high priest Eli concluded she was a drunk.

In the far more capacious men's section of the synagogue tent, her husband, Haim Ba'al Teshuva, scribe and phylacteries maker of Hebron, his arm still in a sling, his head still bandaged in gauze, sat on the floor facing a throng of men packed tightly together undulating like a giant beast stirring in hibernation whenever one or another of them sought to push his way through to make his presence known to the chief mourner and offer the requisite words of consolation. Only when the prime minister of the State of Israel himself, surrounded by his bodyguards with faces as if carved from granite, arrived in a black bulletproof limousine did the crowd part like the Reed Sea to create a passage for his eminence as the first lady who had accompanied him set a silk scarf loosely over her helmet constructed of hair and made her way alone to the women's section. Howie was so overcome by the honor of the appearance of so prestigious a comforter that in violation of religious protocols he rose from his place of mourning to greet him, flushing crimson with gratification at being singled out for such public recognition, to his everlasting shame and regret failing to seize the moment to cry out for all to hear demanding justice and to extract before all these witnesses the promise of retribution. For months afterward he would replay the scene in his head, with the crucial variation that in his internal drama he spoke out and said what he should have said so that as time passed he had massaged the history, recounting the story crowned with his bold outcry, and no one denied him.

From the ranks of religious leaders, Howie was also honored by shiva calls from the two chief rabbis of Israel, the Ashkenazi rabbi in his three-piece suit with the cutaway coat and black fedora smelling of calf-foot jelly *ptcha*, the Sephardi in his brilliant robes and turban and tinted shades smelling of musky patchouli, each arriving separately in an armored limo accompanied by his retinue.

No less keen an honor, which at first served in some measure to render tolerable his grief, was the constant presence of the Toiter, Rabbi Elisha Pardes, who appeared at the shiva directly from the cemetery and remained for the entire seven-day period of mourning. Declaring that since it had been he who had performed the circumcision on the child, which strictly speaking is the duty of the father, he felt himself to be like a father to the boy and therefore it was incumbent upon him to go into mourning too. With a rip like a scream, he tore his white garments and donned sackcloth that one of his disciples handed to him and, bending down, he picked up a fistful of dirt and poured it over his head. For seven days he sat on the floor in a corner of the tent, and in the night he slept there guarded by a few of the Hasidim from his inner circle. Swaying jerkily, refusing almost all nourishment, growing increasingly gaunt and frail, his white hair and beard wild and ragged, his eyes hollow, he looked like a madman who had wandered in from the street, and though he strove to practically erase himself and achieve a level close to invisibility in his corner, several of the comforters who took notice of him approached to drop some coins into the cup half-filled with cold tea on the floor beside him thinking he was a beggar even as Howie pointed out that this personage was no less than the holy Toiter himself, leader of the Dead Hasidim, possibly one of the hidden thirty-six righteous of the generation upon whose merit our world continues to exist.

At the close of the seven days, as they all got up from shiva, the Toiter addressed Howie for only the second time since his arrival when he had expounded on his reason for including himself among the mourners. "You have given the child to the Molekh by exposing him to such danger in the streets of Hevron," the Toiter said in an even voice like a judge passing sentence at the end of a long trial, revealing no trace of anger or emotion. "It is an abomination, idol worship—child sacrifice explicitly forbidden in the Torah, a profaning of God's name for which the punishment is death by stoning. The stone that struck the boy was meant for you and will one day find you."

It seemed to Howie as if those words of the Toiter were like a curse spewn out by an uninvited guest in a fairy tale, like a preview of the stones themselves pelting him, yet to his eternal satisfaction he did not lose his presence of mind on this occasion as he had during the visit from the prime minister, but replied in kind with a reference to the Torah, passages of which he knew by heart primarily from his work as a scribe, in particular from the days when he had painstakingly instructed his wife, letter by letter, in the writing of her pathetic little mother scroll.

"Excuse me, Rebbe," Howie said, "but this time it's not my fault. It's the sin of our leaders and founders who had misguided pity for the inhabitants of the land and didn't kick them out once and for all like the Torah commands us to do, every last one of them, when we returned home to Zion—I'm telling you, Rebbe, it was like we were dreaming. So now they've become 'stings in our eyes and thorns in our sides,' exactly like the Torah says they would, and they hassle and kill us right in our own backyards. Believe me, Rebbe, I know from bitter personal experience what I'm talking about. What? You think I'm some kind of idiosyncrasy?"

This idea—the mandate to ruthlessly rid the land entirely of the Arab infestation, to strike them down like Amalek, man and woman, infant and suckling, ox and sheep, camel and donkey, to blot out their memory forever from the face of the earth—this charge had gripped and taken hold of Howie even before the blameless infant Kook Immanuel had been so barbarically cut down during the rightful exercise by citizens of peaceful assembly and nonviolent protest. What was this Toiter talking about anyways? Was it really possible that he seriously believed there was even one centimeter of our God-given soil that we Jews did not have the right to tread on?

With nearly breathless interest, Howie had been following in the press the emergence of the Jewish Defense League in America under its fiery leader, Rabbi Meir Kahane. Had Howie still been living in the States, there was no question in his mind that he would have been one of the first to sign up to serve as a faithful foot soldier in the JDL ranks to fight the anti-Semites anywhere in the world they reared their ugly heads. There were some, even (especially!) among Jews, who called the rabbi a hothead, an outlaw, a terrorist, for God's sakes. So what else is news? What else would you expect from Diaspora Jews with their *shtetl* mentality, always sucking up, always making nice, always pishing in their pants from fright lest they offend, God forbid. Enough with playing the victim, enough with going like sheep to the slaughter—been there, done that. With the conviction of inspiration, Howie knew in his heart that Kahane had it right. A Jew had to stand up for his own, there was no one to depend on to protect you and look out for your interests but yourself, a Jew had to show the world he had balls. To be called a vigilante was not an insult, it was not a dirty word, far from it, it was the highest compliment. To turn the other cheek—nonviolence—that was the deluded idea of a Jewish boy two thousand years ago who had gone bad—very bad. Oh yeah, for sure, Howie would turn the other cheek, only it would not be the cheek of his face. To carry a weapon in a holster at your waist to defend yourself and yours was a holy obligation, a commandment, like wearing a kippah on your head and a fringed garment on your body. Only the underclasses and the subjugated were denied the right to bear arms, that was a historical fact. Already Howie was never without a gun, even during the shiva. Jewish pride. Jewish power. Never again.

How this translated in Israel was obvious to Howie. The land had to be cleansed of the sons of Ishmael. They were like wild asses, their hands mixing it up with everyone, and everyone's hands therefore lifted against them in self-defense. Whatever they touched they befouled and destroyed. They were liars and thieves and murderers, they were barely human, they lived in filth like monkeys, they ate their own excrement. They only understood one language—the language of force. If they don't pack up and go quietly wherever, maybe to that ridiculous kingdom of the little Hashemite gigolo on the other side of the Jordan River where they are already the majority, then a little friendly or maybe not so friendly persuasion on our part will have to be used to transfer them. Yes, let's face it boys, we're talking expulsion here, forced deportations. Nobody lifted a finger when they did it to us, so where is it written that we can't do it to them too? It was all so clear to Howie, he could barely understand how anyone didn't get it; only a numbskull wouldn't *khop*. Just look at the statistics. They were breeding wildly like rabbits, those Arabs, like a cancer in our body politic, it was only a matter of time before they would outnumber us, before this malignancy would eat us up alive. Surgery was required to remove every last trace and cell of them—it was our only hope for survival—a radical Muslimectomy. As far as they were concerned, time was on their side; they would just sit there playing with their beads and smoking their bubblies and scratching their balls and screwing away like nobody's business and wait us out—the democratic end of Zionism, voted out of existence by its own citizens, the end of the Jewish State. It was plain demographics, pure and simple. Howie recognized that it drove those liberal, mush-headed Jews crazy to hear this simple fact on the ground because—why? Because they knew it was the truth. Don't talk to me about majority rules, forget about democracy, Howie thought to himself. Is democracy in Israel good for the Jews? That was the bottom line. That was the question every Jew had to ask himself at all times, that was the gold standard he had to live by—what's good for the Jews. What does democracy have to do with us Jews anyways? It is a goyische concept. For a Jew in his own homeland there is only one rule—the rule of the Torah. Torah is our constitution, our law of the land.

Howie took for himself the nom de guerre Go'el-HaDam, Blood Avenger, and with two comrades who called themselves Shimon and Levi, they carried out the first of their acts of civil disturbance on the *shloshim*, the thirtieth day after the death of the innocent baby, Kook Immanuel. On Al-Shuhada Street, on the very spot where Kook Immanuel was cut down, they erected in the middle of the night a monument to memorialize him. Its base was composed of a pile of stones to which was affixed a sign announcing that on this place, in the year 5729 from the creation of the world, the baby boy, ten months old, Kook Immanuel, may his memory be a blessing, son of Haim Ba'al-Teshuva of Hebron, was murdered by Arab degenerates, may their names and memories be blotted out. On top of the stone pedestal a baby carriage was affixed inside of which a wooden facsimile of an Uzi submachine gun was placed with the words Kook Hai! scrawled across it on one side in blood red, and on the other side, Nekama! Revenge!

And Kook did indeed continue to live on, at least in that monument, because for every time it was demolished by vandals and hooligans, or defaced with graffiti such as Jews Raus! or Zionism=Racism! or smeared with disgusting body matter, solid and liquid, human and animal, the small cell of zealots led by the mysterious bandit Go'el-HaDam would restore it in the night until it merged with the landscape and no one paid attention to it any longer, circumnavigating it automatically like any other familiar obstacle absorbed by the street. Dogs lifted a leg and relieved themselves against the stone foundation, men threw their cigarette butts into the baby carriage and emptied their pockets of condom wrappers and sunflower seed shells, young boys stuck their chewing gum and smeared their snot on the Uzi and young girls drew hearts on it with initials plus initials that only they could decode.

By day, Haim Ba'al-Teshuva, aka Go'el-HaDam, continued to sit in a corner of the synagogue tent performing what had now become his day job, the scribe's repetitious task of writing the mandated verses and sacred letters on small pieces of parchment to be folded into mezuzot and tefillin boxes, but the bulk of his spiritual energy was given over to strategizing with his comrades, laying out the plans for their operations and movements of the night, an occupation that flooded him with such excitement that, despite a personal loss that would surely bring him down to *Sheol* in everlasting anguish, he felt almost dizzy with elation at having found new purpose and meaning in life. Sabbaths and holidays he rested along with his surviving boy, Pinkhas, welcomed guests in other people's tents and at their tables where he would sigh and express to these sympathetic ears the thought he considered original to himself, about how unnatural it was for a son to precede his father in death, this was not how it was meant to be in the human order of things.

Over the ensuing months, joined by one more man who called himself Avshalom, the band of self-appointed avengers, like the dagger-wielding Sicarii zealots two millennia earlier cleansing Judea of its Roman occupiers, carried on with what they regarded as their holy mission of sowing dread and unrest in the cities and the countryside of the so-called West Bank—Judea and Samaria, the biblical heartland—with the goal of planting in the guts of its Arab scourge a sense of insecurity and unwelcome in their own homes, which was only right, since after all, this was not their home.

Dressed entirely in black to merge with the darkness, with black stockings drawn over their heads, they set out almost every night except Sabbath and holidays, in Howie's Peugeot or some other vehicle with the license plate obscured, to mete out Old Testament punishment like gods of vengeance, maiming and mutilating for the purpose of causing shame and humiliation, but stopping short of killing outright, at least for the time being. For this reason, with regret, because it was such a time-honored biblical war prize, they rejected the idea of cutting off the foreskins of all the pissers against the wall they could lay their hands on and bringing them back as trophies, like scalps collected by Indians, because the procedure could take too long and become too messy and lead to unanticipated bleeding and death; in any event, most of the Arabs in the territories were Muslims and already circumcised in the tradition of their progenitor, Ishmael, who had his *brit* at age thirteen by the hand of his own knife-wielding father, Abraham, a nice bar mitzvah present.

Instead, they opted for such actions as snatching any man they could find venturing out in the night, and occasionally they would even enter a house or courtyard that was open and easily accessible. Three of them would hold down the captive while the fourth would pound a nail through his earlobe with a hammer, as was the fate of the Hebrew bondsman who rejected freedom after seven years of indenture. And what were these Arabs anyway but a nation of slaves with a slave mentality, the descendants of a slave mother Hagar? If the man they caught had a beard, they would shave off half of it, and they would slice off half his garments exposing the buttocks, as Hanun king of Amon did to the emissaries of David to mortify them and insult the Jewish king. But their most satisfying specialty was cutting off both thumbs and both big toes of their captives, as the Israelites did to Adoni-Bezek the Canaanite, and as Adoni-Bezek had done earlier to seventy kings who crouched under his table licking up the crumbs, an eternal cycle of retribution.

For nearly six months the gang of four executed their campaign, reports of the incidents filling the press and the media and provoking marches and stone-throwing demonstrations by peaceniks and appeasers, until the night they were stopped for littering by Israeli soldiers when Avshalom threw an emptied bottle of grape Tempo wrapped inside a greasy Bamba bag out of the window of their speeding car. It shattered alarmingly on the road near Nablus, better known as Shekhem, in the shadow of Mount Gerizim and Mount Ebal, the mountains of the blessing and the curse. Their car was searched, the trunk opened to reveal piles of dried-up blackened fingers and toes, like the waiter's black bowties that used to spring up in the popped trunk of Howie's father's Chevy.

"C'mon guys," Howie said, draping his arm familiarly over the shoulder of the officer clearly in charge, "we're all Jews here. Gimme a break. It's just some lousy Bamba, it's not a bomb-a. Get it? Israeli junk food, fellahs, Holy Land snacks, no problem. Wait, we even have some more in the car in case you're hungry, you deserve a little nosh—our way of saying thank you for watching over us against the terrorists and murderers on our God-given turf. Just tear open the bag, take a minute to thank the One Above by saying a little *brakha*, maybe a *Shehakol*, maybe a *Boreh-pri-ha'adamah*, depending on which rebbe you go by, then dig in and enjoy—delicious, yum-yum."

Despite this generous offer, the four musketeers, already celebrated by some as Maccabim for their bold and original acts of defiance and denounced by others as meshuga'im for their mad and inflammatory exploits, were placed under arrest and taken into custody.

As soon as she heard reports of Howie's detention, almost without thinking, as if moved by a higher force, Ketura made her way along back roads up to the hilltop compound overlooking Hebron, costumed in the knotted kerchief pulled close around her face to conceal her dark skin and alien bird scar, long skirt, and loose tunic of a Jewish settler woman. According to press accounts she had seen, Howie was being held as a suspect in the recent crime rampage throughout the territories but Ketura had no doubt that this was primarily a cynical publicity maneuver on the part of Israeli authorities to placate their superpower patrons and quiet the shrill human rights delegation. It was only a matter of time before he would be released to his own recognizance pending a trial, assuming there would even be a trial, and be hailed upon his return as the anointed hero, a legend about himself that, knowing him as she did, it would not take him long to believe in. Now was her window of opportunity, her only chance to get to Temima. Under no circumstances would Howie in his latest incarnation as stricken father and righteous avenger tolerate her presence anywhere near his tent, this Philistine temptress, this Delilah, this disfigured outcast—not least because she made him squirm in the shadow of his own past carnal sins, but for the moment at least he was officially occupied elsewhere, and Temima, Ketura knew in her heart, needed her now.

Her son, Ibn Kadosh, had long since brought his flock of goats to graze as close to the settler's hill as possible in order to scout out the terrain and pinpoint the precise location of Temima's tent, like a target. Ketura penetrated soundlessly. The darkness and silence inside pressed down like a weight, giving out an otherworldly hum. The space seemed emptied of all life, until, as her vision adjusted, Ketura noticed a rounded heap of stuff, a mound of what looked like discarded rags piled up on a chair that appeared to be stirring lightly. She approached, and peeling off from the top one piece of cloth after another—headscarves and veils, ten in all—Ketura uncovered the hauntingly impassive face of her friend.

"Temima," Ketura whispered.

She had withdrawn to her tent after the seven-day mourning period ended for her son, Kook Immanuel, and had remained there in complete seclusion. She abstained from all forms of intercourse with other human beings, no longer colluding in the teaching of Tanakh against the background of evocative settings, or providing legal responsa for eminent rabbis stumped by such questions as whether a man who wears a toupee is also required to cover his head with a yarmulke, or accepting the morally dubious veneration of visits to the holy woman from petitioners seeking blessings or advice or healing or self-knowledge or whatever other desperate intercession.

The care of her remaining child, the boy her husband called Pinkhas, was entirely taken over by Yehudit Har-HaBayit who simply swept him up into her own brood, though out of pity she would allow him to stand alone for an hour or two each day sucking his thumb gazing with longing at his mother's tent, which seemed to many to be giving off rays of light but which he was strictly forbidden to approach or to enter. Temima's extreme isolation was regarded not as a pathological expression of grief but rather as a transcendent form of the practice of *hitbodedut*, revered as the quest for utter solitude to commune with God by a certified holy woman.

When she had risen from shiva on the seventh day she strode through the crowd clustered before her in the women's section of the synagogue tent directly to a complete stranger and rested both of her hands, one on top of the other, on the left breast over the heart of this woman who seemed to have attracted her so powerfully; the very next day the lump that had just been found in the breast upon which Temima had placed the warmth of her two hands had simply melted away, they later learned, a miracle confirmed by the doctors. Turning from this sufferer, Temima made her way back to her own tent trailed by a swarm of bees as if she were their queen, streaming behind her like ribbons of golden tresses, obliging those who witnessed and later gave a full account of this procession to keep their distance lest they be stung, to allow her to enter unimpeded into the seclusion she required for her holy work separated from other mortals by this celestial escort, like the divine pillar of cloud by day and the pillar of fire by night that parked itself outside the Tent of Meeting in the wilderness to mark the presence of Moses Our Teacher within in private conference with the Lord Almighty, and all of the Israelites stood at the openings of their tents observing this from afar and bowed down low.

Inside the tent, according to reports from the women delegated to deliver her food and basic needs as unobtrusively as was humanly possible and to provide the minimal care she required, Temima also undertook a whole array of self-mortifications—including the fast of speech such as she had practiced after her mother's death when she was eleven years old, along with the midnight lamentation over the destruction of our Temple, may it be rebuilt speedily and in our time, and also the silent recitation of Psalms and immersion in ice-cold water in atonement for the most basic and primitive libidinous sins of body and mind.

Most radically, she took upon herself an extreme form of the practice of womanly *zni'ut*. In an effort to achieve the highest level of female modesty, akin to the male modesty of Moses Our Teacher who was also veiled, about whom it was boasted that the man Moshe was so modest above any other man on the face of the earth, Temima sought to erase and extinguish herself as a woman. Her womanhood, after all, had been the source of all her suffering and the suffering she had brought upon others, both through the expression of her womanliness and through her efforts to suppress or to rebel against it. But the root was one and the same—her existence as a woman—which she now sought to obliterate by burying herself under every article of clothing she possessed.

By the time Ketura finished undressing her, a service to which Temima submitted without resistance, with the passivity of an invalid, eight skirts had been removed, nine tops, seven shawls or wraps, six pairs of socks from her feet and from her hands three more pairs worn like mittens—all this not including the ten layers of face and head coverings that Ketura had already stripped off at the beginning. Not an inch of skin had been visible, an observance of *zni'ut* that even some ultrastrict rabbis who routinely ordered the blacking out of images of women from newspapers and advertisements and set up separate entrances to public buildings for women would have deemed excessively severe, primitive even, like those Muslim ladies in their full-body black schmattehs in the marketplace resembling walking sacks of potatoes—not an enlightened Jewish thing that at least allowed the face to show and the hands from the wrist to the fingertips so that the dishes could be washed.

Howie for his part found it oddly comforting to wander in now and then—it was his own tent after all, he was master of the tent—and sit there gazing at that pile of rags that seemed inanimate but reportedly contained his own wife. And thanks to her fast of speech he could talk to his heart's content to this practically inert protuberance on the chair, without interruption, without fear of mockery or scorn, at ease in the knowledge that she would not betray him and she would not answer back as he recounted at length the details of the exploits of the previous nights—so many and so many spikes driven through earlobes, beards half-shaven-off, clothing half-shredded to reveal hairy *tukheses*, thumbs and big toes added to their collection—until the day came that Temima broke her vow of silence and spat out, "You think you're such a big man, Howie? You're just another pathetic American loser trying to get some respect on the West Bank. Don't you realize you're sacrificing the kid all over again for your own glory? It's plain *avodah zara*, good old idolatry. You're using him dead like you used him alive. Asshole!"

After Ketura had removed all the outer garments, letting them slip to the floor in a perverse kind of strip tease, Temima continued to sit there in silence in a loincloth she had fashioned out of a torn-up white sheet, strips of which she also used to bind her engorged breasts as with a bandage— she had still been nursing Kook Immanuel when he was so cruelly wrested from her—squashing them brutally against her rib cage. She was, Ketura saw, more beautiful than ever, tragic and mythic, her dark eyes even larger and her cheekbones even more prominent from the austerity she practiced, her skin flawless like a hothouse specimen, her body so shapely with its tiny waist, the twist on which her entire female form pivoted, it was no wonder she was so dangerous and had to be buried alive.

Ketura took a large wooden comb from the bag she was carrying and began to pass it through Temima's long black hair, working it gently through the knots and tangles filled with lint and threads and dust and other sheddings that had collected there from the layers of head coverings, and the minuscule forms of life that seemed to have been generated spontaneously. Tucked deep inside all of it as if in a nest Ketura found a bead, a luminous tear-shaped pearl, and she could only smile to herself—despite everything Temima was a woman, adorning herself.

"Stop grinning—it was my mother's," Temima said without moving, "from an earring. Keep it. It's yours—a present." These were the first words she had uttered since Ketura's arrival, and though for Ketura it was as if the limitations of her own thoughts and assumptions, the narrowness and conventionality of the possibilities she could imagine and conclusions she could draw were exposed by Temima's words, she was nevertheless swept away once again by the gifts of penetration of this remarkable woman. However numb and detached she appeared, she knew not only what Ketura had found, but also had parsed Ketura's brain waves and plunged straight to the depths.

"You mother would weep to see you now," Ketura said.

"My mother is very far away by now," Temima replied. "She doesn't care about me at all anymore. She never really cared in the first place. Otherwise, she would never have left me."

Still, Ketura went on, what Temima was doing to herself was very unhealthy—it was a sin. She, Ketura, had climbed this hill at great personal risk. She could have been shot by a trigger-happy settler or a jittery new recruit stationed on this army base if she were recognized as an Arab, or she could even have been assaulted by her own people who wandered in this area, punished yet again for shaming them by daring to move about freely, a loose woman with a death sentence hanging over her head who in all honor deserved to be killed. Ketura's hand reflexively brushed a wing of the bird scarred into her cheek. Nevertheless, she continued, she had not hesitated. She had made this trek because she had heard that Temima had taken herself out of this life and she, Ketura, had come to bring her back. She had come to bring Temima to Abba Kadosh's place in the Judean Desert near the Dead Sea, to cure and revive her.

There was nothing in this for Ketura herself. Yes, it is true that once upon a time long ago she had been a *pilegesh* to Abba Kadosh, one of many concubines, but now of course she could no longer live in his community herself since he had banned the presence of their son Ibn Kadosh, he had evicted and exiled the boy as a threatening element. Nevertheless, out of grinding worry over Temima, because of the profound love she felt for her and the history that bound them together like sisters, the sorrows and travails they had passed through together, she had sought and been granted from Abba Kadosh permission to bring Temima to his compound for a period of recuperation and rehabilitation, as to a spa—to bathe in the rich minerals of the sea, lie in the sun and soak in the healing rays, massages and facials, salt baths and mud masks, enemas and colonic irrigations, wholesome exercise and breathtaking walks, pure water and clean food beautifully prepared free of the taint of any animal product. Temima could stay as long as she desired and then she could leave, no questions asked, no problem.

Ketura went on in this way, not knowing if anything she was saying was having an effect on Temima who continued to sit there as if made of stone. Not far from Abba Kadosh's retreat, Ketura said, were the caves of Qumran where the Essenes had lived in extreme asceticism, where the Dead Sea Scrolls had been found by a Bedouin boy searching for a goat that had strayed. Temima could wander there, it was the authentic biblical epicenter, it was in complete harmony with her interest and absorption in the Hebrew Bible. Abba Kadosh's community was also as it happened purely biblical, it had nothing to do with the rabbis, it was post-rabbinical, the rabbis rejected him and he returned the favor, they didn't even consider him a Jew. And had Ketura mentioned the music? They had a choir of angels there—the heavenly voices of young boys, sweet as honey—and ancient instruments clear as crystal, lyres, ouds, timbrels, bells.

She had no idea which if any of her words had moved Temima—or perhaps it was not something she had said but rather a leap in Temima's own thoughts—but the moment came when Temima rose and dressed quickly, then paused as if frozen, as if she were trying to remember something vital. She found a piece of paper and a pen, sat down at the table and after some further inward foraging wrote a note paraphrasing from the prophet Isaiah—In the wilderness where wildcats meet hyenas, and demon goats call to each other, there too Lilith will repose, and find a resting place for herself. She folded the paper in half and left it in the crater in the cushion of the chair she had occupied for nearly six months. The two women stepped together out of the tent, and made their way along the perimeter of the the camp down the hill.

It was the heat of the day when they left, everyone was inside resting during the early afternoon, no one observed them leaving except for the little boy Howie called Pinkhas who had been given permission to spend part of his nap time standing outside opposite his mother's tent, his thumb in his mouth.

A white Cadillac was waiting for them at the bottom of the hill. The driver was introduced to Temima by Ketura as the two women climbed into the backseat—Melekh Sinai, formerly Miles Sinclair of Bedford Stuyvesant, Brooklyn, New York, Abba Kadosh's right-hand man. A small, wiry black man somewhere in his forties, he was bopping on his stem in his champagne-colored leather seat as if tuned into his own private beat, craning his neck and jutting his jaw forward as if his collar were too tight, swiveling his head to get a good long look at Temima. "Yes, Sister Temima," Melekh Sinai confirmed, "Brother Abba and me we go way way back—to Yazoo City, Mississippi, to be exact, federal penitentiary, maximum security."

Temima took in his round rimless sunglasses, grizzled beard stippled with silver, a pink scar snaking down his left cheek, gold hoop in one ear, white dashiki overlaid with a fringed garment, and a generous-sized white skullcap that somehow she knew covered a bald head as if it were shining through. Melekh Sinai turned back to attend to his driving, expounding over his shoulder that she was not to infer anything nasty or untoward from where he had first had the good fortune to run into the holy brother, the prophet and messiah, Abba Kadosh. Brother Abba, then known as Elmore Clinton of Selma, Alabama, was in bondage thanks to the pharisee pharaohs who as everyone knows are international superpower control freaks, the official rabbinical Jewish conspiracy who rule the world in exile as well as in Israel. So these bigshot guys did not appreciate it one bit that Brother Abba he was exercising his constitutional rights to worship freely as a Jew, descendant of one of the ten lost tribes of Israel, the tribe of Ephraim. Like they claimed Brother Abba was a harasser, a trespasser, a kidnapper of souls, a messianic Jew for Jesus bent on proselytizing among them—and then they throw in for good measure some other garbage about a drug cartel and a human trafficking ring and what not that they cooked up to get him sold back into slavery and put away for good. But Brother Abba he just shouted straight out, he was no Jew for Jesus, he was just a plain old Jew for Jew, he wasn't even Jew-ish,

Brother Abba says to 'em, like two-ish or blue-ish or true-ish, he wasn't a sort-a, kind-a Jew, he was the genuine article, the real McOy, he was a good old Jew boy from the South, shalom y'all, count him in for the minyan, sisters—and count yourselves out.

As for himself, Melekh Sinai, he had the honor of finding himself in Yazoo City thanks to a frame-up pertaining to some respectable young ladies he was doing his best to protect the way all young ladies need protecting, nobody but nobody knows the trouble he'd seen, but as soon as he met Brother Abba, prophet and messiah, he knew like a flash of lightning that he, Miles Sinclair, he too was a lost Jew, he had always felt a soul kinship with those crazy guys with the beards and black hats rushing around his neighborhood, in Crown Heights, worshipping that cool old rabbi guru dude who gave out the dollar bills on Eastern Parkway. So suddenly it hits him like a ton of bricks that he's a Jew too, from the tribe of Zevulun, and ever since then, him and Brother Abba have been joined at the hip like David and Jonathan, our love for each other more wonderful than the love of women, and that's pretty wonderful, sisters, making our life's journey together—liberated from slavery in Yazoo City, go down Moses, wandering through the Diaspora desert, and now here we are at last in the Promised Land, Hallelujah, roll Jordan roll, kumbaya, we shall overcome, amen selah.

A life story so complex and intricate as Melekh Sinai's was far too long for most distances traversed in a country as small as Israel. In less than an hour the Caddy was climbing a twisting road through crags and boulders in every shade on the sand-and-stone spectrum revealing with each turn staggering panoramas of the lowest spot on earth, the Dead Sea, the Sea of Salt, Yam HaMelakh, coming to a sudden halt at what seemed to Temima to be the very edge of a cliff, the point to which her life had now brought her, like the scapegoat on the brink of Azazel. Before them was a gate inscribed across the top with the words BNEI HAELOHIM BERUKHIM HABA'IM. Yet, despite this hospitable welcome, blessing all comers, the entrance to Bnei HaElohim was blocked as they drew up like the entance to the Garden of Eden after Adam and Hava had been driven out for biting into the fruit of the tree of knowledge good and evil, a revolving sword of flame set before it to bar human beings from the tree of life bearing fruits that would render them immortal like God Himself.

Blocking passage into Bnei HaElohim was a regal Nubian ibex framed by the gate, tan in color and a darker stripe down his back, with great ridged horns rising majestically from his head and arching eloquently backward. He stood there perfectly still, unmoving like a statue, taking them in from an elevated plane with the rutting slant and moistness of his eyes, considering them in all their aspects at his leisure as if stroking lasciviously his dark silken beard, a higher form of mountain goat.

"Ah," Temima said, "Abba Kadosh himself has come out to greet us in all his glory—*b'khvodo uv'azmo.*"

"Amen sister, you tell 'em," Melekh Sinai sang out in response, "Abba Kadosh, the whole earth is filled with his glory."

Ketura leaned in across the seat and kissed Temima on the cheek. "This is as far as I can go," she said. She reached for her bag, jumped out of the car, slammed the door, and vanished like a gazelle leaping on the mountains, bounding over the hills.

A full month passed before she met Abba Kadosh for the first time in his human guise. Awaiting her upon her entrance into Bnei HaElohim was a welcoming committee consisting of his head wife, Em-Kol-Hai Kedosha, a heavyset woman in her fifties dressed in a dazzling kaftan of woven gold-and-maroon kente cloth draping down from the prow of her dowager bust, and a stately coordinated turban denoting her lofty position in the community, accompanied by Shira Silver Kedaisha in a green cotton print African blouse and wrap skirt and matching head wrap who had been appointed as Temima's special liaison to oversee all her needs. They were carrying against the merciless sun Chinese umbrellas made of lacquered paper, and Shira handed one to Temima as well. The three women proceeded under these parasols down the path that cut through the center of the village, lined with date palm trees and blooming cactuses and succulents in clay pots. Along the way Em-Kol-Hai speaking in English with an unfiltered New York accent pointed out some of the major landmarks—the Bedouin tents, the largest and most elaborate housing Abba Kadosh himself surrounded by smaller satellite facsimiles each allocated to a wife or a concubine and her children, with similar constellations on a lesser scale revolving around other men and their households.

Two wooden structures stood out for their size. The first, Em-Kol-Hai said, was Health House in which the women gave birth in the most natural and enlightened manner, lovingly supported by their sisters, birth control was of course strictly forbidden in Bnei HaElohim, and where spa services were provided to paying guests and spiritual seekers. Temima's eyes came to rest on a large sculpture in front of the entrance to this building fashioned out of metal depicting a bulb and syringe set at an angle on a stone base as if taking aim like a cannon.

"That's our monument to the enema," said Em-Kol-Hai. "We're renowned throughout the Holy Land as the place to go for the best enemas, five-star high colonics. We believe in full body irrigation, cleansing outside and inside."

The second structure was the kitchen where the freshest food was prepared from the green plants of the earth and the fruit of the trees explicitly given to us to eat by God when He first created the world, free of the taint of anything that might once have had eyes or a mother; alcoholic beverages, with the exception of wine for blessings made from organic grapes, and drugs of any kind from tobacco to you name it were absolutely off-limits, they were pollutants banned from the body as well as from the village, both holy temples whose desecration was a grave sin, all violations severely punished. Alongside the kitchen was a spacious pavilion with a roof of linked trellises bedecked with palm fronds and dried herbs, the floor spread with straw mats and lined with cushions and low banquettes; this was the dining hall, synagogue, village green, all-purpose meeting place, Em-Kol-Hai explained. There were also smaller wooden buildings, bungalows and cottages and huts for guests of the spa and the ashram, and here and there hammocks hung woven from multicolored strings.

Along the way they encountered no signs of human life except for one girl, perhaps thirteen years old, jumping rope while a little boy crawled around on the ground nearby stuffing fistfuls of dirt into his mouth. Em-Kol-Hai stepped up to her, whispered something in her ear, then gave her a sharp smack on the behind, at which the young girl scooped up the child, straddled him on her hip, and ran off into one of the tents. It was only then that Temima noticed that Em-Kol-Hai's left hand was missing; she had whacked the girl with her stump.

They continued on past the hub of the village climbing a short distance until they came to the opening of a large cave in the mountainside. "Our

VIP quarters, our superdeluxe suite," Em-Kol-Hai said. "Your reputation has preceded you. Abba Kadosh, prophet and messiah, regards you as something like a colleague. He has given specific orders to treat you like visiting royalty, like the Queen of Sheba."

This was where Temima was to be accommodated, and there was nothing she lacked. The floor was covered with deep burgundy Bokhara rugs, the walls lined with tapestries depicting in sequence the story recounted in the first chapters of the book of Genesis—the six days of creation and the seventh of rest, a black Adam and Hava in the Garden of Eden, the serpent and the expulsion, the tragedy of the first brothers Cain and Abel—drawn in a delightful primitive style in vivid primary colors with all of the human figures garbed in fur pelts like prehistoric cave dwellers.

Books, writing materials, linens and clothing modest but suitable for the hot climate, proper lighting, everything was provided for Temima's comfort, she could leave the cave at will for her pleasure, but all of her necessities were brought to her like room service. Three times a day her meals were delivered by one of several young girls between the ages of eleven and fourteen, Temima estimated, often carrying in a pouch on her back a little boy no older than three whose hair had not yet been cut. One day she complimented one of them on how nicely she took care of her little brother. The girl opened her eyes wide as if incredulous that there could be in this world someone as uninformed as Temima, and said, "He's not my brother. He's my husband."

This was confirmed to Temima by Shira Silver Kedaisha, her designated lady-in-waiting, on one of the many walks and hikes they took through the stark wilderness terrain and the wadis down to the Dead Sea, excursions during which over time the two women grew increasingly close. Shira had been working as a nature guide in the area when she first encountered Abba Kadosh, prophet and messiah. She held Temima's hand as they climbed the steep cliffs and explored the caves, she named the birds soaring overhead or perched on crags—buzzards, falcons, pelicans, once even a golden eagle, the hoopoe, the bulbul—lizards underfoot, everywhere the ibex. She gathered wild flowers and braided them into wreaths with which they crowned one another as they descended the rocky bluffs past the salt marshes, the mountains of Edom and Moab a twilight purple in the distance on the Jordanian side, and bathed naked in secluded freshwater springs she found for them, or lay on their backs floating on the saltwater bed four hundred meters below sea level, silent and inward in each other's company for hours and now and then talking.

Hadn't Temima wondered about the striking scarcity of young men in Bnei HaElohim? Shira asked. There were in fact very few men in general in the village; it was populated primarily by women and girls ruled over by the patriarchs, the exclusive circle of older men from the original exodus of liberated black slaves who had arrived with Abba Kadosh, prophet and messiah. Some, like Abba Kadosh himself, came with first wives, such as the matriarch Em-Kol-Hai, a Jewish woman from the Bronx known then as Hedda Minsky, a lawyer trained at Fordham night school who had gotten Abba Kadosh out of Yazoo City and into Israel, claiming her rights under the Law of Return, and spiriting all of them under her Jewish skirts into the Promised Land where they have remained ever since as illegal squatters here in this remote and inhospitable corner of the universe not far from the desert canyon where the Romans starved out the band of Bar-Kokhba rebels, the caves of Ein Gedi where the bipolar King Saul pursued the young godfather David, the cataclysmic ruins of Sodom and Gomorrah, the suicide rock of Masada. To this very day the inhabitants of Bnei HaElohim were not officially recognized by the government of Israel as Jews but were classified as a cult or sect, they had no rights as citizens. So much for the ingathering of exiles.

As for the absence of young men in the village, Shira told Temima, it did not take Abba Kadosh long to realize that in a patriarchal community very few patriarchs are required to propagate the seed. Just a handful was needed—in fact, the fewer the better to retain reproductive supremacy and sustain the line. Young men were threatening, they were dangerous rivals for receptive females, they were rogue elements who had to be subordinated or eliminated. It was a situation not so different, Shira said, from the mating strategies of other animal herds in the wild ruled by a dominant male figure.

Abba Kadosh, prophet and messiah, and the old men who accompanied him here on the middle passage were committed to surviving as the main breeders, the dominant males. And so, when a child was born, if it was a girl, she was allowed to remain in the community. All of the girls were called Zippora bat Cushi. No offense intended by Cushi by the way, which for some people has a connotation kind of like the n-word, Shira put in hastily; here in Bnei HaElohim, though, it stands for black pride, she took pains to elaborate. Most of these Zipporas bat Cushis were given at a very young age to one of the old men as either a wife or a concubine—whom she was given to and her destined status in the household always determined by the powers of spiritual penetration of Abba Kadosh, prophet and messiah. You could think of it as a kind of variation of the droit du seigneur theme. A few of the girls, however, were allowed to reach puberty unclaimed until they were married off to a much younger boy who, upon his birth, based on Abba Kadosh's mystical insights into the baby's nature, had been granted the right to stay within the community, a privilege that could of course at any time be revoked depending on the character traits he manifested as he developed, the male aggression factor. This was something you could think of as a variation on the eunuch theme, a beta male. All of the boys, those who were kept and those who were unloaded, were called Zephania ben Cushi. That was the name of the prophet Zephania's father—Cushi—as Temima surely knew, it's straight from the text, maybe he was from the land of Cush, maybe he was black.

In any event, before a Zephania ben Cushi who was selected to remain reached the age of three, as soon as he was old enough to pronounce correctly the words *Harei-at-mikudeshet-li*, one of the Zipporas set aside for this purpose was given to him in marriage. Thereafter, as the wife consecrated to him, this Zippora was charged with tending to him until he grew up as a way of gaining practice and hands-on experience in the care of a husband—feeding him, changing him, cleaning him, playing with him, nursing him when he was sick, and so on. These were the girls carrying their husbands on their backs who served Temima in her cave. But the majority of the Zephanias by far who were born in the village were judged to be budding alpha males, unfit for a patriarchal lifestyle, with incipient wild and disruptive and rebellious and competitive tendencies evident to Abba Kadosh immediately from birth. Every newborn son throw into the Nile, and every daughter let live, as Pharaoh commanded the midwives in Egypt concerning the Hebrew slaves. Within the first year of their lives these Zephanias were taken away and deposited in adoption agencies in Panama or Puerto Rico by Em-Kol-Hai, who as an authorized Jew with the rabbinical stamp of approval could leave the country and return at will; several times each year, she would travel back and forth for this purpose, to unload the latest crop of dangerous black baby boys. This had been the fate of Shira's own baby, her Zephania ben Cushi, she told Temima, taken from her arms and transported to an orphanage in Latin America—"And I did nothing to prevent it," Shira wailed. She raised her voice and wept so loud that a male ibex stopped in his tracks and pricked his ears stiffly upward as she howled, great tears rolling down her cheeks, adding to the salt of the sea.

After she lost her Zephania ben Cushi, Abba Kadosh stopped bothering her. This was the word he used for the act—bothering—since he taught that according to the Torah woman possessed no will or desire of her own and if she did seem to possess a will or desire it was illusion and emptiness, of no consequence. A woman did not choose but was chosen; she was the property first of her father and then of her husband, to be disposed of as they saw fit, she was merely a vessel for use by a man, like your neighbor's house or his ox or his ass or anything at all that belonged to your neighbor, a possession you were forbidden to covet as stated explicitly in the tenth commandment. Not that Abba Kadosh ever exactly forced himself on a woman, he merely believed the act of bothering to be an expression of the male will, initiated by the man. "I will stop bothering you because you are too sad, you depress me," he had declared to Shira one day. The man's decision to stop bothering, Shira explained, was in essence the only form of birth control practiced in the village—that, and breastfeeding for as long as humanly possible.

By now Abba Kadosh had already stopped bothering legions of women, Shira went on, including some time ago his head wife, Em-Kol-Hai, a mother of ten, because, as he said, she no longer turned him on, she was too old and too fat and with each passing year more and more resembled a man, she had a beard of stiff bristles on her chin that she didn't even have the decency to pluck and a dark brooding mustache that revolted him. To tell the truth, Shira said, Em-Kol-Hai seemed very relieved not to be bothered anymore, and since then this woman, who was already such a force, has truly come into her own, effectively running every aspect of the entire Bnei HaElohim operation with, you might say, one hand tied behind her back. Temima had surely noticed her missing right hand. It was cut off when she assaulted an Israeli government official inspecting the village as part of the campaign to get them evicted who had dared to raise a fist to strike Abba Kadosh, prophet and messiah. Em-Kol-Hai did not hesitate for one minute—she went straight for his testicles. This is explicitly forbidden in the Torah. In such cases, even if the woman is standing up for her man, you must cut off her hand, the Torah commands this. You must show no pity—those are the words of the Torah.

As for Shira herself, the musical concubine whom Abba Kadosh had once called his *Pilegesh* of Oud, she was now in charge of the voices; she was the choir director, thanks to her Juilliard training. It was a gospel chorus made up of the beta boys whose voices had not yet changed, and other assorted surviving males for the lower registers. Mostly they sang Negro spirituals or verses from Scripture set to music that Shira composed accompanied by a small orchestra of women sitting behind a curtain playing ancient biblical instruments. Shira herself also conducted from behind this screen while Melekh Sinai stood at the podium waving his arms around pretending to be doing the job and getting all the credit. They performed throughout the country to packed houses, they were very popular, up there on the charts, very much in demand, they even made some records that sold very well and contributed substantially to the income of the community. Hadn't Temima ever heard of them? She should step out of her cave on her own one day into the sunlight and face the music.

But what is the attraction of this man, this Abba Kadosh, that he could exercise such power over you? This is what Temima wanted to understand from Shira. How is your beloved better than another, most fair of women? How is your beloved superior to another that you have sworn yourself to him in this way? They were lying naked in the shade of a tamarisk tree in a secluded corner of the oasis of Ein Feshkha, near the pool of spring water in which they had just bathed. Shira was basking in the memory of how Temima had called her My Batsheva as they washed in the pool; surely the meaning of this was deeper than a reference to Bathsheba abducted from her bath. Shira wanted to reflect on this, but the question Temima had just posed sprang into life between them and would not be still. She sat up, folding her pale lean body, wrapping her arms around her drawn-up legs and lowering her forehead onto the caps of her knees so that her long red hair, wet and curly, cascaded forward. She raised her head, smoothed back her hair with both hands, and looked at Temima through pale lashes. "He is whole, complete, his inner peace and self-assurance are like nothing else I've ever experienced, it's what I've been searching for all my life, it flows out of him to me, to all of us, all of his women, yet he still makes me feel as if I'm the only one, I feel no jealousy, I feel calm, serene, at peace for the first time in my life, he gives me everything I need, he makes me feel as if my life has meaning, for the first time in my life I feel I'm not just matter, I feel I matter."

All this was delivered rhapsodically, as if on a single sustained breath. Shira turned to look behind her at a pillar of salt petrified in an anguished formation—Lot's wife?—nameless, voiceless. "Self-realization by surrender to a higher force," Shira pushed on, groping for the words to explain, convince. "For me, he is the end, the ultimate, like the messiah. Maybe you think I'm brainwashed, but what it is really is the purity of surrender. I am like clay in the hands of the creator—he can shape me any way he wants. Into his hands I entrust my spirit—and with my spirit, my body. He is a force of nature, he can take me where I want to go—carry me straight up to the heights." She gave Temima a rueful smile, coughed out a little laugh as if tuning an instrument, squeezed her eyes shut, then lifted her arms palms upward, opening up in song, letting her voice be heard as if everything that preceded had been recitative and now came the aria—Lord get me high, Get me high, Get me high, Lord get me high, Get me high. Higher and higher, Higher and higher, Lord get me high, Get me high.

The gospel choir was called Kol-Koreh-BaMidbar. Temima's inner eye alit on the verse in the book of Isaiah—A voice rings out in the desert!—from the post-traumatic fortieth chapter, Comfort, O Comfort My people. Melekh Sinai was conducting from a podium in the pavilion, his back twitching to the audience at a specially called town meeting that everyone was required to attend when Temima stepped out of her cave that morning and heard the singing. She approached and stood listening behind the women and girls seated in the rear on the straw mats separated from the men and boys in the front section of the congregation by a line of potted sabra plants heavy with prickly fruit. It was a rendition of the spiritual "Sometimes I Feel Like a Motherless Child"—the sweet harmony of the high-pitched little boys' voices lined up in front, the baritones and basses, including a few full-grown men, in the row rising behind them. The full year of mourning for her baby Kook Immanuel had not yet passed and she was still in need of comforting. It was as if the music were stabbing her heart; no wonder the sages forbade music during this period, not because of its pleasure but for its pain. Off in a corner to the right Temima could see the curtain stirring softly in and out as if breathing. Behind this she knew sat Shira conducting her small orchestra of women striving to stay together with the singers now invisible whom she had rehearsed rigorously in private, passing the baton in the public arena to a man, as was required.

When the performance ended, the congregation rose as one, linked arms, the men with the men, the women with the women, and, swaying from side to side, broke out in the ecstatic refrain from the hymn, "Amen." But in the Bnei HaElohim version, "Amen" was replaced with "Elmore" in glorification of Abba Kadosh, prophet and messiah, whose slave name had been Elmore Clinton; the refrain was transformed into a cry of longing for the imminent grace of Abba Kadosh's divine presence— El-More, El-More, El-more, Elmore Elmore.

The members of the gospel chorus melted away into the singing swaying crowd nearly overcome with the anticipated arrival of Abba Kadosh, prophet and messiah. Melekh Sinai turned his lectern to face the audience, pulled out a Tanakh from the compartment underneath, and set it down on its slanted desk. As if by a chop from above, the singing was cut off, the entire congregation was struck silent and dropped to the ground in full prostration so that Temima, standing alone in the rear, had an unobstructed view when she laid eyes on Abba Kadosh for the first time. He appeared as if he had descended, like one of the Nephilim, a giant son of the gods who had fallen to earth to cohabit with the daughters of men. He was a glowing apparition in white, long white linen tunic with fringes at its four corners each cluster coiled in azure string, loose white linen breeches, a white linen sash and a regal white turban, like the vestments of the high priest when he entered the Holy of Holies on Yom Kippur day. Sunglasses concealed his eyes. He was holding an African walking stick carved out of ebony wood crowned with the coiled figure of a serpent for a handle. From his shoulders and upward he stood taller than all the people, and, despite what must have been his sixty-plus years, he was still vigorous and manly, a hint of cushioning around the middle inviting a place to rest your head, full lips, wide flaring nostrils, rich black beard with no streaks of gray or fading, skin like dark chocolate so smooth, none of its ripeness fled, eyes almost silver, like mirrored glass, with no signs of dimming, which he took off his dark glasses to reveal, fixing them unblinking straight ahead directly upon Temima, sending out beams to pierce her soul. When he judged that he had taken in enough of this bold antagonist, the only other person not counting Melekh Sinai still left standing in the ring, he put his shades back on, turned to his right, and passed his walking stick to his jittery sidekick in position behind the lectern.

With an upward gesture of his arms, his large hands outspread palms up, he sang out in a voice that seemed to come from fathoms deep within him, "Rise up, holy brothers and sisters, rise up, Bnei HaElohim! Lift up your voices—El-More, More-El, we cannot have enough of El, Elohim, Adonai, Shaddai, Yah, Yahweh, more and more and more El!" This incantation levitated the entire congregation as one and transported it once again into its rapturous refrain of El-more, El-more, El-more, Elmore Elmore, until with his massive right hand Abba Kadosh, prophet and messiah, made a slicing motion and pronounced, Cut!—and instantly there was complete silence broken only by a steady rhythmic beat, as of a donkey swatting its fly-infested tail against the trunk of a tree.

"My holy, holy brothers and sisters," Abba Kadosh boomed out. "For thousands of years we of the ten tribes of Israel were lost in the uttermost West, but our hearts—our hearts have always been here in the East, the Middle East. We have suffered countless woes and vexations, my holy, holy brothers and sisters, descendants of the black tribes of Reuven, Shimon, Yisashar, Zevulun, Gad, Dan, Asher, Naftali, Menashe, and Ephraim—six hundred million holocausts, slavery and torture, maiming and mutilation, beatings and blows, death and disease, disgrace and humiliation, but now our wandering days are over, we have crossed the mighty river Sambatyon roiling with stones, we have crossed over the sweet rolling Jordan and come home at last to the heaven of the Promised Land, we black Jews of the ten lost tribes. Even if the rabbis reject us, even if the Mishna despots and the Gemara oppressors—the Talmud tyrants— in their arrogant certitude spurn our claims as authentic Jews, we have the holy Torah on our side, and the God of the original Hebrew Bible says to us, Truly Ephraim is a dear son to me." Abba Kadosh turned to Melekh Sinai at the podium at his right and commanded, "Jeremiah, chapter thirty-one, verse twenty—Read!" Melekh Sinai jumped as if sprung out of a far-off realm in which he had been marinating in daydreams, fumbled to find the place and read out loud in Hebrew, stumbling in his confusion.

"Ephraim is surely the son who is so precious to Me, the little boy I used to delight in dandling. Even as I speak of him I remember him as a child and My innermost self longs for him. Therefore I shall truly truly pity him still. These are the words of the Lord."

Cries of Say it, Brother Abba! and Read it, Brother Melekh! and Amen Selah! and El-More, El-More! and Mashiakh, Mashiakh, Mashiakh, ay-yay-yay-yay-yay! and Hallelujah! rang out from the men's section of the congregation. Women closed their eyes and pumped both arms feverishly upward toward the heavens, many wept and there were some who even collapsed in a faint. Abba Kadosh nodded his head, a beneficent half smile on his lips, then pushed his hands forward palms out as if against a headwind to put a stop to this passionate outpouring. "And He *has* taken pity on Ephraim, which, as you know, is my true ancestral tribe, my holy, holy brothers and sisters, He has taken pity on all of us. He has brought us home—home to the East. The Lord says to us, Welcome home Ephraim, welcome home y'all to the Middle East where you belong, my children. The Lord is on our side, and that's good enough for us. What do we care about the dried-out, meat-eating, neutered old chopped-liver gefilte-fish rabbis when we have the Lord on our side? The Torah is on our side—what more do we need?—and we are on the the the side of the Torah. And that, my dear friends, is why I have called upon you to gather here today, to fulfill as best we can the Lord's commandment in His Torah concerning a prodigal son." He turned to Melekh Sinai. "Deuteronomy, chapter twenty-one, verses eighteen through twenty-one—Read!" There was a bookmark already in place; Melekh Sinai found it instantly and read an abbreviated version: "If a man has a disobedient and rebellious son who doesn't listen to his father . . . they should seize him and take him before the elders of the town . . . and all the men of his city should stone him to death and thus you will root out the evil from your midst and all Israel will hear and fear."

"Unfortunately, my children," Abba Kadosh continued, "because of the difficult circumstances we face in relation to the racist rabbinical bosses who still refuse to recognize and welcome us as fellow Jews here in the East, the Middle East, as much as we might feel obliged to obey to the letter the Lord's command in His Torah with regard to the matter of a disobedient and rebellious son, we cannot at this time risk provoking the powers-that-be by going all the way with the stoning. For this, we must await the blessed hour that the Messiah ben David can shed his incognito and reveal himself to one and all. Nevertheless, my holy, holy brothers and sisters, we do the best we can. Forty lashes we administer to my disobedient and rebellious son, my *ben sorer u'moreh*—'forty lashes but not more,' Deuteronomy chapter twenty-five, verse three," Abba Kadosh said, this time not even troubling to order Melekh Sinai to read—"and, I might add, not less than forty, none of this namby-pamby thirty-nine business of the hypocrite rabbis pretending to be nice guys, we go strictly by the book and our book is the Torah. So join me, my holy, holy brothers and sisters—join me as we complete the required punishment of a *ben sorer u'moreh*, which, I tell you as his father, hurts me more than it hurts him. Count along with me so that you too may partake of this great mitzvah. Sing it out, loud and strong—Thirty-seven, Thirty-eight, Thirty-nine, Forty!"

As the crowd counted down the last numbers in unison with rising fervor punctuated by the whip's lash, a cry of horror sprang from Temima's throat like a demonic creature with a life of its own. How had it happened that she had not noticed what everyone else present recognized as the main event, the occasion for the gathering, unfolding before her very eyes? Perhaps it was because what she now was witnessing was to her mind a primitive relic from an archaic age that her rational self dismissed, rejected, refused to absorb or believe could still happen, perhaps it was because the young boy stripped to the waist, his arms wrapped around one of the pillars that held up the trellised roof of the pavilion with his hands bound did not let out a single sound as the whip scourged his naked back in rhythmic lashes. But now she was screaming, "Savages, savages!" as Abba Kadosh took off his sunglasses and fixed her with his metallic gaze.

"I take it that the holy lady is not aware that in our community women do not raise their voices to be heard in public," he said coolly. "It is most immodest. However, we shall make allowance for you this time—it is an understandable lapse due to your ignorance. The boy—yes, I admit it, this wicked boy is my son—he has been caught prowling around our village. I have forbidden him to enter our camp even from the days when he was a mere infant for I perceived his true nature from the moment of his birth and named him accordingly, the only one of our sons not called Zephania. Yishmael I called him, like Father Abraham's son by Hagar who even that great lady Mother Sarah had to kick out of the house for fooling with little Isaac, same like Father Isaac when he was a grown man fooled around with Mother Rebekah. But boy messing with boy? That's abomination, plain and simple. This here Yishmael, no way I was going to take any chances with him, a defiant and wayward son from the very beginning, I could see that with my inner vision. Now you see his reward. He is a wild donkey of a boy, this Yishmael—and this is what you do to a wild donkey. You flog him until you break his spirit and he learns his lesson."

By now the boy's hands had been untied and he was turned around to face the crowd, held in place by two enforcers, one on each side. Temima recognized Ibn Kadosh, startling in his resemblance to his father she now saw, even more so now as they were positioned within the same frame— the same insolent translucent eyes, a younger, slenderer, lighter-skinned cinnamon-colored version. But it was not just the physical likeness that was so remarkable. The kinship was above all evident in the force of his bearing and pride, in the sensuous connection.

She began to move forward, plowing through the women's section, over the spiky barrier of plants, cutting through the men who moved to prevent her progress, but Abba Kadosh, prophet and messiah, forestalled them. "That's okay my holy, holy brothers, let her come, let her come, bring her on, I can handle her." And as she advanced she was declaiming, "Do you really know your Torah? Did you follow the procedure to the letter? Are you aware that there never has been a *ben sorer u'moreh* and never will be? And do you know why? Because no true parent would ever bring his own child before the elders of the city to be stoned."

"Watch it, sister—you already crossed one line in approaching me, don't try crossing another." Abba Kadosh took Temima in fully with his wolf eyes. "Know before whom you are standing, sister: Abba Kadosh, the holy father—as you are the holy mother. You above all should know that there are times when it is necessary for those in our position to sacrifice one of our children to save all the others."

Chilled by memory, Temima nevertheless plunged ahead. "Let him go this instant," she cried.

Smiling intimately as if he knew all there was to know about her, Abba Kadosh nodded to the two men restraining the boy who immediately released him.

"Come with me, Ibn Kadosh," Temima said. "I will clean you up and bandage you, and give you some water to drink."

With eyes pale gray like ash smoking with contempt, Ibn Kadosh implicated them all; only the corner of his lower lip trembled almost imperceptibly. "I am looking for my mother," he said, aiming his words solely at Temima. "I am thinking maybe she is here with you. My mother she is lost. I must to find my mother." And in a flash he turned, ran off and vanished, swift of foot, the fastest runner in the land, like Asa'el the doomed brother of Yoav ben Zeruya in pursuit of Abner ben Ner, setting in motion a cycle of violence and revenge.

Toward evening of that day the matriarch Em-Kol-Hai Kedosha appeared at the opening of the cave and called to Temima to come out for a moment; there was something of importance that she had been delegated to give to her. Out of respect for this older, enduring woman, Temima rose and stepped forth. Without a word, Em-Kol-Hai handed her a sheet of paper rolled up like a telescope along with a number two pencil. As Temima unfurled it Em-Kol-Hai commented, "Just in case you're concerned, I'm one-hundred-percent okay with this. No problem, honey."

The document was decorated with an ornate border depicting the emblems on the banners of the ten lost tribes of Israel—mandrake, scale, ass, ship, tent, olive tree, and so on, with the bull, the standard of Abba Kadosh's tribe Ephraim, the largest and most dominant, mounted on top. Within this frame was a brief message in exquisite calligraphy: "Abba Kadosh has the pleasure to invite you to join his household." Below that were the words "Check One," followed by three blank boxes, with a single choice next to each—Wife, Concubine, Other. That explains the pencil, Temima figured; another scribe for my sins. Shaking her head in disbelief, she stared with wide open eyes at Em-Kol-Hai while her hands acting independently as if they were not fully attached to her tore the paper into smaller and smaller bits, letting them swirl slowly to the ground, and then she let the pencil drop too. Em-Kol-Hai, heaving a weary sigh, like someone who had lived through this before, a tiresome rerun demanding all the necessary motions once again, squatted down. With the stump of her left arm she pushed the fragments and the pencil together to gather them up more efficiently, then her right hand closed around the entire heap to grasp it. As she performed this chore she said, "I want to remind you that Bnei HaElohim is part of the Holy Land. We do not desecrate the ground of the Holy Land by littering." She rose with a groan, her stump massaging her hip, and stuffed the shredded pieces into a pocket of her kaftan. "He will prevail, sweetie," she said, "he always does. You will find in yourself the correct answer and then you will consent."

Temima remained standing there watching until the heavy figure of Em-Kol-Hai Kedosha receded into the heart of the village before turning and going back into her cave where Shira Silver Kedaisha was still sitting at the table with a notebook open before her, exactly as Temima had left her when the matriarch paid her call. Shira had arrived soon after the events of the morning to plead with Temima not to leave in the wake of her shock at what she had witnessed in the pavilion. As Temima reentered the cave, Shira said, "You don't have to tell me, I know everything. I'm begging you, Temima, please don't go. It will be the end of me. And we have only just started our work." The work was a commentary on the Tanakh beginning at the beginning with Genesis, *Bereishit*, which Temima was dictating and Shira was taking down. They had reached the first two words of the third verse, *VaYomer Elohim*, And God said—God's first recorded words. It had been just after Temima recounted to Shira how the Toiter had told her that merely taking in those two words—the Lord speaking!—left him so overwhelmed he could go no further that the matriarch Em-Kol-Hai appeared at the opening of the cave. Now Shira said to Temima, "Maybe those two words *VaYomer Elohim* were too much for the Toiter, but they're not too much for us. We women move on. Forgive me, but the Toiter is a dead end. We are life. I don't say this to hurt you, Temima. I know you loved him."

Temima closed her eyes. "So. In the beginning there was chaos and emptiness and darkness over the face of the deep and the spirit of the Lord sweeping over the face of the water. And God said, Let there be light. Creation through words. Take words along with you, and return to HaShem."

Over the course of the next week, at unpredictable times during the day, the entire Bnei HaElohim gospel chorus Kol-Koreh-BaMidbar under the baton of Melekh Sinai would materialize outside the entrance to Temima's cave to woo her in the name of Abba Kadosh, prophet and messiah, with verses set to music by Shira Silver Kedaisha from the Song of Songs. Behold you are beautiful, my love, your eyes like doves; Like a rose among thorns, this is my beloved among the maidens; You are completely beautiful, my love, without a blemish; With me, from Lebanon, with me my bride, come; You are beautiful my love like Tirza, lovely like Jerusalem.

Temima was in spite of herself amused, in spite of herself flattered, but as it continued day after day with no end in sight she grew more and more drained and defeated, it availed her nothing to call out from inside her cave Shoo, shoo—go away, scram, scoot, get lost. Melekh Sinai was a well-trained soldier and he was just obeying orders handed directly down from Abba Kadosh, prophet and messiah. Finally, in full awareness that what she was doing might be interpreted as a softening on her part, the first hint of yielding, she handed him a note to pass along to his master in which she parried with a citation also from the Song of Songs—Do not awaken and do not stir up love until it please.

This move earned her a brief respite, but when nothing more was forthcoming, Melkh Sinai appeared one day minus his backup singers at the entrance to the cave to inquire if there was any further message to be delivered to Abba Kadosh. "The message is," Temima replied without hesitation, "And the Queen Vashti refused to come at the king's command conveyed by his eunuch."

The next morning when Temima stepped out of her cave she found gathered there all of Abba Kadosh's wives and concubines, a small crowd, she did not have the heart to count how many, standing in complete silence. Each had her left breast bared over her heart, from the sagging breast of Em-Kol-Hai Kedosha to the small, still-ripe breast of Shira Silver Kedaisha to the promise of a breast flagged only by the bulletpoint of a dark nipple of a little girl four years old at most. The vigil continued for several mornings until Temima could bear it no longer, especially painful to her was the sight of Shira's humiliation. She slipped a note into the pocket of Em-Kol-Hai's kaftan pivoting on a reference to the words of the matriarch Naomi in the book of Ruth. "Shaddai the God of breasts has dealt very bitterly with me."

Two days later, Abba Kadosh himself ascended the slope to Temima's cave trailed a short distance behind by Melekh Sinai leading an ass laden with gifts—baskets overflowing with fruit and bread and olives, dates and figs and nuts, garments and cloths in brilliant colors and intricate embroideries, pottery and jewelry. He stood at the entrance and called to Temima. When she emerged reluctantly he slowly and very frankly looked her over up and down, his silver eyes coming to rest at last on her eyes, not taking them off of her for a moment.

"You have been flirting with me, my holy sister Temima," he said in a playfully chiding tone, his deep voice so soft and intimate she was obliged to move her head subtly forward to absorb his words. "I have heard the true message in your messages, and therefore I have taken the unprecedented step of coming to you instead of you coming to me as by right you ought to have done, as the Queen of Sheba came to King Solomon bearing gifts. I knew the Queen of Sheba in my time, and you are no Queen of Sheba. You're more of an Avigail, the very clever and very handsome wife of Naval the Carmelite with an excellent figure like yours I might add, but even Avigail had the good sense to come to David instead of obliging him to lower himself by coming to her because she foresaw that he was the chosen one and from him would come the anointed line. That was one smart lady, Avigail. She knew what was good for her, sister Temima—learn a lesson from Avigail. For your sake, my holy sister, I am abasing myself and reversing the roles. I have turned myself into a woman for you, sister, I have come to you as a supplicant bearing gifts like Avigail, and I say to you, Leave that worthless, wretched husband of yours, your lowlife Naval, a vile man, a boor, his name tells it all. I am entrusting my fate to you, I am putting myself in your hands."

He continued in this fashion without pause, opening no space for Temima to insert herself. He was placing himself in her hands, he said, by inviting her on a short excursion; he was offering to take her out of the country for a few days, a very risky step for a man in his position who was regarded as a lethal alien by the rabbis and might not be allowed back in again to the Jewish State. But to show his commitment to her he was prepared to take this risk, to trust in her good will and her connections to protect him from the Who-Is-A-Jew cops. He would take her to Amsterdam, to Holland, to the holy grave of the former Marrano, Rabbi Menashe ben Israel, who believed without a taint of doubt the traveler's report that the Indians of America who had welcomed him over the mountains with the Shema Yisrael, Hear-O-Israel, were the descendants of a lost tribe of Israel. Thereafter, Abba Kadosh said to Temima, the holy former Marrano Rabbi Menashe ben Israel devoted his writing and all of his diplomatic efforts to hasten the dispersal of the Jews throughout the world, which must precede the ingathering of the exiles and the messianic age, in accordance with Scripture, Even if your outcasts are at the far ends of the world, from there the Lord your God will gather you and from there He will fetch you.

"I will await your response to my invitation, my holy sister Temima—no pressure," Abba Kadosh said, concluding his case. "Search within yourself, go to the very depths of your being, go down to the lowest place on this earth, go to the Dead Sea below, there your true course will be revealed to you." He turned, took a few paces away from her, mounted the ass that had been unloaded while he was petitioning Temima, and, with Melekh Sinai walking ahead clutching the rope attached to the halter, rode back to the village.

Down at the Dead Sea, Temima walked all day among the seekers after youth and beauty, bathing in the salt waters, soaking under the sun, the ailing and sick desperate for a cure for their mortal bodies, stricken with consumption, fever, and inflammation, with the boils and hemorrhoids and itch of Egypt, with madness, blindness, and confusion of the heart, with infection at the knees and the thighs, pustules from the soles of the feet to the crown of the head, terrible and lasting plagues, malignant and chronic disease. As the sun was setting over the hills of Judea and Jerusalem she heard nearby a song the Toiter used to sing—The pangs of the Messiah, Here they come, Here they come, Today. She saw a small figure in a wheelchair, agonizingly contorted, covered entirely with black mud, taking the cure, surrounded by men dressed in immaculate white, his attendants. She drew closer; his eyes were focused on the void, as if he were blind. "Elisha?" she asked, but he did not acknowledge her, addressing instead the darkening skies beyond.

"It is the Beginning of the Redemption, daughter," he said, "*Atkhalta de'Geula*. The black man is the precursor—the Messiah son of Joseph, from the lost tribe of Ephraim. The staff he carries is the staff of the Messiah, passed down from Adam through the generations to the warrior Hephzibah known in the language of strange nations as Hazel who passed it to her son, the black man Messiah son of Joseph of the tribe of Ephraim, who will in turn find a way to pass it on to you. He is fated to suffer a terrible end. You are fated to hasten the end. You are the end. Whatever he tells you, listen to his voice."

On the only night they spent in Amsterdam, Abba Kadosh took Temima along the canals to the old section of the city near the train station where the prostitutes were on display. They strolled past the narrow buildings packed together as if propping each other up like war casualties, the glass storefronts on the lower levels backlit in visceral red showcasing for sale women for every taste, all sizes and shapes, every color, practically every age. As they window-shopped, he challenged her to put her finger on the G-spot in the Tanakh where prostitution is explicitly prohibited. It cannot be found because it doesn't exist, he declaimed. The harlot was an accepted fact of life, fulfilling a recognized male need. Judah stops off for some necessary recreational relief with a whore by the roadside in Timna, and only later discovers that she happens to be his daughter-in-law, Tamar, who had already buried two of his sons—Er whom the good Lord just didn't much care for, and Onan, whose name has become synonymous with the nasty stuff he thought he was doing in secret. And then there's Rahab the *zona*. The two spies sent by Joshua to check out the land take a little earned break, some R & R on their first stop in Jericho with this ho in the wall, Rahab, completely routine—and the rest is history. And while we're on the subject, how about a round of applause for Gomer daughter of Divlayim, who gets honorable mention by name—the hooker God Himself commanded Hosea to take for a wife as a visual aid to how our people had prostituted themselves.

And speaking of our people, Abba Kadosh went on, in our own holy land of Israel, I'm proud to report, prostitution is a leading growth industry. Percentage-wise, more men in the Holy Land take advantage of this ancient privilege than in any other country on earth, according to the statistics my sources tell me—what with all the stress, the tension, the pressures, religious, political, basic survival, etcetera etcetera, a man needs an outlet, you would expect no less, we Jews are number one as always. Even the uptight rabbis of the Talmud gave the go-ahead to unload in a whore in cases of pent-up horniness; with no outlet short of self-abuse, spilling and wasting your seed like the aforesaid Onan, completely forbidden, naturally, a man could burst apart at the seams. And our whores, by the way, were expected to give tithes from their earnings to the Temple like any working woman, further proof that the business was considered totally normal. His own name, Kadosh—holy, consecrated, separated, set apart—was also relevant to this topic, he declared. The women of his household could be a holy wife *kedosha*, yes, but from the very same root and just as worthy was a holy concubine *kedaisha*, which some might define as a harlot but to his mind was simply another aspect of the feminine emanation of the divine presence, equally holy. Everything on this earth contains both itself and its opposite, Abba Kadosh said; the *kedaisha* is also *kedosha*, consecrated and set apart. These are the deep, deep thoughts of the Kabbalists, the mystics, the Hasidim—they get it. After the Tanakh, they're my boys.

The next morning, in a courtly gesture of gratitude for the night, as a special treat, Abba Kadosh rented two bicycles for the short ride out of the city to the old Jewish cemetery where Rabbi Menashe ben Israel is buried. Temima had never ridden a bicycle before; it was not something Boro Park girls were taught to do, they did not mount, they were mounted, they did not straddle, they sidesaddled in their skirts. But Abba Kadosh insisted, and spreading wide his strong arms, one hand gripping the handlebars and the other firmly on the back of the seat, he held her steady as she wobbled and swayed, the two of them laughing carefree as he ran alongside until he let go and she was triumphantly launched. It was astonishing how quickly she mastered it—but what after all had her life been until then but a fine balancing act? Whatever had transpired between them in the past and however the future might unfold, Temima knew she would always be indebted to Abba Kadosh for forcing her to get up on two slender wheels and go.

"When the messiah comes, it won't be a man on a white donkey but a woman on a white bike," Temima sang out over her shoulder to Abba Kadosh pedaling behind her as they rode over the flat green country-side along the Amstel River to Ouderkerk, past windmills and dikes and quaint little churches and tulips and wooden shoes. Had they not been such a bizarre looking couple as if from another millennium, another planet, Planet Bible, it would have been a flawless picture postcard.

At the gravesite Abba Kadosh reverentially intoned the words, "The Hope of Israel," which was also the title of Rabbi Menashe ben Israel's booklet inspired by the news of the survival of the lost tribe of Reuven in the fantastic form of Andes Indians with painted faces in South America—just another heartwarming example of a you-don't-look-Jewish incarnation. He took a small Tanakh out of his pocket and began to read aloud from the prophet Isaiah: And on that day the Lord will redeem the remainder of his people from Assyria—from Egypt and from Patros and from Cush and from Elam and from Shinar and from the islands of the sea. And He will gather the outcasts of Israel and the dispersed of Judah from the four corners of the earth. And Ephraim will no longer envy Judah, and Judah will no longer torment Ephraim. He turned to Temima and said, "You hear that, sister? First dispersal, then ingathering. That was the holy brother Rabbi Menashe's genius, to hasten the ingathering by promoting the dispersal. That was why he negotiated with Oliver Cromwell to get the Jews back into England almost four hundred years after they were expelled—to bring on the redemption. First it's let my people in, then it's let my people go."

"Ah, Cromwell," Temima said, "God's instrument. Another wild fanatic from another crazy religion, like my stiff-necked Annie Hutchinson—like you." She bent down to pick up two stones, one for Abba Kadosh and one for herself, to leave on the grave as a token of their visit.

"Did you ever see the portrait of Rabbi Menashe by the Dutch artist Rembrandt?" Abba Kadosh went on severely, communicating his irritation by ignoring her remark. "From the looks of him, sister, I do believe our hero had black blood flowing in his veins. He came from the land of Cush." He eyed her disapprovingly. "You should show a little more respect, sister," Abba Kadosh admonished. Raising his two index fingers as if to scold her, he licked them with his long pink tongue and inserted them deep into her ears, twisting them around until he was satisfied. Temima was thinking she might already be pregnant.

Hardly a word passed between them for the rest of that day and into the evening through the flight back to Israel. When they landed at Lod Airport and descended the staircase to board the buses waiting there to transport them to the terminal, a few of the passengers bent down to kiss the holy ground, a ritual with its own decorum that Abba Kadosh furiously expropriated by throwing himself dramatically onto the tarmac, embracing it passionately and weeping as if to attach himself to it with no possibility of dislodging him, his body splayed out like a giant bird that had fallen from the sky as a jeep pulled up followed by a black limousine.

Three soldiers in uniform with Uzis slung from their shoulders stepped out of the jeep, great muscular specimens evolved from the ghettos and shtetls, and while one restrained Abba Kadosh the other two unlatched his fingers from the earth and drew the outspread wings of his arms together behind his back and shackled him. "They're selling me back down the river to slavery in exile—their own brother Joseph from the tribe of Ephraim," Abba Kadosh was howling, his head turned to look behind him as the soldiers prodded him forward into the jeep. His eyes were focused unforgivingly on Temima, and what his eyes were saying to her was, It may look like I'm in their hands, but I am in yours.

The driver of the limousine held the door open for Temima and she climbed in, huddling in its dark corner, making herself small, her arms wrapped around her body for comfort and warmth. She was a motherless child, singled out by a cruel God to be forever alone to her very core, set apart and chosen by Him—Accept Me, Know Me, Love Me, He demanded as He held a mountain over her, threatening to drop it on her head if she dared to refuse. The limo was drawing near to the portal of the terminal building with its massive welcoming sign blessing all comers to Israel not including Abba Kadosh, a black man who insanely had willingly doubled his portion of suffering and humiliation by taking on the yoke of a Jew. Who gave the rabbis the authority to say whether this persecuted and despised man, arrogant and stiff-necked and unctuous and grasping and pushy and perpetually taking offense like the best of us, like almost every other certified member of the tribe, was not also welcome as a blessed comer? And yet, Temima was thinking, it was she not the rabbis who had the power at this critical moment over this man, the destiny of this particular discordant variation on the Jewish theme was in her hands at this moment, but even so, even in the face of that knowledge, she could nevertheless ride on right now, straight to Tel Aviv, she could sit down in a café, order a coffee and a pastry and smoke a cigarette, turn the pages of a ladies' magazine instead of poring over the toxic Tanakh all the time, transform herself into a normal person, become a secular Jew, go to the port of Jaffa and board a ship to Tarsis and land in the belly of a giant sea monster, return to America, forget about being a Jew altogether, start all over again, leave him to his fate.

From the front of the car she heard a still, small voice and for the first time she noticed the shrunken figure in the passenger seat almost completely buried under layers of blankets. "Do not try to escape, daughter," the voice said. "It is your destiny, a decree from above—Accept it! The black man has a part to play. I could give the order to liberate him, but from behind the partition above I have heard it decreed that it must come from you." He nodded to the driver, who indicated to Temima the phone installed for her use in the back of the limo. She made the call to the powers above using her influence. By the time she was ushered through the terminal building to the other side of passport control Abba Kadosh was already there waiting for her, rubbing his wrists reproachfully, offering no gratitude.

Temima awoke early the next morning in her cave, placed into a cloth sack a small toy sewn by the women of Bnei HaElohim and sold in their souvenir shop, a stuffed ibex with curled horns, and, accompanied by Shira, she summoned Melekh Sinai to drive her to Hebron. When in less than an hour the white Cadillac reached the bottom of the hill on the outskirts of the city where the settlers were still encamped in the military base on top she instructed her companions to wait for her there while she ascended to take care of her business, after which she would return to them.

The first person to greet her arrival back at the compound, like Jephta's daughter upon her father's return from battle, was her son, her only one, the one she did not love enough, the boy her husband called Pinkhas who had spent most of his days since her departure playing quietly alone outside the tent waiting for her to come back, sucking his thumb and telling himself stories. "Ima," he cried. "Here I am, my son," Temima said. "What did you bring me?" the boy asked. She took the stuffed mountain goat out of the sack and gave it to him. She sank down to the ground in front of him and pulled him to her, holding him for a long time. "Oh my son," she said, "you have brought me to my knees."

No one was inside the tent when she entered it. She found her little mother Torah at once exactly in the place where she always kept it, basted in dust, and put it into the sack. She had remembered it almost immediately after leaving with Ketura to the desert; even as she had been preparing to go she felt herself agitated with the sense that she was forgetting something vital, and every day since then she knew she must go back to lay claim to it. Now with her little mother Torah in her sack she walked out of the tent where the child was standing guard waiting for her. As she leaned over to kiss him good-bye she heard a voice cry out, "Do not touch that boy, do not do anything to him!"

It was her husband, Howie Stern, Haim Ba'al-Teshuva, scribe and phylacteries maker of Hebron, Go'el-HaDam. Someone had alerted him to her presence; let there be no hope for informers, Temima reflected. Howie had come running out of the synagogue tent from morning prayers as soon as he had received word, he was still cloaked in his great white talit, the black tefillin box on his forehead, the leather straps wound around his arm. She had heard he had been released from custody to house arrest. Who among us is not under house arrest? Temima thought bitterly. With a slight farewell wave of her hand to her son, she turned and began to make her way out of the camp, the child following behind, walking and weeping like Paltiel son of Layish when his beloved Mikhal was wrested from him by the outlaw David. "Ima, don't go, please don't go, Ima," the boy was sobbing.

"Come home now, Pinkhas," Howie said. The child threw himself down shaking and panting, beating the ground with his fists, slamming the stuffed ibex against the hard earth, and raised his voice in shrill cries. Howie lifted him to his hip with one arm around the waist like a bundle, the legs thrashing and kicking. "Let her go down alone without you," he said. "Forget you ever had a mother. Next time you see her will be when you bury her."

His name should no longer be called Pinkhas or even Paltiel, Temima reflected when she returned to the desert, but Isaac, because she had sacrificed him. Maybe Isaac had to be sacrificed because he was a *mamzer*, the product of an explicitly forbidden incestuous relationship, the son of a man who had uncovered the nakedness of his sister, as Abraham himself admitted to Avimelekh king of Gerar about Sarah, It's true she is my sister the daughter of my father though not my mother, and she became my wife. The *mamzer* Isaac was the middle link of the three main forefathers; all of his descendants, therefore, all of Israel, were *mamzerim*, barred from admission into the congregation of the Lord at least unto the tenth generation—outcasts, untouchables, mongrels, lepers, in the absence of a more precise word, bastards—and marked for elimination. But what sin had poor little Paltiel ever committed to deserve such misfortune? Yeshua HaNozri, the star of the sequel, was also a *mamzer*, purportedly God's son with a woman married to someone else, and was sacrificed in Jerusalem. Temima was a woman married to someone else, a forbidden woman; her son Kook Immanuel the *mamzer* was sacrificed in Hebron.

She was pulverized with guilt for the punishment she had brought down upon all of her children—she, a child whose own mother had withdrawn her protection, she should have guarded her children from everything bad, she should have guarded their goings out and coming back, now and forever. Now she was carrying another innocent, another unborn *mamzer*, doomed like all the others. She was still living in the cave by special arrangement with Abba Kadosh, a privilege unprecedented for a wife, concubine, or other in his menagerie, and she could go and come freely thanks to her ongoing contributions to the Bnei HaElohim coffers from the resources available to her, padded with bonuses from the trust fund of Shira Silver Kedaisha, who could not bear the thought of losing Temima. Her cave became her headquarters during this early stage of her pregnancy for her campaign to rescue her gestating *mamzer* from stigma and ostracism and immolation by demanding a divorce from her husband, the criminal Go'el-HaDam.

"Over my dead body," Howie sent back word through Temima's emissary. "No way I'm gonna give that bitch a *get*."

In this way Temima officially became an *agunah*, chained to a dead marriage by a recalcitrant husband who had sole power to grant the divorce—*gufah kanui*, as the Talmud liked to put it, her body is bought, it was Howie's property, all rights of ownership to her body had been acquired by Howie in the marriage transaction when he had uttered the words, Behold, you are consecrated to me. Now she was agitating for him to give her the *get* by pronouncing the flip side of those words, Behold, you are permitted to any man, divesting himself of his personal goods, dumping them in the open marketplace. Since he refused, though, she was in lockdown; she could not remarry in the Jewish tradition, not that she would ever want to marry again in any tradition, she had never wanted to get married in the first place, but for the *mamzer* in her womb, now no more than a tiny worm with no idea what awaited it, there were crushing consequences—branding over generations, shunning for centuries, targeted for extinction. So it was a great surprise, and at first a relief, when a few days after Howie had rejected out of hand her overture requesting a divorce she received word from him that, on second thought, maybe there was some room for negotiation.

It would cost her plenty, however. First of all, there was the matter of child support for the boy he called Pinkhas, over whom she would, as part of her concessions, naturally relinquish all custody rights and visitation privileges. Then there was compensation for himself for personal insult and injury, not to mention loss of face and loss of conjugal rights, damage incurred both above and below the waist, which could run into the very high figures. He also needed a new car—actually at this point a bulletproof van was absolutely necessary. There was also the matter of annual contributions in the platinum circle in his name to the Greater Israel movement and all of its future projects including the ultimate restoration of the Holy Temple on the Mount by whatever means with all of its accoutrements—golden altars for incense and animal sacrifice, golden menorah, golden showbread table, golden vessels, golden ark complete with golden-winged cherubim, golden priestly garments, suitable equipment for the Messiah's entry through the golden gate of Jerusalem on a white donkey, the white donkey itself, and so on. Her trust fund if she truly had one, her inheritance, her allowance from her father, other money and treasure from other sources, the proceeds from the sale of the Ben-Yefuneh Street apartment, and so forth, whatever she had—all of these assets and all that he omitted in his haste, none of these would be off-limits if she ever wanted to see that divorce. Finally, a bit of research on Howie's part had disclosed that the two apartments already underway bought for them by her father, the one in Kiryat Arba and the other in the hostile heart of Hebron itself, were officially in his, her father's, name—the devious old finagler. If she really wanted this divorce she had better hustle and get on his case ASAP, she had better talk to her sneaky old man to transfer ownership and property rights pronto, to him, to Howie, master of the houses.

"Over my dead body, the *momzer*!" her father Reb Berel Bavli spat out across the telephone wires from Brooklyn so that Temima almost felt the need to wipe off her face when she called him. "What? You think I'm some kind of moron?"

She had not seen her father since the circumcision of Kook Immanuel, she spoke to him infrequently, on the eve of holidays to wish him good yomtov, brief conversations at the beginning and end of which he never neglected to rebuke her for not calling enough. The only time he had initiated a call himself was during the shiva for Kook Immanuel; she had simply shaken her head when she was summoned to the phone, refusing to get up. "What a putz you got for yourself for a husband, Tema'le, I'm sorry to say, a real dope, you should excuse me, such a smart girl like you. Can you believe this guy's hutzpah? If I were there I'd wring his fat neck like a chicken—and believe me, when a *shoikhet* like me wrings a neck, you hear your neck-wringing ding-dong loud and clear. Even if I could afford it, you think for one minute I would ever be stupid enough to put anything with any value in the name of such a *paskundnyak* like your Howie? I'm telling you, you'd have to be meshuggeh. For your information, in case you want to know or care, right now I'm sitting here in Boro Park with five daughters to marry off, not to mention a very sick wife it shouldn't happen to a dog who's taking her own sweet time to finish up, making all kinds of demands from me, such as like she has to be buried in Eretz Yisroel the Holy Land itself no less like some kind of fancy lady, when who even knows where her own mama and papa are buried—maybe in a lampshade, maybe a bar of soap, maybe an ash can. A nice respectable cemetery on the New Jersey Turnpike or maybe even in Queens is not good enough for her like it was for your own mama, may she rest in peace—oh no, not for such a hotsy-totsy lady like Mrs. Frumie Bavli, she has to see with her own two eyes the deed for her burial plot signed sealed and delivered before she wraps up her business. I'm telling you, Tema'le, it costs plenty to be buried in Israel, like you wouldn't believe—graves, that's Israel's biggest natural resource, for your information, it will cost me an arm and a leg, it just so happens. I need your problems now to add to my own *zorres* like a hole in the head. I'm sorry, Tema'le, you're a big girl now, you're on your own this time. You made your bed, now you have to go lay down in it. Better you should go back to that little *schmendrik* of yours, Tema'le, that *schvantz* Howie—also, if you'll excuse me, a lot cheaper. Like the Gemara says, *tav lemetav tan* etcetera and so forth, which bottom line means, in case you don't know, it's better for a girl to be married to a jerk, a complete nothing no-goodnik schmuck piece of dreck like what you got for yourself, Tema'le, I'm sorry to say, than to be alone and not married at all."

Short of opening her own purse or yielding on any level to Howie's vindictive extortion, a number of options presented themselves to Temima, each of which she rejected for one reason or another. She could have arranged to have him imprisoned to coerce him into giving her the *get*, but if recent experience was an indicator, serving jail time not only did not faze him in his own skewed estimation, it even enhanced his self-image and made him a hero in his own eyes and in the eyes of his fellow travelers. She could have gone the Maimonidean route, one of the rare instances when the formidable Rambam saw things from the woman's side for a change, and declared him physically repulsive to her, disgusting plain and simple, or she could have petitioned for an annulment on the grounds of failure of full disclosure of a pre-existing condition at the time of the marriage, for surely she would never have agreed to take for a husband a mental degenerate, a violent insane perverted hooligan sociopath who lurked around at night cutting off human thumbs and big toes—but she held back for the time being from proceeding in ways that might shame and blacken the name of her child's father. Of course, she could also have sought to make the case that Howie was in violation of their original agreement with regard to the terms of their marriage and the limitations to his conjugal rights, but there was no prenuptial documentation to attest to their singular arrangement and in any case it was altogether an extraordinary and unique arrangement that would have bewildered and staggered the imaginative powers of the rabbis in a Jewish court of law, turning the full severity of their disapproval upon her head, pelting her as with a storm of blame, declaring her terms null and void.

Above all, Temima was driven by an urgency to settle the matter fast in the hope that the baby in her womb could be spared the stigma of *mamzerut*. It was during this period of intense focus on saving at least this child that she received word that Howie had taken for himself another wife without bothering to divorce Temima, without even taking the trouble to go through the nicety of procuring a dispensation from one hundred willing rabbis since the medieval ban against polygamy of Rabbi Gershom the Light of the Exile was precisely that—a ban with an expiration date and without the force of law, more like the accepted practice among Ashkenazi Jews. The new wife was a little sixteen-year-old girl, Abba Kadosh informed Temima, a Moroccan fresh from Netivot in the Negev desert not too far away from Bnei HaElohim, the headquarters of the miracle worker and faith healer Rabbi Yisrael AbuHatzeira known as Baba Sali with a nose like a kebab and more than one wife in his own personal stable, as a matter of fact. Pardon me, but Bnei HaElohim would have been more than happy to express deliver a nice untouched twelve-year-old virgin divorcée to Howie to compensate for the loss of Temima, a prize package a third Temima's age, an amazing deal, maybe even throw in as a bonus for reparations for any pain and suffering Howie might have incurred a little procedure they could perform on the girl in Health House—a clit slit and other appropriate mutilations, deliver her new but without tags, like they do in darkest Africa for extra insurance to keep her on the straight and narrow, it was something they occasionally opted for when a girl was getting too frisky, Bnei HaElohim's holy sisters knew how to hold a filly down and cut off her ridiculous useless little button with a razor when necessary for her own good. But no, Howie was just too much of a racist and bigot to even consider a Bnei HaElohim girl, not even a black beauty guaranteed virgin who has already been carrying around her nonperforming underage husband on her back for years and already has loads of experience in how to treat a husband right and proper—"Unlike you, sister," Abba Kadosh commented petulantly to Temima. "So your horny old man he goes for this teenybopper instead of a nice respectable Bnei HaElohim girl, a Moroccan with her henna and her cheap earrings with bells that go dingaling when she sashays around the barn like a cow so you always know where she is. Her name is Timna, by the way—kind of a Temima knockoff, you might say."

"Timna, the concubine of Eliphaz, Esau's son—mother of Amalek. You must completely blot out the memory of Amalek from under the heavens—Do not forget!" Temima declaimed as if on automatic.

Abba Kadosh rumbled his deep laugh, which rocked his soft belly that seemed to Temima to have been swelling in recent weeks. He was sitting opposite her in her cave, his legs spread wide. "I didn't expect you to take it so hard, sister." He shook his head with a bemused expression at this further evidence of the peculiar and inexplicable nature of the female mind. No matter how brilliant or accomplished, all women were irrational. "Like I said when I took the trouble to publicly walk unescorted across my entire village and come here in person to see you, sister, I got some good news and some bad news. That little Moroccan chick, Timna, your husband married? That was the good news." His rolling laugh bounced off the stone walls.

Temima would not give Abba Kadosh the satisfaction of displaying the weakness of curiosity by asking directly for the bad news. She sat there in silence preparing herself inwardly.

"Just say the word, sister," Abba Kadosh went on to exhort her. "One word from you, and I send some of my best commandos from Yazoo City up to Hebron to take care of your old man, Howie. Believe me, sister, when they finish with him he will fall down on what's left of his knees and lick your feet if he still has a tongue in his mouth and beg you to accept his miserable little divorce. Howlin' Howie they'll call him, since the guy's name is always morphing anyhow, maybe finally he'll get one that fits him."

Abba Kadosh proceeded with keen relish to run down a list of the various techniques and equipment in his arsenal, from head to toe, electric drill to the skull, pliers to toenails, every variety of sharp or shock-inducing appliance for every orifice and tender part of the body, for every limb and organ, knives and razors, whips and prods, fists and spikes, dogs and rats, darkness and violation, suffocation and drowning, sleeplessness and terror, stretching and shrinking, the full catalogue of tortures straight from Sodom piled in ruins a short distance away. "On second thought, sister, we can save ourselves a whole lot of mess and bother if you'd simply be willing to use your *protectzia* clout with the high and mighty of the land to get his driver's license revoked. Believe me, sister, that will do the trick in no time. You'll get that *get* faster than a speeding bullet, you won't know what hit you."

He sat back with a wide grin, completely at ease in his skin, a quality in him that always affected Temima physically like crescendoing music. "Frankly, sister, it amazes and befuddles me how a smart lady like you has gone and got herself into such a state over this divorce business, puffing up that ninety-pound-weakling husband of yours, making him feel mighty powerful for the first time in his life, like he has you in the palm of his hands and can just squeeze for all he's worth. I like you fine the way you are, sister, *get* or no *get*. What more do you need? And if you're worrying whether that future little Zephania ben Cushi or Zippora bat Cushi in your belly is going to be a *mamzer* unto the tenth generation—well, face it, sister, there's no way any kid with me for a daddy born in Bnei HaElohim hollering to be accepted as a Jew in the State of Israel is going to be anything but an outcast and a pariah, *mamzer* or no *mamzer*. This kid is fated to be blackballed and blacklisted, literally and figuratively, until the last feather in the faded yellow beards of the chicken-skinned rabbis shrivels and falls out. This is going to be a kid handicapped from the get-go, sister, wandering to and fro in the land like a leper with a bell, at home only with the other *mamzerim* in Bnei HaElohim. And what's so bad about Bnei HaElohim anyhow? It is paradise, Gan Eden, like the land of Cush completely surrounded by the river Gihon attached to the Garden of Eden like an umbilical cord. My advice to you, sister, is just to sit back and relax and enjoy the show. But like I said—if you still have your heart set on that *get*, if you still want me to straighten out that dead dog of a husband of yours, that pisser against the wall, that worthless scumbag with blood on his hands—then just say the word. I'm at your service, sister, that's why God put me on this earth—to fulfill your destiny."

Abba Kadosh flashed a sly smile, like a gentleman who opens a door for a lady in order to be better positioned to get a good look at her rear end and give it a good kick. Temima did not say a word, but her eyebrows arced as if into a question mark. "Nothing big," he replied, "just a small favor in return."

He anticipated that his son, Yishmael, the wild boy she called Ibn Kadosh, would be haunting the village again very soon despite the risks to life and limb he knew very well, Abba Kadosh told Temima. He suspected the boy might first stop at her cave to inquire as to his, Abba Kadosh's, whereabouts, or might seek refuge with her as a hiding place from which to pounce like a panther. Should that happen, he was asking her out of loyalty to him, the father of the child she was carrying, and in return for his generous offer to settle the Howie business premium class five-stars deluxe all the way, to inform him immediately when the kid shows up. "He's coming to get me, sister. He believes I killed his mother."

There was a deep pause as this news sank in. Tears pooled in the corners of Temima's eyes and slid down the sides of her face, staining her cheeks.

"Yes, sister, my own son, my own flesh and blood, he is out to kill me—*that's* the bad news. It *is* for me you are weeping now, I take it. Those tears are in my behalf—correct? I do appreciate your sympathy, sister."

He gazed at her coldly. "For the record, sister, I didn't do it, and I didn't order that it be done, though in all candor I cannot say I don't approve. It is an ancient tradition—an honor killing carried out by her own people for her whoring and promiscuous ways that brought only shame to her family and tribe. Stoned to death, probably by her own father and brothers and uncles, with her mother and sisters ululating and dancing in the background, by the way. You might consider it a primitive Arab custom, sister, but as far as I am concerned, it is one of the few practices still upheld by the followers of that ruthless bandit Muhammed, a model to all of us cult leaders, prophets, and messiahs, that I can relate to and respect. Her remains were discovered near Be'er LaHai Ro'i in the Negev desert, in the land of the south, where Father Isaac settled after he was sacrificed. They carried out her punishment in the time-honored way. Buried her in the sand up to the waist, then stoned her to death to uproot the evil from their midst. The flesh of her upper body and her face were already almost entirely eaten away by the buzzards and vultures of the desert down to the eye sockets, like her sister Jezebel, licked clean by wild dogs. The shadow of bird wings rested on the sand, as if peeled off her face. A pearl earring was snagged in the petrified wires of hair plugged into her skull. That's how the boy identified his mother. What is such an earring worth without its mate? What is the value of such a used and defiled woman? She is worth nothing, a woman like that—not even one *grush*, not even a single Philistine foreskin, not even a mouthful of spit, not even half a shekel. She is not counted, and she does not count."

Seven months after losing her Ketura, less than two years after losing her baby boy Kook Immanuel, on a hot and dry day at summer's end in the Judean Desert, Temima was seized by the first pang of her labor, astoundingly fresh in its unnegotiable iron ferocity. She was sitting in a lawn chair outside the entrance to her cave with her Tanakh open on her lap, Shira Silver Kedaisha stretched out on the ground at her feet in the posture of a disciple, left arm propping up her head and a notebook in which to record the teachings at ready beneath the pen poised in her right hand. They still had not advanced beyond the first three chapters of Genesis, the creation of the world through the expulsion from Eden, pondering the mystery of Hava, the original woman, the template, mother of all that lives, *em-kol-hai*. Temima asked, Why did God forbid Adam (though not Hava, at least not directly) from eating from the fruit of the tree of knowledge but not from the tree of life tucked in the center of the garden like the heart in its rib cage? Because in doing so He rendered the fruit of the tree of knowledge the most tempting and irresistible, turned it into the lure to deflect and distract humankind from the tree of life, the garden's real prize. Taking a bite out of its fruit, so good to eat, so enticing to the eyes, so desirable as a source of wisdom, Hava traded the true divine attribute of immortality for the divine delusion of knowledge poisoned with the consciousness of one's own impending death, she relinquished immortality for all of her descendants because that was His will. And what was her reward for fulfilling His will? Painful childbirths, everlasting subservience to man—the curse of Eve—odium and contempt down through the ages too entrenched ever to be eradicated despite lip service, the indelible and immutable image of woman as temptress, root of all evil and sin, polluted and polluting.

Temima grimaced, her breathing sped up and deepened and grew audible, springing Shira to her feet. "Not yet. Let's wait." In a regal gesture, Temima raised her hand palm out as if to slow things down. For some reason she had never taken the time to look into the secret birthing protocols and rituals as practiced in Health House in Bnei HaElohim though she had heard they were extraordinary. But this was her eighth pregnancy and the third baby she was bringing to term, her entrails had loosened. Within an hour after the first contraction had gripped her, a liquid began to seep out of the hollowness of her body through the webbing of the lawn chair in which she was sitting, dripping onto the ground and soaking it; in seconds the puddle was lapped up by the blistering heat as if by the slack tongue of a parched dog. Temima groaned. How much grace will you show when the pains come upon you, the travail of childbirth? the prophet Jeremiah asked. How much dignity?

Hoisting Temima upward with both hands, Shira helped her out of her seat. They went inside the cave where Temima found her cloth bag into which she placed her Tanakh and her little mother Torah, though she hardly knew what use they might serve since they contained essentially no descriptions of such behind-the-scenes women's business as childbirth, absent most glaringly in the scroll of the Pentateuch itself. Yet they were her comfort. I will fear no harm because you are with me. With her elbow linked into the loop formed by Shira's arm, they began an eloquently slow processional as if following a coffin down the pathway from the cave using what Shira called with a muted giggle "baby steps," bringing one foot in front of the other in minimal increments as the fluid continued to leak from between Temima's legs and evaporate almost instantly in the arid soil. All eyes behind curtains and shutters and shades fixed upon them as in exquisite slow motion endowing their advance with a kind of grave significance they made their ceremonious way to the birthing center in Health House as to a place of execution in the heart of the village.

Outside of Health House a circle of ten men was seated on the sand around the enema monument, which Temima now noted resembled the male sexual organ more than anything else in all of its blooming menace. Abba Kadosh was notably absent from this group. The men rocked back and forth reading psalms traditional for childbirth as their leader, Melekh Sinai, chanted over and over above their murmurings like an incantation the blessing from the daily morning prayers, thanking God for not having made him a woman. Temima, with Shira at her side, stood for a while at the edge of this circle listening to their petitions on behalf of women in confinement, and then raised her voice to inquire of Melekh Sinai why he was not also saying the blessing thanking God for not having made him a goy. "The sister is too clever for her own good," Melekh Sinai said, reducing and dismissing her in her exposed female weakness. Immediately two midwives who had been stationed at the doorway a modest distance away from the ring of men came forward dressed in identical immaculate uniforms including long white aprons and white headscarves like sisters of mercy from another century in a war casualty hospital. They relieved Temima of her bag containing the sacred texts, assuring her that her personal possessions would be held in a safe, uncontaminated place through the period of her impurity, her bleeding and discharge, forty days if she gave birth to a boy, eighty days for a girl.

Still supporting herself on Shira's arm, Temima followed the midwives to the suite of birthing rooms set aside for her. It was at this point, with an expression of mortified helplessness on her face, a look bordering on desolation, that Shira detached herself from Temima and entered the larger of the two rooms. Through the open door Temima saw Abba Kadosh wearing only a hospital gown lying on a great plush bed in the center of the room, his head elevated on a lavish bank of pillows, surrounded by all of his women who were not at that time pregnant dressed exactly like the midwives, massaging his belly, applying compresses to his forehead, moistening his lips with ice chips, stroking his arms, his hair, his beard, kneading his shoulders, applying ointment to his chest, taking his pulse, pressing a stethoscope or leaning an ear against his heart and his bloated belly, peering up between his thighs and checking progress with extended arms and probing fingers. Shira stepped into this room, slipped behind a screen, and emerged very soon after dressed like all the others in the costume of a midwife. She went to the basin to wash her hands, then took her place at one of Abba Kadosh's feet and began to rub it alongside a co-*kedaisha* assigned to the other foot. Her duties to Abba Kadosh at this time trumped her bond with Temima, as they had when she had been obliged to supplicate Temima in his behalf, standing with all of his other women in front of the entrance to the cave with one breast bared. Shira could not endure raising her eyes from Abba Kadosh's foot to look at Temima still at the doorway witnessing her debasement, but Abba Kadosh himself, with his head propped high on the pillows, did not take his gaze off Temima for a second. His eyes shimmered with amused triumph and power even as his face wore the mask of agony and his body writhed and his limbs flung out spasmodically though no sounds issued from his mouth, no screams and no cries.

The two midwives delegated to Temima allowed her to remain in the doorway observing the ministrations to Abba Kadosh long enough to begin to absorb the concepts behind the birthing philosophy of the community. When they judged that she had taken in the gist they propelled her respectfully but firmly to the adjacent room, much smaller and strikingly less well appointed than the one in which Abba Kadosh was accommodated, with its narrow austere bed pushed against the wall that separated the two chambers. The younger of the two midwives helped Temima to undress and put on a hospital gown like the one she had seen on Abba Kadosh. While this prepping was taking place, the senior midwife expounded with such fervor on the underlying creed at Health House governing childbearing that the black wen alongside her nose began to twitch like a spider animated by the passionate flaring of her nostrils and the emphatic contortions of her face. It was quite simply and irrefutably the true and authentic biblical way of birth, the older midwife declared. There is not much written in the Scripture about a woman giving birth precisely because it is not the woman who truly gives birth—it is the man. He is the progenitor, the first cause, the child is his offspring in his name so listed and so written as attested to by the begats; the mother gets no credit, and rightly so, she is merely the vessel, the pipeline, the conveyor belt. And Adam lived one hundred and thirty years *vayoled* in his image and likeness and he called his name Seth; *vayoled* Seth *et* Enosh; *vayoled*

Enosh *et* Kenan; *vayoled* Kenan *et* Mahalalel; *vayoled* Mahalalel *et* Yered; *vayoled* Yered *et* Enoch; *vayoled* Enoch *et* Methuselah. And so on and so forth down through the generations giving birth in the masculine conjugation—*vayoled, holeid, yalad.* Already Abba Kadosh was in the throes of childbearing in the next room, as Temima had observed with her own eyes. All he awaited now was to hear her screams through the thinness and porousness of this partition wall that divided them, which he would then replicate cry for cry, only louder and stronger and more heartrending, overpowering her voice and drowning her out to pierce the very heavens; he would take full possession of her labor and travail and claim it as his right for himself and occupy it, thereby asserting prime ownership as the father.

For this reason, because Abba Kadosh's full gratification as the vicarious childbearer depended on her screams, the birth of this her last child was the most difficult Temima had ever endured. She resolved then and there not to emit a single sound throughout the ordeal, not a moan, not a sigh, not an audible breath no matter how violently she was ripped apart or how harrowing the pain—a fast of speech undertaken in the furious epicenter of childbirth itself. Whatever relief screaming offered to a woman in parturition, this she denied to herself. Over the ensuing long hours of labor and delivery she travailed, she suffered. Mute, inside her head that black joke of the Israelites rang nonstop, What, there aren't enough graves in Egypt that you've taken us to die in the desert?—yet she remained faithful to her resolve. If she was to be the ghost creator of this child she would be as silent as a ghost even as her two midwives implored her, Cry out, sister, it's only natural at such a time, make it easier on yourself, sister, scream and yell, twist and shout!

The image she held before her eyes to sustain and strengthen her against involuntary screams was of the boy Ibn Kadosh who had delivered her first child, his flogging in the public square, refusing in his pride to give his tormentors the satisfaction of hearing *his* cries. And then, like the woman of Endor, she brought up from the dead the still-restless and unsettled spirit of Ibn Kadosh's mother, Ketura, with the black bird charred into her skin. Did Ketura planted upright and alive and fully aware in her grave in the desert sand scream out in terror as the stones came flying toward her, hurled at her head, pelting and pounding her from the waist upward, or did she summon all of her powers, an act of sovereign self-control, to suppress the reflexive shrieks so as to deny her persecutors the fullness of their obscene thrill? Not a single one of Temima's pregnancies until now, whether the outcome was a living baby or a dead fetus in a bloody venous sac, had ever been experienced without Ketura at some point faithfully at her side—so she summoned Ketura's familiar spirit to her side now too. If Temima were to succumb and cry out now, she would cry out in grief for Ketura, bird-branded and bird-devoured, but she drew her spirit inward to harness her vow of silence, to honor Ketura through her defiant silence even as the contractions intensified mercilessly and the baby monstrously large like a giant boulder pressing down on the bowels squeezed its way out of her churning womb and tore her to shreds, even as the midwives urged her on, Push, you miserable ungrateful woman, Push, you witch.

Then came the supreme test to Temima's will—head and shoulders preposterously large and wide for the absurd opening squeezing brutally through the passage, and in their wake the rest of the newborn slithering out with not a sound from mother or child. The senior midwife grabbed the baby, a dark underworld creature matted with fur, encrusted with a white cheese and streaked with red blood, while her junior colleague swiftly cut the umbilical cord within a hairsbreadth of Temima's body and set the newborn loose. Without a word to the mother, not even informing her of the sex of the child she had just expelled into this life, the two women ran out of the room, the elder carrying the baby slippery as a freshly netted fish with the hook still in its mouth, her younger sister scurrying behind clutching the end of the long tail of the umbilical cord like a leash, leaving Temima completely alone. They rushed into the adjacent room, shoved the baby with its cord up between Abba Kadosh's legs stuffing it as high as possible, and along with all the other women assembled there they sang out to him, urging him to push with all his might, Push, holy father, push!

Straining convulsively but emitting no sounds—it was a source of extreme frustration to him not to be able to scream to his heart's content, he never forgave Temima for denying him the full pleasure of the experience as was his due—Abba Kadosh discharged the baby a second time into this world. His chief wife, Em-Kol-Hai Kedosha, caught it in both hands, held it upside down by its ankles, and announced, "It's a Zippora bat Cushi. Thank God, one less trip for me." She gave the newborn a sharp welcoming smack on the buttocks setting her screaming to clear her lungs, and the screaming continued at the same heartwarming volume as another woman cut the umbilical cord again, this time as close as possible to the child's navel, the screams subsiding for a short spell only when they set her down on Abba Kadosh's bushy chest with her mouth on his nipple where she foraged in vain until she gathered force again shrieking in furious protest.

In the next room Temima heard the cries and said to herself, as Elijah the prophet had said to the widow of Sidon when he raised her son from the dead, See, your child lives. Abba Kadosh said out loud, "This one will be a handful—we will have to marry her off fast," and bringing his hand flat up to his chin in a gesture of oversatiation he signaled to the women to peel the kid off his chest and take her away from him for bathing and swaddling and feeding and whatever other maintenance might be required by female support staff now that he had done the man's main job in birthing her; Bnei HaElohim was not an uncivilized hellhole like China, we do not dump even girls on a hilltop to starve to death and be devoured by the carrion-eating birds, we find other ways to recycle them. When the two midwives brought the bundle back into Temima's room for breastfeeding, they instantly spotted the mass on the bed—the placenta, a congealing clot like the pile of an embarrassing accident. The older midwife scooped it up in the ladle of her bare hands and hurried in her zealousness back to Abba Kadosh's room to offer it to him so that he might carry through to its proper end the birthing ritual to holy perfection, but he was already rising from his bed and reaching for his clothing to get dressed. "Give that mess to one of my assistants," Abba Kadosh said with revulsion. "I don't do afterbirths."

"Here is your Zippora bat Cushi." The younger midwife shoved a papoose into Temima's arms. The dark skin of the baby's face was sheathed with a thin mantle of fur the sign of a past life in another evolution, the eyes were sealed shut and puffy, the wide nose flattened, the full lips pursed like a gathering raindrop, the head, when Temima removed the little white cap, pointed and dented from having been squeezed and remolded in its arduous passage through the narrow straits of the birth canal into this life. It had not only been she, Temima, who had labored. This tiny being had also been hurled about in that terrible storm, she had wrestled to make her way out through the narrow dark tunnel to the light. She was heroic. Temima was flooded with tenderness for the valor of this little warrior, she felt as if her own heart were breaking. Her name would no longer be called Zippora, Temima decided, but Hagar, in memory of Ketura. Father Abraham took another wife after Mother Sarah's death, and her name was Ketura. Ketura is Hagar, mother of Ishmael, the rabbis teach, the degraded woman summoned back to Abraham's tent after her mistress's death having been banished at Mother Sarah's behest. Even the rabbis were troubled by how badly Hagar had been used, even they sought to make amends in their way in accordance with their notions of what women want. Temima gazed at her daughter and remembered Ketura, discarded like waste, and offered restitution through Hagar's happily-ever-after ending.

She settled Hagar at her breast where the child suckled voluptuously for three full years. Over the eighty-day period of ritual impurity strictly adhered to in Bnei HaElohim prescribed after the birth of a girl—two weeks of menstrual infirmity followed by sixty-six days of blood purification—Temima nursed Hagar in Health House. She nursed Hagar in the cave as she resumed her work on Tanakh with Shira, stopping at each of the stations of womanhood, beginning again with Hava created in the image of man as man was created in the image of God, twice removed. Hagar's teeth cut through her gums, she grew, she walked, she talked; still she continued to nurse with gusto. Sometimes she would take her mouth off the breast to contribute her commentary. She was particularly engrossed during the weeks of discussion of the suffering of her namesake Hagar the black Egyptian slave. "She so black she blue," the child declared solemnly, and she opened her mouth wide and wailed, thin streams of pale milk running down her chin. Another time she pulled her mouth off the breast so abruptly she raked Temima's flesh with her sharp little teeth and exploded into peals of laughter. This happened when Mother Rebekah wrapped her younger son Jacob's smooth arms and neck in the hairy skin of a freshly killed goat to impersonate his brother Esau and trick his father Isaac into giving him the firstborn's blessing—for Jacob really was the eldest according to Rashi the commentator-in-chief, Temima noted with a wry smile as an aside not intended for little Hagar's ears, on the principle of "first in last out," especially in a narrow passageway with no room for maneuvering. And they actually did succeed in fooling the old man Yitzkhak with this gorilla suit. So vividly ridiculous to little Hagar was this great comic scene from the Tanakh that she could envision it as in an illustrated book for the amusement of children. With milk spraying from her mouth, she burst into hilarity, barely managing to get out the words, Yitzkhak—what a retard!

Your curse be upon me, my daughter, Temima reflected.

Abba Kadosh was present on that occasion. Now and then he stopped by the cave to amuse himself listening to the biblical exegesis of these two concubines with an expression on his face as if he were observing a pair of macaques doing higher mathematics. "Where's your respect?" he boomed ominously at the child, who was already back to nursing avidly. He glared at Temima. "Sister, it is your duty to rein in your daughter. If you don't, I will."

"Out of the mouths of babes," Temima responded coolly, fixing Abba Kadosh with a warning glare. And she launched into an exposition of the text to defend her child, asserting that, in fact, Father Isaac—Yitzkhak— may indeed have been "retarded," afflicted with Down Syndrome, maybe he was what they used to call in Brooklyn a Mongoloid, Temima said recklessly to Abba Kadosh. After all, he was the son of an exceedingly old mother, an off-the-charts old mother, Sarah was ninety years old when she gave birth to him, well past her female cycles by her own admission—and it is common knowledge that the chances of having a Down baby increase exponentially with an older mother, not to mention the age of the father at the time of this birth, one hundred years old—And my husband is so old, Temima said quoting Mother Sarah while staring at Abba Kadosh without backing down an inch. Abba Kadosh in turn glared spitefully at the oversized overaged baby still nursing at Temima's breast also no longer in the full glow of its youth, but she pointedly ignored the implication and went on, "Or maybe it was just a case of shell shock, after being sacrificed on the mountaintop by his old man. That would do it. Face it, brother, check out the text—Isaac was a guy who just didn't have a lot to say. And frankly, Abba dear, I don't know why you of all people don't consider Father Isaac a little on the slow side. After all, he was our only patriarch who was monogamous."

Without giving Abba Kadosh a chance to counter, Temima went on to ask if he by any chance knew how old Isaac was when brought by his father Abraham to be bound to an altar on top of Mount Moriah and slaughtered. Thirty-seven years old! Temima answered her own question—according to many commentators. How do they figure that? Since the report of Sarah's death comes almost immediately after the account of the binding of Isaac, it is believed by some that his mother had simply collapsed and expired, maybe a heart attack, maybe a stroke, when news reached her of what her old man had been up to this time, it was the last straw. Mother Sarah was one hundred and twenty-seven years old when she dropped dead, she had given birth to Isaac at age ninety, which would have made him thirty-seven when he was sacrificed. And the loopy question he asks as he so docilely tags along with Abraham to the land of the Moriah—My father, here's the fire and the wood, but where's the sheep for the burnt offering?—and how passively he allows himself to be bound onto the altar without a peep of protest, a thirty-seven-year-old man, there must have been something wrong with him, something not so *beseder* upstairs. Temima tapped her temple with her forefinger, and shook her head. Three years later, at the age of forty, he is married off to a wife picked out by his father and delivered from the old country by his father's consigliere, Eliezer of Damascus—Not one of the local Canaanite sluts for my boy Isaac, the old man had said to the Damascene, promise me, place your hand under my testicles and swear. And how old is Rebekah when Isaac marries her? Three!—according to the commentators. How do we learn this? Because her birth is announced immediately after the incident on Mount Moriah, directly before the death of Sarah. So at the age of three, Rebekah waves bye-bye to her father, Betuel, and her brother Laban and with a shiny new gold ring in her nose she is lifted up onto a camel by Abraham's right-hand man Eliezer of Damascus and led away, she crosses over from Aram-Naharayim to the land of Canaan—accompanied by her wet nurse. You have to wonder—What kind of normal man marries a three-year-old?

On the day that Hagar was weaned, at the age of three and one day, Abba Kadosh, prophet and messiah, made a great feast for the entire community, as Father Abraham had done when Sarah weaned Isaac. By that point in her studies of Genesis as transcribed by Shira Silver Kedaisha, Temima was preparing to dictate her teachings on the thirty-fourth chapter: And Dina daughter of Leah whom she had borne to Jacob went out to look over the daughters of the land. Shekhem son of Hamor the Hivite prince of the land saw her, and he took her and lay with her and raped her.

The feast celebrating the weaning was held in the grand pavilion, attended by the entire village, the men and boys separated from the women and girls by a line of blooming plants, bright reds, pinks, vermillion. In the men's section, Abba Kadosh was enthroned on a peacock chair in pluming extravagant display. His daughter, the freshly weaned child he called Zippora bat Cushi, decked out like a bride in a white dress and white headscarf for this special occasion, was seated on his lap under a canopy held up by four men while his chief wife Em-Kol-Hai Kedosha took her place in an honorary position behind him, screened by the flamboyance of the throne. To symbolically mark the separation of mother and child that weaning signified, Temima was seated at the opposite end of the pavilion amid the women on a lesser peacock chair meant for a queen also under a canopy held up by four women. The gospel choir, Kol-Koreh-BaMidbar under the baton of Melekh Sinai, to the accompaniment of Shira Silver Kedaisha's small orchestra in a curtained-off area, performed a medley of tunes, including the spiritual "Oh Mother Don't You Weep" and a hearty rendition of the Hebrew celebratory hymn, "Siman Tov and Mazel Tov," setting the entire crowd rocking and waving its arms jubilantly.

The dancing and hand clapping and singing of *Siman Tov u'Mazel Tov* continued full force even as Melekh Sinai left his position at the podium in front of the chorus and took his place under the canopy. *Siman Tov u'Mazel Tov* went on throbbing and pulsating as Em-Kol-Hai Kedosha, carrying in her arms Zippora bat Cushi, the child Temima called Hagar gearing up for a tantrum because her face was covered by her white scarf and she couldn't see anything, encircled Melekh Sinai seven times. Since in this instance Abba Kadosh held with the sages of the Talmud who asserted that a girl of three years and one day may be betrothed by sexual intercourse (though prior to that age it would be like sticking a finger in her eye), he now read out loud the marriage contract in full legal Aramaic and recited the seven marriage blessings in Hebrew in the traditional rabbinic style. The cloth was lifted from the girl's face and she was given some sweet wine to sip, which calmed her down. Melekh Sinai slipped a glittery ring on her milk-fattened dimpled finger, which pleased her very much, and pronounced the prescribed words to Zippora bat Cushi, Temima's daughter Hagar: Behold, you are consecrated to me with this ring in accordance with the law of Moses and Israel. Abba Kadosh, prophet and messiah, father of the bride and officiator at this sacrament of matrimony, intoned, May your Yah rejoice over you, as the bridegroom rejoices over the bride. Then Melekh Sinai brought his foot down, stamped on a glass and shattered it. The crowd went wild, roaring *Siman Tov u'Mazel Tov* ever louder and more ecstatically. Melekh Sinai turned to face the congregation, one arm plumbed downward gripping the raised hand of his bride Zippora bat Cushi, Temima's Hagar, happily sticking out her bright red tongue to lick the cherry lollipop that Em-Kol-Hai Kedosha had reached into a pocket to give her. Basking in a shower of *Siman Tov u'Mazel Tov* auspicious signs, good luck and good wishes, the couple stood there under the wedding canopy facing their guests, by the law of Moses and Israel husband and wife.

And Dina
Came Out

You must wrestle through the night until the break of dawn to discover your true name, the name that unlocks your destiny, Temima said to Shira when they came out of the desert, it's a fight for your life that leaves you forever mangled and crippled, it will pulverize your hip, it will cost you dear. Names give you away, Temima went on, repeating a basic tenet she had taught over the years, which is why God conceals His so that uttering even the aliases is so dangerous and charged, but for us in this life it is a matter of uncovering the one that signifies, insisting on who we are.

During that first year after they left Abba Kadosh's patriarchal compound deserting the child bride Hagar ruined for the outside world like a deliberately mutilated infant condemned to a life of beggary, as they wandered the streets of Jerusalem to find their ordained path, Shira's name was the first to be revealed, then Temima's.

When they came out of the wilderness they took up residence at first in the Royal Suite of the King David Hotel, the Toiter's base while in Jerusalem. Impeccably trained management and staff did not betray with even a sniff or flinch any sense that something bizarre or out of the ordinary was unfolding before their eyes as word spread that a holy wise woman healer had established herself in their historic hotel from where it was reported she was performing miracles every day. The grotesquely disfigured and the putridly contagious in all their unseemliness came out of their holes in the ground and streamed through the stately gilded lobby of the hotel like an invasion of locusts and boarded the elevators with their pustules and tumors alongside the aghast guests paying full price and ascended to the sixth floor desperate for a cure. Temima would greet her supplicants with the words, It is not I but God who will see to your well-being, yet she offered comfort, palliative care, temporary relief from all the pain of this life. God is your healer, Temima said, but she at least would do no harm.

Taking direction from the incident described in the book of Exodus when the Hebrews arrived at the oasis of Marah in the wilderness and complained about the bitterness of the water, which Moses then sweetened by throwing into it a piece of wood equally bitter, Temima applied a homeopathic method based on the principle of like curing like to effect healing. She created a personalized distillation of the disease tailored to each suppliant, diluted it in living water, and gave it to the sufferer to drink in order to restore the vital physical and spiritual energy and balance unique to each individual. For a person afflicted with intestinal agonies, for example, Temima might encapsulate the disease by writing out on a piece of paper the verse from the book of Chronicles describing King Jehoram smitten in the gut until his bowels fell out. She would fold the paper as small and compact as a pill, drop it in a glass filled with fresh living spring water, and as the patient drank this potion to the dregs she would chant the words that Doctor God spoke at Marah, All of the diseases I brought upon Egypt I will not bring upon you, for I am the Lord your healer. In a similar fashion, for the supplicants tormented by skin diseases and rashes and sores and eruptions all over their bodies like Job and rot and pollutions and infestations of all varieties, she might drop into the pure water a totemic verse pill projecting one of the Tanakhi lepers, Naaman or Gekhazi or Uzziyahu and also her punished Miriam.

More and more of the wretched and cursed poured into the aristocratic old hotel as Temima's reputation spread through the city and radiated beyond among Jews and Arabs until the order came down from top corporate headquarters for the doormen to direct these instantly identifiable unsightly specimens and human blights to the service entrance of the building; let them follow their pocked and inflamed noses to the stench of the overflowing dumpsters and the reeking sewage outlets and then up the freight elevator assigned to menials and the invisible. Temima was outraged and offended on behalf of her petitioners—I will bring healing to you and cure you of your wounds because they called you an outcast, said the prophet Jeremiah speaking for the Lord—though not as outraged or offended as the Polish head of state with a nose like a kielbasa when he and his entire drunken retinue with flaming red faces were ordered late one night to the dark side of the hotel by a nobody, an Arab hooligan decked out in a uniform with gold epaulets and tassels on his shoulders.

Soon after, Temima with Shira clinging faithfully to her side relocated to the Old City of Jerusalem within the massive Suleimanic walls, taking up residence on the Street of the Kara'im next door to the underground Karaite synagogue in the Jewish Quarter undergoing exuberant restoration in the wake of its reconquest in the Six Day War. Here she remained for more than a decade. It was here that her renown and her following grew, here she solidified her reputation throughout the land as the illustrious guru and Tanakhi luminary, HaRav Temima Ba'alatOv—Ima Temima.

She fixed on the Street of the Kara'im intentionally in order to confront head-on the charges that her approach to Tanakh in its emphasis on the literal text, on *p'shat,* and rejection of rabbinics as the sole and definitive authority was essentially a variation on the Karaite heresy. It is true that Temima was a great believer in text, in *p'shat.* She insisted first upon a literal reading of text without the intervention of commentary and interpretation, exegesis and hermeneutics, *pilpul* and *midrash*, often tendentious and agenda-driven—at times ameliorating, at times exacerbating. This is what she taught. Only by facing the text head-on, without partisan constraints and orthodoxies, can we recognize in the relevant passages the truth about how woman is regarded and valued in the basic scheme of things—and in the face of that recognition perhaps nevertheless not jump off a cliff, make our choice, seek out how to justify the ways of God to women, consider not rejecting it all, man and God.

By settling in the Street of the Kara'im she sought to nullify the lethal accusations that she was an undercover Karaite as she nullified physical illness by dissolving its toxic essence in clear water, like a vaccine containing the weakened pathogen of the very illness it was designed to prevent. You may consider me a Karaite if it serves your purposes to think of me in that way to mock and marginalize me, was what Temima was in effect declaring, since I subscribe to the principle of the Karaite founder Anan ben David, Search the Torah thoroughly on your own and do not rely on my opinion—even if Anan may not exactly have had me or any other woman in mind when he enunciated this principle. Even so, I too have opinions, I too am open to new forms of interpretation and oral law not restricted exclusively to the Talmud and the authorized rabbis, especially in reading the text as it applies to the inescapable reality of how contemptuously we women are viewed and how cheaply valued. But no, I am not in the camp of Anan or the other Karaite or Samaritan fanatics in their strict fundamentalist adherence to scriptural law. I do not sit in the dark for the entire Sabbath because of the injunction against lighting a fire on the day of rest. And I do not refrain from sexual intercourse on the Sabbath because of animal husbandry—the prohibition against plowing.

To Temima's new quarters on the Street of the Kara'im flocked the seekers of Torah enlightenment and the yearners for self-knowledge, also the ailing in body like the afflicted who had been drawn to the King David in their numbers, and increasingly more and more souls racked with mental and emotional anguish, gripped like King Saul by an evil spirit from the Lord, cursed with an unquiet, agitated heart, disappointed eyes, a despondent and despairing spirit, their lives hanging perilously before them, terror day and night, utter loss of faith in themselves, in the morning longing for evening and in the evening wishing it were morning. Sitting knee-to-knee face-to-face with these tormented souls Temima would clutch both of their hands in her own and with her thick-lashed, frank, penetrating eyes gaze silently and deeply through their layers of veils until their personal healing word would rise up or their true name would manifest itself, which she would then guide them in absorbing in an inward flow of acceptance to soothe their spiritual wretchedness.

But most comforting for these souls sunk in the depression of hopelessness and misery like the depths of a black pit crawling with snakes and scorpions, the slough of despond, were the two exercises she instructed them in to be performed simultaneously and in complete privacy even in the most crowded of settings bringing a measure of healing to the chronic human condition of physical and spiritual emptiness. Physical emptiness was relieved through an exercise known in the outside world as the Kegel designed to awaken and strengthen the walls of the lower orifices, two openings for men and three for women, all of these holes and hollows exposed and known before His throne of glory, a technique that involved conscious contractions of the muscles of the pelvic floor surrounding these cavities.

At the same time, spiritual emptiness could be relieved through an exercise known to the inside world as the Silent Scream of Rav Nakhman of Bratslav, a meditation technique that involved summoning up in the mind the visual image of the black hole of the mouth rounded into a scream and the aural sensation of the sound of a scream coming out of that black hole until you are actually screaming full time inside your head in a still, small voice that no one can hear, though occasionally a faint cry might escape from you just as a small trickle might leak out while squeezing the muscles of one of your nether apertures. It did not take long before men and women in public and private places all over Jerusalem and disseminating throughout the Holy Land, from the Knesset to the kiosks to the kitchens, were furiously kegeling down below and silently screaming up above, and no one saw or heard them, and no one knew.

Trailed by bands of wrecked kegelers and wasted silent screamers, along with other assorted seekers and believers, surrounded by an early incarnation of her Bnei Zeruya security contingent, with Shira sutured to her side, accompanied on occasion also by Ibn Kadosh in a red-and-white keffiyeh with a goat slung over his shoulders and a herder's crooked staff in his hand, Temima set out almost every day from her residence on the Street of the Kara'im to find her place in the world in anticipation of her full anointment. She bedecked herself for these excursions very deliberately in the full regalia of a grand rebbe—long satin kaftan of striped silver or gold or brocade like a dressing gown, girdled around the waist with a black rope *gartel* to divide the upper spiritual portion of the body, heart and mind and breath and spirit, from the grossness below, on her head the giant wheel of a *shtreimel*, its ring of thick dark fur fashioned out of hundreds of tails of sable, all of her rich black hair tucked under its black velvet hubcap with the exception of two long ringlets corkscrewing down in *peyot* on either side of her face, and fastened to her chin with a string a false beard symbol of royalty like those shown on the clean shaven faces of the pharaohs made of hammered gold, spade-shaped, jutting forward as depicted also on the statues and sphinx of the mighty queen Hatshepsut.

Garbed in this fashion she strode at the head of her procession through the Old City of Jerusalem, engaging as she walked in intense discussion in the gesticulated tradition of a master with disciples like the strict Rabbi Hillel or the even more strict Rabbi Shammai surrounded by their warring factions or the late-bloomer messianic martyr Rabbi Akiva with his twenty-four thousand squabbling students debating the fine points of Torah—discoursing on a range of topics, on the fleshpots and other temptations of Egypt, on the eunuch minister Potiphar buying the ravishing seventeen-year-old slave boy Joseph for personal sodomy, on Joseph losing his striped shirt to Potiphar's wife burning with lust as her kitchen maids watched from behind a curtain cutting artichokes down through their bones, their fingers dripping blood so dazzled were they by the boy's beauty. Temima posed the question pointedly, Where in the Tanakh do we find a Jewish woman expressing sexual desire in all of its rutting intensity and feverish urgency like Potiphar's wife? The idealized boilerplate Jewish woman, she is stripped of all eroticism, Temima said. Charm is false, beauty is vanity, the God-fearing woman, she will be praised.

As she continued to offer her radical teachings on these and other subjects, Temima led her flock through the ghetto of the Jewish Quarter ignoring the taunts of bystanders—Hey, what's with the beard, Queen Tut? So you wanna be a rebbe, Rabbi Kook-Kook? Immersed in Torah talk they made their way through the newly laid plazas and arched passages of the restored Jewish ghetto into the Armenian and Christian and Muslim Quarters also enclosed within the walls of the Old City of Jerusalem, their dark narrow streets of ancient stones worn slick from centuries of traffic by humans and other mortal beasts of burden. At the head of her flock she meandered through the labyrinth of the *shuk* and bazaars, past men straddling low stools in cultivated idleness at the entrances to shops, fingering their beads, smoking green tobacco, absentmindedly scratching their privates, brazenly following her passage, undressing her with their eyes. Never mind her monumental learning, she was naked to them, never mind her apotheosis in the vestments of a holy man, her nakedness was on full display before them, every female part in its predictable place, a familiar piece of goods, no different from any other woman—her femaleness, all you needed to know.

They violated her with their eyes, their dirty thoughts rose visibly like gassy cartoon bubbles out of their heads, but they were absurdly insignificant to Temima. They were as beneath her notice as the intrusion along her path of the vulgar idolatrous symbols of the three faiths battling over the same dismal patch of blood-soaked turf—the hodgepodge sinking lean-to of the Holy Sepulchre church, the Golden Dome and the Al-Aqsa Mosque flaunting their biceps like bullies in the arena of the Temple Mount, the pathetic Western Wall wringing perverse pride from weeping and wailing. She swept past all of these disturbances in the aura without a glance or a nod or a teaching. She led her congregation out of the garrison of the walled city through the Dung Gate and turned eastward for the ascent to the Mount of Olives, wild dogs prowling among the shattered and crumbling gravestones, Arab boys squatting on their haunches against gnarled tree trunks observing their approach through slitted eyes, picking their teeth.

Signaling with a hand to indicate to her followers to halt so that she might proceed on her own to engage in the practice of *hitbodedut*, she set forth in solitary walking meditation among the rows of graves, searching for the burial place of Rabbi Hannah Rachel Verbermacher, the Maiden of Ludmir, the shocking woman rebbe whose body had been laid to rest in this ancient cemetery almost a century earlier but whose soul now resided in Temima. Temima was the Maiden's *gilgul*, like the Maiden learned and devout, charismatic and mystical, ostracized and motherless, the Maiden's incarnation. Like the Maiden, Temima had also stubbornly refused to marry, the marriages that each of these women had acceded to in the end under duress were nothing but sham and pretense. Even so there was true issue from Temima as there was from the Maiden, contrary to received opinion. The Maiden's daughter was Temima, a pariah like her mother. Temima searched for her mother among the graves, she sought the one her heart loved, she sought her but could not find her.

She took her congregation through the Zion Gate without a glance toward the ghoulish abbey outside the city walls where Miriam the preposterously virgin mother of Yeshua HaNozri had fallen into her final ecstatic trance and was raptured up to paradise. Nor did she manifest any interest at all in the complex of buildings housing the chamber in which Miriam's son ate his last meal before his crucifixion, icons of his grim apostles flashing eerily one after the other like frames in a movie through the long slitted windows as she moved forward. She passed with equal disinterest the yeshiva for the lost boys of the Diaspora strumming their guitars, more tuned out than the stuporous stones of Jerusalem themselves. With similar disdain she rejected David's sepulcher in which almost no sane person believed the king was buried if only because sane people believe David king of Israel is alive and everlasting—like Enoch and Elijah whom God spirited away and they are no more, like some immortal rabbis of surpassing holiness on temporary leave from this life, destined to return in messianic splendor, the Toiter, the Maiden, there were already those who whispered in future days Temima herself. Joined on Mount Zion by Ibn Kadosh with his herd of goats coming up from Silwan, she shepherded her flock southward down into the Valley of Hinnom, Gehinnom, the vale of earthly hell, the ancient garbage dump for all of Jerusalem's bad dreams, receptacle for carcasses and corpses, rotting animals, human sinners stoned, burned, stabbed, strangled, tongues of flame darting into the sky day and night to incinerate the offal, pools of blood saturating the earth until it could absorb no more, the valley of the slaughter where fathers and mothers brought their children as offerings on the altars of the Molekh.

Shira said to Temima, "My band Jephta's Daughters once gave a concert here—at midnight, for women only." Temima thumped her fist against her chest over her heart. "I have sacrificed all my children here," she cried. "O my daughter, I opened my mouth to God and could not take it back."

Or she led her people out through the colossal portal of the Jaffa Gate taking them through the streets of the city along the Jaffa Road through the commercial center of western Jerusalem, the new city. A village really, Temima thought as she moved onward, ugly, provincial, shabby, primitive, greasy plastic streamers hanging in restaurant entryways, porters crossing the road bent over like mules, pianos and wardrobes lashed to their backs, peddlers with their wares spread out on a rag on the pavement—a few rusted hairpins, a dented saucepan, Q-tips with yellow earwax on the cotton bulbs—everywhere rubbish, filth, reeking human and animal waste, the earthly Jerusalem. You must lift your eyes to the heavenly Jerusalem, was Temima's teaching as they proceeded through the streets, Ben Yehuda, King George, Radak, Jabotinsky. Look up, it is stretched out like a bright canopy above, like a luminous hologram pitched over our heads. Truly there is a God in this place but I did not know it. How awesome this place is. It is none other than the house of God, and this is the gate to heaven. *Mah norah ha'makom ha'zeh,* the congregation sang out in response, Shira's strong voice ringing out above all the others. They chanted with palms uplifted, arms pumping heavenward toward the grandeur of the Jerusalem above as their feet trod through the squalor and muck of the Jerusalem below, Shira's voice penetrating the intoxicating, overrich atmosphere in wave upon wave, drowning out the chorus of bystanders providing commentary and gloss along the parade route. The Jerusalem Syndrome strikes again, it's a virus in the air! Messiahs and saviors, an epidemic, God help us, nutcases and crackpots! Take a look at her—a lady decked out like some weirdo rebbe, another crazy for our collection, just what we needed in this city! Just listen to them—yelling verses from the Bible at the top of their lungs, another tribe of loonies let out of Egypt!

Shira continued to take upon herself the holy task of pitching her sonorous vocal cords to neutralize the enemy whose ranks grew in number and strength every day as Temima brought her people more and more regularly directly into the heart of the most calcified piety as if snaking through its blood vessels to her destined place, which was approaching clarification. From the Street of the Kara'im they would make their way out of the Jewish Quarter through the arcades of the Muslim and Christian Quarters lined with tourist shops like hives stuffed with artifacts and souvenirs, the proprietors honeying you in just for a look, into the narrow lanes swarming with locals hunting and gathering, sheepsheads on iron hooks dripping blood in butcher store windows, cushiony brassieres in bright flesh-colored synthetics strung up on pegs, then out of the walled city through what the Arab Semites called the Damascus Gate and the Jewish Semites the Gate of Shekhem depending on where you are going, arriving finally into the constricting artery of Mea Shearim Street, marching under banners admonishing female visitors to respect the sensitivities and uncontrollable urges of the residents by refraining from dressing immodestly, a warning Temima's people abided by in any case on their own terms out of personal choice.

Nevertheless, immediately upon their appearance cries went up of *Beged Ish! Beged Ish!* They pointed to the male apparel of Temima in her rebbe's costume, accusing Temima of violating the injunction explicitly stated in the book of Deuteronomy against women wearing masculine garments, the prohibition against cross-dressing, an abomination to the Lord. Shira would then be inspired to raise her voice to declaim in a kind of recitative between full-blown arias or more familiarly for this congregation a cantor's liturgical chanting between discrete tunes, she would sing out her counterpoint that maybe it is actually the rebbes themselves who have been going around in drag all these years. Since when has a long silk bathrobe tied with a sash and a giant fur pillbox hat and white leggings and black pumps been designated a man's outfit? Maybe the rebbes are the ones who have been committing a transgender violation abhorrent to God by decking themselves out like the opposite sex. At which a roar went up even more furious, *Kol Isha! Kol Isha!* punctuated by a hailstorm of stones. How dare a woman raise her voice in public, how much more so, in song? *Kol Isha Erva,* they screamed, the voice of a woman is nakedness, she might as well just go ahead and take off all of her clothing in the public square in front of everyone as open up her *pisk* like that and actually sing, allow her naked voice to be heard out loud and bring nearly half the neighborhood to orgasm.

As Temima's people ducked for shelter behind cars and inside the doorways of shops, Shira placed herself in front of her mentor and teacher to shield her from the assault and sang out even louder above the voices of her harassers, "Yes, *Kol Isha Erva.* That's me. From now on that will be my name."

Temima raised her head in a show of support for her bodyguard, rendering herself a visible target, she clamped her two hands on either side of Shira's waist like a dance partner about to lift her up and twirl her in the air, she nodded as if she were the ventriloquist throwing her voice, projecting the words directly into the mouth of the golem she had created in her image out of mud as God created man in His image out of earth. "Because if I am silent now at a time like this," sang Kol-Isha-Erva moving her lips definitively with Temima's face rising above her like the sun, "salvation and deliverance will come from somewhere else, and I and my people will be lost. And who knows if it was not for a moment like this one that I have reached this place?"

The powerful vibrations of Kol-Isha-Erva's naked voice now faded as she craned her head to attend with her trained ear to a sound that seemed to be audible to her alone in her state of acute sensitivity and receptiveness.

She made a large summoning gesture with her two hands, calling together all of Temima's followers from their places of refuge. She set out at their head with clear purpose and direction, Temima gladly taking her place as one of the congregation, in her wisdom as a leader deferring to Kol-Isha-Erva's authority, a disciple in the throes of visionary inspiration.

Without doubt or wavering, Kol-Isha-Erva led them through the maze of alleys and lanes, between piles of dilapidated structures propping each other up, blocks of cramped, festering apartments held together as if by clotheslines, attending to the sounds beckoning her that at first only she could discern. But as they moved deeper and deeper into the dark and suffocating hidden cells of the interior the cries began to reach the others as well—Their cries have reached Me, I have seen how they are oppressed. When they burst in through the door of the fetid rooms reeking of stale Sabbath stew and soiled diapers he was beating her with his shoe, his rage materializing down his beard in runnels of white foam. Her cries cut off instantly. "It's me, I deserve it, it's coming from me, the smell, I stink very bad," she called out to them from her degradation curled up on the floor, one hand tugging her headscarf forward to conceal every strand of her hair, the other shielding her face, slashed and swollen. "Go away, it's nobody's business," her words pumped out in bleats. "There are ten children to marry off."

The voice of my sister's blood screams out to me from the ground, Kol-Isha-Erva sang out. Yet over the period of time that she was gripped by these illuminations, this was not the only woman to refuse rescue for the sake of public image and the family's survival, the perpetuation of the myth of peace in the household behind every door at whatever cost. Kol-Isha-Erva was always the first to hear the moans, nearly always she could pinpoint the source with supreme accuracy and assurance as if guided by an unseen beam straight to the rank black hole—a woman battered and beaten with fists and straps, choked and burned in the presence of her mute children, pregnant women stomped and kicked in the stomach. She was practically driven mad by the sights her eyes were seeing.

Now and then, it is true, the source of the cries would elude her as if she were a false prophet. Later she would insist to Aish-Zara that she had heard her cries too and had followed them until they had faded away like a ghost. "You did not allow yourself to be found then out of misguided pride," Kol-Isha-Erva chided Aish-Zara only half playfully.

"People almost stopped believing in me." But there were also those times when the spirit would come to rest on a woman taken in the tribulation of ravaging violence. She would rise up from the lowest point, her nose bashed in, teeth knocked out, eyes puffed shut, black and blue, bleeding, stagger out with them in her housecoat and slippers and kerchief, leave everything behind and throw in her lot with Kol-Isha-Erva, loop herself in a loop of the rope of the school for prophets and transform herself into a prophet so that it could be said about her that she too is among the prophets.

Temima did not restrain Kol-Isha-Erva's visionary ministrations, she did not begrudge her. To the contrary, she drew a portion from the spirit that was in herself and bestowed it upon Kol-Isha-Erva. If only all of God's people would become prophets, Temima declared as had Moses Our Teacher. If only God would put His spirit into *all* of them, Temima proclaimed.

It was said of Temima that during this period of preparing herself to come out in her full radiance as a towering leader in Israel there was not a single instance when she refused a call to assist in the ritual preparations of a dead woman for burial, no matter the time of day or night or the distance to be traveled or whatever the obstacles in her path, and especially if the deceased was utterly alone with no one else in the world. This, as everyone knows, is regarded as a supreme mitzvah, since under the circumstances there can be no expectation of gratitude from the beneficiary, not even a simple thank you.

Yet it was also reported and attested to by every single woman of the holy society who had ever worked at Temima's side in a team of four performing these final ministrations that, without exception, in the last moments, as the veil was drawn down over the face of the corpse lying there in her white shrouds just before being swaddled in her winding sheet, the words Thank You always came out of her mouth packed with sand without spilling a grain, as if emanating from her agitated soul still hovering like a moth rubbing its wings together on her lips before taking flight. They all heard it, they were startled the first times it happened, but then they came to expect it almost as a point of good manners; they recognized that it was meant not for them but for Temima alone, and they bowed their heads in awe. But Temima's head swung back sharply as if struck each time the words shot out of the mouth of the corpse, it was always a blow. The highest mitzvah for everyone else was not available to her, she was not worthy, she performed this service with an excess of pride disguised as humility. Upon Temima was placed the burden of having to strive to fulfill an even higher mitzvah for which she would get no gratitude.

Her quest also lay in the realm of death, that much was clear—but what? Remembrance? Resurrection? Reclaiming the tree of life that the first woman had forfeited? Slashing her way beyond the cherubim and the fiery revolving sword guarding the entrance to the east of Eden and plucking its fruit? Finally, the woman had figured out which fruit was the forbidden one. Knowledge was tasty, delightful to behold, desirable to attain—a pastime, a plaything, a distraction. But choosing life, swallowing up death forever and wiping away the tears from every face—that was the true prize, that was her messianic mission, her thankless task.

Nevertheless, the women who worked alongside Temima under her direction performing the purification ritual considered it a great honor to be joined in their holy society by a personage of such stature. Moreover, they regarded her participation as an extraordinary privilege accorded to the remains lying naked under a sheet, a distinction the corpse was surely aware of at some level of consciousness and could appreciate.

Temima demanded to take on for herself the most difficult and unsavory tasks—washing the waxen feet encrusted and scaled like hooves and cleaning under the clawlike toenails with a toothpick, thrusting her hands into the orifices to drain out all solid and liquid matter like a plumber, extracting whatever they were stuffed with, false teeth, rotting food, pessaries, excrement, gems, money, drugs, once, a piece of wire coathanger, another time, a vibrator like a dead rat. She chanted psalms and verses from the Song of Songs in praise of the beauty of the remains lying stiffly in front of her as she labored, pausing between refrains before exposing the next section of the body to be worked on in order to beg forgiveness of the dead if in any way she had violated her dignity, addressing her by name—so-and-so daughter not only of a father but also of a mother, she had ruled that the mother's name must also be noted and invoked as well.

So it happened one night that Temima repeatedly intoned throughout the meticulous washing of an exceptionally heavy woman weighing more than three hundred pounds the words, Forgive me Frima daughter of Zsuzsi and Rudolf if by any of my actions I have in any way trespassed on your honor. But it was only when she would not be dissuaded from serving as one of in this case three women who held up this massive body while the fourth poured the nine *kavin* of water over it in a continuous stream for the actual *tahara* ritual, chanting She is pure, She is pure, She is pure, only when she felt the full crushing weight of this body through which this human being had experienced her life and looked out at the world, only then did Temima realize with a pang of despair that the dead woman she was raising was her father's wife, Frumie. She had removed the plaintive polish from the nails, raked between the toes, separated the folds of fat to wipe the crevices in between, extracted the false teeth from the mouth, probed inside the nostrils and ears with a Q-tip, combed out every knot in the wispy hair, cleaned the scar over the gash through which the womb had been scraped out, cleaned the webbing of scar tissue where the breasts had once been, cleaned out the orifice where her father had deposited his seed, repeating the name of the dead woman all the while, pleading for forgiveness for any sins this woman might have committed among them surely gluttony, begging forgiveness for herself if in any fashion she had offended her. But not until she had hoisted the great load of the physical remains for the purification bath itself did Temima recognize that this had been her own stepmother Frumie to whom she had been attending all this while. She had invoked her name again and again and the name of her mother and father, she had looked at her closely, examined the moles and bristles on her skin, the sores and spots and discolorations, the lumps and lesions, her acne-pitted face, but she had not taken her in, she had not truly seen her in death to know who she was as she had not seen her in life.

How much older was Frumie than Temima? Five, six years at most. But the body Temima now gazed down upon ready to be dressed in its shrouds was utterly used up. Frumie's girls, the daughters of her father but not her mother, Temima's half sisters, whom she had always conflated with the five daughters of Zelophekhad of the unmentionable sin demanding their right to exist, might even at this very moment be waiting outside the door of the purification room in the direction toward which their mother's feet were pointed, assuming they had escorted her remains from Brooklyn for burial in Israel, which would have amounted to a grudging expense for their mutual father, Reb Berel Bavli. No matter, whatever they shared in common, Temima would not have recognized them in any case except perhaps if they were clumped together in a gang of five, and out of delicacy members of the holy society because of the intimate knowledge they acquired of the deceased took pains to avoid contact with survivors especially those who had in some form once been inside this very body.

She wondered if her father might be lurking somewhere nearby too or even if he had come to Israel. Maybe he hired some loafer to accompany the body stowed in the cargo hold of the El Al carrier through all the stages to the interment in some less prestigious and cheaper cemetery in the Jerusalem environs, the compromise Temima imagined worked out by her father in his negotiations with his wife so that she would give up and die already, just as he had hired a bum off the street to recite Kaddish over her own mother. In any event, Temima had not had any contact with her father since he had turned down her appeal for help in obtaining a divorce from Howie.

Soon after that, he had officially cut her off entirely by declaring her dead and sitting shiva over her for committing adultery with a *schvartze* whom nobody could ever convince him was a Jew even if you stood on your head and spit wooden nickels and talked until you were blue in the face. At least he sat shiva in person, Temima reflected, rather than hiring some good-for-nothing to do the job in exchange for a brisket.

Throughout her father's seven days of mourning over herself, as a point of honor, Temima took great pains to make her living presence felt. At first she called the Boro Park house nonstop on the telephone. One of the girls would always pick up in the way of youth still hopefully expecting their lives to be altered dramatically through a message communicated from the outside world. Temima could hear the girl yelling across the living room to her father sitting on the floor—she could picture it—on the avocado green wall-to-wall carpeting in his stocking feet with the ornate smoky mirror in its gilded frame draped with a sheet behind him, accepting condolences from visitors for her passing. "Tateh, it's Tema," the kid would yell, "long distance, from hell—she wants to talk to you." Naturally, her father did not come to the phone since she was dead. He wasn't like some kind of meshuggeneh in the street, he didn't talk to himself, though as he never failed to point out to others he conversed with that at least if he talked to himself he would be talking to an intelligent person, a person with some brains in his head.

Even so, despite the brazenness of Temima's constant calls, the family tolerated them longer than she might have predicted, probably because the girls kicked and screamed and raised a fuss and threw a fit against unplugging their lifeline, until finally, at the end of the third day, they clamped down and took the phone off the hook. Temima considered coming to Brooklyn herself from Israel and sitting down on the floor beside her father in sackcloth and ashes to mourn her own life like Jephta's daughter or like a character always wearing black in a Russian play, and thereby in the presence of family and friends, mourners and comforters, rub in the absurdity of the whole travesty and farce, but that would have been too much of an effort, that would have implied she cared too much. Instead she arranged through the Toiter to have some of his people march full time back and forth in front of the house carrying signs on poles, Tema Bavli Lives, Tema Bavli Is Alive and Well and Living by the Dead Sea, Reb Berel Bavli—Your Daughter Tema Is Not Dead Meat, and so on, now and then breaking out in joyous singing and dancing, giving the lie to the rumors of death. On the sixth day, by personal order of the police commissioner of the city of New York, the Toiter's demonstrators were arrested for disturbing the peace. On the seventh day Temima rested—not in peace but in indifference.

Now, as she worked with the other three women to dress Frumie in her simple white linen shrouds like the high priest in the Temple on Yom Kippur, the Day of Judgment and Awe, it required all of Temima's inner strength to hold back from bursting out in hacking laughter that would have glided inevitably into savage crying. She looked down, focusing on her task, chanting the order of the dressing in a soft trembling voice—And she shall be attired in a linen headdress, and linen breeches shall be on her flesh, and she shall don a holy linen tunic, and with a linen sash she shall be girded, and God Almighty will give her mercy. She did not inform her companions who this woman was to her even though now that she had recognized her she ought to have been spared this further painful invasion of the physical privacy of someone who, after all, was related to her even if only by marriage, she should have been shielded from revealing the nakedness that belonged to her father, an explicit incest prohibition in Leviticus, a variation on the sin of Ham. May I be lost in the depths of the sea, Temima prayed to herself, may I be vaporized in the atmosphere, may I be swallowed up by the earth rather than have this poor body of mine that I have guarded so zealously to dispose of in accordance with my own desires subjected to handling even by well-meaning souls such as these earnest good women who are toiling at my side at this very moment.

The lifting of Frumie's dead weight to slip on the pants, simply finding a pair of pants that would fit her from among the shrouds, a sash that would go around her waist just once much less three times with a bit left over to tie with a slip knot, never mind such fancy stuff as fashioning it in the shape of the letter *shin* for God Almighty's name Shaddai—viewed from above, with detachment, with no imperative for reverence, the scene was slapstick, black comedy. Temima turned her inner vision to her memory of Frumie pregnant, sitting at the edge of the bed in the Boro Park house where her own mother had once slept and perished, Frumie dressed in her hat and coat with the white fur trimming, her black patent-leather pocketbook in her lap, her suitcase packed ready beside her, all set to escape, crushed by the realization that there was no way to sustain herself on her own, no one who would be left to protect her daughters, no place for her to go—she was trapped. Few and bad had been the years of her life. Now she was released early for good behavior, she had found the only way out. For your salvation I had hoped, O Lord.

Temima was overcome with a desire to give Frumie a parting gift, some token to thank her with for her kindness over the years they had lived together under the same roof, for the generosity of simply leaving Temima alone to find her own way, but that was impermissible. Naked I came from my mother's womb and naked I will return. Shrouds do not come with pockets for little treasures or mementos, in death there is no discrimination between rich and poor, the same uniform for everyone, the same plain pine box put together without nails, in Israel maybe no box at all, affording unimpeded access for the maggots and all the other creatures of decay burrowing in wait. Even between men and women the distinctions fade in death; a devout woman is clad in trousers in death perhaps for the first time in her life just like a man, the restrictions fall away—with the exception, Temima now reminded herself, of the prayer shawl in which only a man is privileged to be cloaked in life, in death his prayer shawl can become his winding sheet.

With a nod to her companions Temima stepped away for a moment from the corpse to retrieve her capacious white talit with its licorice black stripes. It was a traditional prayer shawl, with no extraneous ornamentation and no feminizing accents. She wore it whether praying alone or with others regardless of the time of month in a woman still cyclic, she did not consider it a show of excessive piety or ostentation as a woman to wrap herself in it but rather an essential cocoon inside of which she could achieve the focus and transcendence that carried her to new mystical planes considered unattainable by her sex. She always carried it with her in a special bag in those days should the opportunity for *hitbodedut* present itself, which she performed during this period in the enhanced isolation of the sheltering white tent of her prayer shawl.

The three women working alongside Temima did not question her actions, they simply followed her lead, putting their complete trust in her higher powers. It required the maximum effort from all four of them heaving together to levitate the rigid, putrefying mass of Frumie's body, whisk away the cloth it was resting upon and replace it with Temima's talit with its fringe torn, no longer usable for prayer. As they were folding the talit over Frumie as if shaping a stuffed cabbage, bundling her to be sent off from the struggle of this world to the void who knew where, Temima pronounced the words, "Frima daughter of Zsuzsi and Rudolf, know that you are dead." Only then did the body seem truly to expire, to relax and deflate. The face cloth with the broken pieces of earthenware over the eyes and mouth seemed to flutter and they all heard the words, "Thank you, Tema."

The members of the holy society turned stunned to Temima. One of them dared to inquire. "You know her?"

Temima nodded. "Yes, I knew her. Alas poor Frumie."

The more flesh, the more worms, Rabbi Hillel was wont to say. In almost the same breath he also used to say, The more women, the more witchcraft. This was the more tolerant sage Hillel, the Hillel of the Golden Rule, the Hillel who did not, as did the more severe Rabbi Shammai, swing his stick in the air to whack the prospective proselyte who had the audacity to demand to be taught the entire Torah while standing on one foot, but answered instead, What is hateful to you do not do to your friend.

The rest is commentary.

As word spread throughout the Jewish Quarter and beyond that the dead women prepared by Temima for the next life invariably raised their voices in the final moment to thank her, there were those among the living who also raised their voices—to accuse Temima of witchcraft. Conjuring up the dead, consulting familiar spirits and ghosts, the *ov* and *yedonim*—this is a Canaanite abomination strictly forbidden in the Torah, an encounter with the supernatural we are fiercely enjoined to shun, an odious practice we must ruthlessly extrude from the sanctified precincts of the Promised Land along with its idolatrous priestesses.

Temima's response was sharp and absolute. She let it be known that henceforth she would be called Temima Ba'alatOv, Mistress of the Spirits, to honor the woman/witch (here the two words had elided and become synonymous) of Endor who at the behest of King Saul raised from the dead the ghost of Samuel to ask for a prophecy.

You have sinned, God has forsaken you, tomorrow you will die, the prophet said.

You shall not let a sorceress live, the Torah says. "It depends how we define 'live,'" said Fish'l Sabon, leader of the movement in the Jewish Quarter against Temima. "In that golden age when the Messiah comes, speedily and in our day, God willing, when the Holy Temple is restored on its Mount and the Torah is once again the law of the land, a witch will be put to death by stoning, the same as a person who has had sexual intercourse with an animal. Meanwhile, in these dark and profane times, we shall not let her live in peace."

Out of pity for Fish'l Sabon, Temima tolerated his harassments for nearly a full year. In a sad way, she felt a strange kinship with him. The story was that he too had taken his name—Sabon, *soap*—in a spirit of defiance reminiscent of how she herself had assumed the mantle of Ba'alatOv, in his case to spit in the eye of the arrogant Zionist powers who, with such disdain for what they regarded to be the sheep-to-the-slaughter passivity of Diaspora Jews, had called the victims of the Shoah *sabon* since, as rumor had it, soap was what the fat of their bodies had been processed into by the Nazi psychopaths. You call us Sabon, you obnoxious Zionist snobs? Fish'l in effect was saying. Henceforth, that will be my name, my badge of honor, I wear it with pride.

Of course, Fish'l had not been recycled into soap himself, but he was a survivor—as Temima taught, Who in this life is not a survivor? Orphaned before the age of ten, he wandered alone in perpetual terror somewhere in Eastern Europe, hiding due to the ineradicable scar of Jewishness on his male flesh, joining a band of partisans in the woods where, because of his small stature and undernourished size, he was used to plant explosives on railroad tracks. After the war he was smuggled by Zionist activists out of a displaced persons camp, arriving in pre-state Israel singing the "Hatikva" at the top of his lungs and dancing a hora, then forcibly turned away by the British occupiers to Cyprus. There Fish'l, by then already a young man nearly twenty years old, along with his fellow survivors, was herded yet again, to the everlasting shame of the entire so-called civilized world, into another prison camp behind barbed wire.

No one knew how he eventually made it back to Israel to settle permanently. There were some, it is true, who maliciously and it is generally agreed falsely maintained that Fish'l had never actually been in the war at all or even a bit player in its theater—that he had never even been out of the Holy Land in his entire life, that he was a ninth-generation descendant of a family that sustained itself on alms from the Diaspora and begging from pilgrims in the alleys and arcades of the Old City of Jerusalem, and that his true name was Yonah Seif. For this version of the story, there is very little authoritative support.

One thing is certain, however. Until his public emergence as Fish'l Sabon, as if fully formed like Adam himself the first man without the tenderizing benefit of childhood or youth or for that matter a mother soon after the Six Day War of 1967, very little is known about Fish'l Sabon except that he had been a constant presence at the trial of the Nazi war criminal Adolf Eichmann six years earlier as evidenced by the repeated capturing of his unmistakable image in the background of news photographs and television footage from that historic event. No one even knew how he had made a living until he came out fully and definitively in that triumphant messianic year, 5727 from the creation of the world, though there were some who asserted that he was the mysterious author known as 202500, widely admired and revered as the writer and illustrator of a series of booklets that brought to public attention in painful detail the terrible sadistic sexual tortures of the Nazis, may their name and memory be erased.

For Fish'l, Israel's stunning victory in the Six Day War against such impossible odds was an irrefutable sign that the redemption was underway and the messianic age at hand. You had to be deaf, dumb, and blind not to recognize the mighty hand of God in such an obvious miracle, Fish'l insisted, or damaged even more hopelessly, in the very pith of your soul. It was around this time that Fish'l assumed the title Baba, an acronym heralding the imminent arrival of the Messiah, *B'mhera B'yamenu Amen,* Speedily and in our Time, Amen. Baba Fish'l Sabon burst into the public consciousness by establishing himself as a fixture at the redeemed and repossessed Western Wall, declaring himself its official janitor. Every night he could be seen with a squeegee and a bucket, mopping the stones of the plaza in front of the wall, and once a week, after the Sabbath, when three stars appeared in the darkened sky and the blessing dividing the sacred from the profane was recited with sprigs of fragrant rosemary wafted in the air, Baba Fish'l would come out with a long rubber hose and aim a powerful stream of water full force at the stones of the wall, sending the piteous *kvittlakh* and petitions stuffed in their crannies pouring down in rivulets like copious tears, which he swept up with a brush broom into plastic garbage bins and dumped.

Everyone agreed that the fissures and clefts had to be regularly cleared out to make room for the next batch in the endless flood of pain and supplications, but there were those who were troubled by Baba Fish'l's seeming callousness and sacrilege in discarding with such casual disrespect and hardheartedness these poignant letters many of them doubtless inscribed with the name of God as the addressee, therefore rendering them holy fragments requiring eternal preservation through burial in a designated cache. To these benighted souls, Baba Fish'l coolly pointed out, "A retaining wall, nothing more," with a contemptuous shrug of a shoulder toward the massive stones bolstering the western side of the mountain. "An exterior wall, a prop, a casing, like a pita bread," Baba Fish'l added. Raising his eyes to indicate the plateau protruding above the wall overlooking the plaza with its two domed Muslim edifices, like two invasive tumors, he said, "Up there—that's the big falafel."

Not for a single minute did Baba Fish'l lose sight of this prize. It infuriated him that the Zionist government had so cravenly handed over control of the Temple Mount to the imams of the Muslim Waqf after the war in June of sixty-seven, an unforgivable suicidal multi-culti concession to stroke and make nice to the gentile world that loathed us even more for our imbecile simpering fawning and obsequiousness. Every one of Baba Fish'l's thoughts and actions from that day forth was focused on reclaiming this old threshing floor of Arauna the Jebusite, which David our king who is alive and everlasting had purchased for fifty silver shekels fair and square for the purpose of erecting an altar up there to stanch the plague that was consuming the Jewish people in those days—and, in our own day, too, Baba Fish'l hastened to add, is still eating us up alive.

To build an altar up there once again, to restore the Holy Temple erected on this site by David's son Solomon in all of its splendor so unparalleled that he who had never seen it had never seen beauty in his life—this was the goal to which Baba Fish'l now dedicated himself. To reach this height, he publicly declared himself a Nazir, asserting that he would faithfully adhere to his Nazirite vow of asceticism until the Temple Mount was reclaimed. It was this Nazirite path that rendered the particular offense of Temima's communion with the dead, her necromancy, even more profoundly distressing to him than her all-around witchcraft, which in and of itself was already bad enough. He declared himself a Nazir very soon after he came to the wall as its self-styled custodian in his quest to discover the divinely ordained path from this peripheral station to the Holy of Holies at the summit. Standing in front of the wall with a cadre of fellow seekers he declared, "The first *kvittel* I pluck out from between these stones will reveal to me the way to the top." He inserted his hand, pulled out a precisely folded note torn from a pad with a letterhead that indicated it had come from a law firm in Washington, D.C., and read aloud these words: Dear G-d, Please don't let me go bald. Thank you in advance. Sincerely, Mervin Zupnik, Esq.

In a flash, Baba Fish'l recognized that this was the sign he was seeking. The most distinctive feature of the Nazir, the way in which a person who has taken the Nazirite vow can instantly be recognized, is his hair that he is forbidden to cut, like Samson, because it is in his hair that a man's life force and vital strength reside, it is his crown and glory that he dedicates to the Lord. A razor may not touch the head of a Nazir; the fullness of his growth of hair is the outward mark of his vow as its inward expressions are his abstinence from eating grapes in any form wet or dry, intoxicating or not—the blood of the grape—and his avoidance of all contact with a dead person, even his closest relative, mother or father, sister or brother, son or daughter. With these three strictures the Nazir sets himself apart as holy to God throughout the specified duration of his vow, in certain respects even holier than the high priest himself who can sip his wine while getting a haircut. Extracting from the lawyer Zupnik's note the divine sign he was seeking intended for him alone, Baba Fish'l immediately announced that he was taking upon himself the yoke of the Nazir, sanctifying himself to God for a designated period of time, which, Baba Fish'l affirmed, would be the day on which he would be able to mark the fulfillment of his vow by offering up the requisite sacrifices on an altar on top of the Temple Mount.

Several times a year, without any advance notice, Baba Fish'l and his band of followers would attempt the ascent up the Temple Mount carrying a one-year-old unblemished male lamb for a burnt offering, an unblemished ewe lamb in its first year for a sin offering, a ram without blemish for a peace offering under which he hoped to burn his shorn-off hair upon ending his Nazirite term as is required, plus a basket of unleavened cakes with their libations as well as a portable altar and all the other prescribed accessories and gear. One way or another, with varying degrees of savagery and derision, the pilgrims were always halted in their ascent and prevented from attaining their hearts' desire. Most likely there was a traitor or a mole or a double agent planted in his inner circle, Baba Fish'l suspected. They were blocked not only by the Muslim interlopers and trespassers, as might have been expected from such barbarians, but, far more troubling, by the Israeli authorities themselves, their own brothers and sisters, the vaunted holy nation, the kingdom of priests, who cut them off with astonishing ruthlessness and shocking mockery.

In his most spectacular attempt to end his Nazirite period with the mandated sacrifices, which exploded in banner headlines in all the newspapers not only in Israel but in the nations of the world as well, Baba Fish'l and his comrades loaded the animals and all the other supplies including the porta-altar onto a helicopter paid for by a billionaire American evangelical from Florida and sought to land on top of the Temple Mount, only to be viciously apprehended and placed under arrest by a security force welcoming committee made up of Arabs and Jews, united for the first time in history for this disgraceful purpose.

As the years passed and he persisted without success in his efforts to bring his Nazirite vows to an end by performing the required sacrifices on top of the Temple Mount, Baba Fish'l's hair, which he was not permitted even to pass a comb through lest he break a strand in violation of his ascetic commitment, grew into a wildly tangled ash-colored mass with the coarseness of sackcloth stuffed with straw, ending in long tassels of fused-together locks, the tips so dry they seemed to give off a crackling sound like kindling as he moved about the vicinity of the wall carrying out his self-imposed duties, a small, withered holy man upon whose head the dark mass of a threatening sludge-brown cloud seemed to have settled and would never lift. For a Nazir, it's all in the head, Baba Fish'l taught—not only the hair on top, but also the hole in the face known as the mouth through which he abstains from taking in the fruit of the vine, and the two little holes of the nose through which he avoids even breathing in the secondhand smoke of death by rigorously shunning all proximity and contact.

Temima's communion with the dead carried the pollution of death's aura into the intimate space of the enclosed city in which Baba Fish'l dwelt, contaminating the very air he breathed. Her necromancy, her summoning up of the spirits of the dead with black magic, endangered the forthcoming redemption that he had devoted so many years as a Nazir to bringing about. The Nazir is the Maccabee who reconsecrates. The Nazir Baba Fish'l Sabon would be the soap that cleanses and washes away the impurity of the witch.

Witch! *Makhshefa*! Sorceress! Necromancer! Such slanders and others far more excoriating, calling attention to every part of Temima's body from head to toe—the squirming venomous serpents of her hair, her cloven feet like a demoness, and all the swampy filth and stench in between including the raw nakedness of the tail behind—were found scrawled with paint or marker or chalk on the stones of her quarters in the Street of the Kara'im almost every morning, requiring vigorous scrubbing to remove them by Kol-Isha-Erva supervising a damage-control team. Dumpsters were overturned or set on fire outside her building. Stones were hurled through the windows wrapped in messages tied with string warning that BABA, Swiftly In Our Time, Amen, when the Temple is restored on its Mount, such stones will be cast directly at the softest and tenderest parts of Temima's sinful body in compliance with the sentence of death meted out by the Torah to a sorceress. There were mornings when they opened the door to the street and knocked over slop buckets set down in the night. Excrement smeared over the entryway, used condoms and bloody sanitary napkins deposited in heaps, dead birds, dead cats, dead rats, such were their daily deliveries, and every now and then, for a festive touch, whole rolls of toilet paper unfurled and hung in streamers from whatever projection they could be affixed to or draped over, which inspired Temima to pronounce the blessing thanking God for having kept her alive and sustaining her to this time, marveling at how far the State of Israel had come since the early pioneer years when quality toilet tissue had been such a precious commodity no one would ever think of using it for decoration or a prank, it was a luxury to be hoarded, to be dispensed sparingly, imported from abroad as she herself had done in a special suitcase when she had first arrived in the Holy Land. Blood was slathered on the doorpost one night, along with instructions in gothic script, ANGEL OF DEATH, DO NOT PASS OVER THIS HOUSE. Another time an X was slapped across the front door with tape punctuated by a skull and bones and the warning—POISON, PLAGUE, BLACK DEATH.

The tape gave off a grating screech as she tore through it and once again took her life in her hands by stepping out. She went out on her own to check out the scene, ventured beyond the four walls of her house. Urchins leaped into view like imps from every side screaming Lilith! Delilah! Jezebel!—running in front of her, ringing bells as if to alert the citizens of the approach of a leper, crying Impure! Impure! Stones and shoes, rotten vegetables and eggs and other assorted objects were hurled at her but on no account would she allow her persecutors to keep her a prisoner in her own house or prevent her from going wherever her heart led. Through this pelting storm of taunts and missiles Temima floated regally, divinely untouched like the first time she entered the army camp overlooking Hebron and walked between the raindrops. It was as if she hovered above and beyond all that was transpiring in the chaos of her orbit, she its fixed star.

More difficult to bear though was the relentless stalking by Baba Fish'l himself whenever she ventured outside the city walls in search of the solitude she needed for the practice of *hitbodedut* to strengthen herself spiritually. Temima's people urged her to avoid leaving through the Dung Gate, which was the closest to the Western Wall where Baba Fish'l was always on patrol. Like a hawk he would spy her departing and swoop down at once on her trail. But Temima refused to change course in any way that might even implicitly acknowledge this little Baba's power over her. For a mere woman like herself the Dung Gate would serve, she declared, departing through it was the equivalent of taking out the garbage, egress by the bowel. Beyond it the hills and valleys opened up before her, the purported tomb of the prophet Zekharia, the cone-shaped pinnacle of what legend had it was the burial site of David's wayward and rebellious son, dazzlingly handsome, endowed with such a lavish head of hair it killed him in the end—Absalom.

Like Absalom's grim supporter Shimi ben Gera, Baba Fish'l Sabon came after Temima, he came out through the Dung Gate cursing her the whole way, throwing stones at her and at all of her people to her right and left, he would curse her and say, Get out, get out, you bloody whore, you witch. One of Temima's Bnei Zeruya protectors would demand, Who is this dead dog to curse you? Let me at him and I'll chop off his balls. But Temima would shake her head. Since he is cursing me, said Temima, it must be the case that God intends for me to be cursed. But the day will come when God will recompense me for all the abuse he is heaping on me.

For many months Baba Fish'l Sabon continued to walk alongside Temima and her people unimpeded through the hills and wadis, the valleys of Kidron and Jehosephat, along the brow of the Ofel and by the Gihon Spring, beyond the walls of the Old City, walking and cursing, casting stones in Temima's direction and fistfuls of dirt, until one day Ibn Kadosh came up the flank of the slope from Silwan with a herd of goats and followed along on the ridge beside Temima, taking in the ravings of her oppressor through the shade of the dark velvety richness of his lowered lashes. "Why you let this little rasta lice-head talk to you like this?" he insisted. Temima smiled, pleased to see the lithe form of this beautiful boy again after so long an absence, the glow of his polished mahogany skin. "Never mind," she said, "in the end all is known."

The next time Temima went out of the walled city for *hitbodedut* through the Dung Gate Baba Fish'l did not appear. He did not appear the next day either, or in the days after that. At around the same time the daily bombardments she had been subjected to for so long inside the Jewish Quarter subsided until she grew out of the habit of fortifying herself inwardly in anticipation each time she stepped out, and even the memory began to fade so that it was almost impossible to believe it had ever happened, it was as if she had been trapped in a bad dream.

One morning as she was sitting alone in her study reflecting on the strange case of Elazar son of Dordaya of whom it was said that there was not a single whore in the entire world with whom he had not had sexual intercourse at least once, a story recounted in the Talmud open on her table to the tractate Avodah Zara focusing on all forms of idolatry that are the lethal side effects of mixing with the gentiles, she raised her eyes and saw Ibn Kadosh standing in front of her. She had not heard him enter; she could not say if he had slipped in through the door or the window or descended like a stealth angel from the ceiling, so silently and mysteriously did he appear. He stared down at her sitting there at her table over her Gemara and pronounced, "I want for you to raise from the dead someone for me." Temima's eyes widened in alarm.

Ibn Kadosh let out a dry laugh, decoding her leap. "No, not him, not your little Bob Marley rasta lice-head freak. You think maybe I kill him? Why I want to kill *him*? And if I kill him, why I want to see him again? But not to worry, I already take care of him for you, he don't bother you no more." And from the sheepskin pouch slung across his chest, Ibn Kadosh extracted some photographs that he fanned out on her table. "I give him one for souvenir. You take too. Present."

Temima's eyes ranged over them, all copies of the same image—Baba Fish'l Sabon naked except for his yarmulke affixed with a triangular metal clip to his monumental thatch of hair, trussed up like a turkey, an object resembling a large sausage sticking out of his rear end and a rubber ball plugged into his mouth. Towering over him was a formidable female specimen, on her chiseled blond head a Stormtrooper's visored cap with a skull and crossbones insignia, a tight black leather jacket open to reveal pneumatic breasts, a garter belt hoisting sheer black stockings, tall shiny black leather riding boots with spiked heels digging into Baba Fish'l's pasty flesh as he groveled at her feet, one of her gloved hands yanking his head back brutally by its dreadlocks to force him to bare his face to the camera lens, her other hand with the red swastika armband swinging a whip over his back, spongy and white like dough.

"Special whorehouse in Tel Aviv for Hitler S&M freaks," Ibn Kadosh commented. "Your lice-head is regular customer. When I show him picture he say to me, 'Big deal, for Nazir like me and Samson no law against fucking any way turn us on—only no wine, no dead bodies, no haircut, that's it, don't say nothing about fucking.' What is this Nazir thing anyway—some kind of Nazi gig? But one thing for sure, now he leave you alone forever."

Temima pushed the photos away from her with the squeamish tips of two fingers across the tabletop back toward Ibn Kadosh. Elazar ben Dordaya in the tractate Avodah Zara heard about a prostitute living by the sea whose price was a full purse of dinars. With a purse full of dinars he crossed over seven rivers and came to her. While they were fornicating she passed gas. She said to him, Just as this gas can never return to the place it came out of, so too Elazar ben Dordaya can never return in penance. He cannot be forgiven.

"I get rid of this lice-head for you," said Ibn Kadosh. "I do you big favor. Now you raise up from the dead for me someone."

Temima objected, she had never possessed such supernatural powers as had been attributed to her, she protested. He, Ibn Kadosh, should know this better than anyone. He had attended her in childbirth. She was an ordinary woman—she bled, she shat, she cried, she howled in pain. She had been falsely charged and persecuted by this madman with his pathetic fantasies, the dead she prepared for burial never opened their mouths to thank her, it was a hallucination conjured up by her coworkers in an ecstatic state to fill their own void, they were hearing voices.

But Ibn Kadosh refused to accept this. "I want you should raise up for me my mother."

A vision of Ketura as Jezebel appeared before her inner eye as if on a screen on the back of her lids, Ketura's body turned into dog shit so that no one could say this was Ketura, the shadow of the black wings seared into her face dissolving into the sand. "Your mother is too long dead to be reached. Her spirit is too far away," Temima said.

"I need her. I need for to ask her a question."

The answer came in a bass rumble from below. "Enough already, I told you on the mountaintop but you refused to believe me. I did not kill her, it was her own people, an honor killing."

Temima let out a cry. What were they seeing? An old man, hollow eye sockets, broken bones, his long cloak in tatters, his black flesh shredded, covered all over with dried blood and gravel, a ghost. "What more do you want from me?" the old man growled. "Why do you disturb me now by bringing me up from the depths you have cast me in?"

Ibn Kadosh flung himself on the floor, his body stretched out prone to hide his eyes from this terrible sight. Temima knelt down beside him and stroked his head and long back. She led him to her bed where she tended him for a week, feeding him milk and honey with a spoon until he regained his strength, neither of them rising to take part in the rites of mourning for Abba Kadosh condemned to wander in the next life seeking his own path to mercy, from them he would not find forgiveness.

Reports of his death were broadcast that evening. According to a press release issued by his chief widow and lawyer, Em-Kol-Hai Kedosha, the martyr Abba Kadosh, za'zal, may the memory of the righteous be a blessing, had thrown himself off the mountaintop of the suicide rock of Masada in an heroic sacrifice rather than submit to the Judeo-Romans threatening to seize him and sell him back to slavery in America. His remains when they were discovered had already been picked over by the black birds swooping down from the desert sky, leaving only shredded fragments of one of his striped homespun robes made of hemp, the costume he wore every day except for special occasions, Sabbaths and holidays. Even the signature staff he always carried was nowhere to be found, all of which necessitated a painful delay until he could be definitively identified and properly mourned.

There was a spasm of attention to the violent end of this self-styled Jew, leader of the cultic polygamous sect of outcast blacks in the Judean Desert, and then all interest fizzled out. On the extreme religious right, the notion that this son of Ham who called himself Abba Kadosh like some kind of Christian holy father pope could ever be accepted as a Jew was a joke, not worth pinching your nose to blow some snot down into the gutter. As a small aside it was also noted in this camp that if he had been an authentic Jew he would have known better than to jump from Masada. On Masada you committed suicide by sticking a knife into your heart or you fell on your sword; if you want to be a big hero and kill yourself by jumping, the place to go is up north, to Gamla.

The topic also came up in passing on one of the television news shows when an expert tapped his temple and indulged a speculation as to why anyone in his right mind would even want to become a Jew, and especially a black man—didn't he have enough problems already? It could only be some weird form of masochism. From the ultraliberal far left a buzz of indignation was revived in newspaper commentary around that old question, Who is a Jew? and its logical corollary, If a person considers her or himself a Jew, who among us has the right to tell her or him that she or he is not a Jew and deny her or him full-fledged Israeli citizenship under the Law of Return? We are all guilty of Abba Kadosh's death. All of us pushed him off the top of Masada. The sheer hypocrisy of excluding this Jewish wannabe from the congregation of Israel is intolerable, it is an ethical outrage. In what way are we, the purported light unto the nations in the immortal words of the prophet Isaiah, any better than the racist thugs of America hooding themselves in sheets muttering mumbo jumbo and burning crosses on the lawns of a black family that moves into your all-white neighborhood?

Just such an image lit up in Temima's mind one night some months later as she gazed out of the window of her private quarters on the second floor over her newly established synagogue and study house in the Bukharim Quarter of Jerusalem. Positioned directly in her line of sight a quorum of ten men was performing the lashes of fire ritual of a *pulsa denura* across the street instead of in a cemetery where this curse is traditionally delivered. Temima was well aware that an exception was being made for her sake so that she could witness the rite with her own eyes and take heed, pack her bags at once, and exorcise herself from the neighborhood. For atmosphere, however, a token coffin was set down at the feet of the ten men lined up in a row facing her, each with a yellow star affixed to his breast over his heart and a crumpled Xerox of the kabbalistically potent curse custom-tailored for Temima clutched in both hands. She was not able to identify any of these men, but she did recognize the coffin, it had her name on it, and certainly she also recognized the impressive widescreen back in its shimmering black kaftan of the leader of the group, Rabbi Kaddish Lustiger, son of the Oscwiecim Rebbe from Brooklyn. The old man was also in Jerusalem, she had heard, but no one had actually seen him, he was kept hidden away in a state of raving dementia, so they said, unrecognizable and unrecognizing. It was generally believed that Kaddish had kidnapped his father, a necessary act according to his Hasidim for the sake of the perpetuation of the chosen dynasty, in order to restore the court in the Holy Land on the correct path with himself as the designated heir. Meanwhile his mighty mother, the Oscwiecim rebbetzin, ran a rival court from the old house in Brooklyn over which another son, Kaddish's younger brother Koppel, was poised to preside.

Even before Temima's physical arrival in the Bukharim Quarter,

Kaddish had taken upon himself the task of mounting the campaign against her, ordering his men to harass and attack the Arab workers renovating her headquarters and to plaster posters on walls throughout the neighborhood especially in the crucial media-center intersection of Sabbath Square warning of the danger that her existence in their midst would pose. Now from her window Temima could hear every word of his incantation in a Hebrew richly schmaltzed with a Yiddish inflection, each phrase then repeated in unison by the pack reciting from the scripts in their hands illuminated by the streetlights, first zooming in on her by name as at a bull's-eye—Tema daughter of Rachel-Leah of the family Bavli, also known as Temima Ba'alatOv—followed by the plea that the blasphemous perversions and corruptions she promulgates never come to fruition, May they not come to pass, May they not come to pass, May they not come to pass—culminating with the call to bring down upon her head the full wrath of God, May all the curses listed in the Torah cling to her, all the plagues, all the afflictions, all the malignant diseases of the body, all the derangements of mind and spirit, May her name be erased from under the heavens, May she die immediately.

The angel Metatron was disciplined with sixty *pulsa denura* maledictions for passing himself off in paradise as a co-God, thereby encouraging the heretical dualism in the mind of the brilliant apostate, Elisha son of Avuya, known as Akher, the Other. Temima stood at her window with the curtain drawn slightly back as if she were in a theater box observing herself being played by the actor receiving the lashes of fire, and as she stood there witnessing her laceration her mind expanded with the realization that this trial befell her as a consequence of the spiritual penetration of another Elisha, her Elisha Pardes known as the Toiter, the Dead One.

Since the seven days when they had sat on opposite sides of the synagogue tent in the army camp overlooking Hebron mourning the baby boy Kook Immanuel she had not seen him in any form resembling the flesh she had known that had led her deep into the most dangerous and secret levels of understanding, from text to subtext, literal to allusive to interpretive to mystical, contained in the orchard of paradise. Daughters of Jerusalem, if you find my beloved, tell him this—that I am sick with love. Sick unto death he came to her afterward, his apparition, his ghost, his familiar spirit, directing her into the tent of Abba Kadosh in the wilderness and keeping her there until the correct hour, a figure faded and wasting away, she did not know if it was he or his shadow, if he was alive or dead, he took his hand back from the hole and everything inside her stirred for him. He appeared among the gravestones on the Mount of Olives when she sought her solitude to cry out, a wan and gaunt messenger at dawn with his cloak drawn up across his mouth, tolling a warning bell and calling out Unclean! Unclean!—bearing the news that a grand dwelling place was being prepared for her outside the city walls, on the broad avenue carved out in Jerusalem by the tribal mountain Jews of the Caucasus, now in the quick of the most rigid piety, a divine test of her readiness to go forth without question. Every detail would be in accordance with the required specifications—study hall and house of worship and holy ark on the ground floor, overlooking it the men's balcony, beyond that her private quarters, inner courtyard planted with fig and pomegranate trees.

Within days after she moved into the stately building in the Bukharim Quarter he made his presence known again, masked, backlit with fever, ravaged by mortality, bestowing the estate upon her for all eternity, fusing and welding her to the line of the Dead Hasidim, contaminating her, so that she took to her bed infected and inflamed and did not get up for a week. Rising from her acute contagion she went out again bedecked with the veil, her personal partition that separated her ever after in all her public appearances, rendering her instantly recognizable by the manner in which she was set apart.

Early in that week of confinement Rabbi Kaddish Lustiger stomped heavily up the stairs followed by a small entourage of retainers, pushing past Kol-Isha-Erva as if she were invisible, stationing himself in Temima's room at the foot of her bed that was surrounded and concealed by a heavy burgundy brocade curtain puddling on the floor like pools of melting wax. He began at once to state his position, without bothering to ascertain if Temima was actually present on the great raft within that enclosure; for his purposes he would consider himself completely absolved, in fulfillment of his obligation whether she was there or not.

The notorious path she had carved out for herself, Rabbi Kaddish Lustiger declared, sinning and causing others to sin like Jeroboam son of Nevat that led directly to the destruction of our Holy Temple and our exile from the Holy Land, made it incumbent upon him to set aside any personal connections he might feel toward her through their fathers and shared roots in Brooklyn, New York. At great personal risk, he has brought himself and a few of his inner circle to her infested residence, a recklessness that would now oblige them to immerse their bodies in the ritual bath immediately after departing from her in order to cleanse themselves from her pollutions. He has come to serve notice that she must without a moment's delay remove herself and her malignant teachings and influence from their midst. As the designated successor of the holy Rebbe of Oscwiecim, the town better known by its infamous German name of Auschwitz, he, Kaddish Lustiger, bore upon his shoulders the responsibility to do everything in his power to prevent another Hurban such as befell our people at the hands of Hitler, may his name and memory be blotted out forever. This catastrophe that overtook our people was, as everyone knows, the deserved punishment for the abomination of men lying with men as they would lie with a woman, the very same sin for which the city of Sodom was gassed and cremated and reduced to ashes.

Her unnatural behavior—her insistence on carrying out commandments and obligations that are the exclusive province of men, on wielding authority and participating in ritual and studying and commenting and pronouncing on texts reserved for men alone, on setting herself up as a special case among women, and so on and so forth—all of this can only be explained in one way. She is in actuality a man—a man locked inside the body of a woman. Her external female shell is possessed and inhabited by the dybbuk of a man who in his lifetime was guilty of the grave sin of lying carnally with men as if they were women. Now his punishment for all eternity is to be imprisoned inside the body of a woman. *Midah ke'neged midah*—as he had sinned so is he punished. And what punishment could be more terrible to such a sinner than to be trapped forever inside the body of a woman, a place that in his lifetime he found so loathsome and disgusting? "You are nothing but a vessel," Rabbi Kaddish Lustiger reminded Temima, "a putrid vessel for the fulfillment of the ordained punishment of this male sinner. But unlike the vessels of the Holy Temple defiled by idolators, there is no living water, no ritual bath, no mikva, that can ever purify or reconsecrate you. You can only be cast out."

When he finished he turned at once to leave, neither requiring nor expecting a response from behind the curtain, so when Temima's voice came at him like a heavenly *bat kol* he stopped short as if the breath had been knocked out of his body by a punch in the gut from a hidden assailant.

"I know you, Kaddish," Temima's disembodied voice called out to him as he reached the door. "The inclinations of your heart have been nothing but evil from your youth. When you go to the mikva bath now to purge yourself of me, beware lest you put a naked little boy on your lap again as you have done so many times in the past. It is an abomination."

For a few days afterward there was a halt in the defamatory poster campaign that Kaddish had launched well before Temima's actual arrival when news of her impending residence in their midst had first reached him. During this pause he conferred with his kitchen cabinet as to whether to pull back so as not to antagonize this witch lest she unleash a vindictive barrage of false rumors and calumnies against him, or whether to push forward even more vigorously with their righteous mission of forcing her out of their sphere of influence. They determined on the latter course, setting up as a precaution a squad of swift boys to tear down immediately any counter posters that Temima's people might dare to put up.

The new set of posters slathered on the walls by Kaddish's camp setting out like guerrillas in the night armed with brush brooms and flour paste were far more furious and slashing than the earlier ones had been, like the deadly curses on Mount Ebal, calling on Temima and her cohorts to Get Out Now Or The Land You Pollute Will Vomit You Up, bringing down upon her head Blood And Fire And Pillars Of Smoke, Cancer And Heart Attack, Terror And Torture, Madness And Humiliation, Agony And Death, issuing an urgent warning to the People Of Israel to Guard Against This Nazi Who Will Turn Your Skin Into Lampshades And Your Hair And Beard And *Payess* Into Mattress Stuffing, this *Sotah* Adulteress, this *Makhshefa* Sorceress, this Lilith She-Devil, this Delilah Seductress, this Female Who Commits The Perversion Of Standing Naked In Front Of An Animal For The Purpose Of Mating—An Abhorrent Transgression For Which She Is Condemned To Death Along With The Animal—and so on and so forth. All of this was communicated to Temima who absorbed it with a vague smile, noting only that it was instructive and on balance maybe also even slightly insulting how, considering the immediate provocation, Kaddish's new offensive abstained from retaliating in kind by according her at the very least the dignity of the equivalent label of lesbian—no doubt, Temima observed, because there is no specific ban in the Torah against such woman-on-woman activity, it is not taken seriously, no seed is spilled, it leads to nothing, woman's desire is beside the point and probably does not officially exist in any case, a woman is merely a receptacle, all that is required of a woman is to lay there like a dead carp that is turned into gefilte fish.

For a period of time Temima watched with mild interest while Kaddish's attacks unfolded, as if to gauge the limits of his creativity, until the night she grew bored with the range and predictability of his insults and invective and simply to add interest entered the fray. She gave the order to her Bnei Zeruya bodyguard contingent to fan out and hang up multiple copies of the same poster at strategic points throughout the neighborhood and to watch over them lest they be vandalized in any way. In almost every respect these posters resembled notices that sprang up daily announcing a recent death—Blessed Is The True Judge, Let Every Eye Weep And Every Heart Groan, Oy Vey, We Shall Never See His Like Again—but in this instance the name of the deceased in stark bold black letters was Rabbi Kaddish Lustiger, za'zal, son of the Oscwiecim Rebbe, may his candle shed light.

Kaddish himself was the one who happened to pick up the telephone when the first condolence call came to the house. "Kaddish, is that really you? I expected to get the rebbetzin, you know, the widow, the *almunah*, or maybe God forbid one of your eleven *yesoimim*. Where are you talking from? I'm telling you, I'm so shocked my hand is shaking, I can't even get the words out from my mouth, I didn't expect to find you among the living, much less you should answer the telephone. The notices are hanging up all over the place, about you being *niftar*, God forbid. Maybe it's a different Kaddish Lustiger with a different father the Oscwiecim Rebbe, it shouldn't happen to us. Oy vey, Kaddish, thank God, thank God you're still alive, such a terrible terrible mistake, it should only not be a bad omen, God forbid, it should only not God forbid open up a mouth to the Satan."

Directly after hanging up, Kaddish buried himself in his bed, drawing the covers over his head. In a muffled shriek as if from underground he ordered his wife not to bother him. "Leave me alone, woman. Can't you see? I'm being hunted down by the angel of death." Yet over the years, in times of intense tribulation and stress, relief was always at hand for Kaddish by imagining himself already dead, untouchable by his enemies, indifferent to all outcomes. With a kind of morbid onanistic pleasure he would evoke his own namesake by chanting in Aramaic over and over the Kaddish elegy for himself, Exalted and Sanctified Is His Great Name. But this time the tranquilizer didn't work. The specter of his own death this time had come from outside, he had not summoned it up, it was not under his control. However many times he sought to lull himself with the drone of his Kaddish, no comfort was forthcoming, he was not soothed until, like the holy Rabbi Shimon bar Yokhai setting down the mysteries of the Zohar Book of Radiance in the darkness of his cave while in hiding from his Roman oppressors for thirteen years, Kaddish also dipped into the bottomless well of the kabbalistic mysteries. There in the darkness of his bed he plunged into the mystical depths to retrieve the correct *pulsa denura* curse with Temima's name on it that would bring about the end of his tormentor. He drew forth the white-hot fiery lashes, repeating this *pulsa denura* to himself again and again like a charm until he knew it by heart word for word. When he finally emerged from under his covers and resumed his place in the world as the living heir designate of the Osc-wiecim Rebbe, he wrote out the *pulsa denura* personalized for Temima in a fluent stream as if taking dictation from a voice within, channeling it. Together with his elite strike force of loyalists, he then awaited the most auspicious night to deliver this precision bomb that would explode in the face of his persecutor and wipe her and her abominations off the face of the earth once and for all.

Over the weeks and months that followed, Kaddish and his cadre watched and waited for the powerful spell to take effect. They had full faith that it would succeed, and though they could not predict in what form exactly it would show itself, they knew that the disaster that would soon overtake Temima would be the result of the *pulsa denura* they had planted like a mine.

Reports were delivered to them regularly of the activity at the Temima Shul, the streams of supplicants and petitioners coming and going, men and women, including rabbinical authorities arriving incognito seeking and then taking full credit for responsa to newly urgent questions such as those relating to technology with its God-defying hubris and power for good and evil, like the copper and iron invented by Tubal-Cain and the overreaching of the Tower of Babel. Jews and non-Jews made their way through the upstart Ba'alatOv's quarters, according to the reports of

those who had been sent to spy out the land, among them Arabs emerging as if drugged, cradling precious blessings, hailing miraculous cures,
extolling life-altering insights, the meaning of dreams, of past events, of
future possibilities, and also students and seekers notable for the hordes
of women who packed the sanctuary to hear the words of Torah from
the mouth of this so-called holy woman delivered from behind a curtain
on the elevated platform of the *bima* or at the great *tisch* over which she
presided veiled at Sabbath eve dinners on Friday nights tearing one hallah
after another and distributing the pieces to her Hasidim clamoring for a
blessed morsel touched by her sacred gloved hands.

There were also many eyewitness accounts of sightings, Temima moving freely through the streets, always veiled, always accompanied by her
sidekick, Kol-Isha-Erva, guarded by her Bnei Zeruya phalanx, trailed by
assorted acolytes, a sorry band of lost souls and misfits, from Kaddish's
aspect. Word reached him of how on one such outing she had removed
her gloves and placed her two hands nakedly upon the head of the penitent beggar Yisrael Gamzu, and blessed him ostentatiously as he held
out his cup at his usual post on Malkhei Israel Street in front of the pizza
store, the upper half of his drastically mutilated body, all that remained
of him after his tank exploded in the Sinai during the Yom Kippur War,
potted like a surreal rootless growth in his wagon. Immediately Kaddish
arranged for posters to be slapped up all over the neighborhood denounc-
ing this brazen woman for her lewd immodesty in touching a man, even
one missing all of his lower-level equipment, her shameless flaunting of
physical contact between the sexes in a public place.

It was also communicated to Kaddish, despite some trepidation among
his Hasidim, that Temima on one of her forays through the streets of
Geula and Mea Shearim had encountered his father, the Oscwiecim
Rebbe, as he was being taken out in his wheelchair for an airing by
Ishmael their Arab houseboy, and of how the old man had greeted her
by her childhood name—Tema—grasped both of her hands in his aged
liver-mottled claws and in a quavering voice had declared to her that he
had been waiting to meet her, he had been prevented from dying until he
had the chance to see her once again face-to-face and beg forgiveness from
her for ever thinking she was possessed by a dybbuk and forcing her to
suffer the humiliation of an exorcism, now by the refracted light of the
next life he recognized all she had endured in her childhood, he prayed

she would accept his apologies since only the injured party could forgive a sin between one human being and another, even God could not wipe him clean, he hoped she would grant him full and sincere pardon for the sins he had committed against her so that he could die in peace at last and be allotted a place in Gan Eden when he stood before the heavenly throne to be judged, she was a holy soul put upon this earth for an extraordinary destiny, he recognized that now and bowed his head.

Kaddish dismissed this story entirely. It was not possible to believe some Muslim menial's report that his father with a brain sucked dry like a prune could experience even a moment's lucidity, insofar as such an encounter even if it actually took place could be cited as an example of lucidity. Within the week, however, the old man expired, as if in confirmation of the report that he had been holding out only for the opportunity to be absolved by Temima before throwing off the burdens of this life.

Following all the mourning rituals and a decent interval of thirty days, Kaddish immersed himself in the mikva to purify himself from the taint of death, after which he was declared the new Oscwiecim Rebbe—at the very hour by the clock, as it happened, that his brother Koppel was named the successor in Brooklyn in a private ceremony attended by the mayor and governor and senators of New York as well as other bigshots at which his mother served marble cake and prune compote on real china plates rimmed with gold and cherry heering in genuine cut-crystal goblets. But since Kaddish was in Israel his anointment came first by the world clock, a divine confirmation deeply gratifying, seven hours before his brother's elevation as the earth rotates on its axis seeking the light of the sun.

Yet all this was worth nothing to him so long as he could still see Temima sitting in her palatial house or parading through the streets receiving full honors like royalty. Why was the *pulsa denura* curse he had so painstakingly devised to target this demoness exclusively taking so long to work? Where was his personal God? The veils and cloaks that enshrouded her completely—he could only hope and pray that they were concealing boils oozing pus and inflamed open sores bubbling with worms, rotting white skin shriveling and flaking like scorched parchment off her crumbling bones. It was a comfort to picture the curse festering underneath all those rags, but only a small comfort. Kaddish needed more proof to find peace at last, he had to see with his own eyes.

Draped in black robes from head to toe with a black mesh pane across his eyes like an Arab matriarch just returned from a pilgrimage to Mecca, he entered the Temima Shul on a day a public lecture was announced. He endured the indignity of fighting for a spot in the main study hall in the herd of cows, squeezed in among menstruating females with mouths open like pitchers full of blood drinking in the words of their guru. Apparently, she was giving some kind of talk about Bruriah, the brilliant wife of the Mishna giant Rabbi Meir. Could it be that this witch had the hutzpah to compare herself to Bruriah, practically the only woman in rabbinic history whose moral authority and legal rulings are mentioned, even praised, even on occasion accepted in the pages of the Talmud? Kaddish was horrified. No comparison was possible, *lehavdil elef havdolos*, the two were separated from each other by one thousand separations. But in the end, Kaddish was reminded, Bruriah proved herself to be no less empty-headed than any other woman, despite her arrogant insistence to the contrary, surrendering to the seductions of one of Meir's students who was charged by his teacher, her own husband, with the task of bringing her down for the thrill of winning the argument about the fundamentally unserious and flighty nature of a woman's mind.

When a woman submits to temptation, Temima was offering her sick commentary to this story, it tells you something about her mind. When a man submits, it tells you something about his body.

Kaddish felt sullied by her sarcasm, he needed a bath. In his black shrouds, vile intimate fumes gusting from all the orifices of these females pressing against him, he could hardly breathe. At least Bruriah had the decency to strangle herself afterward, Kaddish reflected, more than could be said for this shameless female up there, she continues to cackle away with her woman's naked voice—about what? About Meir's guilt for destroying a prideful woman? I should be so lucky. Not with hexes and voodoo, Temima was saying, as some among us have been known to attempt to destroy a woman. We shall not name names here because our sages of blessed memory teach that whosoever embarrasses a fellow human being in public has no place in the world to come, it is like spilling blood—But you know who you are. She strained her neck and jutted her chin and swiveled her head as if to cast a hidden seeing eye like the beam of a searchlight over the crowd. How he would have loved to clamp that windpipe of hers with his two hands and squeeze, if only to get her to shut up once and for all. I know you, he heard her calling out into the congregation. Your spells and black magic and hocus pocus and mumbo jumbo and evil eyes and pagan curses and lashes of fire, they are nothing less than idol worship, plain *avodah zara*. Commandment Number One—I Am the Lord your God. There is nothing else besides I Am. I Am, I Am, I Am.

Bruriah's husband, Rabbi Meir Master of the Miracle, is said to be buried standing up, not out of remorse for his sexual manipulation setting up his wife or his ruthless intellectual competitiveness and conde-scension, but rather like a sleeping horse positioned to be first out of the gate when the Messiah arrives to awaken him.

The morning after Temima's talk, the fourteenth of Iyar, the anniver-sary of Meir's death, a warm spring day, Temima with her entire inner circle and protectors left Jerusalem for the north in a caravan of taxis. She performed her *hitbodedut* at dusk on an isolated beach on the shore of the Sea of Galilee, Lake Tiberias, not far from the tomb of Bruriah's husband, an albatross circling in the otherworldly refracted light of the sky over the silvery waters of the Kinneret as she cried out to God as to a mother and pondered the question whether it is preferable for a woman to be destroyed out of love or hate.

They climbed by foot westward to Safed where they stopped at the tomb of Hannah mother of seven sons willingly handed over and mar-tyred in sanctification of The Name. From there they hiked through the springs and past the fruit trees and caves of Wadi Amud, ending up on the eighteenth of Iyar, the thirty-third day of the Omer counting from the lib-eration from the Egyptian bondage of Passover to the acceptance of God bondage forty-nine days later on Shavuot, at the tomb of the purported creator of the Zohar Rabbi Shimon bar Yokhai in Meron. Here, along with throngs of other revelers marking the anniversary of Bar Yokhai's death, the happiest day of his life, they celebrated the *hillula* with torches and bonfires, singing and dancing and feasting among the women and bearing witness to the shearing of the heads of three-year-old boys by the men, and Temima discoursed on the subject of the journey from the cold rational cliff of Meir to the steamy mystical cave of Shimon paved along the way with the heads of children offered up as sacrifices.

When the taxis brought them home to Jerusalem a little less than a week later and they entered the Temima Shul in the Bukharim Quarter, they were struck immediately by the aura of discordance between the familiar arrangement of the sanctuary and study hall, all of its books and benches and tables in place and the eternal light still burning, clashing with the satin curtain draping the ark that they took in instantly out of the corners of their eyes hanging in ragged shreds, as if raked by the teeth and claws of wildcats roaming freely at the end of civilization. When they opened the ark they were sucked into the dark void where all the Torah scrolls had once stood; only Temima's little mother Torah remained, mantled in dust wedged in the blackness of the far corner, forgotten and rejected and branded as a plaything to be dandled by children. The floor of the ark was covered with human feces of various textbook sizes and configurations still steaming.

Even as they were examining the ruins and desecration, four giants entered the building dressed identically in one-piece convict suits in a fluorescent orange synthetic, white crocheted skullcaps drawn over their shaved heads to their eyebrows with two long ringlets flowing down on either side like loose ties that could be knotted in cold weather under their chins that sprouted new beards from a stippling of dark pores. They strode directly up to the ark glancing neither to the right or the left. After removing Temima's little mother Torah and handing it like an ember rescued from the flames to Kol-Isha-Erva, they girded and trussed the ark all around with belts and straps to hold it together and seal its doors shut. The largest among them then bent over as the others lashed it to his back like a wardrobe. They did not utter a single word as they performed these tasks methodically, step-by-step, chanting instead the aphorisms of Rav Nakhman of Bratslav, Gevalt, Never give up hope, Because there is no despair here in the world!—raising their voices to a soaring anthem as they made their way out of the sanctuary into the street, hauling the ark and its contents away with them.

"I had to wait for you to return so that you could see with your own eyes—so that you would not simply conclude that the ark had been stolen along with everything inside it." These were the first words he spoke to her when he came into her private chamber that night. She was lying in the cavern of her bed, her little mother Torah resting in the crook of her arm. His glow pierced the thickness of the curtain pulled closed all around. He parted it and lay down beside her, transparent to the bone, no longer of material weight, a shaft of light no longer connected to his physical being. "I have heard from behind the veil it said of me as it was said of the apostate Akher, Elisha ben Avuya, Return all of My backsliding children except for Akher," he whispered in a hoarse voice. "My repentance alone will not be accepted." From these words Temima understood that this was the last time he would come to her, she would never again see him in this life.

"The greater the thirst, the stronger the pleasure when it is satisfied," he went on, his lips grazing her ear. "The stronger the desire the greater the obstacles. Within the obstacles, God Himself can be found. Your destiny is a tight bud that has yet to open fully and reveal itself. Not the good wife-mother Sarah-Rebekah-Rachel-Leah to bless girls by. Not the Wise Woman of Tekoa or of Abel-Bet-Ma'akhah saving men from their animal nature. Not even Deborah wife of Lapidot setting up shop on her own under the palm tree, judge and prophet, warrior and poet. Yours will not be any familiar female emanation. What will still happen to me I do not yet know, but of this I am certain—the Messiah will come from me through you." And he brought his lips down upon her open mouth and kissed her, transmitting to her whatever infection remained in him that he had not yet passed on.

Early the next morning the four ex-convicts in their orange prison jumpsuits appeared again pushing a dolly on which was mounted a huge steel vault bank safe weighing several tons. Still without uttering a word, chanting only the mantra of Rav Nakhman of Bratslav, You should know that the whole world is a very narrow bridge, they wheeled the safe to the honored spot at the head of the hall where the violated ark had stood. They hoisted and maneuvered it into place, tested the alarm system, checked the security of the tight-fitting door, and handed a sealed envelope to Kol-Isha-Erva containing the code to the combination lock. Three of them then perched on the dolly as on a scooter while the fourth, the giant who had carried the desecrated and befouled ark on his back the day before, pushed his comrades out of the study hall into the street, all of them singing jubilantly at the top of their voices over and over again the chorus affirming the most important point—Not to be afraid at all.

When the four returned again about two weeks later they were dressed in shimmering white, their holiday best, no one would ever have known they had once been in captivity. It was the fifth day of Sivan on the cusp of summer, the anniversary of the death of Sashia, wife of Rav Nakhman of Bratslav, who bore him two sons taken in infancy and six daughters, four of whom survived; therefore he had no heirs and his followers are known as the Dead Hasidim. It was also the eve of the holiday of Shavuot when the liberated Hebrew slaves received the Torah in the wilderness at Sinai— or, as Temima observed referring to the text, at least the men among them received the Torah at Sinai, since it stands to reason that God's command to prepare and sanctify and make themselves pure three days in advance by abstaining from going near a woman could only have been directed to the men. There was thunder and lightning, the mountain was covered in clouds of smoke from God's fiery presence upon it, it trembled violently, the blast of the shofar grew louder and louder. The trumpets blared as the four freed slaves, each one holding aloft a pole attached to a corner of a canopy stretched overhead as in a wedding procession, made their way toward the Temima Shul through streets lined with onlookers. Beneath the canopy other newly redeemed slaves carried the reclaimed Torah scrolls freshly decked out in gleaming white satin mantles and ornate sterling pomegranate finials and lavish high silver crowns like brides, and behind them came more men rejoicing, whirling with all their might and leaping into the air, shouting and blasting their horns, roaring the words of Rav Nakhman, The bride is beautiful, Love is perfect.

Temima, also dressed in white with a heavy white veil over her face, opened the safe-ark with the combination of numbers that equaled three hundred and forty-four totaling *pardes*, the orchard at the heart of which the universe's most dangerous knowledge is guarded. The Torah scrolls were settled inside the ark-safe in their rightful places, the doors were shut, and the white satin *huppa* was taken down from its four poles and hung on a specially designed rod to serve as a curtain over the face of the ark.

Embroidered in gold thread across this curtain were the words, AMONG WOMEN IN HER TENT OF TORAH MOST BLESSED, THE RABBI, THE ZADDIK, THE QUEEN, THE ANOINTED ONE, TEMIMA BA'ALATOV, DAUGHTER OF RACHEL-LEAH OF BROOKLYN. This was Elisha Pardes's final gift to her, she knew now for sure that he had set out and was gone. Temima took her place in front of the ark and surveyed the congregation, the women packing the main stalls, overlooking them in the balcony the men including a few of Kaddish's Hasidim who had been swept in with the crowd and whom she recognized from the *pulsa denura,* conspicuous now for the white gauze bandages wrapped around their heads, arms in casts and splints, black eyes, bruised and swollen faces, leaning on crutches, still groaning in pain days after the battle to reclaim the abducted scrolls, and as she gazed outward she searched within herself for the truth concerning the fate of the beautiful bride once the wedding is over.

Kaddish waited three days from the end of the Shavuot holiday and the Sabbath that followed. On the third night he dispatched his commandos with brushes and pails of flour paste and thousands of new posters still smelling of wet ink to be hung up wall-to-wall screaming in thick black letters that a *herem* is hereby imposed upon the witch known as Temima Ba'alatOv. She is hereby excommunicated from the congregation of Israel. She is to be ostracized and treated as dead. She has no place in the world to come. All God-fearing people are hereby strictly ordered to shun her like a leper lest her defilement rub off on them and contaminate them. Should they unintentionally cross her polluted path or come within four cubits of her contagion they must immediately turn their backs to her and run away, they must stuff their fingers in their ears if she attempts to speak, they must spit three times onto the ground as if to vomit her dreck out of their system and utter the words, Ptui, Ptui, Ptui.

"What does it mean for a woman to be excommunicated, to be put into *herem*?" Temima calmly posed the question to Kol-Isha-Erva who had conveyed the news of this latest assault and then took down the words of her teacher. "Not to be counted in the minyan? Not to be called up to the Torah? Not to be honored with leading the blessing after the meal? To be banned from the study hall? To be isolated and excluded and treated with contempt? To be ignored in public? To be considered unclean and impure? To be regarded as weak and inferior and light-minded? To be kept out of sight and confined to the *harem*? Is it at all surprising that over the centuries no one has really taken the trouble to put women into *herem*? I shall send word to the Oscwiecim pretender that I am honored among women to be singled out for official recognition and, yes, somewhat befuddled as to why he even bothered."

She dictated to Kol-Isha-Erva her thank you note to be delivered to Kaddish, adding as a helpful postscript the personal suggestion that for his own sake he might wish to consult the Gemara Sanhedrin page such-and-such, column such-and-such for a discussion of the cut-off age for abusing a child above which pederasty is considered a sin warranting stoning, but if the urge is too overwhelming for him with no convenient outlet she suggested that he take the advice of those sages who ruled that it is not a capital offense to relieve oneself by using one's own member to penetrate one's own anus.

Temima raised no objections when Kol-Isha-Erva indicated she would make this response public. By no means was Temima of the camp that maintained it is preferable to refrain from washing dirty linen in public out of fear of what the goyim might say or from pointing an accusatory finger at a clerical figure who has exploited his position lest the entire congregation of Israel be stigmatized. She fully intended to air out the filth inside Kaddish's house, but her immediate task was to fumigate the courtyard in front of her own. Kaddish's people had appropriated it as if she no longer existed, the logical outcome of the excommunication imposed against her like a death certificate. They laid claim to the vacated estate. Temima ordered her Bnei Zeruya and other supporters to prevent the trespassers from invading the building itself, but for the interim she was tolerating their squatting outside her door.

They transformed the courtyard overlooked by her headquarters into a bazaar bustling late into the summer night. Young boys escaped from stifling schoolrooms to this new attraction to engage in the furious trading of rebbe cards bearing portraits of rabbinical luminaries with their records and rankings—I'll give you nine Teitelbaums for one Feinstein, five Gerrers for one Munkacz—which they would then flip against the wall panting asthmatically in long intense matches. Married men left their study halls where they were serving the nation spiritually through Torah learning to deal in all manner of goods from lottery tickets to cigarettes to ritual objects to diamonds. Old men were parked in the morning in their wheelchairs under the fig and pomegranate trees by female members of their households where they sat until the moon came up and the chill set in peddling single shoelaces and half-used toilet paper rolls that they had secreted out of the house in their pockets, false teeth belonging to the recently departed or plastic bottles of unfinished pills with the labels peeled off. Throughout the day they all ate nonstop, food that did not require the washing of hands and a full grace after the meal. The yard filled up with the remains, sunflower seeds and peanut shells, wax paper from greasy snacks, candy wrappers, fruit pits and peels, empty soda and juice cans, tea and coffee cups. Cats poked in the rubbish, ravens perched high up on tree limbs, foxes were seen prowling at night.

Scooping up handfuls of this trash they cried out *Schmutz! Dreck! Treyf!* and hurled it at Temima's disciples making their way through this swarming occupied territory to their master's feet undeterred. Nor did Temima in principle alter her comings and goings, pausing at her door in a cocoon of her stalwarts as Kol-Isha-Erva raised her woman's naked voice to order the interlopers off the property at once—The ground you are treading upon is holy, You are banished outside the camp for your sins—which provoked them to turn their backs instantly and scurry to the edges of the garbage-strewn courtyard as far as they could go with their fingers plugged in their ears, muttering Ptui, ptui, ptui! and spitting on the ground. Now and then Temima would deliberately coordinate her departures with their prayers three times a day, as they were immersed in the Eighteen Benedictions of the Amidah with their feet pressed together, forbidden from reacting to any interruption or distraction. While they squinched their eyes shut and murmured to themselves the verses of the silent devotion—May all the heretics perish instantly, Speedily uproot all deliberate sinners, smash them, cast them down, destroy them, humble and humiliate them speedily and in our day—Kol-Isha-Erva would excoriate their master Kaddish as a molester and pervert and pedophile and pederast, and then she would proceed to revile all of them as well for scavenging in this plot, they were like maggots and dung beetles, they were nothing but parasites, and she would order them off the premises immediately if they knew what was good for them. By the time they took three steps backward and bowed their heads three times in three directions and muttered He who makes peace in His heights, Temima and her retinue had passed through their swaying rows, out of the courtyard, and disappeared.

The Bnei Zeruya pleaded to be allowed to break the heads of these pathetic invaders—Come, let us give their flesh to the birds of the sky and the beasts of the field—but Temima rejected this brute tactic, rounding her thumb and forefinger into a circlet and gesturing with her fist, an indication to just be patient and wait to see how events will unfold. On the third day she authorized the police to dispatch two officers on horseback to the courtyard, but she forbade them from doing anything further such as tossing canisters of tear gas into the rabble, a service they had offered to perform, no problem. They were simply to station themselves in the midst of the crowd as a warning, like the queen of England's mounted guard. As the hours passed and no action was taken by these armed men on their lofty beasts, the squatters grew emboldened, calling them Nazis, Gestapo, pogromchiks, Chmielnickis, anti-Semitin', corrupt instruments of the corrupt Zionist state, at other times attempting to reason with them and win them over to their side by stressing the point that, after all, the land they were seizing was vacant as the previous occupant had been officially pronounced dead, it was a land without a people and they were people without land, as the Zionists like to say in their own defense. The children pulled the tails of the horses and dared each other to run under them but the long-suffering animals paid no attention, they stood there stoically and endured, placidly dumping clods of manure onto the ground, contributing to the muck.

Toward evening of the fifth day the police on their horses moved to either side blocking the opening into the street at the same time as Temima's people under the command of the Bnei Zeruya contingent dispersed in the courtyard and jammed the squatters into a huddled mass in the middle facing the doorway of Temima's headquarters. Temima herself emerged with Kol-Isha-Erva at her side. The two women set their feet on the threshold as on a small platform that seemed to be fashioned out of bricks of sapphire, like the essence of heaven in purity.

Kol-Isha-Erva raised her woman's naked voice. "Listen up, guys. Your time is up. The party's over. If you continue to remain here, violating this holy space, you will be condemned to look at the forbidden at mortal peril to your souls."

Temima then stepped forward. "On this day you will know that I live and that it is I who am speaking," she declared through her veil. "*Hineini.* I am here."

She parted her robes. Naked, she revealed herself to them.

I Remember,
O God,
And I Moan

The total span of Reb Berel Bavli's life was one hundred and four years. He let out his last breath and he died, at a good ripe age, old and contented, and was gathered back to his kin, including his daughter Temima who in the eyes of her family had already officially been delivered up to the angel of death and duly mourned. For this reason many months elapsed before she learned of her father's passing. The news reached her during the period when she returned to the rabbinic texts struggling to understand further the point of the life of Bruriah, that token woman sage, if ever such an aberrant creature even existed, the marvel whose clever ripostes occasionally bested even the sharpest minds it was noted to the astonishment of all, such a precocious little performing monkey.

The man said to be Bruriah's father, Rabbi Hananya ben Teradyon, unlike Reb Berel Bavli, suffered a monstrous death, one of the ten sages executed by the Roman occupiers of Judea, burned at the stake wrapped in the scroll of the Torah with water-soaked wool packed against his flesh to prolong his agony, his final vision as the parchment was being consumed by the flames of the letters themselves bursting free and taking flight soaring upward black cinders to the heavens. If the sins of the daughters have any consequence at all, the punishment was also visited upon the father, for the brilliance of this woman, judging by the testimonials, too often expressed itself in the form of ironic, aggressive, show-off coquettishness, which her father might even have encouraged for his personal entertainment due to the sheer cuteness of this brazen talking anomaly, such as when she scolded Rabbi Yossi the Galilean for using too many words to ask her the directions to Lod, "Galilean fool, Did not our sages say, Do not talk over much to a woman?" But there was no one who was punished more mercilessly than this smart girl herself, she was just too smart for her own good, every human connection unraveled in disaster. Not only the auto-da-fé of her father, but her mother killed by the Romans, her sister (or was this Bruriah herself?) sold to a brothel in Antioch or Rome, her two sons struck dead suddenly one Sabbath day, her husband the Mishna luminary Rabbi Meir pimping her for the sake of prevailing, dominating, teaching her a lesson about the essentially light-headed nature of the female mind, climaxed by her own suicide. She even had a brother, it is reported, whom she also outshone in learning, whose life also spun out miserably. He went sour, it is said, turned into a gangster, an outlaw and an outcast, his mutilated body dumped at the side of the road. At his funeral, Bruriah displayed her freakish brilliance, her over-the-top erudition once again by summing him up and disposing of him with a citation of the perfect verse from the book of Proverbs: Sweet may be the bread that a man gains through falsehood, but afterward his mouth will be filled with gravel.

Temima learned she had a brother at the same time she found out about her father's death. Cozbi opened the door to the study heralded by the rhythmic popping of her stilettos to inform her mistress that a fat boy was sitting on the balcony claiming to be her brother, Getzel—but everyone, or so Cozbi reported based on information this stranger apparently had volunteered, called him Glatt. He was just sitting there picking his nose waiting to see her, one of the fringe clusters of his *zizit* caught in his fly. He had brought something from Brooklyn to give to her, Cozbi passed on the message.

Temima shook her head. All Israel are brothers, she commented, but are the sisters also brothers? She had sisters, she was aware of that, half sisters, Frumie's five daughters, but to the best of her knowledge her father's wish for a son of his own had, for his sins, never been granted. She lowered her head to the volume of the Babylonian Talmud spread open before her, an indication that she would not grant an audience to this petitioner, though she registered within that had she truly had a brother, the son of her father but not her mother, he might indeed have been called Getzel, since that was the name of Reb Berel Bavli's own father.

A few minutes later Cozbi clattered into the room again, this time carrying a bag. She set it down on the table, careful to avoid contact with the holy texts. No doubt she had already inspected its contents for any suspicious objects. It was an amazingly used and reused shopping bag wrinkled like the skin of a reptile, smudged with dirt and grease stains, but nevertheless Temima recognized it instantly—the Berel Bavli logo, the two *B*s like the two tablets of the Ten Commandments bisected, cross-sectioned, flipped on their sides with their humps facing in opposite directions but sharing a common dividing line, and the familiar slogan, STRICTLY KOSHER! STRICTLY GLATT! STRICTEST SUPERVISION! When she checked inside the bag she saw the remains of the refueling this brother pretender required for the trek to her quarters, the last bite of a sour pickle, several crumpled napkins and wax paper wrappings from street food such as falafel and pizza, emptied greasy bags of Bamba and Bisli, some flattened Fanta and Maccabi Beer cans—at least this boy did not litter in the Holy Land—and she also saw the book, her mother's copy of *Anna Karenina* by Leo Tolstoy in the Modern Library edition translated by Constance Garnett, aged, soiled, moldy, bloated, water-damaged, the cover ripped off, the spine broken, smelling of brine and blotched with oil and fat. Temima drew her veil down over her face.

"Is our father still living?" were the first words out of her mouth to this brother after she regained control over her emotions, the sight of her mother's worn book like a familiar spirit emerging from underground had threatened her composure, brought her to the verge of raising her voice and crying in sobs so loud they would have been heard in the streets of Egypt.

"What—you didn't know? Almost a year ago already he was *niftar.* By now already, God willing, his soul got called up to the Torah in Gan Eden, or maybe at least they gave him *hagbah*—like maybe they let him pick up that Torah in the next world and open it up really really wide and twirl it around to show off his muscles like some kind of freakin' bodybuilder strongman, his supersized *knaidlakh,* they were awesome. He really dug *hagbah*, it was his friggin' favorite thing in shul. Even when he was already a really old guy he was still strong like an ox, a tank, he could still rip the Manhattan Yellow Pages in two with one single rip. Me? Yours truly? I still can't even do Staten Island."

He elaborated on her father's death genially, an extended footnote, as if by virtue of it being already old news it had lost its sting, the moment of the telling itself, who tells it, how it is told and to whom, could be of no consequence, it could have no special meaning for her the daughter even upon first impact, the shock of this death had already been absorbed by the universe and the earth continued on its course, the sun still rose and set. She watched as he seated himself opposite her without awaiting an invitation, a nicety he most likely had never been taught, and jiggled in place to adjust his apparatus for comfort.

A long silence followed as Temima took in this brother through her veil—a young man, twenty at most, in the uniform of a yeshiva boy, black pants, white button-down shirt without a tie, ritual fringes hanging out from underneath on one side as he worked on liberating another cluster from the teeth of his zipper without a pause in the stream of his jabber, a black velvet yarmulke perched like a cupola on top of the fuzz of his close-cut hair the color of a melting orange popsicle. There was no doubt he was her father's son, the resemblance was comical, manifesting itself almost point for point in the form of caricature. Where Reb Berel Bavli was a gigantic presence, with huge hands and feet, a thick beard oxygenated red in color when he was a young man, shrewd eyes heavily lidded as if to provide screening when closing a deal and a ruddy complexion rough textured like granite, his son Getzel Glatt Bavli was soft and flabby, a blubbery heap, large pudgy hands with savagely bitten fingernails, baby-fine sidelocks tucked behind each ear and sparse coiled sprouts of new beard pale persimmon in color, the small eyes receding as if to take cover from a punch coming his way, his complexion rouged with flush like a chronic case of low-grade embarrassment, the skin powdery white, baby smooth. He was like a chicken stunted in a factory into all breast destined to be pounded into millions of schnitzels, he was a capon, whereas his father was red meat, roast beef, top cut, prime. No wonder the boy was called Glatt, not only because it alliterated so naturally from Getzel, so intuitively, and not only because the father he reincarnated in the form of parody was king of the kosher meat business, but also for the creamy glatt smoothness of his flesh, like the kosher standard for the insides of the lungs of a slaughtered animal, with no adhesions or perforations.

"Blessed is the True Judge," Temima said at last, pronouncing the traditional phrase of acceptance upon learning of a death. She forgave him in his youth and self-absorption for his failure to appreciate the momentousness of such a message when it is brought to any human being, for dropping it upon her so casually, as if it could not in the scheme of things matter that much or have retained any shattering significance even for the ghost of a daughter. The legendary Bruriah, with respect to her own father, Rabbi Hananya ben Teradyon, is reported to have asked how such a man could truly have deserved such a death. I could also ask the same question about my father, Temima reflected as she gazed at this brother. She rent her garment over her heart as was required, in a sign of mourning for a close relative, the cloth giving out a keening screech.

Getzel Glatt now confided that he had always had it in his head to bring her that book. It had always been on his to-do list when he was finished with high school and got to go to Israel to learn for a year or two in some yeshiva or other until his mother found for him a nice *frum* girl to marry. He had always wanted to meet her, his notorious half sister Tema, star of the religious underworld, the temptation was irresistible *davka* because no one was allowed to even mention her name in the house, she was one-hundred-percent *treyf*, she was considered like dead meat. But just *le'hakhis*, just to get everyone pissed off because she was so *assur*, totally off-limits, which in his opinion completely sucked, he made up his mind to actually meet her. Anyways, one of Frumie's girls, the one who sells all those Armani suits and Borsalino hats in her Boro Park basement at a tremendous discount, she explained to him about the book since it was always laying around the house somewhere or other, and that it used to belong to Tema's mother and that she always had her nose stuck in it. So he figured he'd schlepp it along with him to Israel even though it's a pretty fat book you know, and even though he would have to hide it somewhere in his dormitory room under his stuff because he heard it's all about this married lady who fools around with another guy and then jumps on the third rail in the subway—right? A dirty book, *schmutz*, and really long, a million pages—how many times does this writer guy have to say the same thing over and over again? Okay already, buster, we get the point. But he decided he'd take it anyways so that he could use it like a ticket to get in to see her, since she was such a bigshot VIP by now, he heard all kinds of wild and crazy stuff about her, this and that, like she was some kind of lady guru or something, really cool. And *barukh HaShem*, his plan worked—right? See, here he was right this minute, sitting by this room, he couldn't believe it, everyone's banging their head on the door trying to get in but he actually made it through to the *Koidesh Kedoishim*, even with the bodyguards and the secret service dudes and the hot killer babe in the high heels, here he was in the Holy of Holies and he wasn't even hit by lightning yet. His mother would kill him if she ever found out where he was, she would hock him to death, wring his neck like a chicken, yeah, no problem, she would start hollering that he was spoiling his *shiddukh* chances hanging with someone like her, no good girl would ever consider him for a husband if anyone found out, even with all the money they had, his reputation would be in the garbage pail.

Glatt tipped up a haunch, drew a wallet from the back pocket of his pants, slipped out a picture, and flicked it across the table to Temima. "That's my holy mother, the only wife in the history of mankind to survive our old man. She's running the whole business now singlehanded, the whole shmear, wholesale, retail, on the books, off the books." Temima's eyes came to rest on the image of a thickset woman significantly younger than herself with a broad glistening face outlined by a tightly wrapped kerchief, her hands firmly clamped on her hips as if to forewarn you against trying any funny business, a long white butcher's apron smeared with blood. Had she been waving a certified ritual knife big enough to cut an animal's throat with a single swipe, Temima's heart would have embraced her. The time had come for women to step out from behind the counter and the scales and the cash register and the ledgers, and into the slaughterhouse.

So that's the whole story, Glatt continued, upturning the plump palms of his hands. Meanwhile, he was just hanging out in Israel until his mother fingers the right *maidel*, his *bashert'e*. She was checking everything out about the girl, she got this list a mile long with these little boxes and she puts checks in the boxes, she's like his one-stop shopping for a *kallah*, there's nothing for him to do right now but just sit back and relax and wait for the bride to be delivered to him on a silver platter like a stuffed Cornish hen at a catering affair. Bottom line, he trusted his mother one hundred percent, she wouldn't miss one single thing about the girl, don't worry, no different than how she checks out a goose in the market, or a side of veal, inside and out, with her eagle eyes, she doesn't miss a thing, starting from what score the *maidel* got on the Apgar test when she was first born in the hospital—even from before she was born, from if her mother went to the mikva every month when the girl was, you know, conceived, if her mother kept all the laws so that when her father and mother did their business the girl was created in an atmosphere of family purity, blahblahblah, *ve'hulai ve'hulai.* Do they have a television set in the house? How long are her skirts? Does she wear flashy colors? Do her shoes make noise when she walks? Did she get good marks in school? Was she a troublemaker? Does she have a big mouth? Did anyone ever see her hanging out at the pizza store talking to a boy? You know the deal. A nice *zniusdik'e* girl, modest, long sleeves, quiet voice, a good shopper, *eidel, balabatisch,* sweet, sweet. Like his mother says, we're shooting for good looking but not drop-dead gorgeous, common sense but not a genius—been there, done that, know what I mean? He shot Temima a complicitous grin.

Also, they wanted from a family with no sicknesses, no meshuggenehs, no wackos, no inherited crap, that goes without saying, all this his mother was checking out for him. From the business side, they were looking for comfortable but not loaded super rich because his mother wants the girl she should always be grateful for the upgrade, she should come from a family with a father who sits and learns Torah all day, we don't want a father who goes out and works for a living, God forbid, it's a very bad male model example for a young lady—right?—she'll get very bad ideas what to expect from a husband, you know what I'm saying? Anyways, we have plenty of money, thank God, which is the other headache his mother has to deal with now, because Frumie's girls were yelling and screaming bloody murder all day and night for an equal share in the business and the profits, it really stinks, they were driving his mother nuts. They even hired these lawyers and they got hold of some rabbis on their side, Modern Orthodox, you know, touch-me, feel-me. Come on, gimme a break man, it's like a pogrom. Hey, maybe he shouldn't be telling her all this, she was also a sister, he hoped he wasn't giving her any ideas. But like his mother says, by Jews, girls don't inherit, not one penny, period, end of story, whatever a girl gets is like a tip depending on the service, you know what I mean? For sure, his mother won't budge one inch, so it's like this huge fight between the chicks, like cats and dogs, like lady wrestlers in the mud, because *kitzur,* bottom line, *takhlis, tukhes* on the table, his mother has his interests at heart one hundred percent, he is number one in her book, it's like, don't mess with my kid or I'll scratch your eyeballs out. So meanwhile, here he is sitting in Jerusalem just passing the time, learning a *blat* Gemara, a little Yoreh De'ah, maybe some *mussar*, you know the drill. Sometimes he went with his roommate Simkha to the mall to hang out a little, Internet café, whatever, sometimes they went on a trip to a festival, Hasidic rock, klezmer, Reb Shlomo, Jewish soul music, fooled around a little in the mosh pit, Simkha was teaching him a few chords on the guitar, on a good day there was maybe a demonstration so they can get a little exercise, throw around a few stones, turn over some dumpsters, whatever. So that was his life. He wasn't complaining. His rebbe will tell him everything he needs to do when the time comes for him to *pish* or get off the pot, you get the point. Any question he has about what you have do by the girl when you get married, any *qasha* no matter what, worst comes to worser, he can go to his rebbe and ask, because like he said, the *ikkur* is she should get along with his mother, that's the main thing.

Temima sat for a long time reflecting in silence, staring at this brother through her veil, this sluggish, soft variation on the male child her father had longed for so desperately, a sinister joke played by God that ultimate prankster on the strutting colossus who was her father, she riveted him with her gaze seeking to draw in the wounded essence of this son like an undertow in order to return him to himself restored as if after a close brush with death.

"Brother," Temima said at last, "I understand now that you have come to ask me a question about yourself and the true longings of your heart and how our father would have reacted. I understand your suffering, I know your question. For the kindness of bringing to me my mother's book, I will spare you the embarrassment of having to ask your question directly. The answer is, our father would have had no interest at all in what you feel, he would have had no tolerance or sympathy, he would not have cared, no more than he cared how a cow feels. Which bull the cow liked or did not like, or even if the cow loved another cow, the heart's desire of the cow or the cow's broken heart, all this were of no importance to our father, may he rest in peace, as long as the cow stood still and didn't give him a hard time while he cut her throat. In this respect, our father was a traditional man of faith. We have in many ways a very great religion but also in many respects a very cruel one. What you feel in your heart, whom you love or desire, mother, father, girl, boy, all this is beside the point. The point is what you do and what you don't do. The point is practice. But our father is now dead—and there is some consolation. You know how King Solomon goes on and on in the book of Proverbs with so much sensible advice—Listen my son to your father and mother, don't be lazy, stay away from the seductions of 'strange' women, abominations one and all, though as everyone knows the king himself was the biggest transgressor of all in that department. Who can explain the pull of human desire, however 'strange'? Yet when it is thwarted, it is sickness of heart. And when it is realized—even in the face of the loss of all your comforts, the disapproval and rejection of father and mother—it is sweet to the soul, Solomon tells us, it is the tree of life."

Temima shoved the shopping bag containing the leftovers and rubbish across the table to the brother and had him escorted out of her private chambers. She gave orders that until further notice she was not to be disturbed for any reason, including the sudden appearance of a newly declared relative or news of a death in the family. The ensuing days were consecrated to a close rereading of this painfully intimate copy of Reb Lev's novel, in search of her mother. What drew her mother so personally to Anna, such a lost and tragic figure finally? "She throws herself under a train in the end," her mother once commented. "She says to herself, They'll be sorry—but does anyone really care? She's the one who's crushed, she's dead, they're alive, they go on living, nobody cares."

A woman's cautionary tale for herself, for her girl child, a book with a moral, a lesson to teach—was that how her mother saw it? Temima read slowly, closely examining the text, turning the brittle pages cautiously, seeking a fingerprint, a clue to her mother. Anna Karenina, AK, AK47, a weapon that could kill you. Reading it again now after so many years she found herself too often exasperated with Anna, so spoiled and self-absorbed, another brilliant woman wasted. The spiritual struggles of Levin were far more engrossing to her on this reading, sections that as a girl she occasionally found onerous, interruptions in the romance, but would plow through dutifully nevertheless especially because she secretly was convinced that Levin, like his creator Reb Lev, were fellow Jews, their names alone betrayed them. So she could never quite accept the solace Levin found in Christianity, a faith that had always seemed to her to have ecstatically, pornographically, appropriated the blood that the God of the Jews had forbidden to humankind, reserving it for Himself.

Now Levin and Anna were minor characters, footnotes and gloss. She was hunting for the overwhelming presence of her mother brooding between the lines. Page after page, nothing yielded itself up, no signs of a dog-eared corner once folded down, no comment or exclamation point or question mark in a margin, no underlining, no phrase bracketed, no torn slip of paper tucked into a cleft of the spine, no lipstick mark, no coffee stain, no dried bodily fluid, no lingering scent. The stack of pages grew higher and higher on the left, on the right they diminished relentlessly, no treasure could be dredged up from these black depths.

Temima was ready to despair, she was approaching the end, the twentieth chapter of the seventh book, and that was when she noticed the faintest swelling, like water damage, alongside the passage where Anna's brother, Stepan Arkadyevich Oblonsky, remarks, "But what possesses you to get mixed up with railways and Jews? Any way you look at it, it's a stinking business." Here was a glimpse into the disappointed soul of her mother, a slap in the face, a fatal blow. All of Anna's passion and spirit, her operas and balls, a life intensely and daringly lived—this was a world into which Rosalie Bavli was not welcome, a party to which she would never be invited.

One day her mother revealed yet another personal disappointment. Temima must have been about five years old at the time, it was one of her clearest early memories, it occurred not too long after her mother returned home from one of her periodic disappearances of a few days that always seemed to the child Tema to drag on for an eternity; this one, as it happened, would be the last until her mother vanished irreversibly when Tema was eleven. During those absences, she would wander around the house clutching a blanket and crying, "I lost my mama, I lost my mama," a detail she herself did not recall but rather one her father summoned up now and then even when she was a teenager and her mother long gone as an element of the selective mythology by which she was packaged within the family, inevitably appending the observation, "And even to this day my highfalutin daughter kvetches and schlepps around her old schmattehs."

Her mother was lying on the couch in the living room as if recuperating from an illness that had drained her of her vital strength, one arm crooked over her eyes, the other encircling Tema nestled at her side, drawing her close. She was a small woman with high cheekbones and thick brows that met over the stately arc of her Mediterranean nose forming a kind of shade, like a visor, as if to protect from unwanted scrutiny her large dark eyes, always slightly moist, a faint mustache shadowing her wide mouth. Even lying down in her housecoat and kerchief her face was made up; a heavy pearl earring hung from one ear, the piercing stretched into a slit by the weight of the jewel while the lobe of her other ear had split entirely and healed in two cushiony, downy flaps that Tema liked to stroke. In a soft voice her mother said to her, "You're big enough already, Tema, to understand that when I go away it is because a baby inside my body decided it is better not to be born. Even before I had you there were two others who also refused. But for you I cried so much and prayed so hard in shul, like Hannah the mother of Shmuel, that everyone must have thought I was drunk or crazy, and I said to God, 'If you give me a child I will dedicate him to You.'"

From this revelation Tema understood and accepted as her fate that she was the child of a mother who had struck a deal, who had made a bargain with the Lord—a mother who had given her up and had sacrificed her to God for her entire life.

On a Sabbath not long after this, before the blessing over the wine, her father, Reb Berel Bavli sitting at the head of the table, sang as always the hymn from the book of Proverbs in praise of the Woman of Valor, so enterprising and hard-working, a ferocious warrior in the cause of husband and family. As usual, when he came to the verse, Charm is false, and beauty is vanity, a God-fearing woman, she will be praised, his voice swelled as he enunciated each word distinctly, looking hard and meaningfully at his wife who was universally regarded as an exotic beauty.

When he was finished with this obligation, as if on cue, Tema's mother dismissed the serenade in her honor with her usual quip, "A good slave." This exchange had become a regular feature of the family routine when only the three of them were at the Sabbath table, with no guests. But this time, her father's eyes froze and his red beard seemed to flare out tongues of flame; Tema herself could never have known the provocation, she sensed it to be something like a vapor oozing out from under the closed door of their bedroom, related to her mother's recent return from the hospital. "It also tells us about the Woman of Valor," Reb Berel Bavli accentuated every syllable, "that her sons rise up and praise her. But this one"—he fixed his glare on the wife sitting to his left, the closest point to the kitchen—"this fancy-schmancy madam here manages to squeeze out for me only one measly girl and now she's closed for business." He flicked a but-I-love-you-anyway wink in Tema's direction like a dart. "This is my reward for marrying a skinny-malink," Reb Berel Bavli declared. "My next wife, she will be a baby factory—zaftig, zaftig—knocking off one product and one product only—sons, sons, and more sons!" He stretched out his arm and pinched his wife's cheek—a gesture to be interpreted as conciliatory, *shalom bayit*, peace in the household above all else for which the woman usually takes the pinch and pays the price, he was only kidding, it was a joke, a joke.

Tema spoke up. "It also says about the Woman of Valor that her husband is renowned among the wise men of the city, and she's cheerful all the time."

"And not just a measly girl this skinny-malink for a wife gives to me," Reb Berel Bavli pressed on, "but a girl who is too smart for her own good, with a brain too big for her head, a brain like a man, a freak of nature."

Even so, when there were guests at their table, Tema's father would allow himself the pleasure of lifting her under her arms and standing her up on her chair to sing and recite from memory all of the Sabbath tunes and hymns, in Hebrew and Aramaic, despite the questionable nature of such a performance by a girl. There were even occasions, after Reb Berel Bavli chanted the Kiddush over the wine extolling the creation by God of the universe culminating in the seventh day of rest, that he would require her to do so as well in front of the guests although this was a role usually reserved for the male members of the family, demanding that everyone remain respectfully standing as she performed flawlessly. It was as if he were stepping back like an impresario flaunting his discovery, like the opening act who had just warmed up the crowd for the star attraction. Despite his flamboyant lamentations about what a shame it was that such gifts should have been squandered on a female, it shone through—his pride in his little monstrosity. "Not normal, am I right?" There was in his pronouncement an element of taking precautions to avert the menace of the evil eye. "If it was a boy, everyone would be dancing in the streets—a little genius, an *illui*, the next Gaon from Vilna. But on a girl—such a waste!"

In the Oscwiecim *shtiebel* on Sabbaths, Reb Berel Bavli kept his daughter at his side during prayers in the men's section, which took up three quarters of the front portion of the synagogue until the floor-to-ceiling opaque screen partition behind which the women sat on folding chairs in cramped rows smelling of bodily secretions and talcum powder and chicken fat. It was acceptable for Tema to sit with the men as she was still a very young child, not yet even seven years old, the age of the princess Snow White when the magic mirror broke the news to the wicked stepmother that she no longer was the fairest in the land, the age at which, according to Rashi the commentator-in-chief, a female is at the peak of her beauty. How do we learn this? From the extraordinary delineation of Mother Sarah's age at the time of her death as specified in the opening of the portion "The Lives of Sarah" (this was a woman who had no life, only lives)—one hundred years and twenty years and seven years. Why the breakdown and repetition of years? To teach us that at one hundred years Mother Sarah was as pure as a twenty-year-old girl who is not responsible for her actions and therefore it is as if she had never sinned, and at twenty years she still retained the perfection of beauty of a seven-year-old girl.

Tema was already reading Hebrew fluently by then. Throughout the services as she sat among the men her father instructed her in the protocol of prayer ritual—when to rise and when to sit, when to bend your knees and bow your head, when to take three steps backward and forward, when to say Blessed Is He and Blessed Is His Name and when to say Amen, when to pray out loud and when in silence, how to keep up with the cantor as he marks the completion of a passage by chanting out loud the last few lines, how to *shuckle* and sway, how to *daven* in a low murmur moving your lips never reading silently to yourself as if the Siddur were some kind of story book, how to stand with your feet pressed together oblivious to all distractions during the Eighteen Benedictions silent meditation and especially during the *Kedusha* sanctification that the angels themselves sing to God on His heavenly throne, and so on and so forth.

Tema grasped every point instantly, swiftly committing the entire liturgy to memory. Reb Berel Bavli could not refrain from caressing the top of her silken head and giving a proprietary tug to one of her two thick long braids, grinning with pleasure at the men seated around him and muttering, "If it was a boy this is what you would call a one-thousand-percent return on your investment. Nu, so tell me? Am I right or am I right?"

On the occasions when the Oscwiecim Rebbe would rise and lean on his wooden lectern to offer in Yiddish some words of Torah, Tema would listen closely, often posing questions provoked by his talk as she walked home with her father after shul. She also asked questions about the weekly Torah portion, following along with the reading attentively in her Tanakh, including the sections skipped over in most children's classrooms such as the accounts of Lot's daughters impregnated by their father, the rape of Dina, Reuven sleeping with his father's concubine, Judah taking as a prostitute his son's widow, and so on—the dirty parts. She deciphered the cantillation signs and accents above and below the letters like musical notes and rests to aid in the memorization of entire blocks of text that soon she was singing. When they read the portion opening with Jacob's flight to Haran and his dream of a ladder with angels ascending and descending, she turned to her father and asked, "But aren't the angels in heaven? Shouldn't they be going down first?" Reb Berel Bavli beamed. "You hear that?" he boomed to his bench mates. "The very same question Rashi asks. The mind of a man—such a pity!"

Above all her father stressed the obligation to say every word, not to skip a single word of the prayers, though all around her, Tema had already observed, men were *davening* by rote, itching to get it over with for the thousandth time so that they could go home, unbuckle their belts, and stuff themselves with the Sabbath *cholent* stew that would knock them out cold like a sledgehammer for the rest of the afternoon. Her father repeated this instruction so regularly that the men in their orbit would chant the refrain along with him like a chorus, Every single word! No skipping!—until the day they were clutching their bellies with painfully suppressed hilarity, and when Reb Berel Bavli glared at them, an expression of confusion and hurt mixed with fury in his eyes, they pointed to the little girl. Tema was reciting the Kaddish. "See how nice she listens to you?" one of them commented, the only man among them who had no business dealings with Reb Berel Bavli. "Such a good girl, she doesn't skip a single word, just like you said—including the Kaddish. Watch out, Reb Berish, already she has you dead and buried. Either a gold digger or a Dumb Dora—but any way you look at it, the mind of a female after all."

But the greater portion by far of her learning Tema acquired on her own, through personal diligence and will, by applying herself and cracking the codes, her inner being drawn naturally to the material. Nevertheless, to create the illusion of normalcy, every morning her mother put on her weekday wig and makeup, and, holding Tema's hand, they walked together the several blocks to the kindergarten operated by Mrs. Moskowitz in the dark basement of her home near Fiftieth Street under the elevated tracks, which set the entire building quaking and shuddering whenever a train rumbled by overhead or jolted to a stop. There the little girls were taught the letters of the Hebrew alphabet and the vowels, some blessings and basic prayers for specific occasions, upon waking up and going to sleep, for example, or setting out on a journey or finishing your business in the bathroom, and so forth, a few holiday songs along with a warning not to sing them out loud when boys or men are within earshot, as well as instruction on how to help their mothers in preparing the special dishes and cleaning the house for Sabbaths and festivals. They were also given guidance in personal hygiene, such as the importance of wiping one's nose in a ladylike fashion with the handkerchief they wore fastened to the bodice of their dresses with a safety pin.

At story time, they would sit on an old piece of carpet on the floor in a circle flowing from Mrs. Moskowitz in a wooden folding chair holding a bundle that contained her newest baby with her toddlers at her feet as she read inspirational bible tales and legends to them in Yiddish from the Tzena Urena, her eyes gleaming with emotion as she recounted Mother Rebekah's exemplary behavior in offering water from the well not only to quench the thirst of the weary traveler Eliezer just arrived at Padan-Aram where he had been sent by his master Abraham to find a suitable wife for his son Isaac, but also to draw bucketful after bucketful of water for all of his camels as well. "And he had plenty of camels, girls, Avraham Avinu was a very rich man. Do you girls have any idea how much water each and every camel needs and how long it takes for them to drink because they have to store so much up for marching across the whole desert? Girls, I want you to remember how Rivka Imeinu right away ran to feed the camels also even without being asked if you want to find for yourselves a good husband some day."

At play time, they molded hallahs from brown clay giggling behind their hands at the resemblance between their works of art and little turds, they drew holiday pictures and fashioned decorations from construction paper and paste, they dressed up as brides in white sheets, enacting the high point of their future wedding day, after which the rest of their lives would funnel down as expected.

More and more often, Tema held back when it was time to set out for school. For a full week she cried the entire way as they walked there and had to be dragged down the cement steps, weeds sprouting from the cracks, to Mrs. Moskowitz's cellar door where she clung to her mother like a sinking person clawing for solid ground. Then one morning she simply sat down full stop on the floor in the foyer with her arms crossed over her chest, shook her head in a slow flinty rhythm from side to side, her lips clamped tight, and refused absolutely to step out the door and leave home.

"What do you mean she won't go?" Reb Berel Bavli hissed to his wife in their bedroom that night. "Who does she think she is—her majesty the queen or some other fancy lady? Hutz-klutz, Miss Maggie Putz! In this department, she's your daughter, one hundred percent. Since when do you ask a kid if they want or if they don't want? Do I ask a chicken what it wants? You just pick her up and take her there, even if she's kicking and screaming bloody murder the whole way. Don't worry, she'll get used to it, I give you my word. Human beings can get used to anything, just like animals."

But her mother took her in another direction. On the morning that Rosalie Bavli did not paint her face or put on her everyday wig but instead wrapped her head in a dark scarf drawn forward with the ends draped over her shoulders and concealed her eyes behind sunglasses, Tema accepted the hand extended down to her and allowed herself to be led out of the house. The two of them walked together in silence until they came to a hardware store directly across the street from the synagogue of the Oscwiecim Rebbe. They flattened themselves against the shadowy depths of the windowed alcove that led to the store's entrance showcasing different color variations of linoleum samples in a confetti pattern, timers for Sabbath lights, pressure cookers, and so on, their eyes fixed on the Oscwiecim *shtiebel* opposite above which the Rebbe and his family lived.

When they spotted the rebbetzin coming out pushing her shopping cart and making her way up the street and around the corner, Tema's mother signaled by squeezing her daughter's hand that she was already holding tensely. Together they crossed the street and briskly walked down the alley along the side of the Oscwiecim *shtiebel*, entered through a door in the middle, and climbed the staircase that led directly into the Rebbe's dining room where he sat enthroned in his usual place to receive his Hasidim at the head of the great mahogany table covered with an embossed burgundy-colored velvet cloth with the heavy volumes spread open before him. Tema was not quite seven at the time, her hair in its long braids had never been cut, her existence on this earth had been a loan from God in answer to her mother's prayers, and now the loan was being repaid.

Her mother clicked open her black leather purse with the gold clasp, releasing a familiar, embarrassingly private puff of sour aroma, and drew out a fat sealed envelope that she handed to Kaddish stationed at his usual post a few paces behind his father. "Mazel tov," Rosalie Bavli murmured. Kaddish tore open the envelope, counted the cash stuffed inside by flipping through the bills without taking them out, gave a receipt in the form of an acknowledgment nod, then slipped the whole package somewhere inside his black jacquard satin kaftan. He had turned eighteen a few weeks earlier and his marriage to the sixteen-year-old daughter of the Kalashnikover Rebbe had just been celebrated with candlelit processions and rapturous dancing in the closed-off streets of Boro Park and a caravan of ambulances with engines running standing ready to speed away revelers overcome by the press of the crowd and palpitations of the heart brought on by exultation at the union of two such illustrious Hasidic dynasties. Tema observed closely how her mother, still standing, leaned in slightly toward the Rebbe, and with commendable modesty and deference, in the softest of voices, practically a whisper, uttered such words as A special child, A gift from God, You know the situation, You were there when I prayed for her, all of which the Rebbe acknowledged by nodding his head sagely, bunching his beard and caressing it in contemplative downward strokes. Then her mother pushed forward with her request—that Tema be allowed to study with the boys, Talmud, Mishna, Gemara, Halakha, Law, Philosophy, Kabbala, Midrash, Rabbinics, the works, she was a special case, a way must be found, perhaps a partition could be erected in the study hall, maybe a thick curtain hung up in the *beis medrash* behind which the girl would be invisible, but from where she could sit and take it all in.

"Come here, child," the Rebbe beckoned to Tema. A brief silence followed after she approached while he rummaged inside his kaftan and came up with a hard red candy wrapped in cellophane flecked with lint and shreds of snuff. "This is for you, child." He held out the sweet. "But before you eat you must say a *brakha*. So tell me, daughter, which blessing would you say?"

Tema answered at once that she would say a *Shehakol*.

"But my Kaddish here"—and the Rebbe jerked his head in the vicinity of the son behind him—"he tells me you should say a *Borei Pri Ha'etz*, because it is a cherry candy, the fruit of a tree."

Tema shook her head. No, a *Shehakol*. The cherry candy is very far away from the cherry tree. Maybe it was never even near a cherry tree. Maybe it is only cherry-flavored. A *Shehakol*—the all-purpose *brakha*.

"*Gut gezugt*. Well said. In this matter, I must admit I hold with the female." The Rebbe cast an apologetic glance over his shoulder at his son. "But if you happen to have already said *Borei Pri Ha'etz*, that is also good—and you can go ahead and eat *gezunt aheit*. Better just to eat in such a case than to say another *brakha*, so you would not be taking God's name in vain."

The Rebbe smoothed his tea-stained mustache with the pad of his forefinger and gazed at Tema through lowered lids dripping with skin tags like stalactites. "So tell me, child, the Hebrew word for name is *shem*— am I right?" She indicated her agreement. "Is it masculine or feminine?" "Masculine," Temima replied. "Even though the plural is *shemot*, which is the feminine form?" "Masculine," she repeated unwavering. "*Gut gezugt*," the Rebbe said again, and bobbed his approval. "But why do you think this masculine word has such a feminine sound in the plural?"

At that point in her life, Tema did not yet possess the arsenal of terms and vocabulary to set out her case, so as best she could she responded that the simple answer was there was no reason; that's just the way language and all things were, there were exceptions. But then she went on to offer a kind of commentary. Maybe because since we say HaShem, The Name, as a substitute for God's real name, which we're not allowed to say, maybe the substitute also becomes holy—so how can it be anything but masculine?

The Rebbe's eyes crinkled and, to check the laugh he felt heaving up in a surge of subversive appreciation, he pinched his nostrils between two fingers and ejected a loud snort into the napkin upon which the two lumps of sugar had rested for his glass of tea with the half-moon of lemon floating inside. "*Gut gezugt*—very clever. Your voice is the voice of Jacob. You know how to fool and flatter the old man for the sake of the blessing. The blessing is learning."

After that, ignoring her completely as if she had dissolved and lost all substance and faded into the wall, he addressed himself exclusively to the mother. The girl was to be brought early the next morning to the side of the building where his Kaddish would await them. His Kaddish would then direct her into a small room with an entrance in the backyard and a shared wall with the study hall on the inside. Although this room had once been a toilet—it had in fact been an old wooden outhouse to which pipes had been extended when it was annexed to the building—it had not been used for this purpose for many years, the plumbing had long ago been disconnected, and therefore the Rebbe ruled that it was permissible for her to sit in there and listen through the cracks in the wall to words of Torah coming from the adjacent study hall and even to consult in that once-polluted space whatever holy books his Kaddish could collect and set out for her in advance. Since it was wintertime, she should be dressed in a heavy coat and gloves and hat as there was no heat in that room; there was also no electricity, the only light she would receive especially as the short days darkened was the light of Torah filtering through the crannies from the study hall.

"We shall see if her desire to learn is as strong as Hillel's who was found frozen under the snow on the roof of the yeshiva of Shemaya and Avtalyon listening with such concentration to the lecture when he didn't have enough money to pay the fee and enter through the door," the Osc-wiecim Rebbe said to Tema's mother, as if he had just finished proposing to a collaborator a scientific experiment to be performed on a monkey in a laboratory cage.

The aspiring sage Hillel, later renowned for his tolerance and leniency, was rewarded for his devotion to learning with a scholarship, free admission to the yeshiva. But when Tema was smoked out after five months of faithful attendance beginning in the icy days of February and ending in the scorching June heat (in the midst of which, on the seventh of Adar, also the birthday of Moses Our Teacher, she turned seven years old), she was banished from the study hall forever. During those five months she sat six days a week on a plank laid across the blackened cracked toilet bowl in the tiny cubicle filmy with cobwebs, steeped in the acrid smell of ancient urine, and followed along in the tattered books that had been provided for her—Talmud, Mishna and Gemara. An egg that is laid on a festival, is it permissible? The house of Shammai says, Yes, you may eat it on that day. The house of Hillel says, No.

She strained to peer through the chinks to identify her classmates. Boys sat in pairs at each table, study mates, an older more advanced boy coupled with a younger one, none yet a bar mitzvah judging from their prayer sessions, the youngest perhaps eight. Their teacher, a refugee from Vilna known to have once been a prodigy at the Slabodka yeshiva, slight with a scraggly gray beard and pale bulging eyes and an uncontrollable reflex that never ceased to amuse the boys of flinching like a startled rabbit whenever a car honked or backfired outside in the street, paced up and down the aisles snapping the ruler in his right hand against the palm of his left, now and then bringing it down upon the back of one of the boys caught raising his eyes from the page. The house of Shammai says, A man may divorce his wife only if he has found her to be unchaste. The house of Hillel says he may divorce her if she spoils his dish.

Soon it was no longer necessary to peer through the cracks. She knew all the characters, she could distinguish their tones, she could absorb just by listening. A heavenly voice was heard: The house of Shammai and the house of Hillel are each holy, but the law is in accordance with Hillel. When the school day ended, or if physical urgency forced her to leave early, her mother was awaiting her in front of the hardware store and signaled when it was safe to cross the street. There was never a time during those five months when her mother was not at her station waiting for her; her mother was always faithfully there then with the same certainty as she was not there later on. Anyone who might have noticed the girl coming or going dismissed her as a daughter of the house attending to a domestic chore in a broom closet.

If the spirit moved him the teacher would raise his voice and offer a brief lesson or pose a question in Lithuanian-accented Yiddish. When no one came forth with the answer, he would turn to the back of the room with the exaggerated flourish of scholarly disdain for the ignorance of the rabble. "TAIKU?" he would call out, and point with his ruler to a small boy, the only one sitting alone, who would unfailingly provide the correct answer in a soft voice. The boy's name was Eliyahu, which rendered this the running joke of the study hall, since it was common knowledge that TAIKU was the acronym for letting an unresolved issue rest in peace until the messianic age and the resurrection of the dead, when the prophet Eliyahu the Tishbite would return to explain all outstanding questions and problems. But this study hall was blessed with its own Elijah, still present and accounted for, the smartest boy in the class.

On an afternoon in May during a pulsing heat wave, as Tema was standing on the toilet peering out of a small window from which she had scraped off some gelid grime, watching the teacher, the former Slabodka genius, reduced to squirting the younger boys with a water gun to cool them off in the yard during recess, her eyes met Eliyahu's. The next day at recess time he opened the door to her cell and entered. Without a word, he sat down cross-legged on the floor. He was a year or two older than she by her estimation, though he was about her height, small and dark like she was, he could have been her brother, the son her father had been denied. He took out a pocket chess set and lined up the pieces as she sat down on the floor opposite him. Without uttering a single word, he showed her the moves. Thereafter, almost every recess, he came into her place and they played.

On a blistering day in June, as they sat on the floor of the outhouse with the chessboard between them, Eliyahu moved a pawn, then unbuttoned his white shirt and took it off, revealing his *talit katan*, his personal fringed garment. Tema moved her piece, shed her blouse and exposed her undershirt. It continued in this way in complete silence, move after move, shoes, socks, stockings, pants, skirt, underwear, until they were sitting cool and naked opposite each other. The game then went on but in reverse, they did not speak but with each move he put on one article of her clothing and she one of his, until checkmate, when she braided his sidelocks and secured them with her rubber bands and stuffed most of her own hair under the great bowl of his black velvet yarmulke with two ringlets dangling down on each side for *payess*, and then the whistle blew, recess was over, he remained in the outhouse while she stepped outside and into the study hall with the other boys and took her place in his seat in the back of the room and lowered her head over his Gemara, open to Sanhedrin 111a, and read to herself how God rebuked Moses: I am

El-Shaddai Who appeared to your forefathers Abraham, Isaac, and Jacob, yet you alone insist on knowing My true and ineffable Name and you alone question My ways and accuse Me of harming My people.

"Is it possible that Moses Our Teacher, the greatest of all prophets, sinned through lack of faith in the Almighty, by doubting God?" the teacher raised the question as boys sank their heads lower over their volumes so as not to catch his eye and be called on. "TAIKU?" he finally bellowed, and turned toward Eliyahu as to a colleague, a soul mate, the only one in the room who could understand him.

Tema raised her eyes to meet his. "Moshe saw terrible things in Egypt, just like you saw in Europe," she said. The teacher recoiled as if shocked by a bolt from another world. He began to advance toward her with his ruler pointed straight out in front of him like a drawn sword. With its tip he lifted her chin, like an alien specimen dredged from the mud that would befoul you if you touched it with a bare hand. "For your information, I am not at the level of Moshe Rabbenu to question the ways of the Almighty despite all the terrible things I have witnessed, and even more so I have never questioned the Almighty's abhorrence of a female who puts on herself the things that belong to a man," he spat out, referring to the prohibition in the book of Deuteronomy. "*Beged-ish* on a woman is an abomination to God, so it is written," the teacher went on grimly as Tema sprang from the seat of Eliyahu and lurched out of the study hall, past Kaddish smoking a cigarette on the stoop in front of the synagogue, into the arms of her mother who had spotted her at once in her boy's apparel and burst across the street from the hardware store and swept her up as she sobbed desperately, caressing and comforting her and warbling over and over again, Don't cry, Tema, everything will be all right, your father will never find out, nobody will ever know.

Eliyahu also did not return to the Oscwiecim yeshiva, and soon after, Tema heard, he and his family moved out of the neighborhood.

It was not until many years later, when she had already acquired renown as HaRav Temima Ba'alatOv, Ima Temima, that she learned what had happened to him that day when she ran out of the study hall after Kaddish mashed his cigarette under his shoe. One quiet afternoon, when they were still residing on the Street of the Kara'im in the Jewish Quarter of the Old City of Jerusalem, Kol-Isha-Erva slipped silently into Temima's study and handed her a note with a single word written on it in Hebrew—TAIKU—punctuated by a drawing, deftly rendered, of a chess piece, the queen. Temima nodded her acceptance, and soon after a trim, distinguished-looking man, clean shaven and bareheaded, was ushered in, a professor of astrophysics at Caltech, he said—and a chess master, he added with a shy dip of his chin. Kaddish had instantly grasped his strategic advantage when Tema bolted past him that day. He flicked down his cigarette, stamped it out, strode along the alley to the outhouse in back of the building, opened the door, came up behind Eliyahu, and cinched him around the waist humping him over. He flipped up Tema's skirt and pulled down her underpants. He flipped back the wings of his kaftan and opened his pants. He slammed his palm across Eliyahu's mouth as a precaution though he was confident there would not be any screaming, and he rammed himself into the boy muttering the whole time, So you wanna be a girl? This is what it means to be a girl. Nice? Like it? "Your dress was ruined, I'm sorry to say." The professor spat out the dry pit of a laugh. "A bloody mess."

"Kaddish told me what you did today, shame on you," her father said to her in the darkness of that night when he came into her room and woke her up by sinking the full weight of his body onto her bed. "You think you're something special, don't you, some kind of hotsy-totsy? Just because maybe you have a few extra brains in your head, you think you're a boy? You think you're different than every other female what ever lived on this earth? Well I have some news for you, girlie." He threw back her covers, slipped a hand under her nightgown, pincered a nipple and twisted. "You see this thing? It's flat now like a board, but pretty soon it will get big and fat and juicy—and you know why? To attract the male of the species. Man's pleasure, that's what you were made for, that's the only reason why the Master of the Universe in His wisdom created you." The hand moved down between her legs. "I'm doing this for your own good, you should know, to knock some sense into that stuck-up head of yours. You think you're some kind of fancy smarty-pants but you're no different than any other girl. Put an American flag on your face and you're just the same. It's not the noodle that counts it's the knish, it's not what's up there, it's what's down here. So you want I should tell you what's down here? Same by you like by every other girl. Nothing. Zero. A hole." And he plunged a finger inside.

For three years, from the age of seven to ten as Tema's beauty began its slope downward in the eyes of the commentators, she could never know in advance or predict when the urge would seize him and he would enter her room in the dead of night. Weeks would pass undisturbed, she thought she had been cleansed of the terrible sin she must have committed and been found blameless after all, but then he would return. The second time he came into her room she lay on her back in the darkness, feigning sleep. He boosted her flat girl's hips, slipped a pad under her as if to change a diaper, and buried her under the earthly weight of his mortal being. She thought she would suffocate yet she was overcome with pity for him, she was his collaborator. The sudden burst of pain stunned her, but she did not cry out, she continued in that darkness to pretend to be asleep out of compassion for him though he must have suspected how unlikely it could have been that she was still sleeping and taken note in the process that she had surrendered and turned herself into his accomplice. Inside her head she chanted the mantra, mama-mama-mama, until she heard a muffled groan and it was over. There was the wetness of warm sticky secretions and an unfamiliar acrid smell. When he was finished he spent a long time wiping up. She could hear him spitting on the pad, she could feel him rubbing her body between her legs. He drew the pad out from under her and took it away with him, continuing down the hall to the bathroom. Water ran, the toilet flushed. In the morning there were dried blood stains on the insides of her thighs.

The next time she heard him lumbering in the night in the direction of her room she turned on her stomach and remained frozen in that position as if in deep sleep, his co-conspirator as he attended to his pitiful needs. She numbed her mind by counting methodically to herself until his suppressed moan was released and he was done, she did not even reach sixty, she was merely a receptacle, a dumping ground. Thereafter, whenever she would hear him approaching, she would turn on her side, rendering everything that would take place far more impersonal, as if it were happening not to her but to her dark sister curled up on the bed with her face to the wall while she was hovering above like a pure angel with white wings shielding her eyes. She was not present even to him, her being was so irrelevant that even as she was simulating sleep on her side she could on occasion open her eyes and stare unblinking into the darkness like a corpse in its tomb though she would never have risked raising her fist and thumping it against her chest over her pounding heart as she calmed herself by reciting inside her head the ritualized Day of Atonement confession, We have been guilty, we have rebelled, we have robbed, we have spoken slander, we have caused perversions, we have been evil, and so on, until he gasped and was done. One time she heard him beseech her plaintively to touch him as if in acknowledgement that they both always knew she was really awake, another time he asked more irritably as if she were not performing well as a woman, as if she were no good in bed, but still she would not stir inside the webbed net of her counterfeit sleep. Sleep and wakefulness blurred in the nights. She never knew whether she was truly in one state or the other. Dark shadows rimmed her eyes and seeped inward through her skin spreading all over.

Her alien body no longer belonged to her, it was occupied territory. She detached her mind from it by telling herself stories as he made his pit stop in her room and went about his business on his way to the toilet—stories of princesses in locked towers or lost in black forests or smothered in ashes or tangled in thorn bushes or cast into sleeps so deep there was almost no hope of ever reviving them. One of the stories she recited to herself during those nights, she realized only later, resembled in so many ways Rav Nakhman of Bratslav's tale of the lost princess that she wondered if she might have sat at the master's feet as he told it long ago in another life. In Tema's story, too, there was a princess whose father once loved and prized her but she did something to anger him and he cursed her so that she was taken in the night to an evil place from which she could not break free. In Rav Nakhman's story as transcribed by his disciple Rav Nosson of Nemirov since the holy mystic of Bratslav did not write his own words down himself, he recognized how dangerous writing could be, the king is stricken with regret the next morning and sends his viceroy to search for his beloved daughter, the princess. But in Tema's story, the princess must free herself. She struggles over many years and in many places without succeeding, the ordeals of the princess in Tema's story continued as a serial in episodes and chapters through the years over all those nights. Each attempt by the princess to liberate herself would end in defeat caused by some personal weakness in her character. After each new failure she would wake up in a strange place and ask herself a variation of the same question the viceroy would ask when he awakened after going astray and losing his way—Where in the world am I?

On the eve of Yom Kippur in her tenth year, in the morning, her father

Reb Berel Bavli called her down to the kitchen to perform the ritual of atonement. Inside a cage on the floor were a live white rooster and two white hens chosen from among the prime poultry specimens in his slaughterhouse upon which the sins committed by the human members of the household over the past year would be transferred. He pulled out the rooster, gripping it by its legs with his right hand, and swung it around his head three times as it fluttered in a wild panic and shot out pellets of dung, reciting out loud as he performed this rite the verse, This is my substitute, this is my exchange, this is my atonement, this cock will go to its death and I will enter and go on to a good long life and to peace. When he completed his penance, he shoved the rooster back into the cage doomed to be dropped in the soup of the poor, took out a hen and handed it to Tema. "This one is for your sins," he said. "The other hen will be for your mama if she ever manages to wake up in time from all the pills that doctor of hers *schtupps* her with. So just in case she doesn't make it before the Moshiakh comes, you should keep your mama in mind while you *schlug kapores.*"

Tema clutched the frantic bird by its legs as it quaked in a frenzied blizzard of white feathers, but before raising it to whirl it in an orbit around her head she faced her father and said, "For the sins between one person and another, not even God can forgive you, only the person you have wronged. So I just want to tell you that I forgive you."

Her father's face darkened. "What are you talking about? You see that chicken you're holding in your hand? She belongs to me. That hand holding the chicken? Also mine. Everything you have I gave to you—the roof over your head, the food in your belly, the clothes on your back. You and everything you are, body and soul, belongs to me. With what belongs to me I can do with it whatever I want."

The soul is Yours, and the body Your handiwork. Have mercy on what You have labored to make.

By an effort of will, Tema overcame her wish to shut down and fade away. "So you know what I'm talking about, Tateh. It's wrong, you know that. You—we—must stop."

"I'll tell you what, my little genius"—the natural ruddiness of her father's face deepened like raw meat—"I want you should do me a little favor. Tomorrow in shul, when they read the Torah at Minkha, I want you should pay very good attention to the list of your female flesh and blood you're not allowed to lay a hand on and show me in black and white where it says one single word about your daughter." Tema's eyes widened. "Aha, so there's still something left in the Torah you don't know, my little Miss Professor Einshtein-Veinshtein," Reb Berel Bavli hooted.

"Maybe they just left it out—by mistake," Tema responded softly.

"God help us, so now I also have a little *apikores* on my hands to add to all my *zorres*. Is that what they teach you in school, such heresy? Excuse me, but who is this 'they' you are talking about? Didn't you learn that the Torah is written by the hand of God Himself? God makes mistakes? Since when? Such *shtoos*, I never heard such a stupid thing in all my whole entire life, I can't even believe my ears. Bite your tongue, I should wash your mouth out with soap for you. If God leaves something out it is for a reason. If your daughter is not on the list it is because your daughter is not forbidden, plain and simple. Anyways, how can you even know for one-hundred-percent sure with a daughter if she's really your own flesh and blood?" her father added maliciously.

A literalist, her father, a simple man when it suited him. Still, even then, Tema gave him some credit for an inner unease that must have driven him so uncharacteristically to take down the volume and check the text closely enough to put to rest whatever stirrings might have troubled his spirit.

"To tell you the honest truth, Tema'le," her father went on in the guarded tone he deployed with business competitors, "I really don't even know what you're talking about. This is some kind of story you made up, a *baba maiseh*, from all of the fairy tales you fill your head with, all of your mother's goyische books, those *romanen*, all of that make-believe crap. I'm telling you, you're imagining things, nothing happened, whatever you imagine happened has nothing to do with real life. You hear about such things sometimes—girls having such meshuggeneh ideas about their fathers—fantasies. Maybe I should make an appointment for you also with your mama's head doctor. You can go there together, have a mother-daughter outing, and after you empty out all that garbage from your heads in his office you can maybe treat yourselves to a little shopping for some nice new matching outfits for *yom tov*. It will cost me plenty, but what's money when it comes to health?"

The next afternoon, on Yom Kippur day, Tema paid scrupulous attention to the Torah reading from Leviticus chapter eighteen of the catalogue of incest prohibitions. Forbidden was exposing the nakedness of your father, your mother, your stepmother your father's wife, your sister the daughter of your father or your mother, your granddaughter the daughter of your son or daughter, your half sister the daughter of your father's wife, your aunt your father's sister or your mother's sister or your father's brother's wife, your daughter-in-law your son's wife, your sister-in-law your brother's wife, a woman along with her daughter or her son's daughter or her daughter's daughter for this is lewdness, a woman and her sister, a woman in her menstrual uncleanness, the wife of your neighbor to pollute yourself through her.

All of these injunctions are directed to a man with woman (and in one case, a father) as passive vessel, so to cover the territory also included is the commandment that he may not lie with another man as he would with a woman, it is an abomination. In the same vein, he may not lie carnally with an animal to be defiled in this manner. The sole admonition on this roster explicitly invoking a woman in an active role is the stricture against standing in front of an animal for the purpose of mating with it, a perversion. In this entire litany of incest and sexual restrictions seemingly so exhaustive, only a man's daughter is not specifically singled out as off-limits to him.

How had it happened that Tema had not noticed this before? Her father was correct.

Yet after their exchange in the kitchen that Yom Kippur eve of her tenth year, with one stupefied rooster and two dazed hens as witnesses, the pick of the fowl, unless she had been cast from that day forward under the spell of a slumber so deep she truly never again knew where in the world she was, her father Reb Berel Bavli did not enter her room again for his own sorry needs in the night. He no longer found her attractive.

Three months later, in winter, Tema's mother gave her a diary as a gift for Hannuka. It was a small chunky volume bound in satiny ivory leatherette, the border of its cover embossed with an ornate wreath of fuchsia vines, the leaves heart-shaped surrounding the words A YOUNG GIRL'S DIARY in elaborate raised gold script. A gold latch clasped the pages fastened with a miniature gold lock, with its tiny golden key dangling from a thin detachable scarlet cord. "You can write down all your secrets in here, Tema," her mother said. "It's private, for you alone, no one will peek, God forbid." On the first page, also in gold and framed by another garland of hearts, was a quotation from Charlotte Brontë, whose novel *Jane Eyre*, which Temima had found among her mother's collection of books, she had already read and wept over—"The human heart has hidden treasures / In secret kept, in silence sealed." The secret silent pages that followed were all blank and ruled, awaiting the hidden treasures of her human heart over the forthcoming year as if they already existed in the aura and needed only to be captured and stripped of their veil to be revealed, beginning with January the first and ending with the thirty-first of December, two days allotted per page, the entry for each day already conveniently inscribed with a greeting to her newest intimate, Dear Diary.

Dutifully, on the first day of the secular new year, Tema began her entries in her new journal. She cultivated the practice of writing at the end of each day, filling the designated lines, as if no more could happen to her within a twenty-four-hour span than could fit into that prescribed space. Then she would close the diary, lock it with the key she hid in a sock, and slip it under her mattress, on top of the springs.

Today it snowed but I forgot my boots so my shoes and stockings got soaking wet and my feet turned blue. Today at recess Yentie and Faygie were whispering to each other in the corner of the yard, but when they saw me coming they stopped, so I know they were talking about me. Today Mama was up when I came home from school and she gave me some meat soup with kasha and sat down at the table and watched me eat. Today Yentie told me that there's someone who keeps calling her up on the telephone to tell her he's going to kill me. Today my teacher Rebbetzin Klapholz called on me to read but I didn't know the place, so she said the next time she catches me daydreaming again she's going to send me to the principal's office. Today Tateh sent one of his lady workers to my class with a chicken for every girl to show us how to kosher them for when we get married; I will never eat chicken again in my life and I am never getting married. Today Yentie told me the killer called again, so I said, Give him my telephone number so he can call me up and tell me what he has against me. Today I was sitting on a car that was parked in front of school waiting for Mama to pick me up to go shopping for a new Shabbes coat, but she fell asleep and forgot all about our appointment and a man snuck up behind me and dragged me off the car by my braids and screamed at me at the top of his lungs for sitting on his brand-new car. Today I finished another book from Mama's pile, *The Scarlet Letter*; I am a sinner like Hester and deserve to be shamed in front of everyone and banished from Gan Eden. Today Yentie told me that she gave the killer my number and she asked me if he called yet and I said, No, not yet. Today it was freezing cold but the boiler broke in school and there was no heat so we had to sit in class wearing our coats and hats and scarves and gloves all day long but Rebbetzin Klapholz said, It's a very good lesson for you, girls, because it's much more important to save the money to fix the boilers in the boys' schools in case they break, this is a great tradition of our people for the women to sacrifice so that the men can fulfill the mitzvah of sitting and learning Torah. Today I went shopping with Mama for a Shabbes coat and she slipped and fell down the stairs in the DeKalb Avenue Station and her nylons ripped and her knees were bleeding and I heard someone in the subway say she was a drunk or maybe a drug addict. Today Yentie asked me again if the killer called yet and I said, No, not yet. Today on Thirteenth Avenue I saw an old lady in a baby carriage and a little child all wrinkled walking with a cane. Today Faygie tapped me on the shoulder during a Humash test and I let her see my paper so she could copy the answers. Today I told Yentie that the killer finally called me and we had a nice conversation on the telephone and straightened everything out and he promised *b'li neder* not to kill me. Today I passed a store window and saw the reflection of a person who looked like a liar and a cheater and a sinner, and then I recognized myself. Today was my birthday and Mama made cherry Kojel in a fancy mold for me with Del Monte Fruit Cocktail trapped inside and she stuck eleven candles in it and sang Happy Birthday, Tema, and she gave me a booklet called Very Personally Yours for a birthday present with one long-stemmed pink rose on the cover, and she told me to read this book in private very carefully to learn all about the blood that will soon come flowing out of a secret opening in my body; This is a true story, Mama told me, It is not a fairy tale, Everything it says in this book really happens to every girl, You are no exception.

An overdose of Today's and I's—the exercise was growing tiresome. For more than three months into spring Tema had filled in the lines dedicated to each day conscientiously with what she was now abashed to recognize as little more than childish, banal trifles. It was time to change course. She continued to write, but now freely, at any length she desired, straight through the arbitrary stopping point of the inane greeting to this absurd imaginary best friend she now thought of as Dear Diarrhea, and instead of giving an account of the dull events of her girl's life she would focus on a theme, a subject. The subject she selected was self-improvement; she would keep a record of her struggle to work on herself to become a better person, to achieve a higher level of perfection. Her most serious character flaw, she concluded, was Pride. Accordingly she reported on her battle against this enemy Pride to Dear Diarrhea, which she attacked on three fronts until her ultimate downfall and defeat. First, there was her pride in her personal appearance, her pathetic vanity, since everywhere she knew herself to be perceived as a beauty though oddly haughty and imperious for one so young. She confronted this weakness through a campaign of extreme modesty in dress and demeanor—loose blouses with sleeves down to her wrists, dark skirts brushing her ankles, thick stockings, walking silently in padded shoes stooped over with eyes cast down to the ground. Second was her offensive against speaking ill of others, the evil tongue, or even speaking well of others that could provoke a difference of opinion in the form of a pejorative rejoinder—*lashon ha'rah*, a predisposition she acknowledged within herself that implicitly contained a deeply rooted sense of her own superiority. Third was her strategy to obliterate herself figuratively by eliminating the personal pronoun from her vocabulary—I, me, my, myself, mine, and so on into the plural—rendering necessary elaborate circumlocutions to conduct a conversation thereby producing the secondary benefit of constricting all speech drastically. On each of these fronts, all three launched simultaneously, her mother fought her furiously, to the point that Tema reflected it was worth persevering if only to bring forth this desperate gasp of energy from a mother who otherwise passed her days stretched out on the couch in a stupor of medicine and disappointment. All of her mother's counterattacks Tema reported faithfully to Dear Diarrhea not sparing herself the ways in which they broke her spirit and eroded her resolve. "Stand up straight, Tema, don't be ashamed of your body! Give up talking *lashon ha'rah*, Tema, and you take all the fun out of life! Erase yourself, Tema, and you erase me!"

Erase me please from the book You have written, Moses Our Teacher said to the Lord. Tema was felled by the realization that her quest for ultimate humility was the height of Pride—an effort to outdo the man Moshe

328 | Tova Reich

himself, reputedly more modest than any other human being ever to walk upon the face of the earth. She would continue her program of confiding in Dear Diarrhea, she decided, but she would change the subject, she would seek refuge in the impersonal, in lists. She undertook the project of going through the Five Books of Moses in search of instances when God in whose image He created man allows His human side to show in acts of gentle lovingkindness instead of His usual omnipotent divine wrath decimating everything in sight. She listed the two main instances, the one in the beginning when God fashions garments of leather for Adam and Eve in their exposed guilty nakedness and amazingly dresses them Himself (she could see Him sitting there cross-legged like an old Jewish tailor squinting nearsighted as He pokes the moistened tip of the thread through the eye of the needle, then rising like a designer and contemplating His latest creation from every angle with His head cocked to the side, His forefinger pressed against His lips and thumb under His chin), and the one at the end when He buries Moses on Mount Nebo in the land of Moab (there He is, the undertaker, the gravedigger, leaning on His shovel, wiping His brow). But even those two occasions when God is "nice," as Tema put it to Dear Diarrhea, come after He had administered the cruelest of punishments—expulsion from Paradise, exclusion from the Promised Land, the Torah's beginning and end—like a father who gives a present to his child to make up for a merciless beating that will leave its devastating mark forever, ruin the child for life.

In between those two there was almost nothing to add to this list.

So Tema decided to keep another list—a list of instances when her mother seemed happy. This list was also very short. She noted the times she could hear from up in her bedroom her mother playing the piano downstairs, "Ode to Joy," "In the Hall of the Mountain King," the click of her mother's gold wedding band striking the keys of the notes in the bass clef. Was her mother happy at those moments? Tema asked herself. At least she was at peace, there was some relief from whatever roiled her spirit, the item belonged on the list in Tema's judgment. Then there were the times her mother would reminisce about how she would push Tema in her baby carriage and strangers would comment on how beautiful the child was—"People would stop me in the street," her mother would always say when she recounted this memory, pure pleasure uncoiling her face. There was even an occasion when her mother laughed, Tema

recalled, uncontrollably, alarmingly, insanely, which after some agoniz-
ing reflection Tema decided qualified for the list since technically it was
laughter after all and should therefore be deposited for safekeeping with
Dear Diarrhea.

It happened on a Friday night, at the Sabbath table. Her father was
spinning a tale about the past week in the slaughterhouse. So I'm standing there with my knife sticking out all ready to go and this cow comes
along and suddenly she opens her mouth and starts talking to me and she
says, Don't kill me today, I have female troubles. I'm so surprised, you
can imagine, my mouth drops open, one cow is more or less the same like
another cow so it's not every day you meet a talking cow, so I say, Okay
cow, come back tomorrow, I'll kill you tomorrow. So tomorrow comes
and I have my knife out smooth and sharp and along comes this same
cow and again she starts talking and she says, Please, not today, I'm not
in the mood. I'm telling you my knife almost fell right out of my hands
like a wet noodle and dropped on the floor, on top of all the blood and
kishkes, I just couldn't get over it, and before I know it again I'm saying,
Okay cow, tomorrow, we have a date. Then it's tomorrow and here comes
this same cow again and my knife is pointed right at the spot ready to go
in and do the job, and what do you know? Again she opens her mouth
and she says, Please, if you don't mind, another time, I have a headache.
As the story unfolded, convulsive laughter spurted out of the mouth of
Tema's mother, she was practically shrieking with laughter, her chest was
heaving so that she clutched herself over the heart with both hands as if
the breath were about to be squeezed out of her by savage palpitations,
tears flooded her eyes and came gushing down her cheeks streaking her
makeup until hoarse sobs erupted from some feverish depths within her
and she pushed back her chair with a dreadful scraping sound and ran
from the table up the stairs to her bedroom and slammed the door.

Her mother's laughter was harrowing, Tema was racked by it even as
she recorded it. Nevertheless, she resolved to continue her relationship
with Dear Diarrhea, she was not yet ready to give up writing, she set
herself the goal of filling in all of those empty spaces, the void was ter-
rifying. She took refuge in fiction, page after page unfurling the details of
the plot of the lost princess story with which she had numbed herself over
the three years when her father would come into her room, a meticulous
narration of all of the trials ending in failure and defeat endured by the

lost princess in her struggle to free herself from banishment and exile and return to the paradise of her father's kingdom—ordeals by water and by fire, by sword and wild beasts, by hunger and thirst, earthquake and plague, strangulation and stoning, sleeplessness and agitation, madness, poverty, degradation. What had she done to anger him so grievously to lead to such punishment, how had she disobeyed? She wrote and wrote into the early days of summer but the answer refused to rise from the abyss, and then, in a sphere beyond her awareness, her story merged into a retelling of those nights, night after night, when her father would open her door and enter her room. Fire and brimstone, the world had come to an end. Lot's daughters, the same two virgins their father had offered to hand over to the doomed Sodomites instead of the two male guests under the protection of the house these sons of Belial were clamoring for, believed there were no men left on earth for them to procreate with. So they got their father drunk with wine in a cave in the hills near Zoar where they had fled from the conflagration. First the eldest lay with their father and became pregnant by him, the next night it was her sister's turn. The eldest gave birth to a son she called Moab, father of the Moabites, and the younger gave birth to a son she called Ben-Ami, father of the Ammonites. The abomination of the Moabites was the god Hemosh to whom King Solomon built a shrine for wanton, lustful worship on a mountain east of Jerusalem. He also built there a shrine to the abomination of the Ammonites, the god Molekh, upon whose fiery altars the children were sacrificed.

The days grew longer, the school year was over. It was evening but not yet dark, and Tema was sitting in her room reading for the first time her mother's copy of *Anna Karenina*. She was up to Book Two, groping her way back to this world, looking up at the twilight after having lost herself in the story of how Anna's lover, Vronsky, blundered and broke the back of his horse in the steeplechase race. Poor Frou-Frou, there was no choice but to shoot her. Tema was eleven years old and she wanted to howl for this mare who had tried so hard to please her master. She was thinking to herself, this man Tolstoy, here was a rebbe at whose feet she could sit, she would do everything to please him, she would bend her will never to do anything he would disapprove of when she heard her father's heavy tread shuffling toward her down the hallway. He opened her door without knocking but did not come into her room. Still in his work clothes, with sawdust on his shoes, he planted himself at the entrance and said, "I just want you should know that your mama read your diary, all of that dreck you made up about me. You left it where anyone could see. You did it on purpose to hurt me. Now your mama is saying she's going to leave me." Manifesting no interest at all in any response she might offer up, he turned and left. She felt so sorry for him, it left her almost dizzy with hatred.

The next day she waited for her mother to come downstairs, but when by five o'clock in the afternoon she had not yet appeared Tema went up and knocked on the bedroom door. "Yes, come in, Tema," her mother called to her in a muffled voice. When Tema entered the room her mother gazed at her for a long time with her eloquent eyes, then folded back a corner of the quilt and patted the bedsheet, an invitation to Tema to come lie down beside her under the covers. Her mother was still in her nightgown, her hair spread over the pillow like a dark crest.

Tema lay down at her mother's side, nestling close to her body, burying her face in the familiar musty smell tinged with perfume, lily of the valley. "I'm sorry, Mama," Tema said in a choked whisper. Her mother inhaled the sweet young fragrance of her hair and kissed her on the pale exposed whiteness of the part on top of her head.

"It's all right, Tema. It's not your fault. It's my fault. I was a bad wife."

"Why did you read my diary? You promised you'd never look."

"It doesn't matter," her mother said wearily. "I always knew anyway somewhere in my heart. I didn't protect you the way a mother should— forgive me. I put my own interests ahead of yours. Besides, it was just too hard to get out of bed."

Tema shook her head ardently. "It's only a story, Mama. I made it all up, it's not real, nothing ever happened. Tateh says you're going to leave him."

Her mother laughed to herself, a skeptic's laugh, but nevertheless Tema heard it through everything that separated them. "Why did you laugh?"

"I laughed? That was a laugh? Don't worry, *maidel'e*, I'm not going anywhere. Where would I go anyway? Besides, I'm much too tired."

Three weeks later her mother overcame her mortal exhaustion and rose from her bed. She dressed herself in her finest clothing including shoes and stockings. She carefully applied black kohl liner and mascara to her eyes, lipstick, powder and rouge. She polished her nails. She adorned herself in her gold necklace and bracelets and single pearl earring. She dabbed perfume on the pulse of each wrist, in the cleft of her split earlobe, in the scoop at the base of her throat. She coiffed herself in her best wig, a long blonde pageboy all of a piece that she wore only to weddings and other special occasions. She uncapped all of her bottles and emptied all of the pills into her mouth and swallowed them without water. She returned to the bed, drew the covers up to her chin, and lay there with eyes wide open looking back at her life until all the vital moisture within was lapped up by tongues of flame and she was turned into a pillar of salt.

More Bitter
Than Death
Is Woman: Haya

The Teachings Of HaRav Temima Ba'alatOv, Shlita
(May She Live On For Many Good Long Years)—
Recorded By Kol-Isha-Erva At The "Leper" Colony Of Jerusalem

DRAWING from the secrets of the wise and the discerning, and from the teachings derived from the knowledge of those endowed with understanding, I will open my woman's naked mouth in prayer and supplications to beseech and beg mercy before the King who pardons and forgives sins. I have been remiss, I am awash in mortification, whatever excuse I might offer is feeble and of no account. Write it down! Write it down! our holy mother wordlessly commands me every day, several times a day I hear the prophetic voice insisting, demanding, Write it down! Hold nothing back!—but until now in my weakness I have pro-crastinated, I have lacked the strength of character to get my act together and carry out my mandate. It is now well over a full year that we have sojourned here in the "leper" colony of Jerusalem. I have been drained of energy almost to extinction, my fingers have grown numb, the skin of my hands has become scaly, my arms are knobbed and mottled, until now I have not been able to muster the spirit to lift my pen and perform my duty, God forgive me.

Only five souls remain in full-time residence within the walls of our settlement, towering above us all HaRav Temima Ba'alatOv, shlita, who has entered a hidden state, no longer rising from the holy bed, and, in mystical abstinence, no longer communicating through speech. Of the five surviving remnants who have dug in and refused to be uprooted—hell no, we won't go!—the exalted HaRav Temima Ba'alatOv, shlita, is, needless to say, first and foremost; last and not even meriting mention is my insignificant afflicted self. The remaining three survivors in order of appearance include Rizpa, our faithful domestic management associate now donning ritual fringe *ziziot* at the corners of her apron, her dark wizened skin erupted in patches of discoloration, still emotionally powerless to move past her personal mourning and loss through the five stages of grief and achieve closure with acceptance; my prophetess of the past, Aishet-Lot, every exposed part of her massive body white as the salt of the Dead Sea, now promoted to the position of our holy mother's primary personal assistant, still suffering from a severe case of post-traumatic stress disorder with its symptomatic muteness that surely elevates her silent conversations with Ima Temima to transformative heights not to be imagined; and our male help-meet, a nomad (this is not the time to disturb Ima Temima with the question as to whether or not it is appropriate to use the word "Arab" to identify another human being created in the image of God) whom Ima Temima called Kadosh-Kadosh, though I suspect that is not his true name. I recognized him, of course. He was the visitor who would arrive from time to time to the Temima Shul in the Bukharim Quarter—to bless *me*, our holy mother would say, instead of the reverse. Whenever he showed up, despite whatever else of urgency might have been scheduled, HaRav Temima Ba'alatOv would enter a secluded state with him for a long session of *hitbodedut,* in the bedchamber where all business was conducted, with the door closed and no one else present, and when word of this deference to a lowly seeker of obviously no consequence in the world and unmistakably not even Jewish would leak out to the disciples, it only served to embellish our holy mother's legend.

These are the five survivors of our camp, the embers salvaged from the flames. The decimation of our ranks is in no small measure my fault, I take full responsibility, I am prostrate with shame and remorse, I am abject, our holy mother has forgiven me but I shall never forgive myself. All that is asked of me now is to write it down, to hold nothing back, to lift my woman's naked voice and make public confession. I was tested and I failed—flunked, flunked! I stand now on the block as the emissary of our congregation and deliver myself into the hands of the Lord, the high executioner up above: Here I am, impoverished of deed, quaking and terrified, unworthy and unsuitable, a sinner and transgressor, have mercy.

Now at last, in compliance with the admonition of HaRav Temima Ba'alatOv, shlita, to hold nothing back in these pages, I accept that it is no longer possible to avoid setting down a full accounting of what happened here in our "leper" colony starting on the tenth of Tishrei, Yom Kippur, the Day of Atonement, two months and a day after the passage of our high priestess, Aish-Zara, za'zal, from this world to the next. It is my duty to acknowledge that my reluctance to testify to these events, putting the task off day after day, was nothing but a small-minded, self-centered defense mechanism on my part to rewrite history through omission due to the corrosive light these compromising events shed on the weakness and baseness of my own character. Our holy mother's continued silence warns me that I can no longer hide behind the excuse of female modesty or my hypocritical aversion to calling attention to myself in order to be spared the disgrace I deserve for my inappropriate behavior, for all the pain and suffering I have caused, for corrupting and contaminating our community with a sin that festered undercover until it leaked and spiraled out of control to a disastrous climax.

WE WERE still a community of about one hundred souls on that Day of Atonement. How long ago it now seems, a past life, a full year has not yet gone by since that Yom Kippur when it all began but the questions we asked then have already been answered—Who by madness? Who by disease? Who by despair? Who by degradation?

HaRav Temima Ba'alatOv, shlita, did not join us in prayer on that Yom Kippur due to physical issues, but instead remained cloistered over the entire twenty-four-hour period in the holy chambers attended by the only non-Jew from our inner circle, the nomad Kadosh-Kadosh. Everyone else, including Aishet-Lot, who had become the primary caregiver to Ima Temima, was ordered to take the day off to fast and pray as was required, optimally with the full congregation.

During the short break following the afternoon service, high-lighted, to my mind, by its detailing of the frenetic ancient priestly rites and sacrifices and costume changes on the Day of Judgment when our Holy Temple still stood in all its glory on its Mount, may it be rebuilt speedily and in our time, and with its rapturous exhalation of relief when the radiant high priest manages to make it out of the Holy of Holies in one piece, I found myself in the northern garden outside our holy mother's quarters beside the burial spot of our own high priestess, Aish-Zara, za'zal, who had not been so lucky, she had not been spared. There I sat and also wept as I remembered Aish-Zara, za'zal, just as our ancestors also musicians (entertainers like other eager-to-please immigrant population groups) once wept in exile by the waters of Babylon.

So deep in end-stage grief and longing was I crouched there between the still-unmarked grave of Aish-Zara, za'zal, and the sealed door of our holy mother that I did not at first notice the stranger in our midst climbing over the wall until he came scrambling and scraping down and crash-landed on the ground. Naturally, I rose at once to come to his aid, but gesturing defensively with lacerated hands, as if on guard to repel me if I turned out to be a hostile or allow me cautious limited access if I showed myself to be a potential ally, he cried, "The *go'el ha'dam* is after me! This is an *ihr miklat*! You have to take me in!"

The white garments he was wearing as is the custom on Yom Kippur, from his great white crocheted yarmulke pulled low and snug over his skull to the white cloth sneakers on his feet and all the whiteness in between symbolizing purity, a clean slate and fresh start for the new year, were filthy, shredded and bloodied from the ordeal of the gripping chase scene he had just starred in with the blood avengers pursuing him, hot on his heels.

Even then I wondered where in the world he had picked up the notion that our "leper" colony was an *ihr miklat,* a city of refuge, set aside to give asylum to accidental murderers, but he was pitifully battered and distraught, it was not the time to interrogate him, he had the right to remain silent. He was not such a young man either, well beyond the age to be scaling walls. Nor was he in very good physical shape for such an extreme workout, panting heavily, sweating lavishly, clutching his gut. His patchy grizzled gray beard was wiry like steel wool, his sidelocks were white and wispy, but his eyes, set a little too close together, gave off a poignant childlike wounded quality, as if expecting something good and expecting to be disappointed, both at the same time. He reminded me of someone, I couldn't at first quite put my finger on whom.

As I continued to stand there in silence taking pains not to make any threatening gesture or abrupt move—for instance, backing up a few paces and turning to pound on our holy mother's door in this genuine emergency to demand the nomad's help in dealing with this intruder—his agitation began to cool, he calmed down to a degree though he remained wary and alert, and he went on declaiming, "The whole world's going crazy—you know? I'm the main *go'el ha'dam*—that's my job description, to avenge the blood, I'm the blood redeemer, so how can a *go'el ha'dam* be chased by another *go'el ha'dam*? Hel-lo? The buck has to stop somewheres, otherwise you get your endless cycle of violence, blahblah, *ve'hulai ve'hulai.* And where does it stop? The answer is—Right here, lady, in your "leper" colony. Who's gonna come in after me into this joint anyways, and maybe catch the sickness and turn all white and bumpy like a cauliflower with boils like from the ten plagues and pus pimples like you wouldn't believe oozing gunk all over the carpet and all of his body parts that stick out hanging from a piece of skin and then dropping down on the floor one by one, plop, plop, plop, first his toes, then his nose, then his fingers, then his ears, then his pecker—gross, right? So I'm safe in here—right? Until the Moshiakh comes, quickly in our day, amen, the "leper" colony is our *ihr miklat*, my refuge city. It's your job to gimme shelter, lady, like Reb Mick says—'cause there's a war going on, the end of days, Apocalypso, Gog and Magog, fire, flood, rape, murder, and the mad bull lost his way. I'm the main bull, lady, and boy am I mad, I'm real mad!"

All this and more he poured out in English, it occurred to me. There we were in the "leper" colony of Israel but he wasn't speaking Hebrew, he had sized me up instantly as an Anglo. It was a New York accent of some sort, definitely not Upper East Side, nothing I was familiar with, some neighborhood in one of the outer boroughs probably. That was when I also realized whom he reminded me of—our holy mother's son, Paltiel.

Then it all came together for me, like sparks fusing into a bolt of lightning, like prophecy. This was Paltiel's father, aka Go'el-HaDam the blood avenger, aka Haim Ba'al-Teshuva, scribe and phylacteries maker of Hebron, the former Howie Stern of Ozone Park, Queens, New York. I had never met him personally but I knew all about him, there was no mistaking him, this was the man our holy mother, Ima Temima, was still technically married to by the law of Moses and Israel, though, as I also knew perhaps better than anyone, our holy mother's true husband was and remains the Toiter in the line of the redemption and fulfillment of the messianic mission.

Out of concern for embarrassment to HaRav Temima Ba'alatOv, shlita, therefore, without informing anyone of the arrival of this potentially compromising incendiary figure within our gates, I led him along back pathways around the northern garden through the tangled brush and nettles on the east side of the hospital up the stairs under the Jesus Hilfe inscription to the refuge of my room, where I closed the door and offered him asylum.

I HID him in my room for close to six weeks, convinced that during that period, with the exception of Basmat, my cat, I alone knew of this stranger's presence in our midst, and I alone would bear the consequences for shielding a fugitive from justice should his whereabouts ever become known. During that time, I took care of all his needs, from soup to nuts, it pains me to confess. Apart from food and shelter, it would be morally equivalent to a violation of attorney-client confidentiality to give a full blow-by-blow of all the needs I provided for; suffice it to say they were across the board, to my everlasting shame. He called me his "little righteous gentile," I blush to admit, and promised to plant a tree in my honor at the Yad Vashem Holocaust museum when all of this blew over for placing myself at mortal risk by hiding him from his Nazi anti-Semite persecutors. I am equally mortified to confirm that I called him my "Hero of Our Time," but it is my intention in these pages not to spare myself any humiliation or hold anything back except for a pointless recapitulation of the intimate details, which, in any event, would simply reward prurience and idle curiosity, and bottom line always boils down to the same-old same-old tiresome drill between a man and a woman with very limited wiggle room for originality or variation on the theme to the disappointment and boredom of voyeurs and pornography junkies everywhere.

As for attending to his emotional needs, this consisted primarily of listening, of allowing him to talk, which he did practically nonstop when I was in the room with him and we were awake. Fortunately, he did not talk in his sleep, nor did he cry out from nightmares most likely because he was congenitally immune to fear or guilt, nor, to my surprise, did he snore though judging from the position of his septum that was on full display in flagrant deviation when he slept on his back with his nose pointed to the ceiling, coupled with the nasal quality of his voice to which I am acutely sensitive thanks to my musical training and his open mouth that shut only to grind his teeth, he looked and sounded like he would have been a snorer. Each night's sleep, however, I am obliged to note, was interrupted at least once by the thud of poor Basmat's body striking the wall when he hurled her out of the bed across the room. The flow of his talk ran on without pause or interruption or comment from me, which was his sexual preference as well. The only caveats I imposed were that all conversation must be conducted in a whisper, and that above all he was banned from uttering a single word or syllable, either negative or positive, about his so-called "wife," our holy mother, or anything even remotely touching upon our holy mother. In no uncertain terms I warned him that all it would require would be one violation of this restriction and he would be out the door on his rear end in the street before he knew what hit him, at the mercy of the revenge freaks, which is the main natural resource and export of the Middle East.

It was through his endless ramblings, supplemented by my own sleuthing and Internet stalking, that I got full disclosure of his escapades as a blood avenger—not only how many Arab thumbs and big toes he had chopped off, or how many ugly buttocks he had exposed, or how many beards he had half-razored, or how many earlobes he had punctured, for all of which he had already served an abbreviated oddly triumphant jail term flashing his V for victory every time he was hauled out in front of the cameras smiling insanely, but also an exhaustive listing of his more-recent exploits, including shootings through car windows, bombs planted in mosques and discotheques and cafés, buses blown up, packages rigged with explosives, olive groves burned down, wells poisoned, and so on, targeting Muslim extremists and latent jihadists (which, in his world view, encompassed all Muslims), Christian proselytizers, Mormon baptizers of dead Jews, Jews for Jesus, Jewish left-wing intellectuals, homosexuals, Israeli historical revisionists, women rabbis and women wearing prayer shawls or raising their naked voices to cantillate from a Torah scroll at the Western Wall, Holocaust deniers, anti-Semitic European academics posing as anti-Zionists, Zionism-equals-Racism propagandists, international Israel bashers, neo-Nazis, self-hating Jews, women immodestly dressed, the list goes on. The growth curve in his choice of victims was staggering, rendering it exceedingly hard for the authorities to finally figure out that this broad-spectrum violence streak was coming from a single source. For by the time I had given him asylum in my room it was not only the blood avengers who were pursuing him, the law was also on his tail, he was right up there on the top-ten charts of the most wanted. Still, it was not for me to be a *moseret* or a *rodefet*. For the informers let there be no hope. Excuse me, but I would not be the one to squeal or turn him in.

I suppose it is necessary for me to pause here to tap into my unconscious, drawing on my years of treatment with my amazing hearing-impaired Park Avenue mental health therapist, in order to try to analyze my motivations while in no way justifying or turning into an apologist for my transgressive behavior in sequestering an individual who was so clearly the antithesis of everything I had ever stood for during my entire life—a bigot, racist, sexist, misogynist, homophobe, yaddayadda, never mind an outright murderer, a first-degree criminal and felon, not to mention cruel to animals, which speaks volumes about a person. And not only did I take him in, literally and figuratively, at great personal risk, but in doing so I was also endangering our community and all we had journeyed so long and so hard to accomplish at such heavy spiritual and emotional and material cost. Most importantly, though, I was jeopardizing the reputation of our holy mother, our epicenter, our source, to whom I had devoted, and continue to devote, all of my energy and passion, my very life's breath, whose well-being and interests I place above my own without reservation in every way, for whom I would take a bullet anytime, for whom with no hesitation whatsoever I would throw myself away. HaRav Temima Ba'alatOv, shlita, Ima Temima, our holy mother, was and remains the overriding and consuming passion of my life, I can never let go of it and I never will because were I to do so, there would be nothing left of me, I would be eviscerated, hollowed out, empty, I would cease to exist. How then can I explain the root cause of such inappropriate and unacceptable behavior on my part?

What I now recognize and acknowledge, specifically with regard to my relationship with Go'el-HaDam and how it impacted me, is that it was subconsciously my way of connecting with Ima Temima who, when he literally dropped into our "leper" colony that Yom Kippur, was more and more turning inward and withdrawing from us, avoiding association with almost all of the established inner core circle with the exception of the nomad Kadosh-Kadosh. To put it simplistically and, I should add, superficially, when I hooked up with the admittedly somewhat unbalanced and unstable Go'el-HaDam, once again Temima and I were connected through a man as we had been through Abba Kadosh, a'h, in the Bnei HaElohim days in the Judean Desert. Go'el-HaDam was "into" me as once he had been "into" our holy mother. He was the link between us. We formed a triangle, a trinity, a ménage à trois so to speak. I don't want to push this idea any further than is necessary out of respect for our holy mother lest it be misinterpreted as irreverent, coarse, even obscene, though for my part I see it and intend it in purely spiritual terms, a mystical union beyond human understanding, like in the Song of Songs. Whatever my motivations in harboring Go'el-HaDam, they reflect not at all upon the lofty spirit and sacredness of Ima Temima, but rather on my own flawed nature and neediness.

And indeed, when all of this sordid affair involving Go'el-HaDam was winding down to its inevitable miserable smashup, spewing wreckage everywhere and nearly wiping us out, it was our holy mother who got it exactly right and explained me to myself. "The serpent beguiled you," HaRav Temima Ba'alatOv, shlita, taught, "and you ate."

Our holy mother then offered a radical teaching based on the provocative similarity between the words *haya*, animal, beast, and the name given to the first woman *Hava*, mother of all living, the airborne tiny letter *yod* dragged down into the mud and tamed to a *vov*. "When God realized that it is not good for man to live alone, He passed every *haya* and bird of the sky before Adam to choose from and name. According to some sources Adam mated with the female of each kind to try her out, but from none of these did he get satisfaction and he did not find a fitting helpmeet, which obliged God to perform the first recorded surgery to come up with a new and improved model. This one Adam liked, she would serve, and he named her Hava. From Haya to Hava. What do we learn from this?" HaRav Temima Ba'alatOv, shlita, posed the question. "That a woman is an animal—so she is perceived and so she is used."

Our holy mother went on to elaborate, in more words spoken aloud than in several months prior, more words by far than we have since been worthy to hear to this day from the sacred source, that the *wilde haya* wild beast is Lilith, Adam's first wife some say referring back to the conflicting double narrative of the creation of woman—Lilith, the woman created at the same time as the man in the image of God like the man, who would therefore not accept a subservient role, rebelled against the missionary position, would not lie still underneath and just take it, but spread her wings and flew off to *yenne welt*, the land of imps and demons, of Asmodeus and Samael, witch and sorceress, disobedient, uncontrollable, a bird of prey, a raptor, a wild horned goddess, a tigress prowling and lusting and wreaking her havoc on lonely men and newborn babies in the night, not a suitable helpmeet. In contrast, Hava, fashioned through Dr. God's cosmetic-surgical intervention from a spare rib of the man created in the image, was a *behaima*, a domesticated animal, cattle, a cow to milk, a sheep to fleece, an ox to pull the cart, an ass to carry the load, a mare to ride upon, a fitting helper doomed to suffer endlessly, cursed with desire for the man who rules over her.

Whether I was the daughter of Lilith or of Hava, whether I was a Lilith *haya* who had been beaten down into a Hava *behaima*, HaRav Temima Ba'alatOv, shlita, did not go on to specify, nor was it necessary, for both fell prey to the temptations of the flesh, leading to the loss of paradise, shame and death.

OUR HOLY mother's chastisement for my passive-aggressive behavior, admittedly so deserved, was delivered to me in the inner sanctum of the chambers in the northern garden to which I had been urgently summoned by Rizpa and then hastily ushered in by Aishet-Lot, who immediately exited the quarters to resume guard duty outside. Ima Temima, unveiled and in a long white robe, was seated at the table against which what looked like a shepherd's staff or crook was propped and upon which the little mother Torah so familiar to me was undressed and only slightly unfurled on the right tree-of-life roller to the opening portion in which the man passes the buck and blames both the woman who had given him from the tree to eat and God who had given him the woman. So much time had elapsed since I had seen the bare luminous face of our holy mother, its incandescent light like celestial fever, that I was nearly blinded, to the point that I did not at first notice the nomad propped up on pillows in the bed under the quilts, his body from his naked shoulders and upward visible, blotched with a florid rash. "You thought you can hide him, but I know the whole time," the nomad spoke. "When you go back to little love nest, do not look for lover boy. They already drag him out on his fat ass, maybe you see shit marks on floor. We tell to him that maybe next time he go out on the town, he should be suicide bomber. Anyway, good news is, on way to police car, a stone fall on his head, a nice big stone. Maybe some blood avengers, who knows? I think he not feeling so great no more. Bad news is, he sticked the cat in the freezer for good-bye present to you. We leave it there for now so it don't go soft and mushy and stink up the place. Sorry about cat. Cute little pussy."

Ima Temima spurted out what sounded like a dry little laugh, and reached for the staff leaning against the table and clasped it, indicating in this way that the fleeting widening of my eyes when I had entered the room and instantly spotted this vaguely familiar sinister object had, not surprisingly, not escaped our holy mother who sees all. "It's all right, Kol-Isha-Erva, don't be afraid, I don't intend to smite you with this rod, merely talk to you." The beautiful eyes, fully visible, crinkled teasingly and yes, forgivingly, as the holy hand stroked the smooth wood. "Maybe, though, if I let it drop to the floor it will turn into a serpent and bite your heel. Well, as it happens, this staff comes from Gan Eden, from the original tree of knowledge good and evil as a matter of fact. The first couple took it with them when they were expelled, a walking stick to keep them from crawling out on all fours, to aid them in evolving to the upright and human position as they began their wanderings—and they passed it down through the generations. Believe it or not, it's the very same stick that Judah gave to his daughter-in-law Tamar as a pledge when she stood at the crossroads veiled in the manner of a prostitute, to procure her services. Kadosh-Kadosh gave it to me. It was passed down to him from his warrior grandmother Hephzibah."

Our holy mother bent a gracious eye upon the nomad grinning under the covers, baring his teeth like the wolf in the grandmother's bed in the children's fairy tale, showing his gums spotted with sores. "For it is I who am desired at the end of days," HaRav Temima Ba'alatOv, shlita, added enigmatically.

Ima Temima's exposed face turned grave. "For the sake of Zion I shall not be still, for Jerusalem's sake I shall not be silent," our holy mother declared. Turning decisively to the matter at hand, HaRav Temima Ba'alatOv, shlita, referencing once again the expulsion of Adam and Hava from the Garden of Eden (as is true for the Torah itself, every repetition by our holy mother also signifies), informed me that when it became known outside the confines of our walls that we have been harboring within our paradise a snake, a notorious wanted criminal and terrorist, a decision was made at the highest spheres of government to reclassify our "leper" colony as occupied territory—specifically, as an illegal settlement outpost to be evacuated within the next forty-eight hours.

Even our holy mother's extraordinary contacts and *protectzia* could not in this instance prevent the forthcoming ethnic cleansing. It had escalated to a matter of extreme diplomatic sensitivity that touched upon the continued support and patronage of the superpowers at the topmost levels who were demanding the evacuation as a point of honor, as acknowledgement of their authority; the pressure was intense, the goodwill of the protectors was far too vital for the state to risk for such an inconsequential and lunatic fringe figure as Go'el-HaDam. What it boiled down to from the point of view of the state was a serious threat to its basic survival if it failed to evacuate the "outpost"; as for the municipality, here was its opportunity to seize the upper hand economically, for it had long had its eye on this exceptionally valuable piece of real estate in the heart of West Jerusalem and would have liked nothing better than to auction off the property to the highest bidder to be developed into luxury apartments for holiday visitors and commercial centers for foreign investors.

As I stood there with head bowed and eyes lowered accepting this justified rebuke for the catastrophe I had brought down upon our people I could only tremble and weep. "I'm sorry, I'm sorry, forgive me." My throat was constricted, I could barely squeeze the words out, I had lost my woman's naked voice. All I wanted at that moment was to curl up and die, I felt annihilated, I fell upon my knees and prostrated myself at the feet of our holy mother.

Our holy mother took pity on me, raised my head with the staff, and kissed me on the mouth. I could feel the heat penetrating me and spreading throughout my body like fever as I was comforted by the news that permission had been obtained for a very small nucleus of first-circle adherents to remain within the "leper" colony following the evacuation until they too disappeared through natural attrition as the plague ran its course. Thank God, despite my sins, I was one of the elect.

With overwhelming pride I can report that the evacuation, which began the next day, inspired a brilliantly creative protest from the citizens of our "leper" colony now reclassified as an illegal settlement outpost. The remaining hundred or so of our inhabitants came boldly forth to face the police contingent sent in to carry out the *aktion*. Dressed in striped concentration camp uniforms, with numbers tattooed on their forearms and yellow stars of David imprinted with the word JUDE pinned to their breasts or on bands wound above the elbow around their upper arms, some with shaved heads, our brave deportees screamed, Nazis! Stormtroopers! Gestapo! They held up signs, JUST FOLLOWING ORDERS? JEWS DO NOT EXPEL JEWS! THIS "LEPER" COLONY SHALL NOT BE JUDENREIN! NEVER AGAIN!—and so on. The effect was so mind-boggling that the cops withdrew as if whacked with a cudgel, failing to accomplish their assigned mission.

That night the media was foaming at the mouth with righteous indignation and condemnation of the misuse and trivialization of Holocaust language and imagery by cult groupies of a woman guru no less, squatters in a "leper" colony of all places that had been harboring a homicidal maniac terrorist; this was nothing but a desecration of the memory of the six million martyrs of the Shoah, which was an unprecedented genocide to which no other atrocity could ever be given moral equivalency. But in my woman's naked voice I say, with all my authority as director of the school for prophetesses, that if a "leper" colony can be reclassified as occupied territory or an illegal settlement outpost, why not also as a ghetto, why not a death camp? The Holocaust belongs to all of us Jews, it is our communal birthright, no Jew has exclusive rights over it, we all own it to use as we see fit.

Also that night a delegation of top cabinet officials made a preemptive secret pilgrimage to our holy mother's private quarters in the northern garden of our "leper" colony to negotiate a deal for a relatively peaceful and orderly disengagement, providing for only a controlled token protest by our people so that we could save face while also guaranteeing no further embarrassment or trauma for those on the government-enforcement side taxed with doing the dirty work. In exchange for this concession on our part, a quota of select visitors and supplicants would be allowed to continue to enter the radiant orbit of HaRav Temima Ba'alatOv, shlita, and those evicted from the grounds of the "leper" colony along with other followers would be granted the right of return during daylight hours in order to be in physical proximity to our holy mother to whom they were in any event always spiritually connected as by an umbilical cord wherever they were in the world, day or night. But when darkness fell they would be obliged to depart from the grounds of the settlement outpost "leper" colony ghetto death camp and go into exile, leaving only the remnants of the chosen people within, and the gates would be sealed.

The next morning, however, the news was once again hectic with reports of an underground raid on Yad Vashem carried out by "psychos" and "nuts," a happening, it was conjectured, that must have taken place in the early hours of dawn before the Holocaust remembrance museum opened for business, during which an unauthorized exhibition was put up entitled Remember Munich! Pullout Equals Appeasement Equals Shoah!, which showcased images and videos and artifacts from the confrontation of the previous day between our persecutors and our "leper" colony's ghetto fighters and death camp inmates; the floor surrounding the display billowed with concentric half-moons of

hundreds of flickering memorial candles, a very effective installation, I might note, which let's just say I was privileged to view
myself with my seer's eyes. But because of this so-called trespass
and violation, a much larger police contingent than had originally been allocated was dispatched to execute the pullout later
that morning, padded with an extraordinary number of female
officers to physically manhandle our women, along with ambulances, fire trucks, military support and vehicles, including tanks
and helicopters, plus armored buses standing ready with engines
churning to haul away the evacuees, not to mention those usual
feeders-on-carrion who swoop down and swarm to any public
spectacle—the press, bigshots, thrill-seekers, idlers, gawkers, and
other assorted lowlife.

I can only say that as I stood on the elevated landing of the
"leper" hospital beneath the JESUS HILFE inscription and bore
witness to the tremendous dignity with which our people faced
their oppressors, it was as if my heart shattered from sorrow
into millions of cells that soared up to the heavens and became
recombinant in joy. Row upon row of police fully equipped with
anti-riot gear, helmeted and masked, advanced in formation into
our "leper" colony bearing body-length transparent bulletproof
shields in front of them and emitting apelike grunts with each
choreographed step forward. On our side, every woman stood
fearless and inert, frozen in place cloaked from head to toe in a
great white talit, awaiting her fate (how well trained we women
are at staying put and waiting, as if this acquired trait had become
a mutation in our genetic code); our men, fewer in number, were
also garbed in white prayer shawls, each one blowing his shofar.
Visually, from where I was standing, it was black versus white,
a metaphor for the war between evil and good.

As the ranks of police goose-stepped nearer, discharging their
barks and roars, not one of our people flinched or cowered. Nor
did they resist, but neither did they collaborate or participate in
their own extermination or corroborate the canard against the
Jews by going like the proverbial sheep to the slaughter. Instead,
as the police shields came up against them like a barrier wall
they let their bodies slump and go limp in the time-honored

posture of Ghandian passive resistance, Dr. M.L. Kingian, Jr. nonviolent protest, necessitating that each one be lugged out like a deadweight by a minimum of two male officers or four females in a respectful manner avoiding all physical contact with any tender or vulnerable or private body part, especially in rounding up and transporting and uploading our women. As they were being carted out (I must insert here that each time I recall this moment a lump forms in my throat forcing me to consciously stop myself from raising my woman's naked voice and bawling) they were singing with such heavenly sweetness it was as if tears of honey were falling from the clouds—I believe with full faith in the coming of the Messiah, and even if she tarries, despite all that I believe.

FIVE MONTHS after these events, in the first week of Adar, word spread beyond our walls that a coronation would take place inside the "leper" colony at which HaRav Temima Ba'alatOv, shlita, would be anointed the queen the messiah. The faithful arrived in the morning, first a trickle but as the week built toward its climax and the news rippled out they converged in increasing numbers to claim a spot facing the hospital in anticipation of this end-of-history eschatological event. All day they would remain fixed in place to be among the first to greet the queen the messiah, their eyes focused on a hopeful point of light in the distance until darkness descended and they were banished from the grounds. No one knew exactly when the coronation would be carried out, speculation abounded, it could take place with no forewarning at any moment, in the blink of an eye, even behind closed doors or at night, yet the general consensus was that it would be a public ceremony with a multitude of witnesses to affirm that the redemption was already underway, and the likelihood was, it was agreed, that it would come to pass on the seventh day of the month, also the birthday of Moses Our Teacher, another messiah contender according to certain kabbalistic calculations.

The plan was to spread the news beyond the "leper" colony, to broadcast the coronation via satellite TV throughout the world, beam it across the planet, even more mystically into the universe, for it was rumored that the blessed oil would be decanted in a golden stream from the four angels in the upper spheres surrounding the heavenly throne, Michael, Gabriel, Raphael, and Uriel, directly to earth to anoint the head of the designated messiah, HaRav Temima Ba'alatOv, shlita. This is what I heard only after plans for the coronation had been set in motion, for I had no part in it, I fought against it with every fiber of my being when I learned it was in the works, there was no doubt in my mind that in its grandiosity and vulgarity it would be contrary to the spirit and teachings of our holy mother who, with rare exceptions, was no longer favoring us at that time with the personal expression in words or through body language of what was to be considered desirable and what loathsome.

During that entire first week of the month of Adar I remained hypervigilant, on high alert in order to prevent this grotesque carnival from unfolding, I did not shut my eyes for a second, and yet despite my opposition, the procedure was carried out in the shadowy light of a deep purple dusk late on the fifth day, when it was almost dark. It lasted two minutes at most, even some of the assembled still dragging their feet in the courtyard blinked and missed it. Our holy mother (or perhaps it was our holy mother's double), shrouded from head to toe in what resembled a bedsheet like a ghost (though it might have been a prayer shawl or maybe a chador or maybe a hood drawn over the head of a condemned person about to be executed) was pushed in a wheelchair by an individual who looked like an Arab but was, some maintained, an original Canaanite, out through the main door of the "leper" hospital onto the elevated landing that served as a kind of stage or platform against the setting of the JESUS HILFE inscription (ironically, an invocation of a false messiah reduced to the background role of helpmeet for the anointment of the true chosen one who happened to be a woman). The Canaanite with a white keffiyeh pinned across the lower portion of the face like a bandit in a cowboy movie so that only the large aviator sunglasses were visible and robed in a white jellabiya trimmed with gold embroidery along the edges pulled out a half-liter bottle of Two-State-Solution Organic Extra Virgin Olive Oil produced in a joint cooperative grassroots venture by Palestinian and Israeli farmers and poured all of its contents over the blanketed head of the person in the wheelchair alleged to be Ima Temima, though it could just as easily have been a bump on a log (no comparison intended, God forbid) for all anyone knew.

At a certain point in the proceedings a hand emerged from under the wrappings in the wheelchair which, according to the testimony of some witnesses, seemed to wave sedately from side to side like the queen of England acknowledging her subjects from the balcony of Buckingham Palace and by implication endorsing their adoration. But others who also saw the hand come forth from under the layers of drapery asserted that it was gesturing in agitation as if to ward off the sludge and slick of the oil and everything it signified spilling all over the place and making an awful mess.

Assuming that this is not an urban legend and that the apparition under wraps in the chair was actually HaRav Temima Ba'alatOv, shlita, being anointed as the messiah, I am of two minds about the hand that appeared—either it was raised in defiant rejection of the entire idolatrous farce or it was offered in resignation to the inevitability of the ritual that flowed from having been chosen—our holy mother has gone into hiding and has declined through silence to elucidate the mystery. There is, however, universal agreement that at a certain point a cry rose up, nor is there any dispute as to the words of the cry, everyone could make them out loud and clear: Long Live Our Master and Rabbi the Queen the Messiah Forever and Ever—Long May She Live! May She Live Forever! *Tekhi! Tekhi! Tekhi!*

It is no secret that it was I who had raised my woman's naked voice and bellowed out that cry for all to hear. The truth is, we of the inner core circle, with the exception of the nomad who worshipped in his own way as was his right and privilege, had over the preceding excruciatingly difficult months taken to singing out this phrase at various points during our devotions to affirm that the redemption had already begun. I had set it to music so that we could chant it over and over again, like an hypnotic refrain, a mantra, a chorus, breaking out in ecstatic dancing, whirling in a trance until we either took off to outer space from spiritual uplift or melted down from physical exhaustion. The verse was a variation based on the salutation spoken by Bathsheba to her husband, King David, as he lay dying, probably with the exquisite Shunamite virgin stretched out naked in the bed under the covers alongside him warming him up like a human hot water bottle. Years earlier, when Ima Temima and I were still in apprenticeship to Abba Kadosh, a'h, as we bathed in the spring of Ein Feshkha, our holy mother had addressed me as My Batsheva, adding that every human being, regardless of gender, needs a wife. On the first level, this was a reference to what would eventually become my official appointment as secretary, traditionally a woman's role, gal Friday, among other duties perpetuator of the legacy of HaRav Temima Ba'alatOv, shlita, with the responsibility to preserve the teachings and stories and history that otherwise would have been lost by raising my woman's naked voice through speech, song, and above all through writing, a medium our holy mother personally shunned for mystical reasons. Writing is murder, our holy mother would sometimes cryptically say—and yes, I could not have agreed more, writing is very hard, it's hell, it's torture, which is why I procrastinate so much and avoid it for as long as possible and am always pounding as with a sledgehammer to break down my writer's block. So unshakable was Ima Temima's refusal to write, as it happens, that had we been dealing with an ordinary mortal here I would have diagnosed this aversion as an extreme case of graphophobia or another anxiety disorder of some sort. But given the stature of the personage in question, I have concluded that this acute negative reaction to the act of writing was a further teaching from our holy mother concerning how a leader's time might be most optimally allocated. Important leaders, world class celebrities, major public figures, and the like, do not waste their time writing. For that they have support staff, chroniclers, scribes, official biographers, secretaries, speech writers, ghost writers, assistants, aides, clerks, and other such wives like myself.

On a deeper level, though, I also understood intuitively that, like Batsheva, I was first and foremost being impregnated with prophetic powers capable of envisioning the messianic line destined to manifest itself through the coveted neighbor's wife scooped up from her bath, Batsheva, the name by which our holy mother captured me, down through the generations to the end of time culminating in HaRav Temima Ba'alatOv, shlita, and that I was being charged above all with protecting and enabling its full realization. Not for a single moment has my faith wavered in the redemptive mission of HaRav Temima Ba'alatOv, shlita, who except for the irrelevant gender factor is a perfect candidate for the messiah according to the traditionally accepted definitive arbiter Rabbi Dr. Moses son of Maimon, known as Rambam; in an open equal-opportunity nondiscriminatory job market Ima Temima fulfills the Maimonidean messianic qualifications—that's the bottom line. Our belief in the arrival of our holy mother as the full-fledged messiah was, and remains, so strong that even as we ministered daily to the weakening and deterioration of the physical vessel that housed the messiah, and even now after the concealment of the physical instrument, the cry of *Tekhi!* May She Live On And On! still bursts out of our throats spontaneously, not only during prayer but also in the absence of any apparent external stimulus, as if we are gasping for breath—*Tekhi!* And I cannot even count how often our cries of *Tekhi!* were greeted by nods or even on occasion a confirming smile under the veil from our holy mother prior to the concealment, a clear sign to us that the messianic materialization we foresaw and all of our aspirations for salvation were acknowledged and approved by our holy mother. Ima Temima was supportive. Our holy mother would deliver. Our holy mother would deliver *us*—when and how as yet to be determined.

For me, at issue was never the absolute given that HaRav Temima Ba'alatOv, shlita, would sooner or later emerge in messianic splendor but rather the delicate but crucial matter related to how to sell this radical idea in the public arena, not only the heretofore unimaginable concept of a woman messiah that provokes such cognitive dissonance, but also how to factor in commonly held notions relating to death. For to the uninitiated, Ima Temima during the stage prior to the concealment might have looked like just another very sick and very decrepit and very out-of-it old lady in end-stage full-body systemic failure going the way of all flesh. On top of that, there was and remains the heavy business of what in polite circles some might term the resurrection thing, to put it even more bluntly, a second coming, for Jews an extremely sensitive subject, a real sore spot as it relates to a messiah figure. Even in a case that does not involve death, merely concealment, our holy mother's return nevertheless evokes the corrosive myths and madness of Christianity, one of the two of the three major Western religions that had ripped us off so brazenly and persecuted us so relentlessly for being the first, the originals, the chosen ones. Yet despite all that, we await the return, we believe.

In such a sensitive climate, therefore, my strategy was diplomatic—an abiding private faith coupled with working clandestinely behind the scenes to usher in the golden age over which HaRav Temima Ba'alatOv, shlita, would preside as messiah. In a way, I was carrying out a disinformation campaign, for my public stance then was that of an anti-messianist with regard to our holy mother in order not to alert and put on guard the establishment rationalists and skeptics (and needless to say, also the sexists), but what I was in reality was an Ima Temima Messiah Marrano for my commitment to a more secret, undercover process through which I had no doubt the truth would inevitably be revealed on the day of the arrival so that nobody could ever again deny it. The nomad, on the other hand, the impresario of the coronation, pushed full speed ahead for a public in-your-face emanation in order to hasten the coming out of the closet of our holy mother as the messiah. On this matter, he and I were in violent disagreement.

THANK GOD I was informed of the coronation stunt in time to raise my woman's naked voice in this emergency situation and shout out my *Tekhi!* It was at least a form of damage control, for it was critical that any influential cynic witnessing this coronation imposed upon us by the aboriginal Canaanite not conclude that our holy mother was just another messiah-syndrome victim from breathing in the radioactive microbes of Jerusalem's supernatural air, or that the cloaked figure being drenched with oil making deflecting hand gestures in the wheelchair was actually stricken by the impostor syndrome, attributable to a disabling sense of fraudulence at being hailed the messiah. Moreover, the *Tekhi!* is exceptionally potent and healing, especially when combined with Temima, as in *Tekhi Temima!*, two words that in mystical Gematria numerology, each letter of the Hebrew alphabet possessing a numerical equivalent, together add up to 913, exactly the same sum as the very first word of the Torah, *Bereishit*, "In the Beginning." All of this is so incredibly special, I cannot even begin to describe the comfort it afforded us during those dark days, for it confirmed for us how beginnings merge with endings, how inextricably bound up they are with each other, how what might seem like an end (for instance, what the unenlightened might call death) is actually a beginning (the advent of the messiah, the raising of the dead). And as an added bonus, if you flip over the 9, you get 613, corresponding to the number of mitzvot in the Torah, the sum total of negative and positive commandments, the don't-do's and the do's, from some of which we women are so patronizingly exempt. There are times when numbers speak more eloquently than words—mystically, not superstitiously, I hasten to add.

The numerical resonance of the *Tekhi Temima!* hinting at the imminent messianic age when we women will be liberated to fulfill *all* of the mitzvot is so meaningful words are inadequate to penetrate this territory, it requires the perfection, the absoluteness of numbers. Still, I was furious with the nomad for staging the travesty of the public anointment. It was at best age abuse, at worst blasphemy and sacrilege, and so the next day, Adar six, when I was summoned by the chronically grieving Rizpa toward evening to the private chambers of HaRav Temima Ba'alatOv, shlita, I regret to report that I lost my cool entirely, I was powerless to manage my anger.

When I arrived in the inner sanctum our holy mother, unveiled and noticeably more frail, more shriveled and withered and mottled no doubt due to having been dragged out in the cold to

be displayed in the nomad's obscene circus, was in bed alongside
the little mother Torah, the two wooden rollers of its scroll poking out from the covers like rabbit ears perked up at attention
alert to danger. Aishet-Lot was sitting at the table under the
window, not knitting this time but stitching together a garment
of white linen, while Rizpa, compulsively bunching and stroking one of the clusters of ritual fringes at the corner of her apron
like worry beads, remained standing humbly at the door not
venturing to step more deeply into the room. The nomad was
nowhere in sight I was relieved to find. Aishet-Lot set down her
work and rose to hand me a folder containing full instructions
regarding the reburial of the bleached bones of our holy mother's "sister," Ketura, a'h, from their temporary resting place in
Be'er LaHai Ro'i in the wilderness to the northern garden of our
"leper" colony alongside our high priestess Aish-Zara, za'zal.
Most importantly, the packet provided the information I needed
as to whom to contact to expedite the transferral of the remains
of Ima Temima's mother, Mrs. Rosalie Bavli, z'l, from her grave
in the Old Montefiore Cemetery in Queens, New York, also to
the northern garden of our "leper" colony, to be placed in the
same bed in which our own holy mother soon planned to enter
the concealment stage that precedes and heralds the revelation.
"And I want my little stuffed animal in there with me too," an
ancient voice called out.

So unaccustomed had I grown to hearing that voice during
this bleak period that it did not immediately register with me
that it was truly our holy mother speaking, like the little boy
Samuel in the Tabernacle at Shilo who did not realize he was
being addressed by God Himself, that he was experiencing his
first nocturnal prophecy. The consequence of this was that when
I finally turned toward the source on the bed with the question
writ large on my face as to what was this mystical entity our
holy mother referred to as a "stuffed animal" and I saw Ima
Temima's arm caressing in answer the little mother Torah in its
worn, well-loved plush mantle now fully visible from top to bottom, and beneath it, pushing it up into view ever higher, rising
from under the covers alongside our holy mother like the devil

from hell, I saw the fiendish face of the nomad grinning madly, swelling indecently, followed by the red blotches of his neck and shoulders, I was speechless, my woman's naked voice failed me, the sight totally blew my mind.

I have to admit that at this point I lost it completely. How dare he? I reached for the staff propped now against the wall, grabbed it, and began flailing wildly in the direction of the nomad. I was out of control, I was grunting like a savage, I never knew I was capable of such a violent, primitive outburst, I wanted nothing more than to smash him to pieces. Fortunately, he had the animal instinct to leap from the bed to save his own skin, which also spared me from God forbid accidentally striking our holy mother so close by, an innocent civilian caught up in a war zone (a calamity that would have driven me up to a mountaintop to throw myself off like his father, Abba Kadosh, a'h, was thrown), in the process flashing his entire body monstrous with ulcerations and excrescences, grabbing a cloth from the pile on the bed to cover his nakedness as he ran for safety and squatted against the wall snarling like a feral cat with eyes of crystal, reminding me as never before of his father before him who had been the glue connecting Ima Temima to me for which I shall always be indebted to him. At the same time, Aishet-Lot, all one hundred-plus kilos of that monumental prophetess of the past, threw herself on top of me despite the fact that I am her superior in the school for prophetesses deserving of her respect and pinned me to the floor. She detached the stick from my hands finger by finger as I wailed beneath her, and passed it to our holy mother.

HaRav Temima Ba'alatOv, shlita, planted the staff on the floor beside the holy bed holding it erect with one arm extended supported by Rizpa through the night. What I saw with my prophetess's vision from under the pillar of salt that was Aishet-Lot was our holy mother's hand stroking the rod with tender encouragement all night long until the next morning when it budded, then blossomed, then bore fruit.

That was the morning of the seventh of Adar. I had been released early at dawn for good behavior from under my prophetess Aishet-Lot and had taken my place against the wall among the others keeping vigil when the Hephzibah staff burst forth in full bloom and the ancient voice, beloved by all of us, was heard for the last time. "Bitter almonds for women—thorns and thistles for men. We have all been cursed, women and men alike. None of us has been spared. Where I am going no man will ever touch me again. I will miss that above all. In spite of everything, my desire is for him. For your salvation I had hoped, O Lord."

As I said, this occurred on the seventh day of Adar, the birthday of Moses Our Teacher and also, it should be noted, the day on which, one hundred and twenty years later, he died by the kiss of God, which is fatal. To die on the same date as one's birth is a rare privilege of profound import, a sign of pure righteousness, a sign that the individual so set apart possesses godlike qualities, constantly being reborn and dying at the same time, the same moment even, eternal renewal, a perfect circle; such a person is immortal, it is an attribute of the messiah. The stunning truth, however, is that Ima Temima, though born on the seventh of Adar like Moses Our Teacher, did not as some deluded individuals may claim and superficial appearances might suggest also "die" on that date like Moses but rather entered a period of hiding from which we anticipate an imminent emergence in messianic glory.

What happens to the body is beside the point; despite the truism not everyone must die. Enoch, who walked with God and is no more—he did not die for God loved him and took him. Jacob, who might have had a glimpse into the end of days, merely let out a gasp, an agonized exhalation (the penultimate *va'yigvah*) and was collected to his fathers, the text does not in the usual close-the-book way explicitly add that he also died. And Elijah the Tishbite, who as everyone knows will return in the messianic period to answer all unresolved questions and dilemmas, made the most spectacular exit of all, ascending to heaven in a whirlwind in a chariot of fire drawn by blazing horses. Father! Father! Israel's chariot and horsemen! his disciple Elisha cried out.

And so, when on Adar seven, which is also our holy mother's birthday, Ima Temima's breathing grew more and more grating and wheezing, shallow and labored until it became manifest to us that HaRav Temima Ba'alatOv, shlita, had receded to the furthest end of a tunnel like a microscopic dot and entered the concealment space, we also raised our voices and cried out, Mother! Mother!—and spontaneously we joined hands and whirled in a circle raising our women's naked voices and singing joyously, *Tekhi! Tekhi! Tekhi!*—for we understood that our holy mother had merely moved on to the next station in the messianic journey that would soon lead back to us and nail down the redemption. Our universe is filled with all sorts of phenomena we do not see with our eyes but whose effects we experience, belowground and aboveground, surrounding us everywhere, atoms and electrons, for example, the invisibility of God Himself. In the same way, we would soon no longer see our holy mother, our holy mother would go underground as it were into hiding, it would be as if our holy mother were rendered invisible behind a curtain or screen, veiled by concealment as the physical container of Ima Temima had been veiled, but the power and mystery, the wisdom and benevolence of the unseen presence would still remain active and exert its force until the ultimate rising and revelation.

For this reason in this chronicle that I have been charged with keeping I do not now use a traditional honorific for our holy mother to denote a person who has God forbid "died," such as a'h, *aleha ha'shalom*, peace be upon her, or z'l, *zikhrona li'vrakha*, may her memory be a blessing, or even za'zal, *zekher zaddeket li'vrakha*, may the memory of the righteous one be a blessing, which I attach regularly to the name of our beloved high priestess Aish-Zara, za'zal, for example, who has gone on to the next world, and for whose return we long every day with the raising of the dead that will accompany the coming of the queen the messiah. Rather, to the name of HaRav Temima Ba'alatOv I append and always shall append the acronym *shlita*, may She live on for many good long years (the only time, I might point out, that I permit myself to use for purposes of translation the pronoun in connection with our holy mother, which I regard as vaguely tainted with disrespect). This is because HaRav Temima Ba'alatOv, shlita, is not "dead." Simple minds, based on the news of what is said to have transpired, may automatically file our holy mother away, dismiss our holy mother, slap a "death" certificate on our holy mother and consider the case closed. Unfortunately for them, they are not gifted with the spiritual powers or vision to grasp the essence.

For the messiah, death is not an option.

OUR CRIES of *Tekhi!* rang out as we prepared the physical shell and dressed it in the white linen garments sewn by the hands of Aishet-Lot. We wailed *Tekhi! Tekhi! Tekhi!* as we concealed our holy mother swaddled in a great white prayer shawl along with the little mother Torah under a blanket of black earth in the bed in the northern garden in a ritual that others might consider to have been a funeral but was actually a joyous rite of passage attended by thousands upon thousands who had arrived to escort HaRav Temima Ba'alatOv, shlita, on the charted journey to the next level shouting *Tekhi!* the whole way.

Tekhi! resounds in the courtyard of our "leper" colony all through the day as they arrive in their multitudes to stand in pure faith awaiting the return until they are evacuated when darkness falls. Every point in our negotiations with the authorities as to the disposition of our "leper" colony is punctuated with *Tekhi!* To the state and municipality's claim of eminent domain for the construction of luxury villas and apartment houses, commercial centers and educational institutions here we counter, *Tekhi!*—we shall drain this "leprous" swamp and build on this land a palace of sapphire and gold bricks surrounded by lush blooming gardens and fruit bearing trees in readiness for our holy mother's return from concealment and the commencement of the messianic reign. *Tekhi! Tekhi!* we sang out when we dug a grave for the white bones of Sister Ketura, a'h, alongside the resting place of our high priestess Aish-Zara, za'zal, and when we drew back the covers of the bed in which HaRav Temima Ba'alatOv, shlita, is concealed to tuck in the remains of our holy mother's mother, Mrs. Rosalie Bavli, z'l; *Tekhi!* when we carved out a pathway between the bed and the private quarters in the northern garden along which our holy mother will God willing very soon proceed under an ethereal blue canopy in regal splendor to the golden throne with red satin cushions embroidered with silken threads that awaits the end of the concealment; *Tekhi!* when we erected a pavilion to protect from the elements the holy bed where HaRav Temima Ba'alatOv, shlita, is hidden as in a cocoon from which any minute the queen the messiah will burst forth like a butterfly with the most dazzling and magical wings in celestial colors, azure and scarlet and gold, never before seen or imagined on this earth. Long Live Our Master Our Teacher Our Rabbi the Queen the Messiah Forever and Ever! Long Live Temima! *Tekhi Temima! Tekhi!*

In the beginning we rejoiced that the concealment had commenced, and now, almost half a year later, we rejoice even more terribly for with each passing hour we can only be moving closer to the promised revelation. Soon the seventeenth day of Tammuz will be upon us, traditionally set aside to mourn the breaching of the walls of Jerusalem by the enemy invaders and the destruction of the Holy Temple three weeks later, but we shall celebrate with wine and sweets, for the redemption is already in progress when every fast day is transformed into a feast day. The Third Temple stands complete in full magnificence in heaven ready to be lowered to the top of Mount Moriah that the Dome of the Rock now occupies like an illegal settlement outpost. Yes, it will be lowered very soon to its rightful spot on earth the moment the queen the messiah HaRav Temima Ba'alatOv, shlita, rises from the holy bed and favors us by coming out of concealment.

Meanwhile, every day hundreds of petitions arrive from every corner of the globe to our "leper" colony, pleading for blessings, healing, wisdom, answers, justice, pouring out grief, begging our holy mother to come out of hiding—Now! A deep pit has been dug inside the pavilion as a repository into which we empty the petitions at the end of each day like treasured fragments inscribed with the divine name that may never be destroyed but must be buried as if they are human remains. Already the ones at the bottom of the pit have merged with the soil to nourish with their tears everything that grows.

On warm nights we three ladies in waiting of the queen the messiah—Rizpa, Aishet-Lot, and I—sleep under the stars alongside the pavilion, poised to greet our holy mother at the end of the concealment that could come at any moment. My sleep at the pavilion is always fitful and agitated, troubled with guilt by my failure to fulfill my duties as our holy mother's scribe and chronicler, restless with anticipation that any minute Ima Temima may rise up and come out of hiding. I must be ready, I must be alert, it is the moment for which I keep myself alive.

Often I get up in the night to commune privately with the active presence of our holy mother, seeking comfort and counsel. At times I lean over the trench filling up with petitions to HaRav Temima Ba'alatOv, shlita, scoop up a fistful, and study them by the glow of the eternal lamp and the flickering candles in glass cups, an act I perform at the behest of our holy mother calling to me from behind the veil. Like music, human suffering I have come to understand is confined to a limited scale of notes expressed in endless variations, infinite stories. In an unmistakable sign, a petition I plucked out last night was addressed to me rather than to Ima Temima.

"Kol-Isha-Erva," the message singled me out by name, "You know I consider writing to be a crime, with no immunity or pardon even after death. Still, I have gone to the extreme of writing this note and letting it fall into your hands as you scavenged among the private petitions meant for me so that you would interpret it as a sign that it is I who am speaking, I and no other. From where I am now, an eternal place without past, present, or future, I see and know everything, but blessedly I am liberated from the burden of caring. Hava and Adam, prototypical wife and husband, are twined together in the form of two serpents, mouth to tail; they have left the mothers and fathers they never had to devour each other for eternity thereby becoming one flesh. My Elisha is coiled like the serpent of a caduceus or the rod of Asclepius, contorted in agony for eternity with sickness and pain from overindulging on the fruit of the tree of knowledge good and evil. My mother with hair of writhing snakes dangles in front of me the ripe fruit of the tree of life, but I am not tempted. It is better for a person never to have been born, and all the more so not to be sentenced to endless life without parole. I have shed my snake skins, all of them false and diseased—the idea of mother, the idea of master, the idea of messiah. I have ground down the copper snake I held up on a pole to deceive all who had been bitten by the lethal serpents of life into believing that by looking at it they will be cured, and they brought me offerings of incense and worshipped me. It was all vanity and idolatry. Do not believe in it, Kol-Isha-Erva. Do not wait for me. I shall not return."

I regard this message as a hoax perpetrated by the nomad, but I transcribe its contents in their entirety here in these pages in compliance with my obligation to censor nothing, hold nothing back. At first glance, these words purportedly attributed to our holy mother might seem disheartening, crushing. Yet, miraculously, they have fractured and pulverized my writer's block like Moses' serpentine staff when it struck the stone to release the water so that the words have begun to flow. At last I have been able to overcome my resistance and sit down at this table to fulfill my mandate to write it all down, as Ima Temima has commanded.

I think about the times our holy mother would brood on how heartbreaking it is for women to yearn for the messianic age. "Should it ever truly arrive, for there is no real mention of it in the text itself, there will be nothing in it for women, it is a male fantasy," our holy mother would say. But what if the messiah is a woman—a mother? Therein lies true salvation. It is for our mother we always cry out in the darkest night and deepest pain and always in the end our mother comes, she sustains us with sweet cakes, she revives us with apples, she sits across from us at the table, her hand propping her chin, watching over us as we eat and are restored, for we are sick with love and she will never forsake us. Rather than vaporizing my faith, then, the sign given to me from our holy mother has strengthened my resolve to once again raise my woman's naked voice and cry out my *Tekhi!* Ima Temima lives. Temima daughter of Rachel-Leah, You are not dead. The moment we long for beyond all else, when the earth will tremble and the true mistress of the spirit, HaRav Temima Ba'alatOv, shlita, will rise from concealment and return to shine the holy face upon us, is now closer than ever. For the messiah does not come willingly. The chosen have no choice.

Printed in the United States
by Baker & Taylor Publisher Services